1757

BY

JASON BORN

WORKS WRITTEN BY JASON BORN

THE LONG FUSE:

QUAKER'S WAR

SAVAGE WAR

THE CRIMSON GAUNTLET

A FORT TOO FAR

1757

LIONS & DEVILS are:

HELL SHALL STIR

DEVILS IN THE BREACH

WHERE DEVILS TREAD

THE NORSEMAN CHRONICLES are:

THE NORSEMAN

PATHS OF THE NORSEMAN

NORSEMAN CHIEF

NORSEMAN RAIDER

NORSEMAN'S OATH

THE WALD CHRONICLES are:

THE WALD

WALD AFIRE

WALD VENGEANCE

STANDALONE:

GIRL KING (*As Emily Hawk*)

LEAGUE OF THE LOST FOUNTAIN

COPYRIGHT

ISBN: 9781095308424

DEDICATION

To

Chip & Nicole.

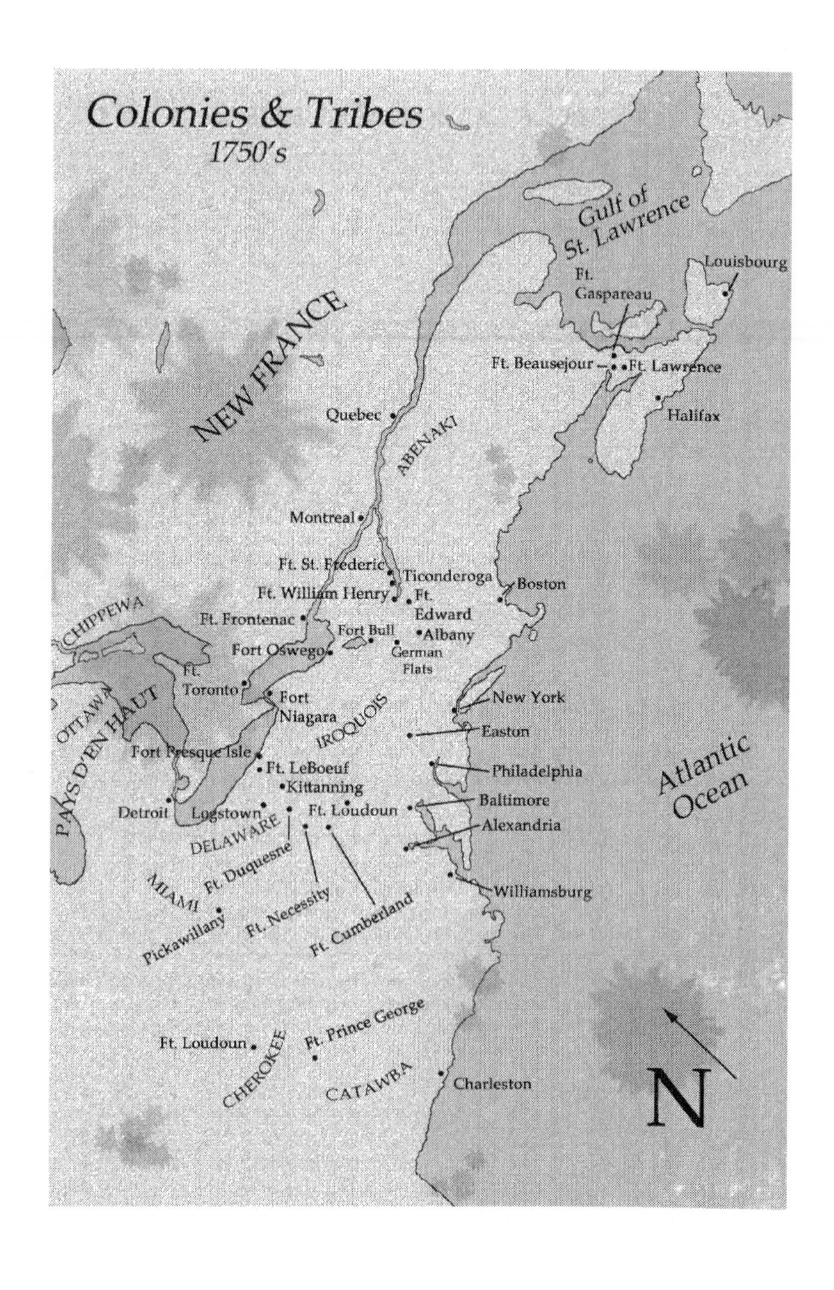
Colonies & Tribes
1750's
NEW FRANCE
Gulf of St. Lawrence
Louisbourg
Ft. Gaspareau
Ft. Beausejour
Ft. Lawrence
Halifax
Quebec
ABENAKI
Montreal
Ft. St. Frederic
Ticonderoga
Ft. William Henry
Ft. Edward
Boston
CHIPPEWA
Ft. Frontenac
Fort Bull
Albany
Fort Oswego
German Flats
Ft. Toronto
Fort Niagara
New York
OTTAWA
PAYS D'EN HAUT
IROQUOIS
Easton
Fort Presque Isle
Ft. LeBoeuf
Kittanning
Philadelphia
Atlantic Ocean
Detroit
Logstown
Ft. Loudoun
Baltimore
DELAWARE
Alexandria
Ft. Duquesne
MIAMI
Williamsburg
Pickawillany
Ft. Necessity
Ft. Cumberland
Ft. Loudoun
Ft. Prince George
CHEROKEE
CATAWBA
Charleston
N

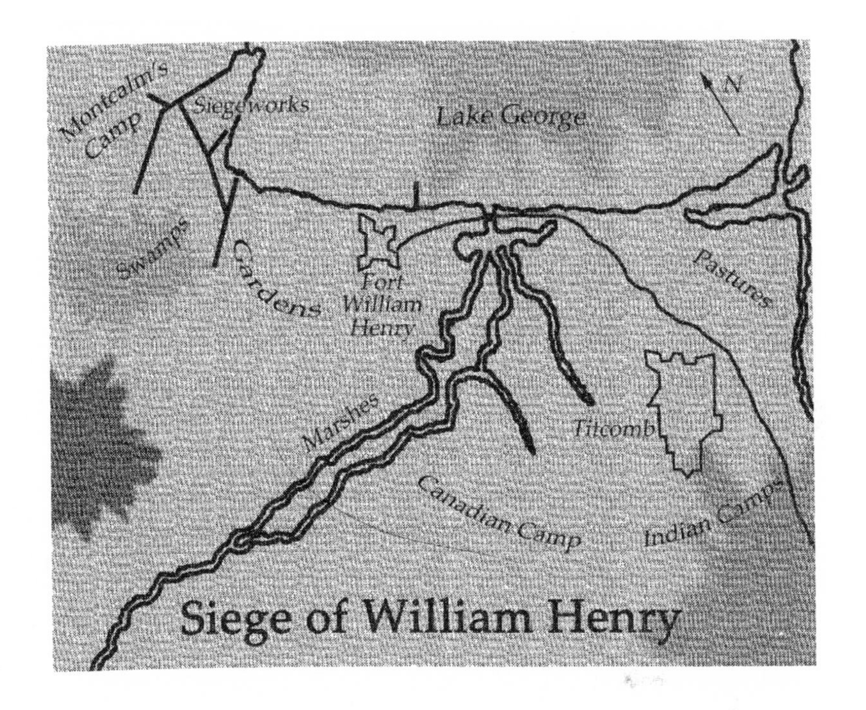
Montcalm's Camp
Siegeworks
Lake George
N
Swamps
Gardens
Fort William Henry
Pastures
Marshes
Titcomb
Canadian Camp
Indian Camps
Siege of William Henry

CHAPTER 1

Shackled, I stooped in the corner of a small log house that served as the jail at Fort Frederick. Only the tiniest of rays snuck in through a handful of gaps in the chinking to provide what an optimist might call light. There was little to do. Mostly, I wiggled my fingers to drive away the pins and needles. Or, I rattled my chain – anything to take my mind from the weeks' long boredom that accompanied my imprisonment. To any observer peeking in, I would appear little more than a wretched animal cowering and scratching around on the packed dirt floor.

The door burst open, flooding the darkness with sunlight. I recoiled, squinting and holding a hand in front of my face. It wasn't time for my daily latrine allowance. A shadow brushed inside and the door was promptly slammed shut. With my eyes sufficiently bleached, I was blind.

"That you Turdwell?" I croaked.

Ensign Turnwell sighed and went to what had become his corner. He tripped over the outstretched legs of a man who snored loudly. Our fellow prisoner had been found sleeping while on guard. As the infraction had been discovered that morning, I expected the army's efficient penalty system to fall upon him at any moment. Straight forward infractions with as many grave implications as dereliction of duty were handled rapidly – and violently. Yet, despite the threat of scores of lashes – or worse – the soldier appeared to have no concern at all. But that is what too much drink could do to an otherwise sentient being. He'd not be the first redcoat to earn the extra crimson stripes of a so-called *bloody back*. And he'd not be the last.

"What happened?" I asked Turnwell.

"Lord Loudoun is mulling it over," he explained.

"What is there to think about?" I asked. "Isn't it bad enough the two of us had to crawl our way out of the woods after the fall of Fort Oswego? Now we rot in here for having done nothing wrong."

"Our accuser is a man with powerful friends," Turnwell sighed with resignation.

"Daniel Webb can go choke on those fingernails of his," I snapped. "He likes to eat them so much! And, boy, what I wouldn't give to have the king's son as a school mate! What has Webb ever got to worry about?"

"But we don't have such friends," Turnwell lamented. "Webb does."

"Oh!" I hissed, throwing a clump of earth at the snoozing redcoat. He snorted himself awake for a fraction of a second before falling back into his stupor. "I never should have stopped at Oswego. Should have kept on going to the pays d'en haut. Instead of being locked in here, I'd be readying to winter with a new wife – maybe another Miami woman. I might have set her with child by now!"

"Why did you stay?" Turnwell asked.

"I don't know," I growled. In truth, I stayed because I had to. What proper Englishman would abandon a fort full of men, women, and children on the brink of starvation? I was no saint in the traditional sense. But I tried hard not to be an outright devil. Sometimes I succeeded. Other times? Well, that's what all these memoirs are about.

The topic was turning too personal. Time to change the subject. "What did you tell them about me?"

My eyes were again getting used to the dark. I could see Turnwell shrug. "The truth."

"There you go!" I scoffed, throwing my chain along with my hands. "It's the gallows for me. For sure."

"I told them you were a hero in many ways," Turnwell admitted, which must have been hard for him. Since the moment I had met him, I treated him so very poorly. "Saved my life. And were it not for the treachery of the Caughnawaga, perhaps many hundreds of other lives."

"But that's not all you told them is it, Turdwell?" I asked. He hated it when I called him that. At least I had refrained from calling him by his fouler nickname for several weeks. We had formed the bonds of friendship while in prison, after all.

"I told the whole truth, Weber."

"But who would have known?" I asked. "It was only you and me who survived and escaped. Even now, the dead bloat in the sun. The rest of the living were hauled off to Montreal as captives!"

"I'm a gentleman, Ephraim," Turnwell answered. "Something you, in your buff buckskins and green gaiters, couldn't understand."

"Gentleman, huh? Could have fooled me," I snarled. "When will they listen to my testimony? I have to set the record straight."

"Soon," the ensign said. "After another year of debacles for our cause, General Campbell wants to put this behind him as soon as possible."

"So do I," I grumbled. "But the *manner* in which we move past it matters a lot to me."

Turnwell nodded. "Loudoun is a fair man. An orderly man. I have hope that he'll see reason."

"And Webb?"

"Webb, I think, wants to see me demoted and struck with the cat o' nine tails." His voice faded.

"And what's the Nellie want with me?"

"He doesn't like you," the ensign said. "Not many do. You're more abrasive than coral."

"Maybe he'll drum me out," I said, suddenly full of hope and ignoring his observation about my temperament. I was not, and am still not, one for introspection. "I don't ever recall officially signing up in the King's service in the first place."

"Webb wants something a little more permanent for you," Turnwell warned. "He said as much."

The door swung open, again blinding me. A shadow momentarily darkened the threshold and I lifted my hands, ready for the guards to jerk me to my feet.

"Where is he, Ephraim?" asked a quivering voice.

"Hannah?" I gasped.

"The rumors are dreadful," she said, standing tall over me. "Was he taken to Montreal with the other captives? Don't lie to me."

I stared silently at the dirty ruffle on the bottom of her skirts. A hundred different versions of the answer raced through my mind. Each of them was wholly unsatisfactory. But the truth, no matter how dressed up I would try to make it, was cold.

Hannah stepped toward me, bent, and began pounding me with the sides of her fists, crying aloud. "I told him not to go! I told him! We'd have figured out a way to survive without the extra money. But he was like all men! Stubborn. Prideful! He was like you! Arrogant! Foolish! Now he's dead. And I've got four mouths to feed!"

I guarded my face but otherwise let her fury rain down on me unopposed. The sentinel had heard the commotion and returned to peer inside. He laughed at my plight. "Let him have it, ma'am."

She had let me have it another time. One fast, hard cross. And in the wake of that particular swing, I had discovered that Hannah could punch fiercely for a woman. Back then, she'd put me right on the ground. But these were not those types of strikes. They were impotent, haphazard, confused, rage-filled thumps that could do no damage to me. Eventually, if they continued, they would only hurt her.

I snatched her wrists, which sent her into a deeper frenzy. "Take your hands off me! You and your ilk got Wellie killed. A kind man. A good father. And better husband. Dead! Let go!"

We struggled mightily for several moments. Hannah was strong. After a time, I began to worry that she'd force me to release her. I'd been malnourished at my posts all summer. Then, since being deprived of my liberty due to the musings of a mad general, I'd not been fed any better. Fortunately, fatigue set in against my mourning opponent first. With a few last tugs and gasps, Hannah weakly slumped against me. Her elbows rested on my knees for a second before she sloughed off, sliding her rump next to mine.

Seeing the fun at an end, the guard growled. "Three minutes!" he hissed, slamming the door behind him.

Our drunken fellow prisoner woke with a start. "Is that a woman I smell?" he asked.

"Pipe down," Turnwell ordered.

"Who are you to make me?" asked the drunk man as Hannah shrunk lower and lower to the dirt, nearly climbing into my side.

"Ensign Turnwell," said the young officer.

"An ensign in the stockade ain't any better than me!" proclaimed the man.

"If you don't shut up and keep your hands to yourself," I warned the man. "I'll save the king's soldiers much aggravation and kill you myself."

Something about my tone caused his lips to snap shut. Meanwhile, I lugged my chains toward Hannah, feeling for her hands. Once they were in my grasp, I realized that they were just as I remembered them. Strong and weathered in the way that all good frontier women were. "Wellie couldn't stop talking about you and the children," I said. "It's not a fib to say that he found happiness in his life with you."

Hannah wept, leaning on my shoulder. "Why?" she mumbled. "Why him?"

It was another question that I'd have rather not answered. But it seemed rude to ignore her pleas. "I asked the same thing when my wives died. Both of them. Still do."

She scoffed, a razor-sharp demeanor creeping in upon her grief. "And do you ever get an answer?"

Nothing agreeable, was my first thought. "Sometimes," I whispered, bringing her hands to my chest. "I cried over the graves of two fine women. But our time together wasn't for naught. I carry their memories. They taught me a thing or two about sacrifice. And, you know, I have children. So, in that way, there's hope. I have hope. I guess." It wasn't the most inspiring speech.

Hannah took back her hands and wiped the tears away from her face. "I never even got to say goodbye to them. Hank and Wellie both died like dogs on the frontier."

"Not like dogs," I said. "Each of them fought for what they loved. For you. For your children. And I know they'd expect you to do what you always do. Rise up and fight."

Hannah turned toward me. I could make out the shape of her face. It was lovely with high cheekbones framed by black hair.

She was one of only a handful of full-blooded Pequot Indians that remained after the never-ending wars between the tribes of the previous century. Originally from Connecticut, her parents had sent her off to a school run by missionaries. She'd been educated in all manners of faith and running a household. In that way, Hannah had become more English than I'd ever be. She studied me. "I'm sorry for hitting you. I just had to find out. All of Albany is in an uproar after what has happened. Everyone's afraid the French will march past the Stadt Huys within days. Seeing you… just brought out my emotions."

I smiled sadly. "I have that effect on people."

"You do," she allowed quietly. Then Hannah glanced at my irons and the bleak surroundings. "And you must have angered someone very important to be in here."

The door shot open. "Alright lovebirds, that's enough!" said the guard as he barged his way in. "Get out of here, squaw. He's coming with me!"

"I'm no squaw! My husband died fighting for this country," Hannah barked, climbing to her feet as I was yanked upright.

"I don't care if you're the queen herself!" the guard said, shoving me into the sunlight. "Time for you to leave, squaw."

Hannah followed. "Where are you taking him?"

The guard laughed, prodding me forward with his bayonet as he slammed and secured the door. "Didn't he tell you? After a little talk with Lord Loudoun, I'm sure he'll be fitted for a necktie from the fort's tailor."

"Tailor?" she asked.

"The hangman, darling. The hangman," he answered happily, leaving Hannah behind in the yard.

And the two of us disappeared into the fort commander's quarters.

CHAPTER 2

Without ceremony, I was ushered into the commandant's office. He was there, on the opposite side of a table with the rest of my would-be executioners. I cannot recall his name. In any case, his identity was not important because, while he sat as a member of the court that would judge me, his voice would merely echo those of the other, more important men in the room. It was their verdicts that mattered.

General John Campbell, the fourth earl of Loudoun, rested in the center chair. My use of the word *rested* here is likely insufficient. Lord Loudoun never rested. For all his faults, and there were many, he was not in any way indolent or lazy. Neither his body nor his mind ever found time to loiter. It was said that he had overseen the precise planting of the trees on his estate in the Mother Country, making sure they stood in perfect rows and columns like good soldiers. And his dealings with the living beings dressed in redcoats or the gentlemen cloaks of Royal Governors was just as demanding. He was essentially viceroy over the colonies in America and he exercised that power with exactitude. His eyes were bright, showing a glimpse of the sharp mind beyond. He was a moderately handsome man, lacking only in much of a chin.

To General Campbell's left sat the fort commander. Since Loudoun's arrival earlier in the year, he'd been effectively demoted and his level of interest on the day of my trial demonstrated distinct boredom. On Loudoun's right were another pair of generals.

Major General Abercromby was second in command over the British forces in North America. He was corpulent in a way that I'd usually associate with a well-cared for sow or plantation owner's wife. His uniform was always clean and in superb condition. But at the same time, it appeared to be perpetually exhausted. The seams had to continually strain to keep the man clothed. They grunted and groaned from the constant exertion of cinching in his ample circumference. Whenever he sat, as he did that day, the seams worked double-time to prevent a most embarrassing split. If they relaxed for just a moment, his pasty flesh just might have unveiled itself for everyone in the room to admire – or, more likely, shun.

And I might be willing to tolerate the old bull's obesity if he had proven himself a capable officer. But it turned out that his soft rotundity was a perfect metaphor for how he handled himself as a general. He worked extraordinarily hard and spent inordinate amounts of time trying to do as little as possible. Even now, much more so than the bored commandant, he watched Loudoun, hoping that he'd not have to make any type of decision on his own.

Finally, to Abercromby's right was my accuser. However, Major General Daniel Webb did not suffer from the same personality maladies as did Abercromby. No. Webb was happy to make decisions. He made all sorts of judgements all the time. Each of them was bad. But unlike you and I, when Webb made poor choices, he suffered no consequences. He was the childhood friend of William, duke of Cumberland, the youngest son of King George II. Webb had a fortress of political cover surrounding him that, it seemed, would forever shelter him from his own failings. You'd think all that protection would manifest itself as swagger and confidence. But if it did, it was lost on me. Webb was constantly anxious, muttering under his breath, gnawing at his fingernails until they bled.

"That's the one, the dirty one," he mumbled when I was presented before the board.

A captain read down the long list of manufactured infractions of which Webb had accused me. How the major general could truly be expected to know any of them was a mystery since Webb had never once made any attempt to ride to within a week of Fort Oswego.

"Insubordination and impersonating an officer in a time of war," the captain finished. He rolled up the page and returned to his post with an impassive countenance.

The truth was that I was always insubordinate. Always. Always. I hated authority. I loathed the rigidity of the army, longing only to be free in the wilderness. That is why I gravitated toward scouting activities. They kept me from the bustle of the stifling camps. So, if Loudoun cared to ask any ten officers with whom I had served, he'd get ten unequivocal agreements. I was insubordinate.

And I *had* actually impersonated an officer while at Oswego. The story is long, and at this point boring to me. Perhaps you'll choose to read about it in one of my earlier works. Suffice it to say, I felt I had a good reason at the time.

"How do you answer the charges, Mr. Weber?" Loudoun asked.

"Hogwash and lies, Lord Loudoun," I said, tweaking my chin up an inch. When a man had no facts to back up his claims, it was important to show bravado, at least.

Webb slammed his palm against the table, startling Abercromby. The latter's jellied jowls vibrated with fright. "I'll not be called a liar by this backwoods bumpkin!" Webb blustered.

The earl glanced at Webb. "You should be used to how these Yankees act by now, Danny. Don't let him get under your skin."

Webb harrumphed. "Quite right, Lord John. Forgive me for stooping to his level. Please proceed in whatever manner you see fit."

"I shall," Loudoun answered as he faced me. "Is that your charming way of denying the charges?"

"It is, my lord," I answered.

"Can you offer any proof of your claims?" Lord Loudoun asked, fingering a stack of papers on the table in front of him.

"Why do I have to offer proof?" I asked. "Can General Webb verify any of the trite fibs he's contrived?"

Webb blubbered angrily. Abercromby set a chubby, comforting hand on his comrade's shoulder. Loudoun ignored them both. "General Webb is a man of some standing in this army and this country. The weight of his word can easily outbalance your own claims."

I blinked, acting confused. "I can see Abercromby carries substantial weight, my lord. I'd sooner carry a side of beef. But I don't think you ought to go around disparaging Webb for his size. It's not his most remarkable or undesirable trait."

"Did he just insult me?" Abercromby asked.

"And me! Proof of his constant insubordination," Webb growled.

"Not another disparaging word, Mr. Weber," Loudoun warned.

At last, I met Loudoun's menacing glare. "What I meant, my lord, was that you mean to tell me that General Webb merely has to accuse and I'm guilty? Unless I come up with some way of proving otherwise?"

Loudoun nodded somberly.

"What proof could I possibly give?"

"Perhaps the testimony of another witness," Lord Loudoun suggested.

"Turdwell. Er, uh, Ensign Turnwell has already done so, Lord Loudoun."

Webb smirked with joy.

"We have heard his testimony in detail," Loudoun explained. "He corroborates your assertions on some matters. On others, he most definitely does not."

"Corroborates?" Webb blustered. "I've said he is guilty! Weber is guilty."

"How could you know?" I asked. "You were hiding hundreds of miles away while we were fighting and dying! Do you know how many friends I watched get their scalps ripped away? Did you know I was standing right next to Colonel Mercer when his head was lopped off by a cannonball? Where were you? Bathing in a hot spring?"

"That's enough!" Campbell barked. My guard prodded me with his bayonet to ensure my obedience. Meanwhile, the general glanced to the other generals on his right and left. "I believe we have heard enough to render a verdict. Does everyone agree?"

"Most definitely," Webb snarled.

"Oh, uh, yes, Johnny," babbled Abercromby, likely contemplating when his next meal would begin.

"Yes, my lord," answered the commandant.

Lord Loudoun fixed me with a stern glare while tapping the stack of papers with his knuckles. "Very well. This tribunal finds you guilty of impersonating an officer in a time of war. The other infractions are hardly worth mentioning since this one alone is normally a capital offense."

"Normally?" asked Webb, his face immediately filled with dread.

"Yes," Loudoun answered efficiently. Then he faced me. "Under the extenuating, quite dire, circumstances at Fort Oswego it seems to me that you acted in the only way you thought possible. And, should events have turned out differently in other areas, may have resulted in tremendous success. Nonetheless, you have committed a serious offense and there must be consequences. Therefore, I sentence you to seven lashes at the post before your peers and then service as scout in the King's army until such time as this current conflict comes to an official end or you are dead."

Momentarily victorious, I laughed out loud.

Webb's reaction was altogether different. He jumped to his feet. "This is preposterous. You're joking, Johnny!"

"I am not," Loudoun said evenly. He looked at my guard. "See him whipped. Afterward, he is free to move about, if he can. Then tomorrow when he has begun to recover from his punishment, direct him here for his orders."

"Wait a minute!" Webb exclaimed. The guard and I halted. "This is a tribunal. And I demand to have my voice heard. And those of these other officers. What if they disagree with you, Johnny?"

Lord Loudoun looked to the other men. Both of them shook their heads, indicating they were happy to support his decision.

"This can't be, John," Webb pleaded, nibbling on a bloody cuticle. A cornered rat showed more decency. "This frontiersman is all malice. What reason can you possibly have to believe he acted for the good of Oswego?"

"His character, Danny," Loudoun explained. "Now, let's be a little more professional. General Campbell or Lord Loudoun or my lord will be fine."

"Lord Loudoun," Webb began, fighting like mad to control his rage. "You and I met this man only once in the spring. He has been under my command since then. I'd humbly say I know his character better than you – at this point, sir, my lord."

That was false. Other than when Webb ordered me placed in irons, he'd had no more interaction with me than Lord Loudoun or a fisherman living in the East Indies.

"That might be true, Danny," Loudoun said icily. I suddenly found respect for the earl. It probably had little to do with the earl himself and more to do with the fact that he was being lenient on me. And I really enjoyed the way he had said *Danny* with bald derision. Perhaps even noblemen tired of associating with the imbecile friends of a prince.

Loudoun went on, gently rapping the pages with his fist. "But I have many statements from respected men. Each of them speaks to Mr. Weber's selfless dedication to his fellow warriors, if not his outright devotion to the king."

"That whole stack? You're kidding," Webb accused.

"No. I am not joking. And if that is all, I have to plan our campaigns for next year," Loudoun said, standing.

"Who? Who would sign his name to any document where the defense of this ruffian was the result?" Webb asked. "I demand to know!"

Loudoun raised his eyebrows, obviously pleased that Webb had goaded him this far. He plucked the first letter off the top of the stack, focusing on the page. "Here," he said. "This letter says, and I quote, *Mr. Weber is a reliable hand in the wilderness. At the start of the present difficulties with the French he risked life and limb in his many attempts to salvage our one and only English fort at the Forks of Ohio before its unfortunate fall.*"

Webb, if he was impressed, refused to show it. "Who?"

Loudoun read the signature. "Ensign Edward Ward."

"An ensign? That's all?"

Showing a little smirk of his own, Loudoun answered. "Why no. I think there is another here." He snapped up the second letter. "Ambassador Isaac Cotton says, *Mr. Weber was instrumental in encouraging the delegates to the Albany Congress to vote in the affirmative for a vigorous, united defense of these several colonies in coordination with the crown against any and all incursions by the French.*"

"An ambassador? From where?"

"Virginia," Loudoun said. He held up a finger before Webb could offer protest. "Oh, look," he continued, taking the third letter. "A Mrs. Hannah Wellbore from right here in Albany recounts in grim detail how Mr. Weber and a compatriot selflessly led more than a dozen women and children out of the burning frontier and to safety, asking for no benefit or compensation."

"Hannah said that?" I asked, feeling warmth spread in my chest.

"She did," Loudoun nodded with a grin.

"A housewife, a Virginia farmer, and an ensign?" Webb asked incredulous. "You're taking their word over mine?"

"No, Danny," Loudoun said. He was truly enjoying this now. "Not theirs alone." He took the next letter. "Here is one written in support of the accused. It comes from Dinwiddie, the king's Royal Governor of Virginia." He tossed that one aside and grabbed the next. "Here is a letter from a certain Colonel Washington, the only man who was able to salvage Braddock's disaster. And here is something from the Honorable Benjamin Franklin, perhaps you've heard of him." The letters were swiftly plucked and dropped as he read. "Colonel Bradstreet, General Johnson, George Croghan, Captain William Trent, Conrad Weiser, Doctor Craik, John Armstrong, and Major William Eyre have all written detailed accounts of the multiple times Ephraim Weber has done heroic deeds for our king. To a word, they affirm his character." Loudoun stared at Webb. "I believe it is safe to say that unsolicited letters from this many respected individuals might rank at least as high as the word of a friend of the prince. Don't you, Danny?"

Webb was flabbergasted. After several unsuccessful attempts at forming a protest, he relented. "I suppose I can see the wisdom in a lenient punishment, uh, in these uncertain times, uh, when we could use the manpower."

"Good," Loudoun said. He gave a curt nod to my guard and me. "Dismissed."

CHAPTER 3

Oh my! I was sane enough to know in advance that being whipped by the cat on my tender back was going to be painful – excruciating. But it was so much more. Unbelievably so.

Turnwell's sentence from Loudoun had been to administer my punishment to me, whatever it turned out to be. The ensign, of course, had said nothing on the subject after he'd returned to the stockade, because he feared that he'd be involved in my hanging or firing squad. I'd not want to be the one to tell me that my end was nigh either. I might have choked Turnwell for simply being the messenger.

But in some ways, this was worse. I do believe the fact that it was his hand that dealt me the blows was punishment enough for the ensign. And to make sure he didn't go easy, a gruff sergeant stood by.

"Give it to him good, boy," the sergeant barked to Turnwell after I'd been bound with my torso naked against the flagpole. A small platoon of warriors had been assembled to witness the meting out of my sentence. I suppose it was considered motivation to see another man suffer for his infractions.

"That's how you talk to an officer?" the ensign asked.

"Sure enough," growled the sergeant. "When the officer is still under my custody as a prisoner. But don't fear, you pus-filled pimple, as soon as that seventh lash is complete, I'll be all nice and proper, spit and polish."

Turnwell growled to himself. "You ready for this?" he asked.

"Hell, no!" I admitted. "But, no matter what, just carry right on. I think it will be best to get all seven done as fast as possible."

Turnwell took a breath. "Alright. Here it goes."

I heard him step forward and then a swift whoosh. Every muscle in my body went rigid as soon as I felt the first stripe stream down my flesh. "Oww!" I shrieked. I'm sure there may have been a few words thrown in that are not fit for print. "Stop. Stop," I begged.

He did. "I'm sorry, Ephraim. I mean, I can't stand you sometimes. But…"

"How touching," said the sergeant. "Now, my stockade isn't some Molly House! So, unless you want me to bring you both up on charges of sodomy, get on with dispensing justice."

Turnwell growled, stepped forward, and struck. My back at once felt hot and cold. I let out a low rumble, realizing that seven lashes with the cat o' nine tails would result in sixty-three stripes down my back. "Just wait a second," I pleaded, trying to regain control over my breath.

The ensign hesitated a great long time.

"Ensign," grumbled the sergeant. "I can see to it that you join the dandy lad against the pole. There are always plenty of men who'd jump at the chance to flog an officer." The sergeant strode so I could see him on the other side of the flagpole. Nonchalantly, he plucked out a pocket watch that appeared so battered that it might not have even worked. "You've got twelve seconds to get in the last five strokes. Starting… now."

The blow came immediately. It was followed promptly by four more.

"Very good, sir," said the sergeant with an official tone. "Ensign Turnwell, sir, shall I dismiss the men and release the prisoner, sir?"

"Yes, damn you," Turnwell instructed, throwing the cat down into the dust.

"Alright, let that be lesson to all of you!" shouted the sergeant as he faced the company of redbacks. "The king's law can barely reach into the forests of this godforsaken land. But the army's law? Well, the army's law can find you even if you try to hide away in the comforts of Hell. Dismissed!"

"And you!" the sergeant barked to my guard, who had stood dutifully silent throughout my ordeal. "After you cut this wretch loose, prepare our last prisoner for his firing squad. Don't think we'll have much trouble with other men falling asleep on duty for at least a few months."

"Aye, sir," said the guard. He pulled a knife, cut my bonds, and watched me tumble into Turnwell's arms.

"We'll get you taken care of, Weber," the ensign said, hoisting my arm over his shoulder.

"That hurts worse," I said, tugging it back. "I can walk." And I did just that, heading toward the gate. It would be a lie to say I was fleet of foot or that my belly wasn't nauseous.

"Aren't you going to the infirmary?" my guard asked, halfway to the stockade to gather up the drunk. "Lord Loudoun wants you cared for."

"I'll be fixed up," I assured him. "Going to town."

"You'll not flee?" the guard asked, wondering about his own hide.

"You heard the letters all those folks wrote about me," I answered. "I'm too stupid to run away from danger."

That was enough to pacify the guard and he went to gather up his next victim.

"Going to Hannah's?" Turnwell asked, pointing to my naked chest. "Like that?"

"She'll know what to do," I said. "Besides, I'd rather have her hands on me than the mitts of some army physician. He probably just pulled his out of another man's guts."

Turnwell nodded. "I'll gather your gun and shirt and bring them down to you."

Again free – at least temporarily – we parted ways. I ambled down the grassy hill, eastward toward Albany and the river. It wasn't long before the shopkeepers, laborers, politicians, and slaves of the city took note of my shambled appearance. I was thin, dirty, hairy, and bleeding. More than one of them gasped after I had passed, their eyes and fingers pointing at my filleted back. It was one of the few times that I was thankful that I did not have eyes in the back of my head. I don't think I could have stomached the sight of my ruined flesh.

I then turned off Yonker Street onto Broadway and headed south, parallel to the great Hudson. On my left was the Stadt Huys, the location of the Albany Congress, which felt like a hundred years before. The peaceful sheep that kept the lawn cut short nibbled away. A few lifted their heads and gave me derisive looks. Their relaxed permanence could do nothing to hide the memory that I'd been shot within the Stadt Huys walls. The mangled scar on my chest throbbed just thinking about it.

Further on my path was the *Beverwijck*, my favorite tavern in town – the only one that would extend me credit. Soon after, I passed the Dutch Calvinist Church. They had a new pastor. Like the former one, this man did a superb job of keeping his front stoop clean. He swept off unseen bits of dust using a corn broom. And also like his predecessor, he greeted me with a circumspect scowl.

By the time I reached what had been Hannah and Wellie's home at the southernmost reaches of town, I was exhausted. I hadn't walked that far in many weeks. And even though fall was swiftly blowing in, the insides of my buckskin drawers were sopping wet with sweat.

"You're that funny man who bathed with the cow last year," said one of the children who greeted me at Hannah's door.

"I am," I said. "Is your mother home?"

Then, without having been formally invited in, I collapsed forward through the threshold.

CHAPTER 4

If you've read my previous tales, you might think me a one-trick pony. There is truth in that assessment, for my skills and my reactions to the world were exceptionally limited. In the normal course of my job, I was frequently injured. Whether acting as a journeyman trader and scouring the countryside for bargains or customers, or working as an army scout and combing the woods for hostiles, I seemed to get shot at, hacked at, or stabbed an awful lot. As a result, if I ever hoped to accomplish anything, I had to push through bouts of severe pain – knocks, bumps, and bruises. Most of the time, I survived in decent condition. However, as return readers are aware, I sometimes pushed my body a little too far. Whether it was stubbornness or stupidity, I do not know. Well – I have an idea which one is more likely, but I'd rather not say. At any rate, I'd pushed myself once again that day after receiving the brunt of the cat's wrath.

It hadn't been sweat that had soaked my trousers as I walked through Albany's streets. My own blood had pooled at my waist and seeped down among my buckskins. And so it was, with sufficient dehydration and fatigue, I had passed out into Hannah's home.

Some hours later, when darkness had already claimed its daily victory over the light, I came-to. Staring at chair legs and boots that rested just a foot from my face, I groaned, lifting my snout from the floor.

Turnwell awakened. He'd sat on that chair, snoozing in the hallway where I'd been dragged. His head bumped the wall. "Stay put," he ordered. The toe of his boot gently tapped my forehead to indicate he was serious.

"I can't move anyway," I moaned. "I feel worse than I did when you clawed me with the cat o' nine tails."

"To be expected," he said. "Stay on your belly. I've bandaged you up."

"Thanks," I muttered. Lifting my head hurt, as it caused strain on my tattered skin. "And Hannah? Her children?"

"The children went to bed a little bit ago," Turnwell said. "Hannah hasn't yet returned from work. You're lucky I came when I did."

"You said you were following," I shrugged.

"I was delayed. Had to watch the drunkard get executed. Then the officers were called to Loudoun. Nothing of note. Just administrative matters – supplies here, companies there. You'd have found every word painfully boring. It was after sunset by the time I arrived here. The kids had dragged you inside and just left you alone." Turnwell chuckled. "They've learned to be self-sufficient. I found them eating a dinner that the oldest had prepared. I think they'd forgotten all about the dying man on the floor."

"They've had a difficult life," I said.

"It seems that everyone who crosses your path has the same experience," the ensign observed. The back door creaked open and then slammed closed. "Sounds like the mistress of the house has returned."

Hannah's footsteps paused for a second. Then they pounded across the kitchen. In a heartbeat she was at the end of the hall. In her hand she held a pistol, fully cocked, and ready to release. "Who's there? We have nothing of value. And if you've touched one of my children, I'll not hesitate to use this."

Turnwell lifted a candle to his face and held up his other hand in surrender. "It's Ensign Turnwell, ma'am. This turd on the floor is Ephraim. We merely use your hall to tend to his wounds."

With a click, she released the cock to half and skittered forward. "His wounds? I just saw him today. Oh!" she gasped as she knelt to me and saw what was no doubt the blood-soaked cloths on my back.

"I just need to rest for the night, Hannah," I explained.

"Doesn't the fort have an infirmary?" she asked.

"He said you wouldn't mind, ma'am," Turnwell began.

"Well, I do," she grumbled as she strode off into the kitchen. I heard her rattling around, cursing under her breath. After more grumbling and some cutting, scraping, and stirring,

Hannah returned to the hall carrying a bowl. "You cleaned his wounds?" she asked.

"I did," Turnwell answered. "And I cleaned the floor where he bled. There might be a stain left behind."

"I don't care about the floor," she explained, gently peeling off my bandages. It hurt fiercely, but I managed to get away with only a whimper or two. "This will sting," she warned as she applied a paste to my oozing stripes.

It did. I gritted my teeth.

Though it was too dark to see, her mixture smelled and felt like a yarrow and honey blend. It was a cure that I, too, had used in the forest many times. After she had covered my back with her concoction, I felt her softly press greenbrier leaves in place until they covered me like a sticky blanket. By then, my injuries had turned just slightly numb so that her touch felt good. To a young man who liked women, Hannah's touch always felt good. "In a week, you should be able to again be up and about," she explained when she'd finished.

"I'll get that, ma'am," Turnwell said and deftly took her dirtied pot before she could protest. He disappeared into the rear of the house.

"I have to be back at the fort tomorrow," I said.

"Go ahead if you want to collapse," Hannah advised.

"I don't have any choice," I began.

"You do, too, Ephraim," Hannah growled. "The army is nothing to you. They do not own you."

"That was true until today," I said. And then explained all that had transpired. "So, if I desert now, they *will* have cause to hang me."

Hannah slumped to her rump against the wall across from me. Her head shook in disgust. "Then why have you come to me?" Around the corner, Turnwell stoked the hearth and had begun heating water to clean the dishes.

The truth was that I was drawn to her. She was lovely – at least ten years my senior, but spirited and lovely. "I thought we could remain friends," I offered.

"You wish for more," Hannah countered in her direct manner. "Quite a lot more."

"Is that wrong?" I asked, settling my head onto my folded hands.

"Were you anyone else, perhaps not," she said. "Have you've forgotten that I just found out I lost my husband?" Her demeanor had hardened in the intervening hours since I'd last seen her.

"No, I didn't forget. It's just that with this war and all, time seems to be running ahead whether I like it or not. The folks I like and love don't seem to give me much time with them. I just saw no sense in waiting."

"Waiting for what?" she asked. "You intend to propose?"

The clattering in the kitchen had fallen off. "Care to join the conversation?" I shouted to Turnwell.

"I would if I thought I could help," the ensign chuckled. "But it seems like you are in a losing battle. I'd rather not yoke myself to your wagon."

"Shut up, Turdwell," I growled. The ensign laughed and returned to his kitchen duties.

"I'm waiting," Hannah said, not smiling in the slightest from our banter.

"Hannah," I sighed.

"Don't Hannah me," she said. "I have four children. You have two of your own, only one of which you managed to find and lend to your parents to raise. I imagine that were I to marry you, you would expect the same conjugal privileges that all husbands want. As a result, in short order there would be one, two, perhaps three more children wandering around. And where will you be? Before today, I could have at least hoped that you might be brow-beaten into staying in the city to provide for your family. But now, the army owns you. They will send you where they will. And given your particular set of skills, that means you will be in the wilderness, facing some of my ancient kin. I do not need to become a widow for a third time over. I need a man who can help feed and clothe these children. A strong man."

"I'm strong enough," I growled.

"It's not physical strength I'm talking about. The fact you didn't know that tells me you have more maturing to do."

"I'm mature!" I barked. "I turn twenty-one in January!"

Hannah took in a long breath. She smiled sadly. "Ephraim listen to me," she said softly. "It is not that you are unpleasing to the eye. You are handsome in a rugged, rangy sort-of way. And whether you admit it or not, you are also dedicated to the king's cause here in North America. Such a sacrifice is nobly attractive. It was because of your many admirable qualities that I had told myself if you again proposed marriage to me *and* vowed to stay put *and* stop drinking, I would agree."

Like a school boy, my heart leapt.

"But I cannot accept you as my husband now. Not until this war is over and you are released from service."

That sounded fine to me. I heard only what I wanted to hear. I could run through the countryside, acting the man-boy for a little while longer, sure in the knowledge that there was a fair woman waiting for me in Albany. "Then if I have my pay sent to you, you will keep yourself unencumbered until that day?" I asked.

Hannah gazed up at the ceiling, peering through it to where her children slumbered. "I'll not lie. The extra income would come in handy. But I'll not take another person's money. Not when we are not yet united before man or God."

"But we will be. I'll count down the days. You'll wait."

She shook her head. "No, Ephraim. I'll not wait. There is no one today, but if a suitable man comes along, I'll not hesitate to become his wife. My life belongs to more than just me. I must think of my children. This war may go on for another ten years."

"But…" I began.

Hannah had already climbed to her feet. My mind said to chase after her. My back said to stay put. Tired, she brushed off her skirts. "I have to get some dinner, Ephraim. Then, before I collapse from exhaustion, I have to get to bed. In the morning, I have to be up and gone before first light for the breakfast crowd of politicians at the *Beverwijck.* My responsibilities can't simply stop just because Wellie's dead or you come crashing into my life." She swept into the kitchen, passing Turnwell, who was on his way out. "I'll get you a blanket, ensign, so you can sleep in the hall while you babysit your friend."

“My friend,” Turnwell quipped. “Ephraim’s not my friend. He’s just a fellow who saved my life. Now I can’t get rid of him.”

Hannah paused in the doorway and chuckled sardonically. “I know the feeling.”

CHAPTER 5

Before that morning, I never noticed how heavy a buckskin shirt could be. Mine now felt like it weighed a ton, pulling down against my wounds. Thankfully, Hannah had helped Turnwell apply a new round of bandages over her more natural remedies. They helped shield my back from at least a portion of the buckskin's tugs.

"You look to be in better shape than any other man I've seen struck with the cat!" said the sergeant with admiration. Over his shoulder, a group of soldiers were cleaning up the mess from the man executed by firing squad the previous evening. His bullet-riddled body was set firm with rigor mortis. As his handlers passed him over their shoulders from the pockmarked wall to an awaiting wagon, they appeared completely at ease. The topics of their discussions ranged from a pretty lass one had seen down in Albany to which of them had the better hometown. Not a single lament went up for their rebuked comrade.

I smiled through the pain and glanced at my companion. "Turdwell hits like a girl."

The sergeant, practiced over many moons of army life, frowned. "Oh, shame on you Mr. Weber for saying such a thing about an officer in the king's military." But he gave me a wink and grin as Turnwell and I walked into the fort's headquarters.

"Why can't you ever shut up?" Turnwell huffed as we wound through the dark timber halls.

"Everyone else seems to like it when I talk," I said. A host of officers came and went. Lord Loudoun had continued his busy ways, planning for the campaigns of 1757 that might not commence for another six months.

"No, Ephraim, they don't," Turnwell countered. "Anyone who has a brain knows that within a minute you'll be ridiculing them for something they cannot help."

"Like their crappy name, Turdwell?" I asked.

"Shut up, Weber," Turnwell said. But he did snort involuntarily as he tried to stifle a laugh. In that moment, I couldn't recall why I had ever hated him, but I had. It was probably because he was a true soldier and took care of his manners and appearance. Despite those obvious shortcomings, I had come to like him very much.

"Go on in, sir," said a private, who stood outside the commandant's door. "You're expected." He glanced at me, none-too-pleased. "You, too."

The private swung open the door and closed it behind us. The room was filled with all manners of officers – except the commander of Fort Frederick was visibly absent. He'd been turned out to take care of his own little section of the world, the men who occupied this very real estate.

Abercromby waved us to a pair of seats along the wall. Webb refused to look at us as Lord Loudoun finished his latest discussion.

"Your association with Governor Shirley did you no favors," Loudoun said.

"I will work with whomever I must to achieve victory for my countrymen and king," proclaimed Colonel Bradstreet. He glanced at me from the corner of his eye and gave me an approving nod. "The Governor was my commander and I did my best at the tasks given me, my lord."

"Well said," answered Loudoun. "We cannot always choose our allies. Nonetheless, despite the difficulties at Fort Oswego, you proved yourself very capable in supplying it once you got your bateaux and trains going. And, I'm glad to say," Loudoun added as he perused a column of figures on a page. "You did so with minimal expense."

Bradstreet quickly produced his own page from a breast pocket. After unfolding it, he set it before General Campbell's eyes. "I've sketched out a plan to save even more money on our efforts of provisioning. Simultaneously, and for the first time in this war, I also believe we can equip all provincials and regular soldiers adequately. We all know an army runs on its stomach."

"You've got my attention," Loudoun said. He pointed to one number in particular on the new page. "Can this be true? You project that we should be able to haul a two-hundred weight barrel of beef at a rate of two pence per mile?" He leaned over to Abercromby. "What did we pay this year?"

Abercromby appeared frustrated that he would have to perform work. His jowls quivered in fear of having to be a part of a moving body. Nonetheless, he fought against his tight uniform and marshaled the strength to twist in his seat. He then rustled through a crate of records, his chair and his voice each groaning. At last, he plucked one out. "Latest estimate puts our expense for this campaigning season at just past… six pence per mile."

"A third of the cost? In one year?" Loudoun pressed.

"If we follow that plan, there is no reason we shouldn't accomplish it and more," Bradstreet said confidently.

Loudoun smiled. "I see its merit. Parliament and the Great Commoner will be quite pleased if we can make this happen."

"With your permission, my lord, we shall," Bradstreet said.

"Granted," Loudoun said efficiently. "You'll take over all provisioning for North America. Anything else?"

"Sir," Bradstreet said, meaning yes. He pulled out another set of plans. "I literally grew up in my father's regiment, the 40th Foot. I fought here in North America during the last war with the French. And while our efforts on the interior remain vital in the current conflict, I know we must also work on the periphery. The French fortress at Louisbourg may seem impregnable, but it can fall. I was there when we took it in '45. I know that I shall be too busy with my new duties, but I believe that anyone who is dispatched to take Acadia will benefit from those ideas."

Loudoun was genuinely pleased. Passing the latest plans to Abercromby, he said, "We shall review your suggestions in detail and incorporate them should such an excursion be deemed profitable. Is that all?"

"One last thing, Lord Loudoun," Bradstreet said in a clipped fashion. Here in the fort, he was nothing like the easy-going frontier soldier I had met in the spring. In the woods he joked with officers and men. No evidence of such improprieties presented itself in Albany. Perhaps, I should have learned something from his ability to separate his actions based upon the situation. "I see that Mr. Weber is now free. That pleases me, sir. Might I have him dispatched to my command. He proved himself capable in ranging for our wagon trains and guarding floating scows."

Loudoun leaned back in his chair, fixing me with a gaze. "It pleases me to see him walking about, as well. But I have someone I'd like him to meet. Someone with a role that perhaps even better suits his skills."

"Sir," Bradstreet said agreeably, tipping his head.

"Dismissed," Loudoun said.

The colonel left after giving me another friendly, farewell nod.

"Weber. Mr. Turnwell," Loudoun said, his voice cutting through the myriad of assembled officers. "Come. I have orders."

Once the ensign helped me to my feet, I was able to walk unassisted to face the seated generals. Webb still found anywhere else in the room to look.

"Do you gentlemen know why our fortunes in this current conflict with the French have proceeded to such dire ends thus far?" Lord Loudoun asked.

Ensign Turnwell was smart. "No, my lord," he admitted.

I was not smart. "Because we let the Frogs win. A gaggle of lasses wearing skirts could have beaten us as poorly as we've prepared. We've taken no advice from anyone who knows a lick about fighting in these woods. From the colonial legislatures to the common soldier, we've been greedy." I glanced to Webb, but showed a modicum of restraint by not saying his name aloud. "And we've been given officers who refuse to fight."

Turnwell, Abercromby, and Webb were aghast. So were the other officers. Not Loudoun, however. "Partially correct, Mr. Weber," he said. "I'll explain to you the parts you've missed. It's because from top to bottom, we have not taken the North American theater seriously. Our efforts, blood, and treasure have been focused on the Continent. But this is not a side show," he said pointing to the table in front of him. "This is THE war. Right here. The outcome will determine which country will form an empire or which will fall to servitude. And I intend to fight with everything I've got to dislodge the French. I'll use every resource at my disposal, and then some. From now on, we are in an all-out war."

I appreciated his enthusiasm. Coming from an intelligent man, it warmed my heart to no longer have to worry about fighting with one hand tied behind my back. "Does that mean the silly rule where provincial officers are inferior to even the lowliest regular ensign is out the window, sir?" I asked.

Loudoun held up a hand. "You've said enough, Mr. Weber. Let's control your tongue before it again gets you in trouble. But to answer your question, no. The rule stands. And, frankly, I endorse it. The real way we are going to defeat the Frogs is to unleash the full might of the regular British army against them. I will command almost all the regulars personally next year in one fell swoop against one of the French strongholds. A smattering of regulars will be left behind in the interior outposts to see that the provisional troops don't crumble from a few Indian barbarians."

For a man so intelligent, he couldn't seem to escape the intense, misplaced gravity of the way men of his class viewed the world.

"Turnwell," Loudoun went on. "I'm told you are proficient with artillery. I wish for you to go to Fort William Henry. General Johnson's duties as Indian Superintendent have pulled him from his post. Major Eyre is an able engineer and currently commands the fort. Learn from Eyre and assist in the fort's defense so that I will not have to be concerned with it while I am gone. Is that clear, *Lieutenant* Turnwell."

Turnwell grinned at his unexpected promotion. Growing even more rigid in posture, he said, "Yes, my lord."

Loudoun faced me. "Mr. Weber, you will accompany the lieutenant. You've heard of Robert Rogers?"

Of course, I had heard of him. Since the outbreak of hostilities, it had been his rangers that had helped stem the worst of the Indian tide from swamping the northernmost colonies. "Yes, Lord Loudoun. He's a legend."

Loudoun raised his eyebrows. "I prefer real men over those from myths. At any rate, he has been tasked with operating around Lake George for the coming year. Now that you are a member of my regular forces, you are to range with his men. I want you to categorize all of his babblings into rules. I want them written, disseminated, and remembered. By this time next year, I do not want to have to rely on colonial troops to serve as our scouts and rangers. I want you to use his tactics to train a band of regular soldiers."

I shrugged. "Hell, sir, I can do that today. I've been in these woods since I was born."

"Did you not hear your commander, boy?" Webb asked.

Loudoun, rather than snapping at each of us like a child, merely glanced at General Webb, then me. He said nothing with his mouth. His eyes were warning enough. Webb curled up in his chair.

"Find Robert Rogers and learn," I summarized.

Loudoun nodded, pointing to the ancient French pistol stuck in my belt. It was the only relic I had retained from my first wife. "Are you better armed than that?"

I peered down at my waist, feeling naked, while shaking my head. "I lost it all in the surrender, sir. My tomahawks, knives, and Brown…" I hesitated, knowing that I had long committed an offense by owning a Brown Bess built from parts pilfered from the armory in the Tower. "And my musket, sir."

Lord Loudoun looked to Turnwell. "See that each of you are refitted from the humble armory below." The lieutenant hastily agreed. "And the two of you carry orders to Major Eyre that he has my permission and encouragement to harass the enemy in any way he sees fit. He shall not be granted unlimited means, but he should make a big noise where he can. I'd like him to draw French resources away from the main point of our thrust next year."

"Which is?" Abercromby asked.

Loudoun scowled at his second in command. "In due time, Jim. We can't have rumors flying about, giving the enemy a half-year of warning."

"Oh, yes. Good show, Lord John."

"Do you understand?" Loudoun asked the two of us.

"Sir!" we both snapped with polite bows.

"Then be off. A train of supplies leaves for upriver in the next day or two. Be with it, *Lieutenant* Turnwell and *Private* Weber."

Hearing me addressed with a rank in His Majesty's army was more painful than all the whipping in the world. For, now I was truly a prisoner.

CHAPTER 6

Over a year had passed since I'd last seen Fort Edward. During my absence, General Johnson and his engineers had completed its construction, shaping it into a perilous obstacle to any Frenchmen dreams of descending all the way down to Albany from the north. It sat adjacent to the Hudson with commanding views over the riverway and the nearby terrain. Fields of fire had been opened from the dense forest on all three landward sides so that their intimidating cannons could decimate any would-be attackers. Edward was our first stop on the way to the remote Fort William Henry.

Because the corridor between Albany and Fort Edward was well patrolled and generally clear of enemy activity, the first leg of our journey was uneventful. Bradstreet's bateaux men were scrappy low-lives who could take care of most problems that might arise. As such, I was free to loiter on their scows. And sleep most of the way. And eat. I ate prodigious amounts of food to make up for the long periods of starvation I'd endured since the previous winter. Salted pork. Salted fish. Salted beef. All that salt made me thirsty. I found rum and brandy among the provisions. By the time we slid into the shingle at Edward, I was properly pickled.

Hannah would not have approved. She often complained that I drank too much. But who didn't drink a little excessively now and then? Weeks or even months could go by without even seeing a drop of alcohol. So, when it was available, I drank. A lot.

I had begun my binge early. For, I had consumed much of the stuff while Turnwell and I had waited for the supply scows to leave Albany. All of it, I had drunk on the good graces of *Beverwijck*'s proprietor. He threatened me often with a wagging finger, but never once shut off the credit pumps entirely. I merely had to drop a penny or two into his hands and he'd renew the flow. Hannah, working constantly in the tavern, had frowned and scowled as I became drunker and drunker. But seeing her displeasure was worth it to me. She had a lovely form and face. They became all the more comely as I drank.

"What are you grinning about?" Turnwell asked as he jostled me from my reverie. I had passed out among a pile of soggy, smelly fishing nets on one of the boats. "You look like the village idiot."

"I must be," I pontificated, unwilling to let go of my continuing daydream. "Do you not think Hannah is the most marvelous woman in the world?"

A burly man carrying a barrel up to Edward brushed past us. "She has her merits," the ensign, I mean, lieutenant, admitted with sufficient decorum. "But right now she is forty miles and two days away and you are in a theater of war. Do you think you can begin to act like a soldier, Private Weber?"

I sat up, sleepier than I'd been before my most recent nap. "Oh, why'd you have to go and bring that up again? Likely ruin my day. Besides, who'll know if you don't tell them?" I asked, pointing to my buckskins. "I don't look like a soldier."

"That is part of the problem," Lieutenant Turnwell said, yanking me upright.

With the lieutenant dragging me, my feet reluctantly plunged through the smooth stones on shore. I lazily swatted at his hand, more to annoy him than actually get him to release me. "Lord Loudoun says that as long as I range, I don't have to follow the regulations." My mouth tasted like I'd spent a month licking rusty iron. "Are you thirsty?"

"No," Turnwell answered abruptly, shoving me forward. "And neither are you. And by the way, Loudoun didn't mean for you to ignore all regulations, just the ones about a warrior's dress. You convinced him that a man must blend in with his surroundings in this hostile country."

"And I intend to, mother," I slurred as we moved into the fort proper. It bustled with activity. Johnson truly had left it clopping on all hooves. It was just as smart as any English fort should be. "Let me quench my thirst," I added.

But Turnwell forcibly turned me from my path when I tried to steer toward a group of enlisted men. They shared a meal – and drink. "No," the lieutenant said rather patiently. "I intend to be at my post by nightfall. The same will go for you. Let's get horses and go."

"By ourselves?" I asked, yanking him in a third direction across the parade ground.

This sudden change of direction surprised Turnwell. But, seeing no liquor at the other end of my proposed path, he followed. "I thought you were Monsieur Wilderness."

I chuckled. "I like that, Monsieur Wilderness. I've never been called that before. I have been called Fierce Dog in these parts. It's a name the tribesmen have given me." In truth, I had bestowed the name upon myself – and it had only modestly caught on. A man shouldn't have to conjure his own forest nickname. His deeds should do that for him.

"So, are you afraid to go from here to Lake George unaccompanied?" the lieutenant asked, taunting. "What is it? Twenty miles?"

"Fifteen," I corrected. "And the portage road is easy. Unless you like your scalp."

"We saw not a single man or woman for our entire trip northward," Turnwell protested.

"You remember Oswego?" I asked, now climbing a set of stairs that had recently been painted white. Even in my inebriated condition, I felt a little ashamed at leaving behind a path of muddy footprints. "There were plenty of Indians there, right?"

He shivered. "How can I forget?"

"There'll be more here," I warned. I sucked a deep breath in and out, willing myself sober and then entered the commander's office.

CHAPTER 7

"We're in the heart of what used to be Iroquoia," Fort Edward's commander said. "Mohawk country. Johnson is an honorary colonel in their army, for heaven's sake! His wife is one of them. We have good relations with the local tribesmen. They've turned neutral, but not hostile."

"It's not the Mohawks I worry about," I answered, setting aside the Brown Bess I'd been issued before departing Albany. It was a fine firearm, bushels better than the old Bess I'd cobbled together at the risk of the hangman's noose. And I'd not be a proper scout if I didn't spend a fair amount of time relating my new gal's looks. You see, if I had a fondness for my old Bess, this new lass filled in the void quite nicely. She was a touch lighter than my original and equipped with a steel ramrod, one of very few guns I'd ever seen with such advanced technology. She wore a cast-brass nose cap that was much stronger than the cheap sheet metal strapped at the front of my last musket. The shape of her lock resembled that of my first, like a banana. But that is where the locks' similarities ended. My new lock was official, stamped, not only with the name Jordan 1747 behind the cock, but also with elements to the front. First came an engraving of a crown, beneath which were the capital letters *G R*, the official cypher of King George. Then, just below the pan was the official crowned broad arrow which indicated that it had been fully inspected and was now owned (like me) by the government of His Majesty. Finally, and probably most importantly, was that a bridle had been added to strengthen the frizzen arm. I cannot tell you how many times I had broken the frizzen at the neck on my old Bess. "Though, as I've had many friends among the Mohawk for many years, I'd still not turn my back during these uncertain times. War makes us all, well, tribal."

"I know that much, lad," the commander said, sniffing the air around me. He could tell I'd been drinking. A blind man with a stuffed nose could tell that. Thankfully, he waited for me to stumble verbally or physically before he outright leveled the accusation. "You're not the only provincial around here who has made nice with the savages. We use colonials as scouts all the time. They keep us apprised of what's going on in the Mohawk villages. Some even bring news from Onondaga."

"It's the distant tribes I'm worried about," I explained.

"Delaware?" the commander asked. "Way up here? The Iroquois would have a bigger fit than we would. Imagine a party of Delaware warriors prancing about in Iroquoia! They'd be dead in a week. And I'd have nothing to do with it!"

I shrugged. "The Delaware, Abenaki, Shawnee, Menominee, Ottawa, Potawatomi, Fox, Chippewa. The word of what happened at Oswego will spread faster than fire through pine needles. Indians will come from all over for captives and scalps from the English. Or, they'll want the same riches Chief Collière received from Montcalm just to stop the slaughter of our helpless wounded."

"I haven't even heard of half of those tribes," he said, exasperated. "An army cannot act upon hunches or gut feelings." He then turned his attention to Turnwell. "Is there a reason you've come, lieutenant? Might you speak in this provincial's stead?"

"He may not look it, sir," Turnwell said. "But he is a member of His Majesty's regular army."

Incredulous, the commander snapped, "In that outfit? What regiment?"

Turnwell and I both snickered.

"What's so funny?" the commander asked.

"Nothing, sir," Turnwell answered. "It's just, well, that was among the first questions I asked Ephraim when I first met him last year."

"What's the answer?"

"None, sir," I piped up. "No regiment. Lord Loudoun made it all official, you see. But I'm to be officially, unofficially attached to Rogers' Rangers. We're told he's lately been operating out of Fort William Henry."

"Rogers' Rangers!" scoffed the commander. He eyed me top to bottom. "Oh, you'll fit right in. Rogers' Rangers. They are no more *his* rangers than they are mine. They belong to the king and royal governors! Huh! And the newspapers act as if Robert Rogers is the only one skilled in frontier warfare. Hasn't anyone ever heard of John Gorham? He was a friend of mine. Even after his death, his rangers are working just as hard as those of Robert Rogers."

I'd heard of Gorham's Rangers. Their territory ran back east a ways. Operated against our French foes in Acadia mostly. Some even said that Rogers had learned his craft from a few of Gorham's veterans. But those kinds of facts didn't matter when it came to selling sheets of newsprint. The hucksters who concocted the tales in the papers were as fickle as a young boy bent on giving his heart away to a girl. Any girl, as long as she smiled right, would do the trick in a pinch when a boy felt those surges of raging manhood. The papers acted the same way with military commanders. They were always looking for the next pretty face.

The commander got his momentary frustration under control. "Fine. Private Weber is to hump in the snow this winter with Rogers and you, lieutenant, are to go to with him to Fort William Henry. Why have you come to me?"

"Two things," I said, answering for Turnwell. I don't think he liked it, but the lieutenant had at least gotten used to the fact that I spoke whenever I chose. "First, we'd like to ride with your next train of supplies to William Henry."

The commandant carelessly tossed his hand into the air. "The roads are safe these days and the two of you could go right now. But I've got more things to worry about than your little schedules." He glanced out a small window to all the bateaux men unloading supplies along with his own soldiers. "By the time we get this batch inventoried and divided, I'd say a train will head for Lake George by tomorrow."

"Fine," I said, thinking I could get another big, warm meal or two in me by then. And a few rounds of rum.

"And two," said Turnwell as I licked my lips. "Lord Loudoun has ordered Major Eyre to be aggressive with regard to his harassment of the French. Until we are told otherwise. Albany will not be able to dispatch any significant resources in that regard, so Edward will have to support any of Eyre's reserve needs."

The commander shrugged. "That is why we're here. If Eyre can give the Frogs a good, hard lesson, I'll do all I can to help. I'd happily go out their personally if it meant punishing a few of those goose-lovers. They started all this by taking over an English fort at the Forks of Ohio, you know."

I knew. I'd been there.

This particular commander was growing on me. He spoke directly. And we shared a hatred of the French.

"Anything else?" he asked.

Turnwell and I exchanged glances. "No, sir," we clipped in unison. For a moment, it was almost like I was becoming a model soldier.

For at least a few minutes.

That night I found a gaggle of young privates. Most of them had just arrived on our wild continent in the spring from Wales. They'd seen nothing of the vast land but York City, the Hudson River, and Fort Edward. And though we were all near the same age, they seemed pups to me. So, while Turnwell fraternized with the other officers in a more appropriate discourse, I led a small platoon of my fellow enlisted men. With expert stealth, we stole a firkin of rum from under the nose of the quartermaster. Then, after promising the night watch a share of money I did not have, we snuck into an ally between the wall and the barracks. We drank. A lot. After they were sufficiently soused, I borrowed playing cards from one of them. We played loo for our wages, again, none of which I had. I cheated. The puppies didn't notice.

To the sound of the reveille drums, I woke up the next morning with more money than I'd had in years. With a splitting headache, I divided my winnings with the sentries who had dutifully looked the other way all night. I was still left with a fair wad of bills and coins.

Then, I sauntered over to where the supply train was assembling at the gate.

"Where were you all night?" Turnwell asked. He was mounted on a horse from the stables.

I plunked my rump in the back of a wagon that was filled with cabbage. "Working," I huffed. And with my feet dangling off the rear, I laid down. Lieutenant Turnwell began giving me some type of reprimand, I'm sure. I heard none of it. I'd already fallen fast asleep.

CHAPTER 8

I do not know how long it took to finish organizing the provisions. At some point, however, the calls of teamsters and the whinny of their beasts rose to a cacophony and I felt my produce bed lurch forward. It rattled and pitched, bumped and bounded. But so exhausted was I that it felt as soothing as a being rocked to sleep against a caring mother's plump, warm chest. Welcome sleep returned before I had even cracked open a single eye.

Hours passed.

Until someone was talking to me. Nonstop. In my sleepy, passed out haze, I recall hearing unending streams of words that seemingly linked together to tell tales. And those tales shifted from one subject to the other, the manner in which they were related to one another known only to the man who did the spinning. I remember hearing something about oysters. Another story involved a stormy gale and a lost albatross. And just when my addled mind thought the teller had latched onto a seafaring theme, I heard one about stepping in a road apple with bare feet.

One of my eyes involuntarily peeked. I was rewarded with a blinding ray of sunshine piercing down through the vast, high forest canopy above. I slapped a hand over the wounded orb and groaned.

"Alright, Sarah Belle," chuckled the voice of the wordsmith. "We've roused him at last. You best go back and give the lad a kiss. See if he's really alive."

There was an immediate rustling over the heads of cabbage. I felt a shadow fall over me, but was too weak to shrink away. I suppose that the silly youth in me still had a little of that eternally springing hope tucked away inside. My mind had already conjured an image of the fairest version of my two wives and Hannah into one beautiful young woman named Sarah Belle. I awaited the lovely brush of her lips.

An aggressive tongue splashed all over my face and hand. It explored my ears, my nostrils, my lips. It was wet and hot. And excited. More excited than any woman could ever possibly be at kissing the likes of me. It licked my hair, brushing it into an upright style akin to the tufts of hair atop the crowns of my

Iroquois brethren. All efforts at guarding my face with my forearms were thwarted by the sloppy, probing mass of muscle. I swung my bent arms back and forth, bumping away the attack. But my opponent was undeterred, intent on finding every new and possible entry point.

"That's enough!" I called. "I'm up!"

But the act of opening my mouth invited a far more repulsive assault. The dog rammed her snout between my jaws like she chased a rat down a hole. Its nose plunged this way and that. The tongue squished its way around my oral cavity, lapping the inner walls of my cheeks and even finding the back of my throat. I gagged. But it wasn't because of the far-reaching and highly offensive tongue. It was the beast's breath. Like a ramrod aggressively fed a shot of lead into the muzzle of a gun, that dog forcefully pumped its fetid concoction of refuse air through my pipes. I could simultaneously smell and taste it. Were I a connoisseur of such things, I might have said it contained hints of dog and cow manure mixed with the essence of rotten venison.

I bit down. Hard. Sarah Belle yipped and immediately retreated.

Laughing now, the storyteller, cackled as the dog raced forward over the cabbage. "That's what you get, girl. I'm sure the French whores don't even act in such a forward way when they are becoming acquainted with a new man. But you'll heal." He made a smooching sound as the cart hit a great root in the road. The front of the wagon rose up and slammed over it. Then the rear axle leapt and fell. "Oh, that hurts my backside," the teamster called. "Sarah Belle meant you no harm. She likes you, that's all."

I spat away Sarah Belle's lingering flavor while wiping the slobber off my face. Then, with mighty effort, I slowly sat upright. Staring out the back of the trundling wagon, I faced a mixed pair of horses tugging a cart filled with barrels of flour. Their giant black eyes gazed through me at the road ahead. I reached out and tickled the supple snout of the prettier one, a bay. Her lips quivered, nibbling on my fingertips.

"What do I go calling you, boy?" the teamster asked.

I craned over the cabbage while scrubbing a quart of sleep from my eyes. From the rear, the teamster was lean, as were most men who lived on the frontier in those days. Nothing like the soft boars who lay around the towns these days moving stacks of papers from this desk to that. He wore a floppy hat with a brim that wrapped all around the base. It was too big for his head and the only things that kept it from sinking over his face were his two ears, which were bent below its weight. On one side, the brim flopped against his shoulder. On the other side, most of the brim appeared to have been chewed away by some creature – Sarah Belle? He wore a soiled shirt with its sleeves rolled all the way down since the chill of autumn had already begun to sink into the dark forests of northern New York. Next to him on the seat, Sarah Belle growled at me.

"Hush now, girl!" he chastised. "Serves you right, coming on to him the way you did. A nice peck on the cheek would have been better. Let that be a lesson." The driver paused for no more than a second before he then said, "If you don't want to share your name, fella, that's fine. Rude. But fine. Takes all kinds, the forest, you know. I'm called Itch. Not what my momma named me. But better than her ideas, don't you think?"

"Ephraim Weber," I said.

"Oh, so you do have a name. Fine name. Weber? German. I suppose you come from Pennsylvania. Stout folks. Good enough, I suppose. But the damn pacifists down there invited all them Indian attacks if you ask me. Haven't seen any attacks up this away since Johnson licked the French up the road a piece last year. Weber? You were there weren't you? Friend of the savages, as I recall. I was down at Edward when I heard all that you fellas had done up here. Fine work butchering those Frog grenadiers the way you did."

"They took a few chunks out of our hides before we repaid them the favor." In truth, the way our cannons had sliced alleys through the magnificent ranks of grenadiers had been a shameful waste of youth and vigor. What had been a brilliant array of soldiers a moment before the guns burst, was reduced to a crawling mess of limbs and innards a second later.

"I'd guess so. Damned Frogs," he grumbled. "And you already met Sarah Belle." The dog's lop ears perked at the mention of her name. Itch affectionately ran a rough hand through the mottled fur on her head. She pressed herself firmly into his palm

Without giving it much thought, I swung my legs into the wagon and leaned against the rattling side board. I then snatched a head of cabbage and bit into it. Food needed to hit my sour belly. Or, without a doubt, my guts would soon begin eating themselves. The cabbage was a crunchy treat, fresh and cool.

Itch turned briefly. He had an average face with an average beard. But his smile was remarkable in that it hiked up much higher on one side, bunching his lean cheek into something that was nearly plump. "Go ahead, partake!" he encouraged. "A man as drunk as you needs something. Of course, cabbage won't improve the smell of your swamp gas any. But at least you might not feel like dying by suppertime. Besides, Major Eyre, the way he talks about you, won't care a lick if you swipe a little food from his stores. The way he says it, you are some fierce warrior." His wary eyes studied me. "I guess he's not seen much in the way of fierce warriors."

I chuckled. Here was another example of a stranger, a fellow forest man. Like those whom I'd met before him, Itch had so easily and quite gracefully slipped into making fun of me. It was how we all acknowledged one another, how we spoke to those we knew in an instant to be like us. Quickly thanking him for the half-hearted compliment, I raised my cabbage in his direction like it was a wine glass.

Itch responded with an approving nod. And now fully satisfied that he and Sarah Belle had safely roused me, he again faced the road. Next, Itch launched into conversation with his team of horses, playing both sides of the back and forth, even arguing a bit about the details of one story in particular. He allowed me a few minutes of quiet to eat my meager meal.

After consuming two full heads of raw cabbage, my eyesight began to sharpen. My mind slowly cleared as the scents of the never-ending autumn forest penetrated what had been my self-induced fog. The fall, a time of dying as it was, always smelled rich and full to me – mature, as if it was something toward which to aspire. It brought with it nothing like the sweetness and boundless opportunity of spring, but a fine aroma, nonetheless. Ripened, brittle leaves had begun fluttering down from the trees. The sight was almost enough to make me forget just how devilish man and the woods could be to mere survival. Almost.

Looking through the poet's natural, fluttering muses, I studied the terrain. Every curve in the path and every leaning oak, I recognized immediately. For, a good scout carried a map of every place he'd ever visited in his mind. And, candidly, I thought of myself as a little better than good.

I quickly craned my neck, peering at a patch of earth we passed next to the path. It was the exact spot where the venerable Chief Hendrick had been slaughtered a year earlier. He and his horse had been butchered to a skinless state by a nasty band of former Iroquois who now served French masters. The ground, as a lasting memorial to the ancient chief, was still stained black from all his blood.

My head involuntarily cocked. A second later, Sarah Belle's did the same.

"Did you hear that?" I rasped.

"It's not polite to interrupt a man in the midst of a conversation," Itch chastised. Then he resumed his heated discourse with his horses.

I gave my cheek a swift, heavy slap in order to better focus. Then I closed my eyes, listening intently.

"That's it," I whispered. "There it was again." Sarah Belle's ears were perked.

"We call that a woodpecker, boy," Itch explained with ample frustration. With an outstretched hand, he shook his dog's head playfully. She immediately turned her attention from the woods to her beloved master.

Meanwhile, I grabbed my new Bess and scrambled out of the wagon, leaving Itch and Sarah Belle to their banter. I guessed, correctly, that Itch and I weren't all that much alike. His fine-tuned forest sense had been too dulled from frequent bouts spent in the great towns back east. And, it seemed, that no amount of liquor could dull my senses when it came to the woods.

"Who do we have shadowing our movements?" I asked the driver in the rig behind, hoping he was a little closer to sane than Itch.

He shrugged. "We've made this trek a lot in the last year. Haven't seen a soul."

That was no answer. "Are you saying we don't have scouts?" I jogged alongside.

His shoulders went up again. "Bradstreet pays me to drive this wagon. I drive this wagon."

"Who's in charge of the train?" I asked.

He looked to and fro. Then he pointed to the van with his nose. "I suppose that pup thinks it's him since he's the only officer around."

"Turdwell," I grunted when I spied the man in question.

A few seconds later, I padded up next to his mount. "Lieutenant," I breathed, feeling queasy. The cabbage was only mildly improving my condition. And in some predictable ways, the ruffage had simultaneously worsened it.

"Remarkable," Turnwell said as he studied me. "It's a miracle you can walk, Mr. Weber. And now that we are in theater, I warn you that I can no longer overlook your shortcomings. I expect you to be the model of sobriety."

I thought of a few pithy comebacks. Heaven knows I adored getting under Turdwell's skin. But there were other matters at hand. "Do you not have scouts on our flanks?"

He shook his head. "I deferred to the men with experience in the area. I was told the French have been content to keep themselves up around Carillon and its environs."

"Times change," I growled. "I think we're being watched. Permission to assemble a troupe…"

The lieutenant's face fell in disgust. "Do you mean to melt into the trees and gamble and drink?"

I said nothing. Only my jaw set firmly, flaring out.

Turnwell knew me well enough. He glanced up into the dark trees, saying, "Granted. Report back at regular, short intervals."

"Aye," I said.

One minute later I had assembled a motley band of scouts from among the train. Three would strike off south and shadow the portage road. I, and two others, would move north.

"Why the hell do I have to listen to some green Pennsylvanian boy?" grumbled one of the men in my party. I never bothered to get his name. His accent told me he was from Carolina. I didn't hate men from his country. But I had found enough of them so egotistical that I had vowed to give all of them a wide berth and avoid entangling friendships.

I spun, getting up in the bigger man's face. "Because this green boy ain't green. He can save your life, you greasy, Carolina bastard. I've spent more time in these woods than most of the tribesmen. There!" I said when the tapping I had heard earlier resumed. "We're sneaking up on that."

The older man's eyes rolled. "On the hunt for a birdie poking at bark. Well, I'll tell you what…"

I slammed a fist as hard as I could into his belly. He made a hollow gasping sound and buckled over, falling to his knees. I slapped a hand over his mouth and drew a knife, setting it against his neck. His comrade was a smooth-faced sixteen-year-old fellow named Thomas Brown. Brown was wide-eyed and still while I motioned for him to stay that way. "If the Indians don't kill you, I will," I whispered into the fallen man's ear. Another tapping sound answered the first. "That ain't no woodpecker, fool. Only you and a Philadelphia gentleman would make that mistake."

I carefully withdrew the knife and my hand, staring into the man's eyes. They were filled with hate, but he obeyed, making not a peep. Some folks were like dogs in that way. You just had to show them who led the pack and no matter what happened afterward, they'd follow.

And that man and Brown followed me silently into the brush.

CHAPTER 9

I was quite satisfied with myself. The so-called woodpeckers were moving rapidly ahead of us, keeping up exactly with the progress of the supply train's progress. The expressions on my companions' faces told me that even they had come to understand that we faced not flitting beasts, but skulking men.

A creek punctuated the forest and was now cutting off our progress toward the roving taps. I came to a dead halt, crouching. "Around that bend to the north," I whispered. "The brook gets wide, shallow, and slow for a piece. We can cross there almost silently and without getting water-logged. Might be able to sneak up on this pack of trackers and give 'em a surprise."

After retracing our steps, we moved parallel to the rushing water. Soon, we again cut westward. As we approached the creek for the second time, I turned and gave my followers a shit-eating grin. The occasional taps were closer than ever, just ahead on the other side of the creek and slowly moving away. "We'll have them in our sights soon enough. Might bag ourselves a Canadian scout or a Caughnawaga Catholic for dinner, boys." This bluster pleased them, even the victim of my blow. They both grinned back.

I spent a solid two minutes peeking from the bramble at the water's edge to make sure no one would see us when we emerged into the relative open of the stream. Satisfied, I cautiously stepped onto a soft sandbank and halted again, partially exposed, partially hidden. I looked down at the fresh footprint of a man. There was no marking of a heel. It had been clad in a moccasin.

I pointed to the mark, to my eye, and then to our surroundings. My men nodded their understanding and crept out behind me, more vigilant than ever. Our movements could not be heard even over the gentle ripple of the creek. Not a rock was scattered. Not a splash was made. We were methodical as we scanned in all directions.

Soon, we passed the halfway point having secured two victories. One, nothing over my ankles had gotten wet. And two, we'd not been killed. The middle was the spot where any lurking enemies would have sprung their ambush. None came. I breathed a little easier and silently finished my trek.

"Good work," I rasped over my shoulder as I stepped onto the opposite bank.

I faced forward and set my weight firmly on my front foot before lifting my rear foot out of the water. Less than a yard from my face, the forest suddenly came alive. A terrifyingly quiet, brown smear flashed from the side. I felt a great crack upon my face. Then, promptly tasting the iron of crimson on my lips, my head snapped back. Every color of the rainbow, and a few more added in for good measure, sparkled in my field of vision. Like a straight, solitary pine felled by a lumberman, I tipped backward. My compatriots did nothing to catch me. I felt myself slough past Brown.

My limp form loudly splashed into the shallow stream before coming to an abrupt halt on the creek bed. But it was not a soft, plush bed. The pain in my rump and back from sharp rocks was only outdone by the great thud of a rock at the base of my skull.

Dazed, the last thing I remembered seeing as I helplessly stared up from the creek was the ruddy face of a white man. In one hand he held the maple limb that he'd used to smack me. In the other, he held a tomahawk, well-used. As he moved swiftly toward me, he wielded the hatchet as if it was an extension of his own body. But I can report no more on the incident. As he crouched at my side, my consciousness fled.

It was probably just as well. I had seen what was about to happen a hundred times.

And no one wanted to be awake when he was scalped.

CHAPTER 10

I came-to in the same position in which I had faded, staring up to the heavens. But it was now some time after midday. The cold creek water sluiced around me. I felt a chill and shivered, realizing that it was probably the cold that had kept the pain of my lost scalp to a surprisingly tolerable level. My head throbbed, to be sure. But it was mostly from the whack I'd received on the front, and then the back, that I felt. The agony on the top of my crown simply blended in with the rest.

It would have been better to not have awakened. Now, no matter what I did, I would have to experience the anguish of the inevitable, slow death that followed a scalping.

Impulsively, I felt at my waist for one of my knives. But with my hand in mid-swing, I realized that the Canadian would have stolen it. Woodsmen of all stripes – English, Indian, German, even Frogs – were resourceful and he would not have abandoned a fine piece of tempered steel to the elements. You may imagine my surprise when I slapped the belt and found the hilt just where it was supposed to be. Thinking sluggishly, I tugged it free.

Holding it now firmly in my right hand, I lifted my left arm up out of the creek. I shook my arm swiftly so the heavy sleeve of my soaked buckskins slipped to reveal my wrist. I then examined the blue and violet veins coursing just below the skin. I'd never harmed myself intentionally. But I had vowed to hasten my departure from the world after so gullibly falling into the Canadian's trap.

The blade went to my wrist. I stared, hesitating. While I had dispatched dozens of warriors in battle, I found I was unable to even prick my own skin.

"Don't look," I muttered to myself.

I sucked in a deep breath. The fresh air brought with it resolve. I exhaled and closed my eyes. Still I hesitated. *One more breath*, I told myself. In went the air. Pause. Pause. Pause. Out went the air. I flexed my blade-wielding arm and shoved.

"Whut in hell-fiyah ah you doin'?" screamed a man's voice as a hand smacked away my extended left arm. "Oh, 'twas a blatant violation of the rules! But not as bad as all that!"

The accent was peculiar to say the least. It was, in one part, Scottish. And another part slipped in that sounded like those who hailed from New Hampshire. But there was a third part that lingered in the words, too. I swore that an Irishman had swatted me.

My eyes shot open, pointing the knife menacingly at my savior. It was the same man who had struck me. The Canadian!

"Mahy, Joseph, and thah son! Whut's gotten into you?" he asked. "Knife to the wrist?"

Adjusting the blade so his thigh was within striking distance, I otherwise remained stationary. I wasn't willing to move an inch out of that soothing water, lest I encourage the pain from my scalp to announce itself. "I aim to finish what you started with that tomahawk, you Canadian Frog." Then, examining his belt for the dripping remains of my hair and flesh, I wondered what it would be like to see something that had heretofore been an intimate part of my own body.

The truth was something else. It was as obvious to my assailant then as it is to you now. But I was oblivious to the fact that I'd not been scalped. Chalk it up to drink or the blow or bald stupidity.

He laughed merrily. "Canadian? Frog?" The man craned his head around toward the bank I'd not yet reached. A host of other laughs joined him. "Did ya heah that one, lads? Me! A Frog!"

Then with blinding speed he twisted. And to this day, I cannot describe how it happened. I only know that in the first instant he was guffawing. In the second, he knelt next to me in the creek. The man now held my own knife so the tip just pricked the skin of my cheek. His other hand firmly blocked my ability to reach for any of my other weapons.

"You ever pull a weapon on me again, even a toothpick, and you'll find that I can scalp in a mannah wahse than any savage could imagine," he whispered in my ear. "And if you evah so much as hint that I might be a Canadian or Frenchman, when I'm dune cuttin' you from limb to limb, I'll move on to yoah muther and fahthah." He slowly pulled his face back so that it hovered a foot above mine. His eyes stared straight into my own. "Ah we cleah?"

The alpha male had claimed his position in the pack. While I knew I was not at the bottom, I was equally aware that I was no longer at the apex. It was comforting to know one's place.

"Clear," I said.

He smiled broadly. As he rose to his feet, he gently set my knife upon my chest and offered me a hand.

Before I gave mine to him, I reached up and felt my pate. What for a split second I thought was oozing blood, was just the water in the brook. My fingers clasped a full hunk of my unruly hair.

He grunted as he hiked me up. My assailant even held me steady for a moment as I swooned. "I'd not take it as a thing to be embahhassed of, lad," he said. "All me men, even the most experienced ones have had to be taught a lesson the hahd way now and again. Though, in truth, few do it within the fahst minute." Then he carefully spun me to face the way from which I'd come. Pointing to the shallow ford, he added, "But I guess you'll not violate this rule anytime soon. Nevah use a well-known ford when in hostile country. Else you want to invite ambush."

I gingerly rubbed my snout, which felt the size of a melon. Then I touched the back of my head. A tender egg had blossomed beneath the scalp. He was right, I'd not soon forget his rule. "How many rules are there?" I asked.

He'd begun guiding us out the western side. Some five paces in, there was a clearing filled with twenty and three loitering frontiersmen. Two of them were my own newly minted scouts, Brown and the Carolinian ass. They each wore fresh black eyes that matched one another. One of the unfamiliar woodsmen, a freedman, answered for his boss. Laying on his side, gnawing on a slab of salted pork, he said, "Let's just say, you've got at least a hundred more lessons to learn."

I eased myself down, groaning along the way, onto a fallen tree that was rotting into the forest floor. "Are they all this painful?"

The leader laughed heartily and stepped into the midst of his men. "How 'bout it, boys," he called. "Do ya learn all me rules with as much pain as this one?"

To a man, his green and brown clad warriors grinned. Some shook their heads wistfully, as if reminiscing about the most wonderful times of their lives. "Worse," they said in unison. Then they laughed in the way that only men who had shared extreme past hardships could – merrily.

My two fellow scouts and I exchanged frightened glances.

"Welcome to Rogers' Rangers, Mr. Webah," said the leader, extending a hand of friendship. "I've been expecting you."

CHAPTER 11

"Private Weber!" snapped an ensign who barged into the second story of the barracks at Fort William Henry. Normally, I shared this particular room with thirty men, but was now alone. I'd come in late, just before dawn, from a night patrol in the woods. Defying both the Iroquois and the English, hostile Indian activity in the area had gone from nothing a month earlier to something dangerous. With each passing day, it seemed to steadily increase at an ever-faster rate.

And despite my non-stop running with the rangers, Lord Loudoun's correspondence eagerly encouraged me to catalogue Rogers' enigmatic rules. But there were so many succinct rubrics that he'd honed over the years, that I had been forced to spend many of my waking hours – when I was not skulking about the woods – writing and distilling the peculiar man's wisdom.

"Ya!" I answered, sitting up on my straw mattress. Pages with my notes pertaining to the so-called rules were strewn about. Though I hated the bunks, I had pulled my work in with me just to catch a momentary nap.

A weightless parcel fluttered from the ensign's hand to my feet. "Mail," he barked before leaving. Carelessly, he left the door ajar, allowing both the cold and light to stream in.

Other than the occasional missive from Loudoun, I rarely received mail. Never was it of a personal nature. And though this parcel bore none of the normal trappings that marked it as official military business, it seemed to me this letter was no treat. "You could have waited to wake me up!" I grumbled to the empty room. Then I dove down under my wool blanket and curled into a ball, pinching my eyes closed.

Soon, I shivered from the blustering cold. Wind whipped through the open window that faced north to Lake George. And now with the door open on the south toward the parade ground, it had no reason to stop. It swept with fury through the room, sending all my hard work on the damned rules fluttering about. Furthermore, no amount of pinching could seem to blot out the light. "Damn officers. Damn army," I grunted, sitting up and snatching the letter. A moment later, I had climbed from the bunk and meandered around the room, breaking the seal.

October 15, 1756

My son, My namesake

I write to inform you that I have been asked to take part in the coming Easton Conference between Pennsylvania and the Eastern Delaware. My fellow brothers in the Society of Friends, chief among them Israel Pemberton, have organized what I think is our best chance for a lasting peace between our peoples. I have agreed to attend.

Though it will be a difficult and bitter reminder to see Chief Teedyuscung, who is meant to represent the Delaware at Easton. My friendship with the man runs deep and I can say that, from my perspective, it shall never cease. After all, he was instrumental in holding our family together following your sister Trudie's death all those years ago. I'm sure you remember, though you sometimes choose to forget.

However, after the passing of his wife in that horrible massacre by Captain Armstrong and with what happened with your mother recently, I am finding it difficult to contain my darkest feelings. But the Lord, in His mercy, is full and generous. I believe that I shall be able to properly represent all sides in matters to bring this bloody conflict to a swift resolution. But I'm told the Iroquois will send a delegation, which will likely complicate matters for everyone. You know how they hate the idea of any tribes becoming independent of their control.

The papers reported that you were charged with some type of treasonous activity following the heinous events at Fort Oswego. I hope the claims are false. I further pray this letter finds you in good spirits despite your incarceration.

Your siblings are in fine health.

I miss your mother terribly.

Your Decent Father
Ephraim Weber

The letter had taken longer than two months to find me. *What the hell happened to my mother?* I asked myself. This was my father's first letter to me since I'd run away from home more than a decade earlier. And it was more infuriating than if he'd simply retained his original streak of no communication.

And what had driven a wedge between my father and Chief Teedyuscung? Why would my father think I cared about that? Why would he think I cared that he was involved with the peace process? Having been at the tip of the sword for five years since the birth of the bloody conflict, I understood what was required for peace. My pacifist old man had no idea. You see, the hearts of men had become hardened. With every new killing on the battlefield or in the settlements, those bloody muscles became like granite on both sides. The only way peace was coming to the frontier was for one side to beat the living shit out of the other! I meant to stand tall over the French. They wished to do the same to me. To believe anything else was wishful thinking or sheer stupidity.

And why the hell did my father have to *hope* that the grounds for my arrest were false? Of course, they were! He should have known better! I was not a model soldier. But I was, and was sure to always be, loyal to His Majesty, George II of England – even though I did hate many of his redbacks. Damn officers. Damn army. Damn redcoats.

I wadded the page up and threw it into the low-burning fireplace. "Family," I cursed, watching the edges catch fire. The only difference between family and strangers on the street was that I could more easily ignore what the latter had to say.

Then I really swore up a storm as I grabbed the note back, stomping out the flames. "Family. Damn family," I grumbled as I re-read the missive.

And a memory, long tucked away, resurfaced. I was there, so young, just a child. Trudie was there, lying down in the grass. There was an Indian warrior of some renown, young and strong. He was squat of stature, but carried himself with a broader air. There was a woman. It was my mother. She'd fallen to her knees, sobbing, covering her face with both hands. We were in a clearing in the woods. Smoke blew in from the other end of the meadow, burning my eyes. Though squinting, I could see that my hands held a hatchet, not a war hatchet or tomahawk. It was a clunky implement made for splitting small logs for the cooking fire. Nonetheless, it had been used as a weapon. The blade was drenched in blood.

"I swear. I do swear, Ephraim," said little Johnny Anson as he burst into the barracks.

I reacted with a start. "Do that again and I'll nip off your ears!" I shouted, pointing the business end of my blade in his direction.

He carelessly looked at the steel as he entered the room. It wasn't the first time I'd made a blustering remark to the lad, whom I had helped save from an Indian massacre. His pa had had a farm out near a placid lake that the Seneca called The Chosen Spot. I couldn't save Johnny's father, though, and so had left the orphan at William Henry to learn the trade of soldiering from Major Eyre.

"Oh, Ephraim," Johnny said, plopping down on the floor next to the fire. He'd grown a foot since I'd last seen him. The boy still weighed no more than loose change, but someday he'd be a substantial man. "I swear a fire right warms the bones. What's wrong?" he asked, finally noting my damp cheeks and the burnt page.

I crunched up the letter and jammed it in a pocket. "Just a list of provisions for my next scout. Rogers is a stickler for planning."

"And that makes you sad?" the boy asked innocently, reaching across the floor to pluck up several of the pages of my first draft of Rogers' Rules.

"No!" I yipped, rubbing my cheeks dry. "Use the sense God gave you, jackass. A coal popped in the fire and got itself in my eye. I'd like to see if you don't shed a tear when an ember worms its way in there!"

Johnny nodded with complete understanding. "Saw a man lose an eye right in this fort from the very same thing last winter. Maybe you shouldn't get so close."

"And maybe you should leave me alone!" I growled.

None of my irritability could tamp down the boy's enthusiasm for life. Though he'd known nothing but tragedy, life's storms seemed to roll right off his back. Strong lad. He'd taken to engineering at the fort like a bird to the wing. And he was still good in the forest, a natural. "I will. I will. I swear it," Johnny said with his usual affection. "I'd never bother you unless it was important. Major Eyre and Cap'n Rogers want to see you."

I sighed heavily. "But I just got to sleep a minute ago."

Johnny smiled brightly. He slapped my knee. "The major told me you'd say that. If only I could be as smart as him!" he said wistfully. "Anyways, he said to remind you that you are under His Majesty's orders these days. No more excuses for you."

"He said that?" I asked, with a curled lip.

"I swear."

And I swore up a tempest as I gathered my gear.

Damn officers. Damn army. Damn redbacks. Damn king!

CHAPTER 12

I liked few men. I liked Johnny, but he was not really a man – just a boy. He'd not yet developed all the traits that I so often saw in full grown men – as in the attributes that I myself exhibited in spades. Nonetheless, Major Eyre had made it onto my extraordinarily short list of men I admired. He was confident and, most importantly, competent. General Johnson, all the soldiers, and even I deserved a little credit for our victory at Lake George. But it was Major Eyre's quick thinking, organizational skills, and engineering prowess that truly tipped the scales in our favor. And he had continued in that vein since I had left. The walls of Fort William Henry had started as low, snaking mounds with fractured wagons tipped atop them to provide us with cover. Since then, they'd been transformed to monstrous stone, timber, and earthen works that only a determined cannonade could hope to thwart.

Even that morning, as Johnny waited on the landing outside the door to allow me to finish dressing, saws sawed, hammers hammered, and chisels chiseled. The toiling sounds of the workers filled the air.

"Can't help but admire her," Johnny said when I stepped out. "No matter how many times a day my eyes take note, I stare in wonder. I swear, I love her."

I glanced out over the earthen and timber curtain wall, which was topped by a parapet complete with sharpened fraising. The main section of the wall was fifteen feet high and thirty feet thick. Past it to the north, the ground sloped rapidly down to Lake George. I took in the picturesque waters. The threat of a bleak winter's swift descent did nothing to spoil the majestic view. My intelligent father would have said the scene was an example of God's general revelation. I thought of it as heaven. "I love her, too."

Johnny saw my gaze. "I mean the fort, Ephraim. Can you believe it? I had something to do with building her!"

I jabbed him in his ribs. "I know what you meant. But will it be enough when the Frogs start hopping?"

I'd offended the boy, which was just what I intended. "Oh, I swear, I might ring your neck one day, Ephraim. But I'll wait until I'm bigger. Won't be long now. Of course, it will hold! No Frenchman will dare getting near us. Not after they remember how we cut them down last year. And not once they see how frightening this place has become!"

When faced with a determined foe, I'd had the misfortune of seeing many impregnable dens prove to be quite pregnable.

Johnny went on as he skipped down the steps. "Listen here. A fool can see that our walls can withstand a beating. But it's also what's inside and outside that counts. You know, we've built bomb-proofs under all the barracks? Ammunition and the injured will be safe and sound. The four bastions have embrasures filled with cannons. Major Eyre has made sure we can hit targets a way out in the woods. But we can also provide enfilade." He paused, smirking, proud that he'd properly used the term for firing lengthwise along the outside of a wall to help protect a fort from attack. "And our dry moat, it surrounds us on three sides, draining into the lake. At the bottom of the moat we have a palisade of sharpened logs. Each are a minimum of eight feet in height. And lastly, out beyond the ditch is the glacis, a fifty-yard stretch of sloping land that is so wide open that a blind gunner working without powder or shot would have no trouble picking out white-coated Frogs for target practice."

I patted his shoulder. "Did you learn all that from Major Eyre?"

"Sure did," he answered proudly.

"And was he also the one foolish enough to fill you with such confidence? I haven't seen yet a device of man's making that cannot be dismantled by another device of man's making."

Johnny spun, burning with hot anger for a split second. But by the time he opened his mouth, he'd eased his emotions back. The boy just wagged a finger. "You're always just tryin' to upset folks, Ephraim. I'd take offense if I didn't know you any better." Then he ducked into the headquarters and I followed after.

When we'd found our place at Major Eyre's table, a servant came along and served breakfast. While waiting for the others to arrive, I ate two helpings of eggs and bacon with vigor.

Likewise, Johnny downed a prodigious amount of food. He might have grown while sitting there.

"Good to see you downing something so healthy for a change," Lieutenant Turnwell said when he arrived. "Have you stayed away from the rum?" he asked.

I plucked up my glass and showed him that it was filled with too-sweet wine. "Indeed," I said. And, in truth, I had been free of the evils of liquor since I'd arrived on the lake's shores. "How goes it with your cannon crews?"

He shrugged, as the servant set his food before him. "I believe you know Major Eyre had them in exemplary condition. My task was simple from the start. But I hope that I've done nothing but enhance their already ample skills. We've improved loading times as well as accuracy."

"So, you've brow-beaten the gun crews enough to hate you?" I summarized.

Turnwell scowled. Johnny Anson laughed. The servant grinned, but was too smart to make any other motion to indicate his approval.

"I am a stern, but fair commander of my men," Turnwell answered.

"Good to hear," Major Eyre said as he swept in. He was energetic, usually solving five or six problems simultaneously while in the midst of conversations with a half-dozen other men on a variety of topics. Today was no different. He craned over his shoulder to address a captain. "You'll continue to focus all efforts on the main structure. Not a hole big enough for a mouse's ear to slip inside! Do you hear? But in the spring, first thing, before the last snows melt, I want all efforts put toward fortifying Titcomb's Mount on the southeast. I should think a modified structure with two strategically designed bastions and a flexible terre-plein should be adequate to prevent the French from using the mount to establish their own base of operations during a siege. Employ young Mr. Anson in your efforts."

"Yes, sir," the captain answered dutifully. The pair sat.

"And you'll have his supplies ready before he needs them," Eyre said to the head carpenter, who trailed in.

This man gave a quick, efficient nod, but said nothing, a fact that endeared him to the major.

"Good. No equivocating." Eyre attacked the next man in the line of officers who were arriving. "The ships. Are they dry?"

"They'll be up out of the water by week's end," answered the lieutenant in charge of our docks.

"And the disposition of the guards around the lakeshore…" Eyre asked.

"Set. Tight," was the simply reply.

And on and on it went. It was really the way in which wars were won. Sure, battles held the honorable place of glory. They were the stage. They were where individual units or commanders, actors all, could make their marks, achieving greatness by force of will, or luck. But I'd come to understand that it was the terrifically boring details where long wars between two evenly matched opponents were won. And despite the mundanity of the topics discussed that morning, from the vegetable gardens and their planned organization next spring to the storage of dried goods, Major Eyre's rapid, efficient approach made them all seem exciting.

"Tell me about the situation with the tribesmen," Eyre said facing me.

I was, without a doubt, the lowest ranked individual in the council. Even Johnny probably registered higher in the eyes of those around the table. It was the first time I'd been invited to participate in such a discussion since arriving back at William Henry.

"Me?" I asked.

"Mr. Weber," Eyre said. "I've known you to be a little more articulate than that."

"Usually you ask Rogers," was my reply.

"He's not here right now. I'm asking you," Eyre explained.

"Iroquois are just as frustrated as we are," I said. "A bunch of foreign tribesmen have been skulking about for weeks. They hunt food that belongs to us and to the Six Nations."

"What's a bunch?" Eyre asked.

"A night hasn't passed when we haven't come across a pack of warriors or scouts. We've exchanged gunfire on ten occasions. Two of our men dead. Eight injured. I'd guess we've done the same damage to our foes."

"How many invaders, then?" he asked again. "Any French or Canadians among them?"

"Only tribesmen," I said. "Of course, they are no doubt providing valuable intelligence to Louis. And it's hard to say on numbers."

"Pretend the lives of the men in this fort depend on it. And if that is not enough, pretend that the lives of our fellow subjects in these colonies depends upon it. And if you require further motivation to hazard a guess, pretend the honor of your king is at stake in the realm of global affairs. And by the way, all of those things are true. No pretending must be done."

"More than one hundred. No more than three hundred. They move about in small bands," I answered swiftly.

Eyre took in the information and spat out another question. "And the tribes involved? Is there something to be gleaned?"

"They *are* coming from further afield, but nothing I haven't yet seen," I said.

"So, the Frogs haven't extended their influence and brought in new slugs of warriors," Eyre surmised.

"No, sir," I answered.

"But they will," Rogers said as he came into the room. He carried a large item that was wrapped in dripping wet leather and slapped it in the middle of the table. Dishes rattled and an ensign had his lap stained with wine from a toppled glass. "Hell. They ah!"

"Enlighten us," Eyre instructed, ignoring the woodland warrior's gruff entrance.

"Thanks, Majah," Rogers said. He meandered around us in a relaxed manner. "I've just retahned from Fort Cahrillone."

"I don't recall authorizing such an expedition," Eyre interrupted.

Rogers beat the air with his palms to tamp down the major's concerns. "You didn't. Thah was no expedition. Only me."

"You went to Ticonderoga by yourself?" Eyre asked. He was not exactly incredulous. For he had worked with Robert Rogers long enough to anticipate some form of surprise at every turn.

"Ya, ya," Rogers answered dismissively. "Bettah than goin' with a hahd of Ephraim Webah's who wouldn't know foorest stealth if it came up and gave 'em a kiss on the ahss."

"What did you find?" Eyre asked.

"Webah's been right about one thing. He's been croakin' about Oswego and its effect on the Indians. I've seen it with mine own eyes. The savages ah comin' in from all ovah. Tribes I've nevah seen ah up nahth. Comin' from the west, nahth, and east. Convahging on Cahrillone. Some ah camped inside. But othahs ah sleeping in lodges set up outside. No' enough room behind the walls."

"Numbahs?" Eyre asked. "Excuse me," he said, clearing his throat. "Numbers?"

"You wah right the fahst time," Rogers quipped. "Upwahds o' thousand tribesmen. Times two o' French bastahds."

Eyre sighed, considering the news. "Then we shall be prepared to harass them as soon as the weather breaks in the spring. No sense in giving them the freedom to lay siege to us first. I shall draw up plans."

Rogers pointed to the leather clad item on the table. Water had begun to leak from it, pooling in a large puddle that dripped between the boards onto the floor. "No sense waiting. We'll hit the Frogs fast and hahd right away. I've got yoah plan all set. She's right thah."

Intrigued, Eyre studied the item. "What is it?"

Rogers reached past the commander and lifted a flap, then another. A chunk of ice about the size of a week-old piglet greeted us. "We'll avoid all thah patrols and skip right to 'em. That, my lads, is ouah key to victory."

CHAPTER 13

I never wrote back to my father. I'd made no inquiries into his deteriorating friendship with Chief Teedyuscung. I'd not asked what happened to my mother – she may well have died – Lord knows she drank a frightful amount more than I ever had. And I'd never sent any questions to him about the well-being of my son, whom he and my siblings now raised. It's not that I did not have those questions. I clearly did. But the thought of penning them all in a coherent manner seemed an insurmountable task. Every time one of the queries sprang forth in my mind, fiery, frustrated rage burned in the depths of my guts and soul.

Meanwhile, in the depths of the New York forests, the mercury plummeted. Flurries swirled. Squalls descended and drifts abounded. The ice chunk that Robert Rogers had brought back to William Henry from Fort Carillon up north melted under our stupefied examination. The puddles, creeks, and our toes froze. Slowly, but very steadily, the waves rolling along Lake George developed a skin of ice that thickened every single day.

It was a frigid, black morning in mid-January of 1757 that I stepped out onto the ice of Lake George for the coming trek – forty grueling miles. Over the many years since those fateful days, I've told my tale in many snug parlors back east. At first, I used to think that residing so close to a great, blustery ocean would allow my listeners to understand the dangers we faced simply in traversing the monstrous sheets of ice. But no. They all listened respectfully enough, saying, *Oh, my!* in all the right places. But their expressions told me that they believed our march across frozen Lake George was no different than when they'd sent their precious daughters out on a calm ice-covered pond with fancy skates imported from Mother Britain.

Within fifteen minutes of leaving the barracks, one man had been climbing over a massive chunk of ice that had frozen upright in our path. His snowshoe skidded, his ankle popped, his knee wrenched, and, as he tumbled over the other side onto stalagmites of granite-hard ice, he tore his cloak and face. It took two men to carry the injured warrior between their shoulders back to William Henry. And even though we were still within sight of the sputtering torches atop the fort's parapets, we were already down some three percent of our fighting force of Rogers' Rangers.

By the time we got further onto the lake, the going on foot grew easier. Where the ice was visible, it was rough and rippled from the last, lingering effects of the currents below and the breezes above right before the surface had frozen. Where the ice was covered, our webbed shoes carried us atop snow that ranged from a few inches to several feet thick. But what I remember most was the wind. It whipped and smacked our faces directly from the north, burning like lightning down from Lake Champlain before gaining more speed over Lake George's deserted surface.

"Pleasant day," observed a ranger next to me. "You really think we'll surprise 'em coming up the backbone of the lake?"

"Unlikely to be any patrols out here," I growled. Then I opened my right eye in order to see who bothered wasting such precious energy by talking. I gazed past the ice-caked scarf I had tied around my face. It was Thomas Brown. "Why the hell didn't you stay on as one of Bradstreet's bateaux men and teamsters?" I asked.

He smiled, leaning further into the stiff wind. "Pay sure was better. I could count on a hot meal every other day when I was traveling between forts."

"So, why'd you join Rogers after he gave you a black eye?" I asked, sucked into his inane conversation, despite my better judgement.

Brown shrugged. "I guess I wanted to see more of the country than just those busy roads."

"With your eyes closed?" I shrieked.

He peeked one open again. His lashes had bits of icicles dangling from them. "You saying I made a mistake?"

"No bigger than the rest of us," I admitted, feeling the sting in my cheeks. We had been somewhere in the middle of our column, which had come to a sudden halt. He and I dropped to one knee, readying to fire in either direction. What we might have hoped to hit, given the limited visibility, escaped my imagination.

"Lowah yoah weapon," Rogers grumbled. "Comin' through." He strode up past me from where he'd marched at the rear. He always changed up the order of the march so that no one ever became bored or too sloppy with his job. Rogers had started out in the van. He was scheduled to be there again soon enough. Just not now. "Slowing down my advance and we ain't even past Tea Island," he groused to himself. "Stahk! Lieutenant Stahk! Why the halt?"

Lieutenant Stark trotted back. "Man on point said he heard a creak in the ice."

Rogers spat. "With this gale he couldn't heah himself break wind! Get this column moving or we'll freeze to death out here. I want to be encamped up neah Nahthwest Bay out of the wind by nightfall."

"The ice, sir?" Stark pressed.

"Whut do you want me to do about it?" Rogers barked. "Piss on it and wait until that freezes?"

"Skirt toward shore," Stark offered calmly. "Toward shallower waters and thicker ice."

Rogers considered the suggestion. "The longah we ah out heah… I hate to add miles to the jahney." But soon he began nodding. "West. Lead us to the westahn shoah and then nahth again."

Just as Stark was tipping his hat in understanding, from the van and over the howling wind came a single, echoing crunch. It was instantly followed by screaming men. And splashing water.

CHAPTER 14

"On ya bellies!" Rogers' bellowed. He sprinted to the front. "Ropes fahwahd!" Another crash sounded with a round of new shouting. Just before Rogers' disappeared into the snow-filled haze, he dropped to his knees and waved us forward. "Spread out! Skahmish ohdah! Toss in the lines. Five men to a rope! Not too close to the hole!"

Brown and I swept our muskets over our backs and crawled into the thick of the mess. Rogers swatted my skull with a mitt as we passed him by. "To the right, boy! Left is full!"

We veered right and found an empty spot of ice next to a roiling mass of water and half-frozen men. On the left of the arcing rupture, our fellow rangers had already begun tossing in life lines and hauling out shivering men. Then, some three feet distant from the edge, I unslung the section of rope I'd been tasked with carrying, passed it back to Brown and a few other soldiers behind him.

"Got it!" they announced.

I launched the line. It smacked the face of a man who struggled in the middle of the fissure, which may have measured two rods in diameter. The confused, waterlogged victim slapped wildly for the rope. "It's behind you!" I screamed over the wind. "Right behind you!" He flailed manically. With every passing second, he sank lower, his arms seized. "It's right there!"

Quite by accident, his hand crashed onto the rigid rope and shoved it below the surface. I thought we'd lost him, when his whole, stiff body followed suit. Only his beaver cap floated. But just as my hopes sank with him, the rope slid through my woolen mittens. He'd latched on as he'd sunk. "Pull!" I announced.

Operating on our bellies and sides, we tugged. We'd brought in two yards of rope before the frozen ranger surfaced, his body no more fluid than an ingot of steel. He clutched the line with both hands, preciously close to his chest. His eyes were determined, his mouth flexed tight. "Faster!" I encouraged.

Hand-over-hand, ever swifter, we drew him in. At last I could make out who was at the end of our rope. It was Amos Conwall, the lone Stockbridge Indian member of Rogers'

Rangers. He created a small wake and uttered no complaint when his hands slammed against the sharp edges of the ice. But I did shout. "Oh, that's cold!" I said as his momentum sent a small wave of frigid water over the ice. It took but a second for it to seep into my clothes and chill my bones.

We heaved on that rope, but Amos didn't budge. He was wedged partially below the ice and was in no condition to paddle his body around. "Grab my ankles, Brown!" I ordered, crawling forward.

I felt a hand slap on one ankle. Then, using the rope as leverage, I tugged myself closer to the hole. "It's a damn foolish idea to take a bath at a time like this!" I scolded Amos, stuffing my arms into the water and wedging them beneath his shoulders.

"Sh-shut up, Weber," Conwall chattered.

With my elbows planted firmly against the ice, I hoisted him up. He weighed a ton. "You'll have to help!" I shouted when his belly was level with the top of the ice.

With all his might, Amos leaned forward while kicking his legs back or crawling or flailing or whatever it was. I rolled as he fell toward me. Then, he crashed down beside me, his feet still dangling in the icy pool. "Pull us, Brown!"

The ice fractured again at my waist level. Down we went. A million pins pricked my face. A billion, more than the stars in the sky, assaulted me everywhere else that had suddenly become submerged. Already frozen like a log, Conwall whooshed out faster than I. But I managed to hold onto the icy locks of his long hair, praying quite earnestly that Brown's grip was better than his conversation.

An eternity later, I was back on the sheet of ice, considerably colder than the last go-'round. We repeated the process, this time with a little more finesse, and our positively frozen victim climbed out a second time. Brown efficiently pulled both of us back in the blink of an eye.

"Drag 'em away," Rogers ordered from somewhere within the howling snow squall. I felt my body being unceremoniously towed to thicker ice. "Give 'em yoah extra wraps. Now! Get 'em outta those clothes. Now!"

Soon I was naked in the midst of the blustery ice sheet and climbing into clothes that were much too large. And since they'd been in a man's pack, they seemed no warmer than the outside air.

"Damn ya!" Rogers barked. "We'll have to risk the woods for tonight. Need a fire."

And after taking a hasty roll call, our company of rangers limped to our night's camp. We'd progressed less than half the distance Rogers had expected that first day. But, we'd rescued twelve men from a frigid death.

Unfortunately, eleven never made it out of that icy pit.

CHAPTER 15

"How'd you know I was coming?" I asked Rogers on our fifth day of travel. After our dreadfully frozen ordeal, we'd all thawed well enough. I lost no appendages. But two or three other men would likely lose several fingers and toes. They and their blackened digits were sent back over the lake to seek medical attention at William Henry.

Our trek since breaking through the ice had mostly involved avoiding the ever-growing presence of scouts from the many foreign Indian contingents we had seen. Had I been given the opportunity to share a pipe in the lodge of a local Iroquois sachem, I am sure I would have heard him rail against the bald affront to Iroquois sovereignty from those unwanted tribal interlopers. Alas, the Covenant Chain between London and Onondaga had been, at least temporarily, severed. As such, I'd not be invited to sup with my old friends anytime soon.

Nonetheless, Rogers was superb in this game of cat-and-mouse, truly in his element. While I and the other soaked rangers had thawed by the fire on our first night, our commander led a pack of enemy scouts on a wild goose chase, far away from our position. Providence had blessed him with abilities that surpassed the average frontiersman. Even with my decade of experience of surviving in the woods, there were many things I learned over those days of ranging. I dare say that most woodsmen would benefit from time spent with Robert Rogers. If they could stand it, that is.

"I smelled ya from a mile away, lad," he whispered, hoofing gracefully overtop the snow. Deep into enemy-held territory, he was where he belonged – at the point of our column. I'd just joined him.

"Not right now," I clarified, thinking that in some ways he'd begun to believe the myths written in the newspapers about his innate tracking skills. I acknowledged that I smelled as bad as any of the rangers that day, but I certainly didn't reek enough for Rogers to catch wind of my approach with just his snout. "The day we met." I pointed to my scarred face. "You whacked my skull."

He gave me a sideways glance. "Did I knock any sense into ya?"

I shrugged.

Rogers grinned. "Thought not. Maybe next time, then." He shifted directly into issuing an order. "Pass the wahd, Weber. We'll be outta the woods soon. Onto Champlain."

I did so, encouraging the men to be extra vigilant. Not that such an admonition was necessary. We'd been able to spend most of our trip atop Lake George, avoiding dangerous ice, while traveling in the worst weather and darkest times of night. But since reaching the northernmost end of Lake George, our company had been forced to skirt around on land, successfully avoiding patrol after patrol. The French Fortress of Carillon, what we, the English, called Ticonderoga, sat on a commanding hill, guarding all northward movement of men and goods. Their eyes and ears looked a far direction in all points of the compass. We had given it a wide berth. And we now approached Lake Champlain north of Ticonderoga.

Rogers held up his hand. In a staggered line stretching almost a quarter mile, we instantly stopped amidst the trees. He pointed to the ground and I dropped to a knee, Bess ready. The rest did likewise as Rogers skipped over the drifts with his snowshoes. He paused behind a thick briar, studying the desolate lake that stretched out under the clear, frigid blue sky before us.

After many long moments, he pointed at me with one finger and waved me ahead.

"Y'evah been this fah nahth, lad?" he asked, still examining the scene for danger.

"More than once," I rasped. "All the way to Montreal a few times since I first began working for Croghan."

He nodded approvingly. "Croghan. Hahd of him. Fellow Irishman. Good tradah. That explains it."

"Explains what?" I asked.

"How I knew you was comin'," he said simply. He pointed southeastward, careful to keep his hand deep within the brush. "Whut do ya make of that?"

I peeked out onto the lake, seeing nothing but intense sun reflecting off the ice and snow. He was testing me. I was sure of it. "Rule twenty-four," I ventured.

"Whut in hell ah you on about?" he whispered.

I'd begun categorizing his dizzying number of helpful maxims into something that could be remembered. So far, I had boiled down the many dozens into twenty-four, with more to come. "If you are to embark by any means over water, ice included, I suppose, then leave at the start of evening so that you have the entire night before you to pass by the watchful enemy undiscovered."

He paused, giving me a bewildered look.

"It's one of your rules," I said, sheepishly.

"I know that!" he barked quietly. "I wasn't gonna go walking out in the open on a bright, sunny day and make myself and my men tahgets!" He pointed, this time with more emphasis in a specific direction. "That. Whut do ya make o' that?"

I'd clearly failed his test, whatever it had been. But I gave it another go. I squinted through the blinding sun. Small whirlwinds of snow rose and fell from the barren lake beneath the cloudless sky. Rogers patiently waited, not once hurrying me while I studied. And I was just about to give up when I noticed that one of the blustering tornados moved steadily northward – against the wind.

Rogers saw that I saw. "That fancy lahd likes you, lad. And fah good reason. I see that now. A good reputation in these woods is ahned. That's how I knew you wah comin'."

He saw my confusion and continued. "*Lahd Loudoun*. The fancy *lahd*. Fellow Scotsman. Even though he's from the Mothah Country, he can't be all bad. Wants to whip the Frogs and takes no lip from govahnahs. He sent wahd you'd be coming my way."

I frowned, momentarily ignoring our quarry on the lake. "But he'd only just decided that I was to be spared from the hangman's noose," I said. "Then I came straight to you. A letter couldn't possibly have beaten me."

He shrugged, waving Lieutenant Stark to us as the other men shivered in place, watching every waving branch, attuned to every forest sound. Rogers then added, "Guess the good lahd had already made his decision befah that show trial."

"Loudoun's in charge. Why waste time on a show trial?" I asked.

Rogers acknowledged Stark, but answered me. "Gotta keep those other generals happy. Pompous pigs who ah pals with one o' the princes." He then addressed his second in command. "Shahp-eyed Sue, heah, has seen a sled comin' nahth from Cahrillone. Slow and steady. He wants to run a plan by ya."

Another test of some sort. Stark furrowed his brow, just as perplexed as I, but awaited my explanation. "Must be mail traveling north to Fort St. Frédéric from Ticonderoga," I started slowly.

The lieutenant peered southeastward, saw the distant sled, and gave me a surprising grin. "Weber noticed that?"

Rogers winked at me. "Tell him what ya think we should do," he encouraged.

A hundred of his maxims spun by in my mind. "Rule twenty-three," I said, fairly confidently.

Stark looked at Rogers, who, in turn, looked at me for enlightenment. I could see I had a lot of work to do in summarizing Rogers Rules of Ranging to these men, Rogers included. "When in pursuit of a party that has lately been near a fort, do not follow in their tracks. A rear guard, especially near a fort, is likely to be most alert and fall upon you. So, we should head them off at a narrow pass and ambush them."

Rogers smiled. "That's as good a summary as any I've hahd. But thah won't be any nahrow passes out on the ice."

A minor failure on my part. I recovered quickly. "The sled is taking its time. We send our own party up ahead swiftly. They lay in wait behind a snow bank, of their own making if need be, and surprise the sled. We take them as captives and we'll soon know, not only the forces arrayed against us at Ticonderoga, but also those at Fort St. Frédéric."

There were a few seconds as both experienced warriors thought about my proposal. Then Rogers gave the lieutenant a nudge. "Assemble a platoon, Stahk. Take Webah with ya. Move fast in case they do have a reah guahd. Bring me back those captives. Then we'll decide which is easier prey, Fred or Cahrillone. Maybe we can burn one to the ground tonight before the garrison can wake up."

The lieutenant's eyes lit up. "Aye," he rasped efficiently, before tearing off to the rear to choose his men.

I stood, crouching, to follow. Rogers snagged the fringe of my coat. "Good instincts, lad," he complimented. "Sometimes, ya have to be aggressive."

"Thank you," I said, again standing to leave.

He yanked me back a second time. "And when yoah done writin' me rules, give me a gandah, will ya? Befah ya send them on to the fancy lahd. I might have some changes to make. Thah my rules, aftah all."

"Of course," I answered hastily. Then I fell-in at the rear of the platoon of fifteen men who'd already begun rushing north along the lake's edge behind Stark.

CHAPTER 16

Despite the cold air hovering above the frozen lake, the French sleigh driver had set a leisurely pace. The explanation for his dawdling was simple enough for even me to ascertain. Next to residence in a city, garrison life, especially in the frigid winter months, was the most tedious experience a man could endure. Day after day of shivering on guard duty, breaking through layers of ice in the troughs of livestock, and watching supplies dwindle were the most exciting occurrences for which a man could hope. None were welcome. So, if a soldier or teamster had been given the task of traveling from one fort to another with a sack of mail and he felt secure within his own territory, it was common for the man to dally.

And the teamster clearly had no concerns. Lying on my belly atop Champlain, I waited impatiently for him to fall into our trap. From behind a pile of snow I'd shoved into a hill some fifteen inches in height, I peeked at him. He glanced about at the distant forest, not searching for potential dangers, but rather like he was on holiday in Paris, taking in the sights. His head moved from side to side as if it danced to an inner melody.

Then I heard his tune over the clomp of the approaching hooves. The driver roared loudly and cheerily with a voice only a mother could find endearing. His two comrades, meant to be guards, belted out with him at the tops of their lungs. Though a French ditty, it was a delightfully bawdy song. And it took a little knowledge of the lingua franca to understand its playful meaning.

La boulangère a des écus
Qui ne lui coûtent guère
Elle en a, je les ai vus
J'ai vu la boulangère aux écus
J'ai vu la boulangère

La nuit pour mieux veiller dessus
Je crois qu'elle ne dort guère
Mais son trésor est connu
J'ai vu la boulangère aux écus
J'ai vu la boulangère

"Lieutenant," whispered Brown.

"Shut up," Stark answered from behind his section of our little hillocks. His thumb stroked the cock of his Bess.

"But it's Rogers, sir," Brown pressed. "He's trying to tell you something."

"What?" Stark growled. He and I both craned to see Brown, who pointed westward to the shore we had lately departed. We followed his finger. There, barely perceptible among the trees, was Captain Rogers. He waved frantically.

"What's he want?" I asked.

Stark grumbled. "I don't know." Then he glanced back to the sled, which was nearly upon us. "Now!" Stark shouted, diving into his duty, forgetting his commander.

In a highly pre-organized fashion, we jumped to our feet and descended to the sled. Four men ran to the single horse. Two snatched its reins from opposite sides and yanked back, while the other two fearlessly blocked the beast's path. A handful of rangers circled around the back of the sleigh to prevent anyone from escaping that way. The rest of us went straight toward the startled driver and his passengers.

One of the French guards, overzealous, jumped to his feet and leveled his St. Etienne musket at us. Anderson, a ranger, and Baker, a volunteer from the 44th, beat him to the punch and blew twin holes in his chest. He rolled over one side of the sled, snapping his neck on the ice in a manner that added insult to, well, death. Seeing his comrade thus treated made the second guard instantly release his musket and throw his hands in the air. "Je me rends!" he shouted.

Meanwhile, I took the opportunity to unleash my perennial hatred of the Frogs out onto the bewildered driver. The last words to his song still lingered in the air when I brought the butt of my Bess sharply against his cheek. He tumbled from the seat and onto the ice. "The baker's wife may have a big one," I said as he swooned. "But that's the only ass end you'll lay eyes on today."

I had thought myself funny.

"Shut up, Weber," Stark said. "It's broad daylight. Get these two prisoners bound and into the sled. I want to be under cover in less than five minutes."

"I don't think we're going anywhere soon," Brown suggested, still nervously gaping toward the western woods. "The captain is coming to us."

Sure enough, the rest of our company had sprung from the trees at the shore. They came toward us at a gallop, arrayed in a wide skirmish line, not the normal, thin column that Rogers employed during an advance.

My muscles tensed and I peered over their shoulders, searching for a pursuing enemy. There was nothing except the unending dark woods beyond.

"Lieutenant," clipped Amos Conwall, who'd been tasked with watching southward to Carillon with his jet-black eyes. "More sleds are comin'. Frogs are out in force."

Stark didn't need to look to know that we were in trouble. "Brown, Conwall, Anderson. On the sled. Now! Take it to the western shore. We'll cover you."

"Right, sir," said Brown, the former teamster. He jumped into the seat and took the reins with an experienced hand. After pausing just a second to see the French captives manhandled into place, Brown slapped the horse's rump sharply with the leather straps. "Yah!" he rasped.

"Skirmish line!" Stark ordered as at least a half score sleds barreled toward us. "We need to finish them all or else they'll raise the warning."

The dozen or so of us formed a ragged line, each man dropping to his knee or behind one of the snow mounds. Then we did the hardest thing for a warrior to do. We did nothing but let the enemy come. Our ambush had been spotted. The drivers whipped their beasts ever faster, trying to close the distance before Rogers and the rest could reinforce us. A few of the Frenchmen had stood in the pitching sleighs and fired wildly on our position. Their flying lead harmed none of us. And even when one or two balls plunged into the snow perilously close to me, I did not move.

It was hard not to react. My heart pounded into my throat. My arms and hands twitched with excitement. "Wait!" Stark instructed. He'd not even bothered to lift his musket to his shoulder. It sat at the ready across his raised knee. "Wait." We did. "Pick your targets, boys. Make the first volley count. Then advance!"

"Advance?" Baker asked.

As his answer, Stark ordered, "Fire!" In one swift motion, he hefted his Bess, aimed, and squeezed. *Cr-crack!* His pan flashed. His muzzle burst. Then Lieutenant Stark's effort was followed by the patter of our guns.

A horse whinnied, rearing, blood spurting from its front quarter. The driver of another sled clutched his belly and slumped forward onto the ice. I watched as he was run over by his own sledge. Wood splinters shot from side boards. More than one French curse word was hurled at us alongside an increased ferocity of shot.

"Load and close in on them!" Stark ordered, already withdrawing his ramrod and jogging forward.

"Whut in hell!" bellowed Rogers, panting. He and the rest ran past us, dropped, and poured more hot lead toward the enemy. "Can't ya see when I'm wahnin' ya, Stahk?"

The lieutenant raced up past his commander and let fly another round. *Cr-crack!* "They would have seen us anyway," he answered.

Rogers grumbled, but said no more as we advanced, slowly encircling the enemy in a step-wise fashion. The two lead sleds had been halted altogether, their passengers either dead or wounded and scattered across the ice. A few more sleds in the middle of their supply column had slowed to a confused trot. This allowed our rangers to attack with greater accuracy. More and more of the Frogs died.

Seeing the carnage, the last few sleds in the line foresaw only futility. They cut away from the pursuit. Their teamsters frantically lashed the huffing beasts, turning in a tight arc, up on one runner, to drive southward.

"After 'em, lads!" Rogers shouted, putting even more energy into dashing after his quickly retreating quarry. "Don't let 'em get to Cahrillone!"

We sprinted for a quarter mile. When at last we stopped, leaning on our knees and sucking in giant swaths of the arctic air, it was clear our mission against the French had suddenly changed for the worse. The sleighs drove on.

Within the hour, our presence would no longer be a secret to one of the most fearsome forts in all of old Iroquoia.

CHAPTER 17

Rogers and Stark were no sluggards with regard to brute strength or decision-making. No sooner had we given up our pursuit of the sleds than they pivoted our path in the opposite direction. The captain jogged over the ice amidst the fractured train.

"Patch up all the Frogs ya find alive. But leave the badly wounded behind," he instructed. "They'll only hindah us. Leave them for the French to nahse back to health."

"Aye," said Stark. With the flick of his wrist, a dozen men set about dragging wounded enemy soldiers from the ruins of our confrontation. Meanwhile, the lieutenant had begun rustling through strewn baggage for any correspondence that might be of use.

"Webah," barked Rogers, peering up at the sky. It had begun to morph from sparkling blue to a mix of gray and black clouds that appeared to be pregnant with snow. "Take as captive any Frenchman who can walk."

"Sir," I responded, tapping the brim of my hat. Soon I was grabbing a young Canadian by the ear. "Se lever!" I growled. The scratched, frightened man stood and obediently began a line, onto which I added more of his compatriots.

Not even ten minutes passed before we had rejoined Brown and the others at the wood's edge. We promptly cut the horse loose from the first sleigh and drove the creature back onto the lake to give the Frogs something else to chase.

Though early afternoon, the descending weather made it as dim as dusk. Between mild grumbles, Rogers said, "See yoahselves and the prisonahs fed. Lost ouah chance of sahprise. No attack this time. We've got a fast mahch ahead of us."

Without further instruction, the rangers pissed against tree trunks or plopped in the snow to eat and drink. They exhibited joy and relief. In a strange example of repose in hostile territory, they laughed, sharing tales of the just-completed battle in which we had suffered no casualties. They even modestly taunted our string of captives, poking them in the ribs or messing their hair as if they were spritely children. I'm sure the Frenchmen and Canadians would have slit our throats if given the chance, but I'm comforted with the knowledge that, given the circumstances, the prisoners were treated with proper decorum.

And I must take a moment to explain something for you folks in the genteel sections of York City or Philadelphia. It is important I note that Rogers Rangers were not overly calloused or oblivious. To the contrary, they were deadly conscious of the menace that might soon descend from Ticonderoga. But those men were equally aware that at least some of the calls of nature should not be overlooked. If meals or mirth could not find a place while on campaign, I'd say, *why bother going at all*?

"So, we came all this way over that ice for nothing?" Brown mused, gnawing on half of a week-old biscuit. He'd shared the other half with a Frog. Silly boy.

"Seven prisoners," I explained, eyeballing one of the young Frenchmen. He looked like the young officer who had murdered my first wife. He wasn't the same man, for he had long ago been killed himself. But the lad's countenance brought back wretched memories.

"Yet, we had hopes of crippling the French for the entire summer season with only our small band," Brown complained. "For naught," he sighed.

"Tell you what," I said with ample sarcasm, throwing a snowball into the Frenchman's face. He reacted with a sharp yip and growl. "You go on by yourself, Brown. Attack a French fort on high alert. Let me know if you survive past a minute."

Stark and Rogers strode into our compact circle, arguing. I was fortunate that neither had seen my launch against the French toad. "It's just ill-advised, captain," Stark explained.

"Do you want all the Frogs at Cahrillone nippin' at yoah heels?" Rogers barked. Then he pointed to the darkening heavens. "And thah's that! You want to add two days to our retreat!"

"If it is necessary for our survival," Stark answered.

"No!" Rogers shouted, breaking one of his rules for stealth. "We move fast. We rush to last night's camp. And get onto Lake Geahge as soon as we can!"

"Captain," Stark pressed. "We agreed upon a different rendezvous point this morning in the event we were required to retreat."

"Webah!" called Rogers, huffing away from his lieutenant. "Get the prisonahs up and moving. They'll lead the way and sahve as a shield."

"Sir," I said, jumping to obey.

"And if ya evah strike one of 'em again without my pahmission, I'll make it so you can't walk fah a month."

I swallowed, knowing that Rogers always made good on his threats. "Yes, sir," I said, waving the prisoners up from where they sat together.

The Frenchman with the patch of red on his cheek from my snowball fixed me with a smug stare. Apparently, he understood enough English.

Yet, I still wasn't bright enough to shut my mouth. "But from what I hear, captain, you propose to violate parts of rules five, ten, and twenty-two."

Rogers veered sideways and rammed his fist into my chin, nearly sending me out of my snowshoes. "The lieutenant is the only man who may question me," he barked as I rolled out of a snowbank and onto my knees. "And stop tellin' me about numbah this and numbah that! Line 'em up. We ah leaving."

Not a single man uttered any protest. Most of his rangers had long ago learned to follow orders without hesitation. Those who may have still harbored a bit of freewill at dawn, efficiently absorbed the lesson that had fallen so violently from the captain's hand to my person. They were lined up behind the captives and me within just ten heartbeats.

Two to three hours of deadly silent travel passed by. The temperatures had steadily climbed, allowing a sweat to break out beneath my wraps. Then the precipitation commenced. Snow at first. Then it changed to everyone's favorite version of sleet – cold, wet, and sharp. The sweat mingled with the rainy snow and made me shiver. I marched with my shoulders permanently humped in order to drive away at least a portion of the misery. Yet, not a complaint was uttered.

Our captives were at a disadvantage to us. They had no snowshoes. Every time the Frenchmen's legs got tired from lumbering through the knee-deep drifts, they'd slow their pace. And even though I glided across the top of the snow because of my webbed feet, I slowed my rate to match theirs. Rogers had not bothered to grumble. He merely locked a bayonet in place and, without holding much force back, used it to prod my rump. I had quickly learned to do the same and, in turn, poked the last Frenchman with my bayonet.

The captives growled under their breaths, but otherwise marched on.

We passed through the previous night's camp. Rogers gave his second in command a self-satisfied grin while we loitered for just ten minutes. Then the march was resumed.

Two miles separated us from Ticonderoga as we curved around southward. I saw no sign of man or beast. There was not a single foreign moccasin or boot track. Not even our own footprints from the day before had survived the storm thus far to indicate that anyone had dared venture out that winter.

The Frenchmen soon picked their way down a sharp slope. It led to a creek that bisected our path. One of them slipped, whisking away on his back with his bound hands in the air until he came to a crunching halt on the brook's ice. The others were more cautious and grasped exposed roots or trees. While chuckling at his misfortune, I, too, was careful to stay upright.

"Through this little notch," Rogers announced proudly, pointing down the creek with his elbow. He'd scooted onto the ice and helped the fallen prisoner to his feet. "And we'll be back on the ice of an English lake." The captain patted my back. "Yoah doin' fine, lad. Keep the Frogs humpin'."

He was a strange man, able to reprimand his men and enemies with intense, swift brutality in one moment. Yet, in the next instant, he was as gregarious as if we'd all enjoyed the same rum-soused party.

"Allez," I said to the lead Frenchman. He groaned from exhaustion, but marshaled the will to move. Soon we all crunched our way over the creek between the momentarily tight, steep walls.

Click. Click. Click.

My eyes and ears shot wide as I lunged toward the bank nearest the sounds, slipping and sliding along the way. Rogers had heard the same thing. He grabbed the rearmost prisoner by the collar and threw him next to me. "Descendre!" he shrieked. The other six Frogs scrambled after him, ramming their backs against the root-entangled cliff.

You see, we had walked into an ambush that, so far, was not going according to the plans of the French. But not every one of their pans would have been fouled by the damp weather.

CHAPTER 18

Cr-crack! Click. Cr-crack! Cr-crack!

Enough of the French muskets arrayed above us were erupting to make life difficult, death easy, for us.

Rogers flicked off a leather pocket that he used to keep his pan dry. A second later he leaned out toward the center of the brook and selected a target in the scrub above. *Cr-crack!* He ducked back to safety, swearing in force before he swiftly reloaded.

I ventured placing my torso in danger, too. Then, I chased a target with my muzzle and gently pressed the trigger. Bess belched. A Frog fell wounded as I pressed up against the bank and a hail of shot cascaded down to my former position. The injured man rolled off the edge, over my head, and slammed down hard on the ice, gasping. Baker, took one swift stride forward and bashed his hatchet into the wounded Frog's throat. That's when I studied, not the steaming blood that streamed from the gash, but the man's uniform. I recognized his baby blue cuffs, his blue waistcoat, and the laced-white insignia upon his brimless cap. We'd been attacked by a regular regiment of His Most Christian Majesty's notorious grenadiers. Hand-selected, these warriors hailed straight from Europe with discipline and tenacity driven into their very souls. The dead man and his living, shooting comrades belonged to the Languedoc regiment. I'd faced these giants of the battlefield before and survived. But once was more than enough.

There was no time for fretting. While I reloaded, a few of the prisoners began crawling away down the frozen river. I snatched the leader's trousers and dragged him back, brandishing a knife in his face. He understood my meaning without a word.

Click! Cr-crack! Click! Click! Cr-crack!

Providence had stretched his hand out over the English that day. Our folly in following our same tracks back home might not lead to our end, after all. The French attack was being thwarted by the weather. Less than half of their weapons were discharging properly.

Still, it was enough to keep us in place. We fired back and forth, exchanging more than three choppy volleys.

"Webah!" Rogers hissed, periodically sticking a finger into a hole that had been shot through his cap. "From shouts and sounds, I count upwahds of 250 of the bastahds." He pointed up the creek to the rear of our column where only twenty rangers had made the descent before the ambush had commenced. "Weah sitting ducks down heah." Another ranger seemed to die every minute.

"Where's Stark and the rest?" I asked.

"Listen," he shouted with a grin, while again leaning out to shoot. I focused my hearing back the way we had come. A terrific racket, above the rest of the din, sounded from upstream on the northern shore. "Stahky's pulled ouah reah of the column up to that hill we passed befah we dipped down heah."

"We need to get to them," I breathed as chunks of ice blew into the air, turning to powder as balls of shot rained from above.

"Aye," he agreed. "Needs to be swift." Then he shouted for the rangers, who were stuck upriver from us, to hear. "We'll fiyah and fall back behind you. Then you do the same." Everyone understood his job and no responses were required.

"Get those tahds up and ready to run," Rogers instructed me, indicating the prisoners with a derisive jerk of his snout.

"Up!" I commanded.

"Non!" said the Frenchman whom I had beamed with snow. His comrades folded their arms, unwilling to move. Apparently, the proximity of their rescue had made them less than compliant.

Rogers would have none of it. "We only need a few of them to talk to the majah. Kill one. The rest will listen."

"Sir," I said in hasty agreement. Then it hit me. "Sir?" I asked.

He extended two of his fingers and jabbed them forward like a stabbing dagger. "Kill one. The rest will fall in line."

"That's murder, sir," I said weakly. If you've read my tales, you know I was no stranger to violence and death. I had thumped a good many men in fights, fair and unfair. I had killed while others had tried to kill me. To my knowledge I had never murdered a prisoner. Well…

In a flash, Rogers' war hatchet bashed the skull of one of the Frenchmen. Blood spattered me and the other captives, who looked on in horror. Except for the man at whom I'd thrown the snowball. He saw an opportunity and lunged forward, snatching my musket with his bound hands. We struggled over the weapon, yanking it between us.

If he'd expected his heroics to rally the others, he was mistaken. The rest of the prisoners remained frozen against the northern bank. Rogers lugged the head of his tomahawk out of the crumpling warrior and promptly brought it against the back of the man who attacked me. The captain let out a vicious roar. His victim shrieked and we both tumbled into the middle of the brook.

A renewed bout of shots fell upon us from above. The dying Frenchman took them all in his back, as my shield. By the time I sloughed him off and scrambled to cover, Rogers had murdered a third captive, this time with his pistol. He yelled at Baker. "Kill the rest. If they won't obey, we can't maneuvah." Rogers then glared at me. "It ain't mahdah to kill the enemy. We ah an exposed force undah attack. Even the Frogs agree on that."

Four prisoners died within the next ten heartbeats. It was as brutal as anything I'd seen from the tribesmen in times of war. It was swift, but gruesome.

"See why you have to submit, boy?" Rogers growled to me. He wanted no answer and for once, I was smart enough to give him none. "Fiyah and maneuvah in two squads," he rasped to those of us still alive. He waited a few moments for us all to have a loaded gun. "Now!"

The half of us at the front stepped back into the center of the creek to get a direct shot at the enemy. We fired as one, forcing them to duck, then ran upstream, past the other half of rangers. "Reload!" Rogers ordered as he skidded to halt at the north bank. We did and the second half of men stepped back, fired, and ran beyond us.

With our next volley, Rogers led us up the slope and onto land. Our small squad crouched behind bushes or trees reloading as the next band made their way up the hill. In this step-wise manner we raced back toward Lieutenant Stark's position on the hill. It was right where Rogers said it would be.

Our pursuers chased us, but were hampered by the snow.

Nonetheless, by the time those of us who'd been on the river dropped into the relative safety of Stark's men, we had been reduced by six in ten.

The battle on snowshoes had begun.

CHAPTER 19

"Where are the prisoners?" Stark asked. The shooting had momentarily ceased as both sides came to terms with the new arrangement.

"Dead," Rogers huffed, offering no further explanation.

Stark nodded his understanding, then pointed to our sad numbers. "The rest of the rangers with you? Lost?"

Rogers snarled. He ripped his cap off and threw it in the snow. Blood poured from a wound in his scalp. He dabbed at it with his palm. "A ball in thah fahst volley struck me skull. Damn that hahts."

Stark snapped his fingers and Anderson ran up to our commander. He followed Rogers around, bandaging his head. Rogers ignored his presence. Instead, he went right on issuing orders. "Set a pahrimetah. Consahve ammunition. Don't let the bastahds get around behind us. We need to get out o'heah before help arrives from Cahrillone."

"So far, from what I've seen, we face just Frenchmen and Canadians, sir," Stark explained crisply. "They don't know how to maneuver in wilderness like our tribal friends. We ought to be able to peel away in ranks soon enough."

Then a screech, a pair of screeches actually, tore through the stormy afternoon. They were followed by the staccato chants of hell hounds. The eyes of all the rangers looked eastward down the hill we'd just ascended. A dozen Ottawa warriors had emerged from the enemy lines and surrounded three wounded rangers, who had been forced down on their knees. The first ranger had a gaping chest wound and teetered, barely alive. As a warning to us, one of the enemy warriors snapped the captive's head back and sliced off his scalp. The blade zipped like hot metal through lard. He finished by kicking the ranger in the back with the bottom of his buckskin boot. The dying man tipped into the snow as his scalp was raised high and hailed with further hoots from the victors.

The next pair of rangers were injured, but far from dead. Thomas Brown shivered on his knees, having been stripped of most of his gear. At least three trails of blood oozed from his extremities. A knife wound here. A war hatchet slash there.

Robert Baker crouched next to Brown. He was in a similar state of abuse.

I waited stoically for them both to be deprived of their hair and flesh as well. The bloodlust of battle was difficult to extinguish once it had a foothold in the hearts of men. But instead of ensuring Brown's and Baker's slow deaths in the snow, the Ottawa warriors yanked them up and bound them right before our eyes. With spears, they prodded them into the French lines.

"They'll share terrible deaths," Stark whispered.

I nodded. For, I'd witnessed many ritual killings in the tribal villages. But there were worse things than death. "Or lives as slaves in the pays d'en haut," I mumbled.

Rogers elbowed away from his makeshift physician, who had not completed his task. "Only French and Canadians, eh Stahk? The damned tribesmen might already be swahling around our ahss," he warned. "Sneaky devils. Sneaky as me!"

Musket fire erupted on the north as a great band of Ottawa did, in fact, try to skirt around our flanks. We weren't going anywhere anytime soon.

CHAPTER 20

We fought like hell against the Frogs and their trespassing Indian allies, exchanging shot for shot and death for death for several hours. Our position ebbed and flowed as we traipsed over the hill's ridge. Periodically, we'd sally down against our foes just to prevent them from massing against us. It was apparent that we were greatly advantaged by the fact that we were all outfitted with snowshoes. Our rangers could move three times as fast as the enemy, which made up for the drastic difference in numbers. Through it all, at least the snow and sleet had stopped, a welcome relief. But the mercury dropped rapidly as evening swiftly drew nigh.

"Heah," Rogers said as he made his rounds at our rough perimeter of panting warriors. "Whisky."

I took a great slug of what he offered and warmth flared immediately from the center of my chest outward. It was a welcome sensation after hours of frantic fighting. My heart rate slowed. My breathing eased. I noticed I was hungry.

Rogers patted my shoulder. "Keep the powdah dry, boy. And eat a small meal. Just because night is neahly upon us don't mean ouah day is done."

I nodded. "The Ottawa might try to skulk in among us tonight."

"Ya," he said. "Be ready to break out. We might try to get to the lake undah dahkness." The blood from his head wound seeped through the hastily applied bandage. It had soaked his hair, neck, and shirt. He appeared pale. If possible, his speech was even more difficult to understand.

I nodded again, having pulled a ration of salted fish from my pack. "We were lucky that no one else from Ticonderoga made it to reinforce the French," I said with a mouthful. "But as sure as thunder follows lightning, they'll be here by morning."

It was Rogers turn to nod. "Sahrry about Brown. Know you wah friends."

I hardly knew Thomas Brown. But we'd joined Rogers' Rangers on the same day, so I suppose we were as close to one another as anyone. "There's not much we can do for him now," I breathed.

"No," Rogers said coldly. Then he shuttled atop the snow to the next man in the line. "Heah. Whisky," he said to Amos. The Indian ranger thanked him and they settled into a brief conversation. Conwall had seen perhaps thirty and five summers. He was grizzled and lean and had showed proficiency in the field. He asked for a second taste of Rogers' spirits.

The French and their allies had, at least temporarily, pulled back out of range of our muskets. They likely supped and rested. If they had plans for their Indians to attack in the night, they'd want to preserve their energy. Or, if they merely waited for greater numbers to arrive in the morning, they likely judged it foolish to accept casualties. In the latter case, all the Frogs had to do was keep us penned up.

First one, then a second, and a third campfire was struck down below in the distant trees. I heard the clatter of pans and the growing careless chatter that came as tired, cold men began to hunker down for the night. If the sun had actually been visible through the cloud cover, it would have been moments from slipping below the horizon.

I sat for a good many moments as utter darkness and cold descended upon us. Rogers permitted us no fires that night, as he wanted our eyes accustomed to the pitch black. And the forest at last became one big shadow.

My stomach rumbled and I again dug in my pack, finding a frozen flake of maple syrup and a hard biscuit. I married the two and took one bite.

Musket fire erupted from the north – of the enemy camp – directed into the enemy camp. I swallowed the bite, unchewed, and stuffed the rest safely away for later – I'd never knowingly abandon such a precious commodity as food. Any ease I had felt from the too-brief respite was gone. My senses snapped to attention. I saw and heard and smelled and felt everything.

Below, the French camp was in total disarray. Some of their soldiers had begun firing up toward us. Others offered shot toward the newly arrived, yet unseen, third force on the north. No. It was suddenly on the east, firing into the scattered camp of the

French and cutting down confused, white-clad warriors. The Ottawa braves hooted, ducking, but receiving the same punishment from the east. No. It was on the north again. Whoever it was, was moving the plane of their attack as swiftly as any I'd ever seen.

"Whut in hell is going on?" Rogers hissed as he slid next to me. I told him, noting his worsening pallor, what I had seen. He took no longer than a heartbeat to consider the latest change in our situation. He poked me in the ear. "You men on the front, fall back silently to the reah. Weah leavin'."

"What about our saviors?" I asked, pointing to the latest place where the unrelenting fire had come. The gunfire came in very controlled bursts or rounds of three muskets, too swiftly to be just three men. But with enough delay to be something less than a full regiment.

He flicked the same ear. It stung. "That's the thing about saviyahs, lad. They do the savin'. We do the thankin'." Rogers jumped up, swooning for a moment, and disappeared into our lines. "Stahk. Prepahe to fall back in ranks."

With one last look at the firefight going on below, I did just what Rogers had suggested. I thanked Providence for those unknown men in the forest. Then I rushed back with my fellow rangers.

Our escape route down the western slope was circuitous before we again turned southward. Behind us, the battle at the French camp went on for perhaps ten minutes longer before it sputtered to a halt. The remainder of our march in the enemy woods was silent, without incident. And though we had been within minutes of setting foot on the northernmost point of Lake George at the start of the battle, it took three hours of rapid hoofing to again reach what Rogers had called an English lake.

The night was bleak. The wind had picked up to something I'd call stiff when we set off on our retreat over the ice. We had made it less than a half mile onto the vast sheet of emptiness when, in a very peculiar fashion, a voice called out in a most friendly manner. "That you, Rogers?"

Shocked, everyone of us halted, dropping to our knees and raising our guns at the sound. The captain did not answer.

"Only Robert Rogers would attempt such a fool thing as tramping over a frozen lake with nary enough men in tow to take on two French forts. So, you don't have to answer, but I still know it's you, Rogers," called the voice from the darkness. It approached from the east.

I peered at the profile of Rogers' hard face in the dark as he listened. His brow was, at first, furrowed in confusion. Then a flicker of recollection softened his expression. And, while I cannot say his face eventually showed joy, it at least no longer expressed concern. He slapped the butt of his musket onto the ice and used it like a cane to help stand. His gait had become rougher throughout the retreat. The head wound was slowly draining him. Rogers then faced squarely at the shadowed form that steadily approached. "That you, Bumppo?"

"Ha," answered the man in a friendly manner. "Bumppo is what generations and Providence called me. But mankind has seen fit to bestow upon me a varied form of names."

Two more figures, tribesmen, emerged from the darkness. They shadowed the first man, who was called Bumppo, a name I thought sounded familiar. Though I was sure I had never actually met a man with such a unique surname.

They finished their approach. Bumppo and Rogers stood two feet from one another, each eyeballing the other like rivals often do. It was Bumppo who offered his hand first.

Rogers allowed it to hang there. Lesser men than Bumppo would have wilted awkwardly away. But this man, this apparition, held his hand between their slim bellies patiently. It appeared he might be willing to wait the whole night through. All the while, he never took his eyes from Rogers face.

Meanwhile, I noticed the newcomer's Indian friends as they stood silently. They were of the ancient tribe called Mahican, just like Conwall. Most of the Mahican peoples had long ago been decimated by the Mohawks. I had met very few in my life, perhaps ten, all old. However, one of Bumppo's companions was young, perhaps my age. He was a handsome man with the remarkable features that occur when someone is the offspring of two nations. The other warrior was twice again as old.

Rogers eventually took the hand. "Up, lads," he whispered so his voice would not carry too far over the lake. "It's an old friend."

Bumppo smiled. He was not a handsome man. Nor was he homely. But neither was he average. The shape of his cheeks and nose were severe enough to be disconcerting. His flesh was weathered and if I had to venture a guess, I would say aged thirty winters. "I'm glad to hear you refer to us as friends, for I believe it with my heart. Elsewise, I and my companions would not have come to your rescue back there outside Ticonderoga."

Rogers immediately dropped the handshake. "We didn't need any rescue."

Bumppo shrugged. "Many men with as fearsome a reputation as you might say the same thing, Robert. But by any measure, you and your rangers were pinned down before we attacked the French camp."

I squinted into the darkness, willing my eyes to see farther and in richer detail.

"You won't see anyone else, son," Bumppo explained. "It's just the three of us."

Rogers scoffed. "Thah was enough gunfiyah coming into the French camp to indicate they faced a company or more."

With genuine humility, the three new arrivals exchanged glances. "My brothers, the English, owe us for many abandoned muskets," said the older Mahican.

Bumppo patted his friend's shoulder. "In time, Chingachgook. Let's get these tired men to William Henry first."

"We know the way," Rogers said, peeved.

"So do we," Bumppo said jovially. Without asking permission to join our troop, he struck off southward toward our fort. The Mahican men followed.

Rogers grumbled but fell in line behind them. He waved our column ahead and we all crunched over the lake.

"Do you think our brothers will pay us for the muskets?" the young Mahican timidly asked Bumppo.

The woodsman chuckled at the younger man. "Uncas," he said. "We both know that the only reason you and your father are so eager to see pennies fall from King George's purse into your palms is so that you may pay the price for your bride and renew the line of your people."

"Good luck with that, Uncas," Anderson hooted from behind. "No woman will have Conwall. I think he's a kinsman of yours. He's been so desperate to bed a high-breasted female, any female, some of us think to get a plump pet possum for him to hold at night."

The men, including old Conwall, shared a laugh as the shy Uncas looked away.

Chingachgook craned his head back to gander at Amos. "Stockbridge?" he surmised. When Conwall nodded, the older Mahican said, "No. Not kinsmen. He's of the Westenhuck clans. We are of the Fireplace peoples. Uncas must continue his pursuit. Besides, it's a noble goal for the boy to have, Hawkeye," said Chingachgook, defensively.

Bumppo chuckled again. "It is," he agreed joyfully. "But your son has the womanly goal of emotional love in his mind as much as the noble ideal of progeny. I dare say," he continued, glancing around as if to discover any spying eyes. "And without the burden of the fairer sex about, I am willing to wager that Uncas even hopes to experience the joyful act of creating a family as much as raising the products of his vigorous efforts."

Chingachgook laughed along with the woodsman. The older warrior even jabbed an elbow into his son's ribs.

"Wait," I said suddenly from my place in the column. "You're Hawkeye? *The* Hawkeye?"

Bumppo glanced over his shoulder at me. "That is one of the names the forest dwellers have imparted. It is the one that most in these parts call me. And I, too, have become partial to it. The French, our enemies in this current war, call me La Longue Carabine, which strikes me as strange since a carbine is something quite short." He hefted his extraordinarily long rifle. "Not like this." He then set the rifle across his folded arms and looked to his companions for help. "What else do they call me?"

"Straight-Tongue," Chingachgook answered, proudly. "For plain talk."

"Deerslayer," Uncas answered.

"You're legendary," I breathed, more enamored with him and his reputation than I had ever been upon meeting even a grand Philadelphian like Benjamin Franklin.

Rogers huffed. "Listen to me, Webah. I prefah to call him The Pigeon or Lap-Eah. They seem fitting to me."

Hawkeye stopped dead in his tracks and spun. I thought for a fraction of a second that he was going to strike Rogers for the perceived insult. The captain believed the same thing and braced for the impact. Instead, the woodsman came straight to me. "Weber. Ephraim Weber? The one called Fierce Dog?"

I was astonished. "You've heard of me?" My face flushed with pride. To be recognized as an outstanding frontiersman and trader and scout by my peers was all I had ever wanted. Well, that and riches. And a wife. Two or three wives, if I could swing such a sacrilege. I liked rum, too. Madeira was good. Whisky had its place. Cards, all gambling really, I wanted plenty of that, too. In truth, in those younger days, I still had many unfulfilled desires.

"Of course, I have," Hawkeye said nonchalantly as he returned to his place in the column. "I was educated by Moravians. Peaceful folk. Providence saw fit for me to meet some of my fellow peaceful neighbors down in Penn's Woods. Many years ago, I met a Quaker there with the same name as you."

"My father," I guessed.

"I see that now. It makes a touch more sense. I never could marry what I knew of the kind man I'd met back then with your reputation for brutality. Word of your exploits has raced through the tribes."

I beamed.

"But this name and reputation of yours will not do," Hawkeye went on. "Why should a man under the authority of Providence be fierce other than in a defensive way? And a dog? The tribes love their dogs as much as any colonist. But dog? The way it is whispered in the villages, I believe they mean it more like cur."

My pride sank a little. But it was still buoyed by the fact that a nickname I had conjured for myself in the midst of hand-to-hand combat some years earlier was spreading far out of the reach of my own voice.

Chingachgook then leaned in toward Hawkeye's ear. "Isn't that the same boy the Delaware call Shit-for-brains."

"Shh-shh," Hawkeye rasped. "One name at a time. The boy is young and has time to do what the ministers might call repent."

But it was too late.

Rogers had heard my old nickname.

CHAPTER 21

And to some people, especially Rogers, it would become my new nickname. No longer was I, *Webah!* No. In the clearest English Robert Rogers ever employed, I became *Shit-for-brains*. In all situations. No matter what strife or scrape in which we found ourselves. Trudging over the ice. Fishing through the ice. Cooking over a fire. He enjoyed raising his pinky, as if he drank in the affected fashion of the eastern ladies and dandies. The captain would then utter my moniker in the sort of clear phrasing that King George II might use when speaking before his Parliament.

So, it was with somewhat great relief to me that the captain's ample energy stores at last gave out when we crossed into William Henry. His head had clotted during the first night of our retreat. Then the wound had re-opened during some exertion. Then it had clotted. Then re-opened. Rogers performed every action with vigor. He was not known for doing anything gingerly.

Things moved rapidly for him once he collapsed on the parade ground. First, his limp form was carried to a dinner table for a physician to inspect the cause for the blood on his head. To probe, the doctor used one of the forks an officer's wife had been using to eat her beets. A hole of some magnitude was quite unsurprisingly discovered. Next, a sled was outfitted to transport Rogers to Fort Edward and probably Albany. Given the amount of blood that had caked in his hair beneath his cap, I thought it likely that the sleigh might cart him directly to a grave. The time that elapsed from our arrival to his departure was less than an hour.

But it was another week before we had our meeting with the energetic fort commander. And during that week we discovered that our scouting dimensions shrunk ever-closer to William Henry's walls. Immense bands of enemy tribesmen began moving about the forest in such large numbers that any force smaller than a hundred men was at risk of being overwhelmed.

"What happened on Champlain that invited all this?" Major Eyre breathed. I stood in his headquarters with Stark, Hawkeye, Chingachgook, and Uncas. "Half of the men were lost, a good many the first night. This was to be a simple operation for woodsmen such as you. The objectives, in order, were reconnoiter, take prisoners, harass supplies and foraging, and, only if assured of success, to set fire to one of the French outposts." Eyre was in no way prone to outbursts. And even though the major was clearly upset by the outcome, his emotions remained in the exacting control one might expect from the consummate engineer.

Lieutenant Stark shook his head firmly. "The casualties on the first night couldn't be avoided. The break-through happened very fast and the captain reacted with speed. He saved the lives of many men."

"Why didn't you turn back once your numbers were so depleted?" Eyre asked. He simultaneously read a report from Lieutenant Turnwell on the preparedness of the artillery crews. The major scribbled questions in the margins.

"Major, sir," Stark began. "We are accustomed to operating undermanned and under harsh conditions. For the captain to urge us forward after what happened on Lake George was considered typical."

Eyre thought about the answer and nodded, moving on. He handed his correspondence to an aid who raced out to draft a letter. "And the first ambush?"

I couldn't help but feel partially responsible. For, in some ways, it had been my plan that led to the debacle on Lake Champlain.

But Stark stood his ground literally and figuratively. "It was our first and best chance at taking hostages. The captain noticed the other sleds approaching and made all attempts to warn me. But with operational control, I deemed it necessary to continue on with the attack."

"Had it gone without a hitch," I explained. "We would have had a good estimate of French strength."

"I can give you that, if you want it," Hawkeye said plainly. "Chingachgook walked right into both French forts. In the middle of the day. And just in the last couple weeks."

Eyre gave the older Mahican warrior a circumspect eye.

Chingachgook shrugged in a disarming manner. "The French fathers wouldn't know the difference between a Mahican and a Mohegan."

"But the Ottawa would," Eyre pressed.

"And they did," Chingachgook said.

His son chuckled into his palm, immediately embarrassed by his own outburst. He cleared his throat. "My father runs pretty fast for a man of his years. Well, when a band of the enemy have their blades drawn and are in pursuit."

"I suppose so," Eyre agreed. "How many at Ticonderoga? St. Frédéric?"

"The French are building up their numbers. We saw many white coats up north in Quebec," Chingachgook answered. "They will have to go somewhere in spring. They most likely plan to move straight through Lake George, all the way to Albany. Fort St. Frédéric already hosts a growing number. Perhaps a thousand Catholic Indians – Nipissing, Abenaki, Caughnawaga, and many more tribes that I have not seen in these parts in a generation."

"Montcalm practically invited them when he paid off Chief Collière to halt the massacre last year," I muttered.

The Mahicans both nodded their agreement. Chingachgook resumed his report. "Another three thousand Frenchmen at St. Frédéric. Almost identical numbers of French and Indians at Ticonderoga, but the tribes represented differ, more Chippewa, Potawatomi, and a dozen more."

Eyre pinched his lips. "That's half again as many as what Rogers counted a month ago before this latest expedition."

Chingachgook agreed. "The French have turned Champlain and the rivers into a highway of sleds this winter, ferrying men and supplies."

"And Governor-General Vaudreuil has made no secret of his wishes for the coming year," Hawkeye added. "Every street rat in Montreal and Quebec knows that he wants to destroy William Henry and Edward. Then he'll send his Indian raiders into Albany to finish the job."

"Why should we trust you men? What took you all the way to Quebec and back?" Stark asked. "And if you are allies of the English, how did you move about safely?" His last question was aimed directly at Chingachgook.

The older Mahican looked at the younger. The younger shrunk in embarrassment and looked to Hawkeye, who grinned broadly. "Oh, trust as you will, lieutenant. The only words of assurance I can offer convey the truth of the tale. Uncas is rich in heart and courage. But when it comes to both speaking outright in front of his red-coated English brothers and in his treasure of the king's coins, he is poor. Destitute even. As a result of the first, I'll answer your question, lieutenant. And it is as a result of the second that we found ourselves up in Canada."

"You see, the handsome boy finds his mind drifting into the realm of feminine charms, of love and family. But also of the plight of his people at the hands of Iroquois and Frenchmen, and a thousand other unnamed bandits from the human race." Hawkeye went on to describe in some detail how Chingachgook had found a young Delaware princess whose father would allow her to be married into the dwindling Mahican tribe. But it was to cost Uncas a lot. "So, Uncas here, lovelorn as he was, enlisted our help. We went up to Quebec and found a smuggler. Bought ourselves several crates of muskets stolen from a garrison up there and mules to haul them – all on the credit of my name."

Eyre held up his hand. "You were going to transport St. Etienne muskets from our French enemy to our Delaware enemy?"

Hawkeye shook his head with a pleasant nature. "Naw, sir. The muskets weren't going to the Delaware, Eastern or Western. Chingachgook and I know our duty to the rightful king of these parts. Our aim was to bring the guns here. We figured that the Frenchmen with a hundred fewer muskets would make you happy. We just hoped that you'd be good enough to pay us a little something for our trouble."

It was a tale that was too preposterous to be a lie. Eyre smiled. "I suppose we could break open the treasury's chest. Just turn in the muskets to our quartermaster. If he finds them in good condition, bring me the receipt and I'll see you paid."

Uncas looked sheepishly at Hawkeye. "That's just it, major," answered the frontiersman. "We don't have the muskets or the mules anymore. You see, we were transporting them down here, when we heard the battle over near Ticonderoga. I think you'd call it the second ambush. We went over to investigate and sure enough, Rogers had his rangers balled up something awful. Well, being friends and neighborly, we helped him out."

"While Rogers and Stark and Fierce Dog fought the Frenchmen, we spent the rest of the afternoon loading each and every musket," Chingachgook said. "We placed them all around the northeastern edge of the French camp while the enemy kept probing the hill. When night came, we attacked. We had to abandon all the muskets when we retreated to Lake George."

"It worked, too," Stark admitted, immediately believing their version of events. "They caused chaos throughout the enemy. Enabled us to slip away without further casualties."

Major Eyre studied Uncas. "Well, son, I'm afraid we cannot compensate you for something that likely wound up in French hands anyway. But I can offer my heartfelt thanks for your sacrifice as you helped preserve Rogers' command."

"I was afraid of that," Hawkeye muttered. "It shows good sense on your part, of course, major. But it means that we will have to continue on our journeys, finding a way to raise the funds for Uncas and his bride."

Chingachgook yanked his head toward the door. "Looks like we'll be trapping all winter."

"One pelt at a time is a slow way to buy a Delaware princess. But it's the surest," Hawkeye agreed.

"Where will you go?" I asked. I knew that the beaver now grew in the greatest number in the Ohio Country. "Betrothed or not, I'd be unwilling to risk too deep into Shawnee or Delaware territory to trap these days."

Chingachgook grinned. "We'll stay in this area and take all we get. My people have a lot of pelts to harvest from what used to be our lands. And I don't mind one bit that the Iroquois might be unhappy about it."

Eyre stood to formally see them off. "Then I shall not say a word to my Mohawk friends about your small trespass. We'll call it our little secret. But it will be up to you to stay out of sight. If you're caught, I will have little power to do anything."

Hawkeye and the others bowed before stepping to the threshold. "I'd not worry about us," assured the frontiersman. "We know how to make ourselves scarce." They closed the great oaken door behind them.

"How many rangers are fit to scout?" Eyre asked Stark as soon as we were alone. He'd chosen to forget running through the details of the second, more fatal ambush in the creek bed. The major found his seat behind his desk.

"With the sicknesses that crop up each day, we now have less than forty available," the lieutenant answered.

"If I want to have eyes up past Shelving Rock on the east and Northwest Bay on the west, what do you suggest?" the major asked.

Stark and I exchanged a glance. "Not possible, sir," the lieutenant answered.

Some commanders would have turned as red as their coats and babbled until their underlings spouted off the things they wished to hear. Eyre merely asked, "Then how far can you give me with so few?"

"All forty would have to scout together," I began. "There's no two ways about it. With all the enemy activity."

Stark nodded. "And since we have only one platoon left…" He glanced at the ceiling, calculating daily marches and attrition rates in his head. "I'd hate to see us range farther away than three or four miles on a trip. At least until we can build our numbers in the spring."

Eyre growled quietly. "That barely gets us to Kattskill Bay."

Lieutenant Stark agreed. "I'll take the men up as far as Long Point on the east. Still Bay or a little farther on the west."

I watched through the window as Uncas and his two older companions walked out through the fort's gates and into the heaps of snow. They had spent what small money they had purchasing traps from a trader who'd temporarily set up shop in the livery. The iron jaws and chains dangled from their great packs. I silently wished for Providence to watch over Uncas as he completed his noble quest.

Johnny Anson came barreling in the opposite direction, kicking up snow as he went. The boy was always in a hurry, but I took a second look, half expecting to see flames pouring from his rump. He raced out of my view toward the door to the headquarters. I shook my head and chuckled under my breath.

"There's nothing humorous about it, Weber," Eyre said. "Until we can get help enough to rid us of these enemy bands, we're nearly blind."

"No laughing matter, sir," I explained to the major. "It's Anson."

Eyre frowned, but then we all heard Johnny in the hall demand admittance. Despite the guard's denial, the door promptly flew open.

"I was out on the lake fishing with a few of the men," Johnny chattered in a frenzy. His nose was pink. "I swear. I do swear up a storm! Looked north and thought I saw a bank of gray fog rolling over the ice. But, I swear, it's too cold for fog. Even the fish kept asking for blankets!"

Johnny Anson was funny. But he was no fool. "What did you see?" I asked, running to the window to check the watchmen up on the wall walk. One of them pointed northward over the lake's surface. He called to his comrades and one of them produced a spyglass.

"An army of Frenchmen! Heavens! I saw Canadians! And tribesmen! Swarms of them all!" the boy said. "They're walking over the ice. Looks like they liked Rogers idea so much, they stole it!"

The sentries on the wall had begun to sound the general alarm. Johnny's fellow fishermen, not quite as swift on the hoof as the boy, bolted inside the fort. They waved for the officer in charge of the gate to see it closed. Several carpenters who had been working down by the shore scrambled in with their tools just as the gates slammed shut.

"How many?" Stark asked.

"More than a thousand, I swear!" Anson said. "Less than two."

"It's a siege. In the dead of winter," I breathed. "How many men at our disposal, major?"

"Johnny," Eyre barked, again rising to his feet. "They can't have brought artillery in these conditions. Tell the watch to prepare to thwart an escalade. I want hooks, poles, pitch forks, anything long on the walls to shove ladders away. Inform Lieutenant Turnwell that I want canister loaded in all of his lake-facing pieces."

"Aye, sir," the boy chirped, ripping out the door.

Major Eyre looked in my direction, peacefully. "Including the sick and infirm and the women and children, we have 474 souls in the fort."

"We could be outnumbered three-to-one," I stated, quite obviously.

"I'd think that all the toiling we've done on our fortress over the past year will do better than even the odds," said the major, confidently. Eyre then indicated the door with an outstretched hand. "But let's go see for ourselves, shall we?"

CHAPTER 22

"What are they waiting for?" Johnny asked, following the major around like his shadow.

Eyre had been studying every detail of the enemy through his superb glass for about ten minutes, making notes, drawing circles with numbers of troops and their disposition. He scratched arrows in the directions he assumed they'd disperse and to which we'd have to respond.

"Rigaud," Eyre clipped as he slid his smooth-working scope together.

Johnny snatched the glass before the major was able to tuck it away. "The governor-general of New France himself? Where?"

Eyre did not fall into an acerbic tantrum as many commanders would. He merely helped Johnny point the telescope in the proper direction. "There," said the major. "Do you see the man marching about in front of the French regulars?"

Johnny squinted. "The little one?"

"That's him," Eyre said, reaching for his glass.

Johnny yanked it back, and peered through again. "Why, he looks like a woodsman sawed him off. He's a head shorter than all the rest. And he's wiry. Skinnier than a snake."

Eyre moved swiftly and swiped his own spyglass. It was in his satchel before the boy could make another move. "And probably just as wily as a snake," he warned, perusing his notes.

"What would the governor-general be doing way down here?" Stark asked.

"He's not," Eyre answered. He took a moment, jotted down an order, and pressed it into the hand of an ensign. "To Mr. Turnwell, please," he said. The lad trotted off to Turdwell who, upon reading the missive, set about shifting a large group of his men to several other guns that faced west and east.

"That's not the marquis de Vaudreuil. The man marching about on the ice happens to be the younger brother of the governor-general," the major finished. He stood with his hands folded behind his back patiently observing the distant, stationary scene unfold on the frigid lake.

“So, is it patronage or skill that got him his position?” I asked. In the English army, unfortunately, it seemed to come down to connections more often than aptitude.

“Their respite is complete,” Eyre announced, not taking his gaze from our foes. The enemy had begun moving directly southward over the ice, splitting into three evenly sized battalions. A set of mixed tribesmen was under the command of a French officer on their right flank. Another French officer led the Canadian provincials on their left flank. Rigaud walked in the center of his regular troops, which were set on a course directly toward us. “We shall see soon enough how the good, young François earned his commission.”

CHAPTER 23

Then the turds again came to a halt. All except a single officer, wrapped snug in thick layers of coats, including a rich bear hide that drooped down to his ankles. He was accompanied by two Canadians. One of them frantically waved a scarlet flag of parley – red of course, because the Kingdom of France had a flag with small rows of buttery fleur-de-lys on a stark, white field. They crunched their way over the lake directly toward us.

"Mr. Anson," Eyre clipped. His mouth twisted in mild amusement at the sight of the approaching envoys.

"Sir," the boy answered.

The major pointed down to where a pair of laundresses toiled at washing officers' shirts despite the cold and pending battle. "Ask one of those ladies for a swatch of cloth large enough to wrap around a man's head. Then take it out to the lake shore. Blindfold the approaching officer and escort him into my quarters. His companions may wait at the edge of the ice for his safe return. Please inform them that should they venture closer, they will be fired upon."

"Just me, sir?" the boy asked.

Eyre glanced at the laundresses plunging their pink hands into the steaming water barrels. "You may take one of the women, or perhaps Mr. Weber, if it will make you feel better, Mr. Anson."

The men on the wall laughed at little Anson. He grinned in a fetching manner. "I think I'll take Ephraim, sir."

"That's what I thought," the major said. Then he descended the step and went across the parade ground to his office.

Anson gave me a wink and raced off to perform his duty. To the hoots of my fellow rangers and regulars and colonial troops, I followed, shoulders slumped. "There goes Ephraim Weber. After he's done babysitting, he can defend a wall, and then darn your socks!" Or another one. "Careful of his hands, the lather from the suds bucket has chafed them. They're not as delicate as the other ladies'."

Thankfully, their jibes were shut off when the man door that was fitted in the great gate slammed closed behind Johnny and me. But they resumed with even more vigor as we walked beneath the north-facing curtain wall. I heard honking calls from my comrades for a good minute as we crossed the glacis beach. Eventually, however, the men tired and shut up. Or, we had gotten out of earshot.

Less than two minutes later, the lanky lad and I stood alone upon the frozen beach. Johnny quickly grew bored as we watched the enemy party's approach. The lad made a game of kicking chunks of dirty ice at the frozen carcass of a gull.

"You should have brought a laundress if you were frightened," I grumbled, burrowing deeper in my coats. My nose was cold. My fingers burned from the cold.

"Oh, I'm not scared," Johnny said as the ball of ice he'd just booted, struck the dead bird, sending its petrified corpse skidding out onto the lake. "I swear it. Thought you might like to get out of the fort. You're always complaining about life in the garrison during winter. Come to think of it, you complained in the warmer months, too. You complain a lot. About a lot."

I had. It's part of what made me a soldier, I think. "Mind your business," I growled. This brought much mirth to the boy.

He was still giggling with his hands stuffed in his pockets when our guests arrived. "Major Eyre sends his regards, gentlemen," Johnny said with as much confidence as a seasoned diplomat. "And though he didn't say as much, I am sure he has a willingness to share a quart of claret with you. It might help drive away the chill."

In passable English, the officer responded cordially. "A kind gesture, boy. Would you be willing to continue your benevolence and guide us to the major?"

Johnny unfurled his blindfold. "I'm afraid I've been given just this one scarf, sir. And I am told that you are welcome to come with me at your arm. However," he added, pointing his mittens at the Canadians. "If those men take another step southward onto King George's territory, they will find they are most unwelcome."

The officer peered back at each man and curtly nodded his ascent. He lowered his hood, showing white tufts of curly hair jutting from beneath his cap. Johnny stepped behind the Frenchman and deftly tied the blindfold.

"Les Anglais," mumbled one of the Canadians. "Mangeurs de merde."

The officer hissed angrily at the man. On the other hand, I chuckled, using what I thought was decent French. "Les Français. La merde que les Anglais mangent."

The officer's anger subsided. He chortled at my barb in a good-natured manner. Though blinded, he poked the foul Canadian in the chest as if he wielded a foil. "Touché." Then, when he again faced forward, he extended both arms. "Lead on, gentlemen. I am in your care."

Johnny took one and I seized the other. We gently tugged him forward. And we'd not traveled two rods when his Canadian guards decided it was safer to simply return to the rest of their comrades scattered over the lake rather than tempt fate and our marksmen on the wall. It took a solid five or six minutes to guide the blinded officer over the rough terrain, over mounds of earth, and around the fort to the main gate. "Step," Johnny warned as we entered the man door. The officer kicked the sawn planks at the base below the threshold to get his bearing and carefully stepped inside.

Across the bailey, we went. Not until we were behind the closed door of the major's quarters, did we remove the Frenchman's blindfold. He blinked, brushing away a piece of fuzz that had stuck to his eyelash.

Eyre stood formally behind his desk. He bowed elegantly. "Major William Eyre, designer, engineer, and commandant of Fort William Henry and honored officer of His Majesty King George II." He indicated an empty guest's chair, before which sat a glass of wine. "I welcome you inside from the cold. And I wonder. Are you and your party lost? Do you require directions and provisions for your journey home?"

The French officer smiled thinly. He, too, bowed deeply. "Captain François Le Mercier at your service. I've had the honor of being at two major engagements in this great conflict while in service of His Most Christian Majesty King Louis XV. I was there when your Colonel Washington surrendered at the pitiful excuse for a fort."

Eyre interjected. "And you were on these very shores two years ago when General Dieskau valiantly led his men to their deaths against my General Johnson's cannons. I saw you run away in fright." Eyre paused, letting the image sink in. "And do not believe I think you cowardly for such a demonstration. Any sane man would have done the same had the force around him been so decimated."

Le Mercier frowned. "Oui," he admitted. "I have been on the winning side of one contest and experienced a setback on the other."

"Quite," Eyre said. "Won't you sit down so that I may fully understand what it is you need of me today."

Captain Le Mercier peeled off several layers of hides and cloaks, piling them in Johnny's arms. He and Eyre sat simultaneously and, in an eerily similar fashion, reached for their glasses of wine. Each sipped, allowing the warmth to penetrate the cold reaches of their bodies.

Eyre leaned back in his chair and set his hands peacefully across his lean belly. There he waited for what seemed an eternity for the Frenchman to begin his discourse. After a time, Johnny unceremoniously dropped the Frenchman's coats into a heap in the corner and began to fidget like the lad he was. But not too long after, I, too, wiggled my toes or fingers to drive away the tedium.

After clearing his throat, Le Mercier began. "François-Pierre de Rigaud de Vaudreuil, General, has led his troupes de la marine and countless auxiliary savages over the frozen French lake with the aim to take this fort for His Most Christian Majesty. The good general has given me permission to grant you full honors of war should you decide to surrender with haste. Your officers will graciously be permitted to retain personal effects." He lifted a long finger. "Though I caution you to leave behind some items if only to gratify the Indians. Living in these parts long enough has, no doubt, informed you that the savages require a certain amount of spoils to satisfy their lusts."

He let that hang. Eyre said nothing in response.

Le Mercier went on. "But please do not harbor any apprehensions or fear from mischief from the savages. We have brought with us sufficient regular soldiers to protect any surrendering enemy from their misbehavior. I must add that you and your men will be carefully escorted to any place you wish to go."

I peered at the back of the Frenchman's gray head. Briefly, I saw the butt of my Brown Bess rammed a time or two against his skull. In truth, however, the weapon remained fixed against me. A man could dream.

For his part, the major was unmoving. His face was unemotional. He was at complete ease.

Le Mercier set his empty glass of wine on the desk. "I thank you for that, sir," he said. "But now that I have given you all of the carrots my gracious general has offered, I fear I must shed light upon the stick. Should you and this garrison choose to resist our rightful efforts, a true calamity would ensue. Moreover, if the fort falls by force, the cruelties of the savages cannot be altogether prevented no matter how compassionate my commander and I wish to be. A time of battle can bring out the worst among the natives, you understand?"

Seconds dragged to minutes. Two minutes dragged to five. Eyre remained silent.

Le Mercier pushed himself from the chair. "I can see that a young officer like yourself must want to discuss such important items with your trusted men." He rapped his knuckles on the desk. "I believe my general will grant an extension of one hour to our truce for you to deliberate."

"There is no need to discuss things further," Eyre said evenly. Though calm, to hear his voice after so long of silence was such a surprise that it startled me.

Captain Le Mercier smiled in our direction and returned to his seat. "Good. I'm glad you have sense. If you have a quill and paper, we can work out the details here and now."

"I have pen and page," Eyre admitted. "But they shall not be necessary. Please inform the Governor-General's petit brother that I unequivocally refuse to surrender. And your threats of mistreatment by your allies does nothing to dissuade me from my course. We may face a thousand of the tribesmen, for all I know. And yet we expect to be equally illtreated whether the fort was surrendered upon official articles of capitulation or taken by storm." It was the major's turn to let his words hang in the chilled air. The Frenchman waited for more. "Mr. Anson!" Eyre barked suddenly.

"Sir," Johnny squeaked.

"Assemble the captain's clothing and see him properly wrapped from the cold."

"Sir!" Johnny clipped, grabbing the mess in one giant armful.

As we helped Le Mercier dress against the cold, Major Eyre slid into his own cloaks. "I do hope you enjoyed the wine, captain," he said cordially.

Le Mercier grimaced. "It was as fine as could be expected from these English colonies," he mocked.

Eyre tapped his hat into place and seized the door open. "I had it imported from France," he said, shrugging. "I guess His Most Christian Majesty's soldiers are not the only of his citizens that are to be found wanting. His vintners could use a bit of education, too." The major nodded his goodbyes and ducked out.

"Touché," I said, poking the Frenchman's chest with my own finger foil.

CHAPTER 24

"Inform Mr. Turnwell that he must relieve the guns facing east and west of their crews," Eyre instructed after the three massive blocks of our foes set their first steps upon the land. Not a half hour had passed since Johnny and I had returned from leading the blindfolded captain back to the ice.

The major's runner stood planted in place, confused. "He only just reinforced the western and eastern walls a moment ago. At, uh, by your orders, sir."

Eyre gave a curt nod of understanding. "It seems they shall no longer be necessary. This particular Rigaud is not as crafty as his older brother." He indicated with his hat toward the mass of attackers. "The crews not employed on guns are to assist the men on the walls. See them armed with muskets." The major paused to make sure the messenger understood. "Also, I'd like Mr. Turnwell's most proficient crews manning the cannons that will provide enfilade across the north wall." The messenger repeated the orders back precisely. "Oh," Eyre added as an afterthought. "And see that Mr. Turnwell fires when ready."

The runner smiled and raced away.

Less than ten seconds later, the northward facing guns belched in unison, sending fire and smoke into the frigid atmosphere. Loads of iron grape heated the air and pelted the shores. Tribesmen, Canadians, and regular soldiers were torn limb from limb. Braves bled. Troupes de terre and troupes de la marine were instantly tattered. Even the brilliant, white-coated elite men of His Most Christian Majesty's best regiments found their blue facings and turnbacks unceremoniously slapped down into the snow. Two of the ladders had been dropped when their carriers were shredded by our cannoneers. Men stepped over their dying comrades and ripped the scaling devices from quivering hands. After only a brief, collective hesitation, the Frogs resumed their steady progress.

"Fix bayonets," Major Eyre instructed those of us perched with muskets behind the parapet. "Hold your fire." Save Colonel Washington, he was as calm as any commander in the midst of conflict I'd ever seen.

Rigaud led his men up the sloping glacis. To my astonishment, his flanks did not duck away into the woods on either side for cover. They marched almost abreast of one another, defeating the purpose of the three separate units. As one, they converged on our northern wall, which is what Major Eyre had somehow come to anticipate.

"Fire!" shouted Turnwell. His crews sent dozens more of the enemy reeling or crumpling into the dirty drifts of white. "Probe the piece!" Those cannoneers worked feverishly.

"One well-timed volley, men," Eyre instructed the rest of us as he strode slowly on the platform behind. He checked his watch and made a note. Then he peered over a gunner's shoulder. "On my command." I brought my Bess to full cock and picked out a foe I thought should die.

In the meantime, Turnwell's crews had spewed another round of death down into the enemy ranks. Hundreds of small balls ripped into them, immediately splashing the white winter canvas with copious sums of crimson red. The attackers were drawing near. In French or one of the Algonquian tongues, shrieks and curses were audible now. Whimpering and crying could be heard tucked in the brief intermissions of cannon fire.

Rigaud fearlessly drew his sword while pressing a group of warriors forward. They lugged a ladder on their shoulders. "Courir!" he screamed into their ears. All along their ranks, men broke into a sprint for the last twenty yards to the base of our curtain wall.

"Fire, lads! Release your Bess!" Eyre yelled.

A wall of orange flame and white smoke spurt over the parapet, momentarily obscuring my view. Two hundred small nuggets of lead raced into the sky. More than half would miss. We all knew that. But even they had an effect on the charge, as frozen earth and chunks of ice and rocks erupted from around the Frog's feet. More than one foe tripped over from fright.

And the half or so of our shots that found their marks? Devastating. As the north wind blew the smoke back into my face and over the fort, I saw the results. Some four score men had been hammered back from the front rank, ramming the men in the second. In that instant, their escalade was thwarted. Though the

French and their tenacious, if unimaginative, leader did not yet know it.

I must interject my narrative with an observation. Though it is difficult for me to admit anything positive about Frenchmen. The moment that followed our musket discharge proved that even Frogs were capable of being men, warriors. Those attackers yet able, plunged through the stumbling masses of their friends, sloughing off fear and wounds in a manner that even the ancient gods of the Romans may have found worthy. Seeing them advance struck me, just fleetingly, with admiration and fear. But those feelings quickly swept to the only thing that could help keep me alive – hatred.

"On your bellies," Eyre called to us. "Atop the parapet."

We scrambled up the earthen and log structure, inching forward to peer over the edge and through the fraising. Frenchmen at the bases of the northwest and northeast bastions had propped up their ladders and the swiftest among them scaled like cats.

"Use the poles, boys!" Eyre chanted. "The poles."

All sorts of items, all of them long, were passed up from the terre-plein to the parapet. Pitchforks, muskets, boughs from maples, anything and everything were used to pry the tops of those ladders from our works. Eyre's men worked in pairs, shoving, while the Englishmen on their flanks provided covering fire straight down the wall. Only a single Frog, heroic in some fatalistic way, managed to get his fist wrapped around one of the sharpened stakes that made up the fraising. His fingers were sliced off with a knife and he plummeted down onto his brethren.

Meanwhile, it was worse for the attackers at the section of the wall between the northern bastions. And anyone who has even contemplated attacking a fort should have been able to foresee the senseless carnage. Rigaud led the bloom of his men into that killing zone. Then, as simply as a country girl might pick wildflowers, his choicest blossoms were plucked. Nay. They were slaughtered.

Turnwell's sets of cannoneers who were charged with providing the enfilade, did so with deadly precision. At close range and with an unrelenting pace, Lieutenant Turnwell poured grape onto the white and gray clad shoulders of the regulars (the streetwise Canadians and Indians had long begun the retreat). The lieutenant was in his element, demanding more and more from his crews. He perspired in the cold. His men sweated buckets. The guns steamed, creaked, and smoked. "Fire!" Turnwell shouted. "Faster!"

Most of the ladders themselves were as fractured as the bodies who had lately been carrying them. But one, and only one, ladder was provided enough momentum from the charge at the center of our northern wall. Its base was planted in the ground. And quite shockingly, the men who wielded it braved the lethal game for a longer duration. They thrust the ladder up so it slapped against the curtain. Up went a man. Then a second. Rigaud stood at the foot of the ladder, no coward, urging one man after the other up, up, up.

All of them were swept from their climb with another blast from the enfilade cannons. Pieces of the splintered, lone ladder rained down onto Rigaud's head. Sections of his men's entrails splattered his hat. "Battre en retraite!" he called.

"Cease fire!" Eyre barked as soon as the French drums began beating the retreat.

Three or four of our muskets pattered after them before halting. "Fire!" yelled Turnwell. His crews obeyed, sending more lead balls into the enemy's back.

"Cease fire!" Eyre called.

"Probe the piece!" Turnwell ordered his crews. They jammed the wad-screws into their muzzles, searching for any remains of the last charge.

Eyre turned away from the retreating enemy and marched along the terre-plein, setting a direct course for Lieutenant Turnwell. The major did not scream. But despite his calm demeanor, I knew that what was to follow was not going to be good for the captain of the guns. From firsthand experience, I knew that Turnwell was not one to stop killing a beaten enemy until they were well out of his range.

"Sponge!" shrieked Turnwell, spit firing from his mouth like the iron and lead he shot. "Quickly now! They're getting away."

"Load. Single charge. Single canister now. They're putting some distance between us and I want some heft behind that grape," called Turnwell.

"Very nice work," Eyre complimented Turnwell. The major's voice was startlingly tranquil.

"Thank you, sir," the lieutenant said as the rest of the men on the wall had come to regard the confrontation looming on the inside of the fort more interesting than the one that had just ceased on the outside. We gaped at the pair of officers.

"A shame about your hearing," Eyre suggested coolly.

"My hearing?" Turnwell asked, his eye ever on his toiling warriors.

"You aren't the first and you won't be the last to have his ears claimed by the roar of the guns," Eyre explained peacefully.

Turnwell smiled and laughed. "I hear fine, sir." Then he turned to his gun crews. They were all in ready position. "F…!"

"Hold your fire!" Eyre interrupted.

The cannoneers peeked back at the two officers, their smoldering botefeux held precariously aloft.

"But we've got them on the run, sir," Turnwell protested, incredulous.

"That was precisely our aim," Eyre countered. "Unload and clean the piece," he told the crews. They jumped to it, swiftly and safely removing all that they had just stuffed into the guns.

"We need to teach them a lesson," Turnwell continued, wiping grime from his brow.

"We have," Eyre said, walking back along the wall. "Well done, boys," he complimented those of us who had faced the ladders.

"But they aren't yet beaten," Turnwell protested firmly.

Eyre stopped and very slowly spun on his heel. I readied to hear what a proper British officer could do to dress down another officer who insisted on testing the former's authority. But first I should add that I agreed with Turnwell. He was a goat and all. He was an arrogant turd. But we were in the middle of killing our fellow man. And when in war, I'd say it was important to kill as many of the enemy whenever possible, lest they come back and kill us.

"Mr. Turnwell, fifteen hundred brave Frenchmen and their allies came from the frozen lake today." There was no vitriol in his voice. The major pointed over the curtain. "Two hundred of them will never see another summer. Wives are made widows. Children have become orphans. I am not a butcher. I serve my commanders, king, and my God. To be sure, I fear my king and commanding officers. But I fear the eternal wrath of my God even more."

He quietly turned and resumed his path. "Lieutenant Stark," said the major.

"Sir," said the ranger, leaping down from the parapet.

"Keep a sharp eye on the enemy. Should it look like they intend to remain in our environs, come to me this afternoon with plans for a midnight sortie with your rangers."

"Aye," Stark said, already watching the enemy disperse across Lake George and into the woods on the northwest.

Eyre stopped again, recalling something. In time, he slowly strode back to Turnwell.

"You are a fine gunner and fine officer," he whispered as those of us on the wall had begun to disperse. "But if you ever disobey an order again, I shall have you in irons quicker than a pissing race horse. Is that clear?"

"Yes, major," Turnwell said fully deflated, while tipping his cap.

Eyre nodded and climbed down the stairs. Without looking back over his shoulder, he called, "And just what are you smiling at Mr. Weber?"

I had been grinning like a joyous fool. I truly did love it whenever another man found himself reprimanded in a public fashion. So often, it was me. I savored the change of pace. It was especially grand when Eyre's method was so subtle, yet firm. "Nothing, major," I chuckled.

Eyre reached the yard below and craned up to see me. "Before you head out with Lieutenant Stark tonight, you'll help clean the stables. That might teach you to pay attention to what concerns you."

I hastily wiped the grin from beneath my snout.

While a smile turned up in Turnwell's lips. And on Stark's. And on Anson's. And on a hundred others.

My comrades were all turds.

I loved them very much.

CHAPTER 25

"You stink like shit, Weber," Stark muttered in the dead of night.

"Maybe that's why the Injuns call him Shit-for-brains," rasped a ranger from Connecticut, giggling.

"They call me Fierce Dog!" I growled, intentionally brushing a pine branch that strained with snow.

His head was instantly salted with fluttering ice crystals. He brushed it dry with good-natured cheer. "And Shit-for-brains," quipped the ranger, barely stifling an outburst.

"Enough," Stark warned. That one word was sufficient. We obeyed the lieutenant just as we would have Rogers. He was not as colorful a character, but his proficiency in the woods was clear and deserved respect.

Our troop silently moved over the snow through the forest. I knew every tree and animal path like the back of my hand. So did the other rangers. We needed neither sun nor moon nor stars to guide us. And we were not given any of them that bleak night.

My shoulders were sore. I had spent the afternoon mucking pens of horses and hauling the manure into a great heap. Then, as Stark and Eyre had planned the very raid I was now on, they had instructed me to move the pile from within the fort to the edge of one of our gardens just outside the walls. It had been my pleasure to handle the same scoops of dung at least three times.

On we marched. Deathly silent. Any stray piece of metal had been wrapped with cloth. Nothing clattered. Our light footsteps were the only sound as we floated overtop the snowbanks with our webbed shoes on the circuitous route. Stark had led us far southward from the fort, away from danger, for about a half hour. Without warning, he had then turned us west, a direction in which he guided us for three quarters of an hour. Then it was northward for well over an hour.

Finally, we moved southeastward. Stark had us attacking the giant French camp in the woods from the north, the most unexpected way. For the past five minutes, we had heard the clangs of camp and seen the glow of fires. We were close and it was imperative we remained fully gagged.

"I worry that even the French goose-eaters will smell you coming," Stark whispered out of the blue. "Really. Weber, you should bathe occasionally."

The nearest three rangers chortled.

"Shut up," Stark warned. He stopped, buttoning his lips with his fingers while giving an evil eye to us all. Then the lieutenant made a series of hand signals that were transferred down the line to the forty-odd rangers who followed.

The offensiveness of my stench momentarily forgotten, the first half of Stark's rangers wheeled left, with him as their axle. The rearmost half of men advanced obliquely right until the first one reached what was our front line. That man then became the axle of their wheel.

The entire operation, something that we'd practiced a thousand times a month in all conditions, was completed in less than a minute. Not a soul in the enemy camp was wise to our presence. That's when the lieutenant peered down the line of men that were staggered around trees or over the undulating land. He held up a pair of fingers indicating distance and pointed forward. We didn't step ahead until his first foot moved toward the slumbering Frenchmen.

My heartbeat was rapid. As was typical. Our progress was slow, methodical. As it should have been.

Stark came to a halt after we'd advanced two rods. We stopped with him. He then asked a series of questions to the man on his right using nothing more than hand motions. That ranger relayed the query all they way to the last man on the right (west) flank. The answer returned just as silently.

The lieutenant interpreted the meaning. He then instructed the right flank to advance one rod on his mark and those of us on the left to advance two.

Crouching now, and stepping as deliberately as a maid gathering eggs in a clogged henhouse, we descended on the enemy.

There they were. I saw their curled forms under blankets, shivering to stay warm. Some nearly hugged the campfires, even each other. We faced a mixed bag of sleeping Canadians and tribesmen. The regular soldiers were all the way at the southern end of the encampment, facing the most likely direction of a sortie. I rather liked that we would oppose provincials and Indians. To be sure, Abenaki and Canadians were dangerous enough. But a proper French regiment could form up a shoulder-to-shoulder line right quick, even from a dead sleep. They could easily send two volleys in our direction while we were scattering away. We'd have been dead before we knew it.

Stark had us pause there, observing them in silence. It was a brief period to calm ourselves and remember our roles in the coming fight.

But while we knelt in the snow, our breaths billowing above us, the lieutenant adapted his original plan, which was for the right flank to pick targets and fire. They were then to shift left as we fired. Two or three volleys was our entire design. It was enough to cause the French to lose sleep all night and worry, while we escaped over the ice and returned to the fort along the shortest route.

All of that was now thrown out the window. The lieutenant, raised on Rogers aggressive tutelage, had seen an opportunity for boldness.

Blades? I asked myself as the meaning of his signals became clear. *Into the camp?*

There was no question. I found myself rising, knife drawn. Then as silently as a hawk gliding on air currents, we walked right into the backdoor of the enemy's abode.

Did I mention that there were over a thousand of them?

And forty of us.

CHAPTER 26

I slit the throat of a Canadian provincial soldier. With his windpipe severed, he couldn't speak as he died. But his teary eyes spoke volumes. He'd been a farmer in Quebec, I was sure of it. His king had appealed for volunteers. Being a patriotic man, he had answered the call. That, and his wife was pregnant with their fourth child. That, and for two seasons in a row the Canadian harvests had been awful. He needed the money. That's why he had agreed to travel so far while bearing arms for a cause he cared little about.

His wife would never know that a Quaker runt had slaughtered her husband while he quivered in a foreign forest.

Stark stabbed a man through his blanket in the back. He made only a dying gasp.

We must have killed thirty enemy soldiers in that cowardly way that night, stepping around first one fire, then the next. Caughnawaga Catholics were killed. Abenaki Catholics were killed. Canadian Catholics were killed. "Revenge of the Huguenots," rasped one ranger as he buried his blade to the hilt in a chubby Canadian's back.

One time only, one enemy warrior, while Conwall's ranger knife slipped between his ribs, moaned a sad, end-of-life peep. The warrior who huddled in the blanket next to him had sensed something was amiss. He sat up from a sound sleep, flipping the blanket off while grabbing his war hatchet. Amos removed his knife from the first victim and plunged it into the startled man's neck. Our presence had remained a secret.

Lieutenant Stark held up his hand, preventing us from advancing too dangerously far. While fanned out over a piece of wooded ground some two rods in diameter, we again knelt. The fires crackled peacefully as we took stock of our situation.

A stick cracked from further south within the camp. The head of every ranger honed in on it. I squinted toward the source, but was blinded from the firelight.

But we could now be seen.

"Yankees!" shouted a Canadian who had awakened only to expose his rear to the night winds and relieve himself. He dropped the wad of straw he had planned on using to wipe and bolted into camp, loudly raising the alarm. "Yankees!"

"Do you see him?" Stark asked, still crouching by a fire and trying to see around it.

"I do now," I said confidently, hoisting my musket.

"Drop him," the lieutenant ordered.

My new Bess felt good in my hands. Her skin was smooth. She was precious. With a gentle tug, she sparked to life, ripping the peaceful night to shreds. I winged the fleeing Canadian so that he rolled forward, smacking his face into a tree. "Finish him and get back here. We're leaving," Stark clipped.

"Aye," I said, tossing him my musket. He'd already begun reloading it for me as I ran over the snow to the wounded man. We couldn't have him telling his comrades just how few of us there were. Then, without joy and without remorse, I stabbed him in the chest. He had rolled onto his back and used his feet to shove himself away from my approach. All that action accomplished was to bury him in the deep snow. He was stuck. "Aidez-moi!" the wounded man screamed as I shoved my blade next to his sternum. I smelled him release that which had awakened him in the first place.

"Onto the lake," Stark growled when I returned.

The entire camp came to life with shouts and drums. We raced single-file eastward onto Lake George. "Hold up!" Stark ordered when we were thirty yards from shore. "Skirmish line."

I knew what he wanted to do.

In the moonless night, we dropped down onto our bellies in a line that ran parallel to the shore. Torches and shouts filtered northward through the camp, pausing occasionally at the trail of dead men we had left behind. I heard the queer Quebecer tongue. I heard men using the Lenape languages, spewing hatred for our kind. Eventually, about fifty of them found our tracks and chased after them toward the lake.

Their leader, a French captain, called them to a halt at the shore. He held a torch far in front of his face, willing the light to shed some type of omniscience for him. He peered around, seeing none of us while stepping slowly onto the ice by himself.

"Wait," Stark said, barely audible.

On came the Frenchman. When he'd surmounted the piles of ice near the shore, he waved his other men forward. They followed his lead, carefully picking their way up the short heaps of ice chunks. They peered out past their torches. I saw the fear in those eyes.

When the majority of them stood at the crest of the ice hill, Stark used the discharge of his weapon as the order to fire. *Cr-crack! Cr-crack!* Forty muskets barked. Two score and five Canadians and Indians toppled backward off the ice. Their captain impotently raised his pistol and pointed it in our direction.

"I'm getting out of here before this place gets too popular," Stark said as he got up. He smacked me on the rump. "Come on, stinky."

And we didn't stop running until we were safely behind the closed gates of William Henry.

CHAPTER 27

The French felt obliged to sleep-in the next day.

As such, the rangers were permitted to do the same. And we did so with unashamed resolve, wadding ourselves into balls while sharing bunks and blankets to drive away the bone-aching chills we'd experienced while on the scout. But slept, I did, even while the French camp remained incited to panic.

Then, after waking around midday and observing the enemy inactivity from the wall for five frigid minutes, I returned to the barracks. For the time being, the Frogs seemed content to do little more than watch us watch them. With a biscuit and tea breakfast, I set to work on Rogers' Rules of Ranging.

I wrote a concise rule about canoes and paddling. But it could even apply to men patrolling on foot. Each ranger (or boat) in front of the other was responsible for the man immediately behind him. This way, no one would be separated in the dark or fog of battle from the rest of his raiding party.

I often referred to the scraps of paper on which I had jotted down Rogers' and Stark's musings. There were hundreds of them focused on one specific item of wilderness warfare or another. And I felt it was my job to marry the ones that were similar into one general rule. No commander could be expected to teach raw recruits scores of rules. Men of the forest really only wanted to learn a few. As it was, I felt that the twenty-eight I had come up with were twenty-seven too many.

One of my last two tenets dealt with setting a proper attack against a foe that was crossing a river or lake. It felt familiar. Not only had I violated this particular one of Rogers' Rules on my first day of meeting him, but he had followed another one of his canons in setting the trap for me. I remember touching the knot that had formed permanently beneath my eye from the great branch he'd brought to bear against my face. It was still tender after all those months. Even today, after five decades, my face is misshapen there, complete with a lump of scar tissue to join the spider veins. "An old war wound," I brag to the Philadelphia ladies. Though they don't ever seem impressed.

Turnwell walked in. I simply glanced up through my brow. "You're in the wrong place," I reminded him as I scratched my quill across the page.

"An officer goes where he will," explained the lieutenant. He dropped his lean frame into an empty chair. "How's the book?" he asked, pointing to my piles of pages that were covered with the turkey tracks I called handwriting.

"Should end up being just one sheet long," I said as I began my last rule. "You know British senior officers aren't capable of reading much more than that." I snickered to myself.

Turnwell chuckled, too. "Why should a gentleman work so hard when he might employ a good ensign to do it for him?" He was a decent fellow, I suppose. For a turd.

"You rangers did good last night," he said after a long pause.

My pen froze. I looked at him. "Did you just compliment a band of provincials?"

The lieutenant stuffed his hands in his pockets and leaned back in his seat, staring at the huge beams in the ceiling. "I wouldn't go so far as to call it a compliment. Everyone knows that it takes ten colonists to equal one decent regular soldier."

I nodded, returning to my ink work. "That's more like the Turdwell I know," I said joyfully. He said nothing in response, happy to just sit inside away from the wind and bitter cold. Despite the siege, it seemed like just another dull example of a day in garrison life. I thought a little about my last rule, I mean Rogers' last rule. It took three or four tries to get my thoughts in proper order.

"What will you do when this is over?" Turnwell asked as I stacked my working pages together and placed my final draft on top.

"I don't know," I said, rolling them all up and stuffing them in my leather satchel. "I suppose Stark will have us out and scouting before the French are halfway up the backbone of Lake George."

"Not the siege," Turnwell clarified. "I mean the war."

It was at that moment that I first realized the war had changed me – perhaps permanently. In the early years of the great conflict, all I would ever do was dream of returning to my life as a trader, a soon-to-be-rich trader-on-the-come. But setbacks, and killings, and murders, and razing, and running, and whipping, and imprisonment, and punishment had conspired to make me like most everyone else in the entire world – shortsighted. I didn't think much beyond the day. Sometimes I found myself thinking about the next week – would it be warmer? My heavens, I was no different than anyone else. It was a terrifying realization.

I risked honesty. "Who's to say it will ever end?"

Turnwell's brows raised. "Every war ends."

I knew that to be true in most meanings. But I shrugged. "I don't know. The Catholics and Protestants have been killing each other for a good long while. The French and the English. I'm told the Saracens have been on the warpath for a thousand years."

Turnwell waved me off. "Of course. But this war will end. In a generation, it will renew itself under a new title and new guise. A fresh batch of men will fight against one another in the names of the latest set of English and French kings – probably another George and Louis. Nonetheless, our time of military glory will be long past. What will you do when this is over?"

"Why don't you just tell me your grand plans?" I suggested, unable or unwilling to think beyond my sentence as a private in His Majesty's army. "You obviously have an idea."

The lieutenant studied me. "You won't make fun of me."

I threw my hands in the air. "Me?" I asked, with a crushed expression. "Of course, I will. What type of friend would I be if I didn't ridicule you for sharing your deepest desires?"

"We're friends?" he asked.

"I obviously misspoke," I deadpanned.

He nodded in agreement, but marshaled on with an earnestness that shouldn't belong in a warrior's repertoire of sentiments. "I think I'll settle here in one of these colonies," Turnwell announced. "It's all so untamed. As if a man, determined, may accomplish anything. The land itself doesn't seem to have the encumbrances that we find in the old countries. And the attitudes of the inhabitants – sure, their liberty mindedness can be a bother to betters – but they operate as if everything before them is a wide-open road on which they may travel. And if they come upon a rut, it doesn't bother them. They just fill it in. They go around it. If they need a new road, it is built with haste. A bridge? It is constructed. These farmers and merchants don't appeal to the king for three decades to commission a body to see something done about it. They do it themselves. There's something to be said for the convictions that give rise to such activity."

He was right of course. More right about the differences in the air and men of America than he or I knew at the time. "Uh-huh," I said absentmindedly. My keen ears back then, picked up some chatter from up on the wall.

"That's it?" he protested. "You've nothing more to say? I've just given your fellow countrymen a compliment."

"Good for you," I ventured, sliding into my cloak and slinging my Bess over my shoulder. "Even a squirrel will occasionally find his nuts."

"You're a pain in my ass, Ephraim," Turdwell growled.

"As I imagine you were to your mother," I said, walking out past him.

I was stopped by a provincial who had the unfortunate circumstance of being sentenced – sent, I mean – to William Henry for winter garrison duty. "Frogs are beginning to hop," he said before he continued springing around to the remainder of the hidey-holes in the fort to roust the rest of the men.

Lieutenant Turnwell heard the call and jogged out onto the walk with me. "Don't you think you'll marry that Indian woman, Hannah?" he asked. "I thought you had plans."

I shrugged, climbing the step. "When I see her face, she's the most beautiful, desirable thing on this green earth. But when I'm in the woods, I think only of the hunt, deer, bear, war, trade, money, rum."

"So, you don't think you want to settle down?" he asked.

We paused, facing one another at the top of the steps before we went our separate ways. No shooting had begun from below.

I considered his question. "If you mean, will I ever marry again? Yes. I suppose so. A wife in my bed is something I want.

If you mean, will I have more children and actually have them running about my feet? I suppose so. Especially if their mom survives long enough to give me a hand. But if you mean, will I ever settle down? Will I act respectable like some kind of gentleman? No. I'm not Colonel Washington. I admire him. He is something to which we should aspire. I'm no Major Eyre. He, too, is someone to emulate. But I won't settle down. 'Til my dying breath I'll be fighting something. I'll be killing the French. I'll be blazing out the forest. I'll be climbing heights. Settle down? What the hell, Turdwell? Who wants to do that?"

I spun to join the rest of my rough rangers on the wall. A few of them grumbled to me for fraternizing with a redback.

And the French came again.

CHAPTER 28

In his first charge, the French commander Rigaud had already demonstrated his lack of innate brilliance. But it turned out he was not a complete dolt or sadist, willing to sacrifice his men for his pleasure. On the contrary, Rigaud had gleaned a vital lesson from his attempt at a rushed escalade. And just in case Rigaud had forgotten the grim tutelage we'd bestowed upon him in his first thrashing, the corpses of his men still lay scattered about as frozen reminders.

From the western woods, bands of howling tribesmen and provincial Canadian sharpshooters peppered our curtain walls with regular fire. It was just enough to force us to duck our heads behind the parapet. Meanwhile, a company of regular French warriors skirted from that same woods over the lake, heading east. So far, these latter men were careful to keep out of reach of Turdwell's grapeshot.

"Mr. Turnwell," Major Eyre asked from what had become his designated position on the terre-plein during times of conflict. He stamped his feet and balled his fists to drive away the cold.

"Sir?" Turnwell answered crisply.

"Do you have any ideas for discouraging the rabble in the woods?" he asked, the minor incident the day before forgotten. "They are a nuisance I'd rather dismiss."

"I do," Turnwell answered cheerily. A second later the lieutenant's demeanor flashed to red as he addressed his crews, barking orders that were efficiently relayed to each gun chief. It took but a moment for them to remove the canister they'd been prepared to fire and replace it with solid shot.

Smoldering botefeux hovered over touch holes as the lieutenant turned for the final confirmation from his commander. Eyre offered a gentlemanly nod. "That will do just fine, Mr. Turnwell. Proceed vigorously, making sure those auxiliary troops fear coming within three rods of the edge of the woods."

"Sir," Turnwell clipped, only briefly gripping the brim of his cap in salute. He spun. "Fire!"

I was momentarily deafened as the guns on the northwest and southwest bastions revealed their ugly power. It was a terrifying, awesome sound. The destruction they belched was a magnificent sight. Twelve-pound balls of iron were hurled with blinding quickness at our enemies. Turnwell had his guns aimed low. A ball bounced once on the glacis, sending a huge tuft of ice crystals into the air. But the plume of snow was just beginning to erupt when the hurtling iron shot sawed off a tree that was about four inches in diameter. Its annihilation blazed onward, plucking the torso from a crouching Canadian before disappearing into the depths of the forest. Three other cannonballs performed similar grim tasks, fracturing trees, ricocheting, mowing down rows of men. Turnwell joyously spurred his cannoneers to further action.

"Very good," Eyre said out loud, but mostly to himself. The major then turned to those of us armed with muskets. He'd previously oriented the majority of his rangers and infantry on the northern and eastern walls. "Lieutenant Stark," he called.

"Sir," Stark answered.

"How many of your rangers are armed with rifles?"

"About half," came the quick reply.

Eyre again looked out over the lake where the French soldiers had begun arcing southward toward shore. They were still out of reach. "And how many of them are crack shots with their rifles?"

Stark grinned. "All of them, sir."

The major did not take it as a false assertion. "All rangers with rifles on the northeast bastion. If a Frenchman comes in range, see him dispatched."

"Sir, if the Frogs show themselves up close, why not put them all on the ground the way we did yesterday?" asked a young captain. "With effective canister?"

"A good suggestion," Eyre offered congenially enough. "But the French aren't going to approach the walls. They're going to do the only thing they can do. They'll skulk about our outer structures. And I don't want to be the one to destroy my own works with cannon fire. These men have toiled for a year and a half building them." He then tersely lifted a gloved hand, indicating that he'd appreciate swift movement from the rangers.

"Yes, sir," said Stark.

"Yes, sir," said the captain, reorganizing his regulars to make room for the rangers.

Men rushed about, bumping shoulders and cursing at one another for no good reason.

I felt I was a good shot, but was not armed with a rifle. A Bess was a fine musket. But her smooth bore could wreak havoc on the intentions of even the sharpest-eyed marksman. Therefore, I found myself lying on my belly while stuck on the parapet of the northeast bastion, but away from its apex.

The woods on the east now obscured our view of the attacking French. Below, between us and the forest, there was an extra barracks and stable in the foreground outside the wall. Both were unoccupied at the moment. There was a sawmill along a creek and a few dug cellars for storing extra food. All we could do was peer over our abandoned works and wait for the attackers to make their plans known. We listened to the guns on the west roar. Turnwell's response had been fiercely effective. Only the occasional musket ping or defiant Indian war whoop sounded in reply.

"I see 'em, major!" called the best marksman among the rangers, a lad that was younger than I. I'd seen him shave only once and yet his face was always baby smooth. He went by the name of Nero and was the lone freedman in what had become Stark's company. If Nero's eyesight was as sharp as his piercing green eyes, then the French would have something to worry about.

Eyre peered in the direction indicated, surveying the scene. We all did. A company of white-clad Frenchmen knelt at the very edge of the eastern woods on the beach. Though it was broad daylight, a half dozen of the men carried blazing torches. Their commander waved frantically to his nodding troopers, but they were too far away for us to eavesdrop on his orders.

"That's what I was afraid of," the keen major admitted. "They're going for our boats."

Sure enough, some fifty paces away from the enemy position, scores of our bateaux were neatly lined up in rows. We'd even lugged our sloops onto dry land for winter. They sat stoically waiting for better weather with their tall masts slightly askew. And still there were more targets for the enemy's torches. The bateaux and sloops were joined by a gaggle of randomly assorted scows and longboats. Under normal conditions the major had regular patrols around the boats to prevent theft by Indians or venturesome colonials. But our sentries had all been pulled behind the fort's walls for safety.

The major very quietly and sternly said, "We cannot afford to lose a single craft, men. They don't have to take our position to defeat us. If they take those boats, we lose our ability to harass them in an offensive manner for an entire campaigning season."

"I'd not worry, major," assured Nero. He breathed on his fingers to thaw them, nearly sticking the entire tips into his mouth. "Any one of those Frogs comes hopping out... Let's just say he'd wish he'd never left Paris."

The boy had no sooner made his boast than he brought his rifle to his shoulder and sighted down the long barrel. A heartbeat later, through the muzzle smoke we saw a French soldier lying on his side on the beach. He was not yet ten feet from the edge of the woods. The torch he had been carrying was now snuffed in the snow. His hands shook frantically as he probed the gaping wound in his hip. Horrified shrieks from the now dying man filled in the gaps between the cannon blasts.

"That's just what I had in mind," Eyre complimented Nero, who methodically reloaded his piece.

Three more brave and foolish French runners met a similar fate at the hands of Stark's rangers. All I did for those early moments was shiver and watch. Drifting snowflakes began to fall.

But the French – simpletons, asses, and turds, to be sure – slowly learned another lesson. After their fourth straight death on the beach, they regrouped just inside the woods. I remember praying that they just got tired and went home. It was cold and all I was permitted to do was concentrate on just how cold it was. I stuffed my hands in my sleeves. I stuffed them in my cloak. I stuffed them in my pants. They were becoming as nimble as granite.

But the French – simpletons, asses, turds, Nellies, and sodomites, the whole lot of them – stayed put. Concentrated musket fire erupted suddenly from their spot in the frigid woods. Shot whizzed by overhead or smacked into the curtain wall. One unfortunate ranger was hit on the crown of his head. By the time we dared peek out again, a new line of two dozen Frenchmen had showed itself. They were clustered around the place where their comrades had fallen. Only now, they had formed a skirmish line. And fired.

We ducked.

And this time another line of Frenchmen had appeared, this time farther out toward the bateaux. They knelt, readying to fire, as the previous line, along with a set of torch carriers raced ahead.

"I believe you know what to do, Mr. Stark," called Eyre.

"Aye," Stark said. He ignored the threat of the coming volley and took aim. *Cr-crack!* A Frenchman fell, his knee blown to bits. "Pour lead into them, men. Don't stop for nothing!"

At least I had something to do. Even as deadly fire rammed all around, I raised my head and Bess. I began firing into their ranks, moving swiftly just to warm myself. I tried to keep count of my pace at one point, but lost track. Let's just say I had loosed four rounds a minute.

Another ranger was hit. A round slammed into the top of his shoulder, causing his arm to hang limp and his rifle to topple over the wall. Johnny Anson and a couple of the other lads dragged him back into the waiting arms of the doctor and two of the officer's wives who served as nurses. They slapped their palms over the spurting wound. But he was dead by the time they managed to haul him to the steps.

The beach was now littered with dead or dying Frenchmen. But the bastards persisted, pressing ahead in leapfrog fashion. Whenever a torch bearer was hit, he was promptly abandoned, but his precious cargo was seized by the next man in line.

"They're getting too close, gentlemen," Eyre encouraged. We fired as rapidly and accurately as we could. Then a half dozen of them dove behind the first of the bateaux while the rest of the regulars retreated back to the woods for safety. "Any man who sees those Frenchmen hiding behind that bateau slain will have my eternal gratitude and a bottle of Madeira."

Our muskets and rifles all efficiently skipped to our shoulders. Madeira was more valuable than gold. It's rich, sweet, and nutty hints made for a joyous evening in the bleakness of the frontier.

But my trigger finger was seized with frozen pain so that I was afraid I'd not be able to use it when called upon for action. While still aiming toward the boats, I tried to straighten the digit to loosen the knuckle. But the damned thing was stuck fast at the joint. I gently tugged it in the other direction, toward me. It jerked hard against the trigger. The cock slammed its flint across the frizzen, sending a shower of sparks onto the fine powder in the pan. Before I knew what was happening, it burst into flame, sent its message of ignition through the touch hole, and caused the packed powder in the barrel to do the same. The super-heated air expanded, roughly shoving the seventy-five caliber ball out the muzzle.

And into the ribs of a Frenchman who had stood up at the exact wrong moment. He had his arm cocked, readying to launch his torch up into the biggest prize – the nearest sloop. The Frog slumped down, dead, but his torch landed atop the very bateaux he and his comrades used for cover. The flames splashed efficiently over the flat deck.

The other rangers all craned their heads toward me.

"Excellent timing, Mr. Weber," said Major Eyre. "At least the burning boat will flush the others out. Despite the fire, you'll still get your Madeira." He stuck a finger up in warning. "But no more boats aflame. Am I clear?"

"Yes, sir," chirped everyone on the wall, eager to receive his own expensive gift.

Four separate rangers killed four more of the enemy men who crouched behind the burning bateau. Each of the dead had tried to do the heroic thing and crawl or sprint to the next boat. Even heroes – no – *heroes especially*, die swiftly. The last one left alive had some time to ponder his next move.

Meanwhile, Rigaud stood at the edge of the woods, hidden behind a tree, shouting orders to the man pinned down on the beach. Over and again, the commander screamed for him to move.

But the last torch bearer had to know that something like a hundred muskets and rifles were aimed at the narrow corridor he must follow. I'm sure his heart beat into his throat and a good gulp of acidic bile had worked its way into his dry mouth. Such were the symptoms of a man about to do something exceedingly dangerous, and foolish.

I saw a flash of white, crouching as it ran. I squeezed the trigger. Scores of *cr-cracks* announced their intent to kill him.

"You missed," Stark accused. "All of you! Blazes!"

"Guess God occasionally takes pity on even a Catholic," grumbled the man next to me.

"There is still a bottle of Madeira that needs a home, boys," Eyre announced. "I'm not choosy about to whom it should go."

The Frenchman's torch reached up onto the deck of the bateau behind which he hid. Lead balls tore splinters from the boat within inches of his flesh. But he stayed fixed in place. The torch's flame quickly transferred to a coil of rope. Then it passed to the planking and beyond. The hand and torch ducked to hiding.

"That's a second boat, lads," Eyre growled. "I'm taking back one of the bottles, you'll have to split those remaining among you."

Those of us fortunate enough to have won the Madeira grumbled. More determined than ever now, we raised our weapons and waited for the turd to make a mistake.

He poked his head out and two dozen rifles and muskets unloaded. But the only thing on his person that was damaged was his hat, which was plucked from his crown, shredded into three separate pieces.

"That man is too lucky!" Stark barked. He had shot as well and he expressed his frustration by hammering his ramrod with extra vigor.

"Mr. Turnwell!" Major Eyre called angrily. The lieutenant, his guns still blazing at the west, raced over. "I want you to lay into the bateau that is aflame. The second on the right. Send a ton of solid shot through it until it is no more than sawdust and ash. Make sure any living thing behind it is no more. Your aim must be true. Hit nothing else."

Turnwell nodded and corralled one of his crews to the best piece for the job.

"Keep the runner in place, Mr. Stark," Eyre instructed. "And those men watching him from the woods."

"Aye, sir," Stark said. He promptly had his rangers begin pattering away with small arms.

B-Boom! Turnwell's aim was low. Therefore, his first ball was short, but it bounced right, ripping a three-foot-long gouge through the burning prow. The ball then traveled up and out over the lake before hammering down through the ice. As his crew reloaded, Lieutenant Turnwell tightened the elevating screw a whisker to drop the breach and lift the muzzle. *B-boom!* The second ball was right on target, smashing through the planking and bursting out the stern just where the man should have been.

But the terrified Frenchman had run again, evacuating his dangerous residence at exactly the right moment. Honestly, his quickness and the fact that he yet lived surprised us all. We watched stupidly, as he ran to the next boat in the line.

And he didn't stop there. Shocked again at his boldness, I watched him sprint in the open along the line of boats. A few of our men came to their wits and opened fire. Ice shot up around him. Splinters flecked him from the perfectly good bateaux that he passed.

"Someone drop him," Eyre commanded warily. "Before he gets somewhere dangerous."

He zig-zagged. His comrades in the woods cheered him on. We jeered at them with insults and lead.

Straight to the first sloop he went, rifle and musket balls peppering the frozen earth around him. Then, suddenly he was behind the sloop.

Turnwell looked at the major for direction. "We're not firing on her if that is what you wonder," Major Eyre answered coldly. "That is one of our chief defensive and offensive weapons for the coming campaign!"

"But the sloop is as good as gone now," Turnwell protested. "Why not try?"

"I'm not going to be a laughing stock in the French barracks all winter," Eyre growled. He crossed his arms, grumbling. "Imagine, blowing up my own boat."

"But don't give the toads any glory," I shouted. "Let the lieutenant wallop the sloop to bits. Then, at least Rigaud can't claim he accomplished anything."

Eyre momentarily considered the suggestion. The pissing competition between French and English officers might have been as thick as the competition among the English officers themselves. But it was too late, the cheering from the eastern woods rose before the smoke or flames. Soon enough, however, we saw that the brave torch man had done his duty. The stern of the sloop was ablaze. The fire spread, undulating like a snake, as it crept from strake to strake.

Balls of lead killed three of us at that moment. The invigorated French attackers from the woods moved out in force to help their lone survivor. More torches came. More muskets leveled in our direction, shooting at us. Our heads ducked.

Eyre succumbed to the changing circumstances. "Turnwell, populate these cannons and fire upon our grounded fleet. Any white or gray coat that moves." The captain of the guns obeyed, not cheerily, for it never felt honorable to destroy that which your own men had built. Fifteen minutes later we had slaughtered forty of the attackers' number.

Thirty minutes later, every single ship, boat, or tub we owned that had been remotely seaworthy was up in flames or shattered to bits. A massive conflagration arose, belching fire and smoke into the heavens. I dare say it was high enough that a sharp-eyed chap from York City might have seen it. From a hundred feet away, I could feel its heat baking the flesh off my face. It was a welcome respite from the cold. Meanwhile, the French regulars retreated over the lake to their camp in the northwest forest. Despite their losses, they veritably skipped.

And the worst of it all was that I had lost my Madeira. We'd all lost our Madeira. For Major Eyre had lost his rewarding mood.

CHAPTER 29

Two more days went by with our unwelcome visitors close at hand.

The third day was much like the second. This time, however, the damned Frogs concentrated their torches on our outbuildings. Back and forth, we shot at one another. Nonetheless, by nightfall, every structure outside our walls was ablaze. The sawmill was reduced to rubble. The extra barracks, gone. We had killed some thirty regulars and perhaps a score of Canadian provincials. But our triumph in numbers of those killed or wounded was an ineffectual balm.

The fourth day proved to be the last of the siege. The French mustered early. We mustered. For eight hours we stared at each other, only the occasional musket shot going in either direction. Volleys of curses were the most common missiles exchanged. But by mid-afternoon, the Frogs realized they had accomplished all they could have hoped under the harsh conditions. Without artillery in their train, any further assault on William Henry was futile. As such, they packed up and silently slinked over the lake, careful to stay hidden in the woods until well out of Lieutenant Turnwell's range.

Fort William Henry and its garrison were intact. We'd suffered few casualties. And since it was the French that had decided to withdraw, by definition we had held the field. It was a victory of sorts.

"What a disaster," Eyre muttered. Two full months had passed since Rigaud's siege. All the French bodies had been buried in a common grave.

The major's boot kicked up the ashes of the sawmill's remains. And though Eyre was not the type of man to stew on losses with inappropriate focus, Rigaud's attack had lodged somewhere in his craw. He stared up at Titcomb's Mount, the small rise less than a half mile southeast. The only snows that remained in the area lurked in the shadows, melting a little more each passing day as spring steadily established its hold. "We need supplies to rebuild the mill before we can go about fortifying

Titcomb. And before we can rebuild our lake fleet. In the meantime, we are vulnerable to a full siege this summer."

"Aye, sir," Stark said from the opposite side of the creek. The lieutenant and I had just returned from a ranging. At the same time, the forty men who had been with us filed back into the fort for rest. "You'd best keep a full guard out here while the men rebuild. We came across a party of more than a hundred tribesmen up across from Tea Island today. Drove them off with effective fire. But they lurk. I fear that with the fair turn in the weather, they'll grow bolder. It wouldn't take much for a score of them to fall upon our work parties and retreat with a dozen scalps before we were the wiser."

"Understood," Eyre groused. "But I'm awaiting work supplies from Edward. I've sent them a petition each week for eight weeks. Normally, their commander has been very accommodative. I need saws and men. But Fort Edward tells me they are waiting for the same supplies from Albany."

"Let me guess. Albany then says that York City has everything they need," I summarized.

"Correct," Eyre answered. "Lord Loudoun is planning something big and sucking up all the materiel from Boston to Charleston. I don't know what it is, but I know it has nothing to do with us up here. I swear, if the French don't kill me, this British army will."

I knew the feeling.

"What's that sound?" Eyre asked suddenly, his head cocked. "Fifes? Drums?"

Stark and I skipped over rocks through the cold creek waters. "We caught sight of at least a regiment of redcoats and others coming this way from Fort Edward," the lieutenant explained. "Moving slow. But lively. We didn't announce ourselves."

"We watched them for a while. Red waistcoats. Coats were red, but had tails a good half a foot shorter than most. Orange facings," I added. "Their black leather caps with the standing front plate tells me they are the 35th."

Eyre's mood brightened. He looked to the charred remains of his fleet on the beach and then back to Titcomb's Mount. "I wasn't informed of such a thing. But I care not. Give me two weeks with more men and materiel and I'll have this place ready to receive whatever Rigaud or Montcalm sends this way." The major craned his head. "Mr. Anson! Johnny!"

"Here, sir!" Johnny answered. He'd been looking through the glass atop Eyre's transom. The boy waved his arm. In response, a distant man who had been holding a stick upright took five long strides before setting the stick back against the ground. "Taking the readings you asked for." The boy peered through the glass, and notched another set of numbers on his sheet.

"Yes, of course," Eyre said. "Good lad. I'll finish that. Set out with Mr. Weber and extend my warm welcome to the men coming. Make a count of officers so that we may begin preparations for a meal in my quarters."

"I'd best go with them, sir," Stark said. "Safety in numbers these days."

Eyre nodded his approval and marched to the transom.

Fifteen minutes later, we met the vanguard of a long train of redcoats, the rear of which, we could not see. A white-haired officer rode a handsome beast at the head. We prepared to fall-in with their pace, but instead the commander held up his hand and brought the entire column to a halt. His drums and fifes ceased their playing instantly.

"A set of Rogers' Rangers I presume," he said with the deep brogue of a proud Scotsman.

"Aye, sir," Stark said. "Major Eyre sends his welcome to all of you. Winters are long in these parts and we've not had much contact with our neighbors from Edward."

The Scotsman shivered, eyeing a stubborn drift of snow by the road. "Aye, indeed. A fright longer than even back home on my father's lands."

"Colonel," Johnny blurted, standing on his tiptoes as he scanned the endless lines of men. "Sorry to interrupt. I can count as good as the next. Probably better, actually. A fair sight better, I may say. Swear it! But would you mind saving me time and giving me a count of your officers. Major Eyre wants to host a feast for you tonight in his dining room. We want a warm meal ready as quick as we can."

The Scotsman grinned. Most folks, if they had a heart, grinned whenever Johnny spoke to them. The lad was all-go, all the time. "What a thoughtful idea. You run on ahead and inform the major that we bring twelve regular officers with us. Another score of provincials at the rear claiming the honor, as well."

Our eyebrows lifted in surprise. Johnny voiced it for us. "Sakes. I swear! That's a host of angels if ever I saw any this far out. Thirty-two officers. I don't know if we have room for all of you in the major's dining area."

"We'll make due," the Scotsman answered congenially. "Run along."

"Quick as a wink, I swear it!" Johnny chirped, spinning on his heel and rushing northwest.

Stark then graciously swept his arm out, indicating the way along the portage road was wide open. "Mind if we accompany you, colonel? It's a pleasant scene to see so many more Englishmen in these parts. We could use the help in driving away the enemy. They skulk about like ghosts."

The colonel spurred his horse. His column slowly filed behind him. "I'd love to spend some time with true men of the wilderness. Robert Rogers has become quite famous for his daring raids, you know. And, I imagine, his disciples are just as courageous."

Stark and I shared an eye-roll. "I hope we don't disappoint you, Colonel…" I said.

"My manners momentarily fled me," he explained, embarrassed. "This country and its ramblings, they sink into the very bones of a man. Forgive me." He tipped his hat as he rode. "Lieutenant Colonel George Monro, at your service."

"Lieutenant Stark with the rangers," Stark said. "This is Private Weber. He doesn't look like much, but he's a fighter. Despite his shoddy dress, he's in the king's regular army, something neither Rogers nor I may claim. Lord Loudoun personally dispatched him to us."

Monro's eyes sparkled. "It pays to have good friends, Mr. Weber. May it be so that you live up to General Campbell's expectations. It is a delight to meet you both."

"Have you heard anything about Captain Rogers?" I asked. "His recovery?"

"I'm sure he'd be pleased to hear you asked. I met him in York City as I passed through. He was up and about, pale but improving. And though I was told he spoke with a Scottish accent, I could hardly discern a thing he said. Made the entire episode so much the more enchanting." Monro peered about him, taking in the remoteness of the wilderness. "Such a strange land and people. As for Rogers, I suppose he'll miss this campaigning season, but he'll be back in the marches soon enough."

"Good to hear," Stark said with genuine affection.

"I've heard they'll make him a major soon enough," said Monro. "The king and these governors do like their heroes."

"Heroes wind up as dead as any man," I said.

Monro laughed. "Aye, they do, lad. But always remember Caesar's wisdom. According to the bard, at least. *Cowards die many times before their deaths, the valiant never taste of death but once.* I saw a version of the play in London some years ago."

I didn't know who the bard was. I didn't know what a bard was.

Yet, I was instantly relieved that Colonel Monro, seemingly a lover of heroes, would not be my commander. Hero worshippers had a penchant for taking chances with the lives of their men. I'd take the methodical, yet competent, leanings of Eyre any day. The major would be better for my health. "I owe Captain Roberts correspondence," I said. "I had hoped that he'd be back to receive it personally. But I'll have to place the letter in the hands of the post."

"You do that," Monro said happily. "I'll see it put with my official letters to ensure its timely delivery."

I smiled. It was difficult to believe that I may have just met a colonel in the British army who was not an arrogant ass. Arrogant, to be sure. But perhaps not an ass. Perhaps. I reserved my judgment since we'd only just met. "Thank you, sir. I'll have the package in your possession before you ride out from Fort William Henry."

He smiled back, patting the neck of his beast while surveying the woods. A few of the earliest buds had begun to poke from the end of talon-like branches. "I should hope so," he said cheerily. "Glad to help."

"That brings up a question, sir. What's a colonel doing escorting men and supplies between Forts Edward and William Henry? Most of the trains that come this way are lucky to have a twenty-year-old lieutenant in the van," Stark said. The woods had begun to recede and open to our little abode on the lake. The pasture, which sat north of the road, for our grazing livestock had tufts of brown-green grass beginning to grow and we'd turned out a score of cows from within the fort to begin mowing it. A pair of the beasts chewed their cud, studying the approaching mass of men with practiced disinterest.

Monro tutted playfully. "I should think it would be apparent, lieutenant. The 35th Regiment of Foot and I are your relief."

"*And* you?" I asked. "Not just the regiment?"

He nodded, noting the terrain. Monro glanced leftward to Titcomb's Mount and over to the lake. "Yes. I'm to command William Henry." He patted his breast pocket to indicate the orders he carried.

"What of Major Eyre?" Stark asked. I was glad it was his voice that sounded. Mine would have been quite a lot surlier.

"I hope he'll stay on, of course," Monro answered. "He has a reputation for being a fine engineer."

"And commander," I said in defense.

Monro shrugged, avoiding commitment to a particular point of view. "General Webb has decided that with the losses William Henry sustained over the winter that it is time for a change in command."

"With respect, sir," Stark began. "But Major Eyre's defense during the raid was superb. We lost only a handful of men."

"And the entire fleet of boats for Lake George," Monro countered.

"Does General Campbell know about this?" I asked.

"Lord Loudoun is quite busy planning his own offensive operations," Monro explained as we drew nearer the fort. "That is why he has other fit officers working beneath him."

There was nothing fit about either Abercromby or Webb. Abercromby's belly might swamp a longboat. Webb's military acumen would get lost in the vast void of an upturned thimble. "Why not send the commander from Fort Edward here?" I said, remembering the able man I'd met on my way to William Henry. It's a shame I cannot recall the man's name.

"He's been relieved," Monro answered. The colonel was clearly growing tired of our inquiries. "Lieutenant, would you be so kind as to guide my officers and me to headquarters. Private Weber, please file to the rear of the column. There you will find companies of provincials from a host of countries. New York, New Jersey, and New Hampshire. And even Massachusetts, I think." The colonel pointed to the nearest part of the clearing that encompassed part of Titcomb and the land that sloped toward the fort's southeast gate. "Have them make camp here."

My little world, such as it was, had been upturned. "Who will command Fort Edward then?" I asked as I turned to obey.

Monro took note that I had begun to heed his command. It was the only thing that prevented him from unleashing what I would come to know as the pure fire he was capable of spewing when his anger mounted. "General Webb has decided to go to Fort Edward himself and command from there. When it suits him and his timetable, of course."

And now my little world had been defecated upon. For, Major General Daniel Webb was the soggiest, stickiest cow pie I had ever known. And I was sure his stench would soon reach the fifteen miles from Edward and completely foul the banks of Lake George.

CHAPTER 30

Soon, I had helped the provincial officers organize their men into neat rows outside the fort's walls. Two or perhaps three hundred canvas tents would soon line the portage road, extending westward into what had been our gardens. Men pounded stakes and tugged ropes. Others lugged barrel after barrel, firkin after firkin off wagons, drays, and carts, piling foodstuffs all about. Dogs had appeared with the train. A pack of them now ran wild. They barked incessantly. Boys, drummers and camp followers, cursed in order to prove their manhood to the more seasoned colonial troops. Somewhere, a set of babies cried. They had accompanied their mothers, who had accompanied their husbands on the trip.

Paws suddenly slammed into my back, nearly shoving me over. "Get off me, you cur!" I yelled, cocking my arm back to take a swing at one of the roving canines. The beast leapt up as I spun, slamming its wet nose and slathering its wetter tongue all over my face. I recognized the stench. "Sarah Belle!" I laughed.

"Ephraim Weber?" Itch called. He pushed off the wagon against which he'd been leaning and ambled over. "I'd have bet a Spanish Dollar that you were dead! Why, the day you stole the king's cabbage from my wagon and went off into the bushes, I thought the savages had made a slave out of you! Or worse."

Barely able to shove the front paws of his excited dog off my chest, I shook the man's hand. "Lord Loudoun had already made sure I was a slave… to the British army. No tribesman would have me."

Itch looked confused. His gaze moved from me to his dog and grew suddenly stern. I welcomed his imminent rebuke to Sarah Belle. If only one had come. "This Weber doesn't get it, do he, Sarah?" Itch set an exasperated set of hands upon his hips. "Everyone's a slave to something. Some men find they are slaves to more than one master. I'd think a Quaker would know such a thing. Don't you?" he asked his dog. After a moment of silence, Itch returned his attention to me. "I knew a man, a seafarer from Providence, he loved money, whores, and adventure. I'd say he was a slave to all three. Why couldn't you be a slave to both the

British and the tribes if they saw fit? Sure enough, the sins don't mind sharing their slaves with other sins. Lots of time, they encourage such camaraderie among themselves. For, what man who is slave to drink can long keep himself a slave from other vices?"

I stared at Itch. He stared at me, impatiently waiting for a response.

"I was joking, Itch," I said. "I wasn't captured. I went off that day and found Rogers. Fell in with his rangers, as I was supposed to all along."

"Oh, he was messed up fierce. Came through Fort Edward a few months back. I thought he might die. Rogers likely thought the same. Sarah Belle and I hauled him down to Albany on a sled over the Hudson. Cold trip. My trousers froze to the seat. Twice. Doctors there at Fort Frederick took one look at the captain, gasped, and sent us on to York City. I imagine he's buried down there by now."

I shook my head. "Just heard that he'll make full recovery."

"Bartholomew!" he swore. "Man's made of iron. No wonder the papers make such stuff of him."

"He's something," I allowed. "Don't know about iron. When he was shot, he bled like you and me."

"Hey, Itch!" shouted another teamster. "What in hell are you doing? Get your wagon moving. Got more provisions to drop here."

Itch formally lifted his floppy hat. "Best be goin'. Told we stay here tonight and head back to Edward in the morning. Got no commander there now. I hear one is coming. A real British general, they say. Third in command over all this mess. Can't wait to see him."

"I can," I muttered.

"Name is Cobb or some such," Itch guessed.

"Webb," I growled.

"Uh-huh. That's it. Like the spider."

"Hurry up, Itch!" called the teamster.

"Coming, old fool!" Itch yelled, reluctantly sauntering back to work. "Sarah! Get!" he chirped. Sarah shoved off me and raced circles around her master, nipping at his fingers and knees. "Why can't you handle any of these tasks?" he scolded the dog. "Just when I get to making friends with someone, you can't seem to get any work done." He sighed, tossing his hands in the air. "I suppose it's my lot in life for associating with the likes of you, Sarah Belle."

He waited at his wagon before climbing on. When Sarah didn't bound up ahead of him, he groused. "Oh, I didn't mean anything by it. Don't be so fragile. You ain't no soft lady. You'll always be my Belle." His palm swatted the wagon seat. Sarah happily leapt aboard. Her master followed and the pair bounced their way down next to the pasture where the other teamsters would camp for the night.

"Thanks for your help in getting organized, son," said a colonel from New Jersey. He approached, drinking hot tea from a steaming cup. He offered me one of my own.

"Following orders, sir," I said. "Thank you," I added after my first sip.

After giving me a simple nod, he and I turned our backs on the hustle of his growing camp. "John Parker," he said. We stared over the calm waters of Lake George. The surrounding hills still didn't appear fully green from a distance, but the chilly north winds blew down the distinct, sweet scents of spring.

I introduced myself and we shook hands. "Shame what happened to the boats," Parker lamented as he watched miniature cyclones of ash kick up on the shingle.

"Yep," I muttered. "But a far cry better than had we lost the fort and our men."

"It is that," Parker agreed. "But I'll feel better when we can get craft on the water again. It's only proper for Englishmen to control the seas, be they large or small. And a naval flotilla will help discourage a full siege from the French."

"We'll all feel better," I agreed.

"Better about what?" asked another provincial colonel. He walked up to us, the sun setting at his back.

"We were just saying that it will be nice to have control of the lake again," Parker answered. "Colonel Frye, this is Private Weber of the rangers. Frye is from Massachusetts."

"Been here long, Mr. Weber?" Frye asked.

"You could say that, sir," I said. "Fought here two years ago with General Johnson." I pointed along the alley upon which they'd begun to encamp. "This looked much different back then. Felled trees scattered about. General Dieskau and his grenadiers attacked right down this path." I shivered. "Lord help them. It was bloody."

"A good day for King George," Parker said.

"One of the few in this war," Frye added, surveying the road and camp. "Two years? You have been here awhile. Scouting all that time?" he asked, eyeing my soiled buff and green buckskins.

"Mostly," I said. "Spent some time up at Fort Oswego last summer."

Colonel Parker shook his head. "A bad day for King George."

Frye frowned. "One of many. Too many bad days for the cause of the English."

We then fell into that silent period that so often accompanies newly acquainted men. It was not in any way awkward. I sipped my tea. Parker sipped his tea, watching the lake intently. Frye stood, arms folded, peacefully observing his men at their work.

"Won't you and the other provincial officers join the regulars for dinner in the fort tonight?" I asked, swallowing down the last of the warm liquid. It felt a solid defense against the wet, cool air of spring.

"The fact that you're asking means that Colonel Monro did not see the benefit of inviting us," Frye said. He shrugged. "I prefer to eat with my men and their kinsmen, anyway. There is such a thing as spending too much time with gentleman from the Mother Country." He casually flicked the brim of his hat and excused himself.

"Oh, colonel," I said before he'd gotten too far. "Colonels, I mean."

"Yes," asked the pair of men.

"Tonight, and every night, please be vigilant, sirs. I've spent more time alone in these woods than a two-score-and-ten-year-old Mohawk. They are as comfortable to me as a good pair of stockings, broken in. But, were I to sleep outside the fort's walls these days, I'd want a set of sentinels guarding my bed. A set that won't be tempted to fall asleep. Else they, and I, would wake up with our throats slit and scalps gone."

The pair of provincials exchanged glances. "We'll heed your advice, Weber," Frye said. "Good night to you." The Massachusetts colonel changed his direction toward the camp piquet.

Parker finished his tea and accepted the return of his cup. "Perhaps, I'll catch up with you and your rangers in the coming days," he said as he angled over toward his New Jersey Blues. "The British like to use provincials as laborers and fort babysitters. I'd like to get my men into the action at least a little."

"Why in hell would you want to do that?" I asked, thinking that most of his regiment would be better served in camp. "Sir," I added meekly.

Parker shrugged. "Last year, half of my men sat in a tiny outpost in New Jersey. The most excitement they saw was when a storm blew over a tree and knocked down a barn."

"I'm not sure how I can help get you out of camp. Lieutenant Stark runs the rangers while Rogers is recovering. But Colonel Monro will have something to say about where you go and what you do."

Parker waved me off. "Lieutenant Stark, eh?" he answered happily. "I'll look him up. You've been most helpful." He crossed the camp to a small, growing fire where his men had begun to prepare dinner.

And I slunk off to the barracks, giving little thought to the two new colonels. Soon, I fell into my prickly, hard bed. As is the case with most active young men, I fell asleep in seconds.

Deep in the night I was awakened by the hoot of an owl. While suddenly staring at the black void above, I heard his talons scratching at the roof of the barracks. He hooted again. It was a low, slow monosyllabic song. I punched my rough pillow and tugged my coarse blanket up around my neck before settling down to drift away to unconscious bliss.

But as tired as I was from ranging all day, I tossed. Though exhausted, I turned. For, all night after that hoot, I half expected to be awakened by the drummer's call to arms. Sometimes, when I was wide awake that night, I found myself staring at the timbers above. First, I wondered if the owl had actually been a wily tribesman, calling his comrades to battle. That is when my thoughts spun on a thousand warriors sweeping from the woods and their canoes on the lake. With hatchets drawn, they sluiced through the teamsters and provincials, creating a hundred rivers of blood.

Other times that night, I slept. At least, I think I did. Unfortunately, when asleep, my nightmares proved worse than my waking dreams. Much worse.

CHAPTER 31

"Ow!" I grunted, sitting up on my straw mattress from a deep sleep.

Stark let go of my ear. He'd twisted it roughly. "Quiet," he whispered. "Get Conwall. Both of you, get your gear and provisions. We're going on a scout."

"Just the three of us?" I asked, rubbing a plug of crusty sleep from my eyes.

"That's what I said," Stark answered as he hiked his weapon and left the barracks.

"Damned army," I muttered, pulling my woolen blanket around my shoulders. I sat there, staring at the wall, in the pre-morning chill. Only a handful of embers remained in our fireplace. "Damned officers," I groused over and over.

At last, however, I crawled out of my sleeping box and shuffled over to where Conwall slept. I looked down at his Mahican features in the dark. He lay on his side, drooling on a pillow that he'd sewn himself. He'd stuffed it with feathers from an assortment of game birds he'd shot the previous autumn.

I spat on my finger and swirled it over his closed eye. "What the hell?" he asked, swatting at me while rolling away.

"Pipe down," I rasped. "We're to gear up and meet the lieutenant at the gate."

He grumbled in low tones as he yanked his blanket over his head, cowering beneath it as he wished aloud for a magical change in his circumstances. Five seconds later, he threw the cover off and seemed unsurprised that he was still in the chilly barracks and that I hovered over him. Conwall's palm wiped away my spit from his eye. "You're a turd, Weber."

"Sure thing," I mumbled.

Not ten minutes later, Conwall and I were fully fitted with packs of ammunition, foodstuffs, and extra clothing. We trotted down the steps to the inner yard. All was quiet. Only a few wary sentries stood at attention, surveying the horizons from the ramparts above.

Stark noted our approach and ducked out through the open man door in the main gate. We followed and it was closed and barred firmly behind us.

"I don't think you'll have much use for your writing instruments," Stark observed as we made our way along the eastern wall of the fort.

I patted my satchel of pens, ink, and paper. "Thanks for reminding me. Wait here."

"Weber," Stark hissed in protest as I took off down the portage road. "Weber."

"Be right there," I called.

Conwall and Stark grumbled.

It took me just a minute to filter through snoring men and smoking campfires of the teamsters' camp. Sarah Belle slept on her master's feet, which stuck out from under a tarp as his snout crackled in the back of his wagon. One of the dog's ears involuntarily perked. Then the beast hopped to her feet and bared her teeth at my shadow.

"Sarah, dear," I whispered. "Just me."

Her snarled lips instantly dropped and her tongue lolled. Sarah let me freely scratch behind her ears. She then stretched her paws forward while offering a great yawn and groan. "Go on. See if Itch is alive. Go on," I encouraged, shoving her under the tarpaulin.

Sarah eagerly crawled over her master's chest and slathered his whiskered face with kisses. Itch moaned, but made no move to stop her liquid assault. "Keep on it," I said, pushing her rump further inside.

Her pace increased as she joyously tasted all the leftover crumbs that Itch had stored in his beard from the previous night's meal. Sarah aggressively shoved her snout into his ear, sniffing loudly.

"That's about enough of that, Sarah Belle," Itch grumbled.

"So, you're alive," I said.

At the sound of my voice, Itch jolted upright, his head forming a center tent pole beneath the tarp. Sarah tumbled against the bed planks and began barking madly. A sharp knife poked me in the chest. "I hope you be a friend, friend. Else you'll be dead.

But I don't have any friends who'd be so stupid as to sneak up on a man when he sleeps. So, I guess we're not friends. It may have been nice to know you."

I felt the blade tip lunge forward. A heartbeat later, the knife was on the ground and I held Itch's hand cocked awkwardly behind his back. "Is that any way to greet a long, lost acquaintance," I scolded him. "Besides, you might want to be careful who you go attacking in such a way. You could get yourself hurt."

"Ephraim Weber," Itch proclaimed with surprise. "Same goes for you. Best be careful." He jabbed me in the check with something cold. I looked down to see that his other hand had efficiently aimed a loaded pistol at my face. He released the cock and carefully set the weapon down.

Sarah Belle's howls had startled a half dozen other dogs among the teamsters. Mutts yanked at ropes, barking furiously. Hounds loped about, sniffing and yapping. Masters shouted. Up in the provincial soldiers' camp, more dogs joined the fray. Barking. Barking. A wolf howled in answer from somewhere off in the distance.

Itch and I shook hands among the growing chorus and I pressed my satchel to his chest. "See these are forwarded down to Captain Rogers. They are important. There's a letter in there from me. I suppose he'll want to respond back before I submit the rules to Lord Loudoun."

"Rogers? Loudoun?" Itch asked. "Use the damn post."

"Just do it," I hissed. "Please," I added, somewhat out of character.

"Oh," Itch said, with sarcastic gravitas. He playfully wrestled with his dog's head. Sarah Belle growled with glee. "The Quaker said please. Guess we have to help him now, old Belle." By now, three-score men and officers were awakened up in the camp. They split the dark quiet, shouting at their loud curs.

"I just don't trust the mail. Monro offered to place it in his correspondence, but... Some officer or clerk might try to take credit for my work. Good Lord knows it's happened to me before. I take all the risk and get none of the glory. I want it to go directly to Rogers. You understand?"

He tapped his forehead as a man might tip his hat. "I do. Never fear. I know a train of men on the circuit all the way down to York City. So, wherever Captain Rogers lies, this pack will find him." He patted the satchel.

I grabbed his hand and pushed a few coins into the palm. "For your trouble." For the first time in years, I had money in my pocket. It felt good to share it.

"Trouble indeed," Itch huffed. Then he carelessly tossed my satchel up into his wagon and slumped on it as a pillow. Sarah Belle whined happily as she joined him. "Be there quicker than you can say, *King Louis wears ladies' skirts*."

"Thanks, Itch," I said, punching the bottom of his bare foot.

"Uh-huh," he mumbled. And I jogged back toward the fort.

Conwall sat on his pack and smoked a long, white pipe, made of bone that had the look of one from out Nantucket way. Stark pointed to the clamoring camp. "All that noise your fault?"

"Me?" I asked, feigning a struck pride. "No."

"Right," Stark said. He hauled up his kit and scampered ahead.

Conwall rolled his eyes while gripping his pipe tightly between his teeth. His pack was soon up and we all set out.

"We must have a specific objective," I offered. For the better part of two hours, Stark had led us around the western edge of Lake George. "Just three men out? When there are so many enemy lurking? That's a break from Major Eyre's protocol."

"Eyre's not in command anymore," Stark explained. He skipped over a rotting log, then bound over a narrow ravine.

"You scared, Weber?" Conwall asked. Without requiring an order from the lieutenant, he'd snuffed out his pipe when we were still within eyeshot of the curtain walls. The sweet scent of his tobacco would give us away as surely as a shout of warning.

"Yes," I admitted. I stared directly at Conwall in the bright morning light that filtered through the trees. "Only an idiot – maybe like you – wouldn't wonder why we are going out here."

"Turd," Conwall grumbled.

"Why are we out here, lieutenant?" I asked.

"Scouting," he answered simply. "We've begun a rotation of scouts, with rangers always out and about. It's the proper way to keep eyes and ears awake at all times."

"That's undeniable. But for months, we've been scouting with forty or more men at a time. And even then, there have been a few scrapes we could barely escape. These woods are quickly becoming French woods."

"Colonel Monro is not an idiot, if that is what you think," Stark said firmly. "He wants as much of the forest covered as he can get. He made that clear at dinner last night. And we can't do that if we all move in one large pack." The lieutenant rested his loaded musket across the folded arms at his chest. Sometimes we walked near the lake. Other times, our path took us a half mile from the waters. Stark led us wherever the footing was solid and our view was best. He paused, scanning a small bay.

"No. But we can stay alive if we stick together," I pointed out.

"Do you deny that a few men are nimbler than more men?" Stark growled, fixing me with a glare.

"No..."

"Then shut up." He resumed his course. And that was the end of that.

I didn't like it. Conwall didn't like it. Stark didn't like it. But I had been the only one dumb enough to question the orders. We snaked our way northward away from William Henry.

Six hours of walking passed by. We'd not seen anything unusual, except all the lingering signs of the large force of tribesmen we'd fought against the day before. The trail they provided could not be hidden and it was something that only a blind London clothier would have missed.

"Up to the pinnacle?" I suggested. "Ought to get a glimpse of where the tribesmen made camp last night."

Stark glanced up at the rounded peak to the west. Without a word he nodded, veered off the trail, and led our ascent. In a little more than a half hour he plopped his rump onto a small, rock outcropping at the top and broke out a portion of smoked beef. "Check the perimeter," he ordered, scanning eastward over the dozens of unnamed islands that dotted the lake. "Tell me if you see any smoke."

"Meet you in the middle," Conwall said to me, pointing straight westward. He chose a northerly route. I struck off south.

After putting a quarter mile between the lieutenant and me, I began arcing westward. The mountain sloped downward from there and I could see a fair distance through the budding trees. A lone doe sipped water from a stagnant pond. Occasionally, she would lift her head and orient her ears in all directions, listening for intruders. I watched her intently, knowing that she'd be a better scout than I could ever hope to be. When her head again dropped to the pond, I continued on, confident that no one lurked in that sector.

I progressed less than a rod when I heard a dull thud echoing from the pond. Freezing, I peered back to the doe. She, too, had frozen. Her ears were perked forward toward the mountainside and her eyes examined the forest floor. All four of her legs were rigid, straight beneath her shoulders. Neither of us moved. Had we heard the same thing?

A minute went by. Then the doe slowly lifted her left foreleg, its knee far forward. She slammed the hoof down against the earth. The dull thud.

Now I was interested. Crouching, I moved deliberately. Then, I situated myself behind a tree that angled down over the slope with gravity. I laid against it and peered around with one eye. The deer was still in place, unmoving. Soon, she lifted the same leg and rapped her cloven hoof against the soil. *Thud.*

I was sure she had a fawn or two in the thicket behind her. A doe rarely acted with such aggression unless she had offspring to protect. And so, willing my eyesight to focus through the bramble at her rear, I squinted, searching for movement. There was none to find. But what had at first looked like sunlight streaming through breaks in the canopy and falling on the forest floor turned out to be the flank of a tiny deer. It was an obedient creature, frozen in fear, just as its mother wished.

But I was too far away for the doe to react thus. I followed her gaze across the pond. Nothing. I scrutinized the western bank. Nothing. The small shoreline curved around to her. Noth…

There was a tribesman, heavily clothed in skins and with his flesh painted. He crept slowly toward the beast, a bow in his hand.

The deer jerked her head and finally saw him, her hunter. They stared at each other, unmoving. I smiled, thinking that the young hunter had wasted too much time. He'd lose his quarry as sure as a gal in a brothel loses her skirts.

Twang. Twang. Twang. Zip. Zip. Zip. Thump. Thump. Thump.

An arrow pierced the doe from the opposite side of the hunter. Its stone head crushed one of her ribs as it slid into her heart muscle. The creature reared before toppling over backward. Her fawn, no both of her fawns, I hadn't seen the second one, had already fallen dead.

The bushes came alive. Fifteen warriors emerged from the eastern edge of the pond. They jogged through thorns or splashed through the edge of the water as they descended upon their prizes. A heartbeat later they'd begun efficiently field dressing them on the spot, occasionally sampling bites of the organs as was their custom. Then the western bushes rattled. Thirty tribesmen walked out to join the decoy who'd been spotted by the doe. One of them whistled, carelessly, I thought, for being in so-called English and Iroquois territory.

An entire company of braves, representing a half score tribes, none of them Mohawk, jogged ahead at his shrill command. "Up," called the decoy as he pointed toward the pinnacle shrouded in woods behind me. He spoke French, which was a language that most of the tribes could understand. "We'll camp here tonight. But make sure our brothers, the English haven't skittered out of their holes today."

More than fifty lads, all in charcoal paint and carrying hatchets, war clubs, muskets, or bows fanned out and trotted up the hill.

I rolled back against the trunk and stared up into the mass of trees that hid my two silent comrades.

I gave little thought to my next actions.

CHAPTER 32

There will, no doubt, be some of you who are prone to second-guess me. As you sit in your soft chair on your softer, plumper rumps, you'll proudly say to yourselves, *that was a foolish thing for Ephraim to do. I wouldn't have done such a thing. If he'd only have done such-and-such. His life would have been easier. It was the safest course.*

Nonsense.

I certainly could have crept up the long trunk of the angled tree and disappeared amongst its highest branches. Even without leaves, no one would have seen me. Even tribesmen aren't all-seeing in the wilderness. They are men, after all. Some are lazy. Some are strong or valiant. Some are weak. A good many could benefit from the miracle of spectacles. The tribes, just as the English, take all kinds. And so, not expecting to see anyone hiding in a single tree out of millions, none of those braves would have looked up. I'd have curled there until it was safe to descend and slip, unnoticed, back to Fort William Henry.

Good idea, you might say. *That's probably what I would have done.*

Coward. Selfish coward.

Not that the thought didn't cross my mind.

But those rangers, even Amos Conwall, were my brothers. They were more my brothers than the sons of my father and mother. They and soldiers of their ilk were more my siblings than my sisters. Of course, I was not stone cold. I still retained a fondness for the Weber boys: Caleb (God rest his soul), Frederick, Hiram, and Thaddeus. I loved my sisters: Gertrude (God rest her soul), Caroline, Eleanor, and Harriet. But save for Caleb, as he died in my grasp at the end of Braddock's March, none of the others had ever suffered under arms or true deprivations along with me. Battles, toils, pain, cold – all of it had served to weld me to my new brothers as the hearth and hammer of the smith welds old steel to new.

With my back pasted against the trunk, I sucked in a swath of air for what was to follow. My hand felt the grip of my knives, hatchet, and pistol in my belt. From memory, I knew where each would be, but before a battle, it was best to be sure. I lifted my musket, readying.

Like a hinged door, I brought my right shoulder around to the left. The butt of the Bess nestled just where I wanted her and I gazed down her long barrel until the naked chest of an enemy was at the other end. *Cr-crack!* The ball hurtled and the man slumped before his comrades could even make a sound.

But then there was a sound. Oh, it was a din. Galloping hell hounds make less racket. Those tribesmen unleashed their war whoops and fearlessly drove up the hill. From my waist, I snatched the antique French pistol with which I had become quite fond. It was as inaccurate as an addled navigator. It was as unreliable as an inebriated sentry. But it had belonged to my first wife and, therefore, I cherished it. Levelling the short barrel at the nearest brave, his belly actually, to adjust for the sloppiness of my aim and the gun, I squeezed. Smoke puffed. The muzzle skipped. The shot was low and left. It grazed his right shin. But it was enough to drop him.

"Maybe a hundred enemy coming our way!" I bellowed, now sprinting up the hill. Branches snagged my cheeks and poked my eyes. Through a little blood and tears, I raced on a straight course toward the lieutenant. I bounded up a large boulder. I tripped once over a gnarled mass of vines that dangled low between two trees. "Just don't shoot me, you idiots!"

Cr-crack! Ping! A ball ricocheted off a tree, dangerously close to my ear.

Cr-crack! Conwall had stepped out and fired at the nearest pursuer. I didn't bother to turn and see whether or not he'd been skilled in his aim. "Who's the idiot who brought a whole war party against us?" Conwall asked as he fell in next to me.

We nearly ran into Stark as he raced toward us on the crest. "Here!" he barked, dropping to one knee. His musket skipped to his shoulder and he hugged it tight, like a man did his pretty wife. He eyed his prey and let her loose as Conwall and I leapt behind cover next to him. I spun just in time to see another warrior fall, gripping his bloody groin.

I frantically reloaded. So did my companions. I saw a running target, aimed, and fired. Then I reloaded. Stark and Conwall performed just as rapidly, perhaps more so.

Whispering now, Stark said. "We'll keep this rolling fire up. For just a minute." Our enemy had halted their pursuit as they settled in behind obstacles and took stock of just what they faced. "Want to keep their heads down as long as we can. But it won't be long before they realize they outnumber us twenty to one."

"Drop your packs. Make yourself light," the lieutenant ordered between his shots. He'd already stripped his gear, stuffing only ammunition and a small sack of foodstuffs into his shirt.

We copied him. Stark kept firing at anything that moved. He hit nothing, but his efforts were enough to thwart the advance.

But when enemy shadows began swinging left and right, Stark hissed. "Don't shoot your next load. You'll want that for the retreat."

"Aye," Conwall said, stuffing his ramrod securely beneath his barrel. He climbed onto the balls of his feet, crouching at the ready. I did the same.

"Stick together for maybe a quarter mile," Stark rattled quickly. "Then split up. Make it hard for them to find you. Don't stop moving. You know Rogers training. Don't take any expected route. I'll see you at the fort in a few days." Without waiting for any response, he stood, ran forward at an oblique angle. Tufts of leaves and other detritus popped at his feet as the enemy finally had a visible target. Stark slammed his side into a tree. "Go!" he rasped. Then he fired and began another set of insane maneuvers.

Stark was an experienced woodsman. Had the world never heard of Robert Rogers, perhaps I'd have been charged with making sense of his forest warfare tenets. But, then again, *Stark's Scouting Statutes* just never would have had the same ring as Rogers' Rules of Ranging. Given the lieutenant's proficiency, Conwall and I obeyed. We unashamedly left him there, figuring that he'd best get some sense and follow on our behinds a few seconds later. Or else, he'd find that the nights grew chilly without the benefit of his cap of hair.

Crouching low to remain obscured as we rapidly descended the hill, Conwall and I sprinted. "Wish we had those forty other men," Amos admitted.

"Yep," I said, cursing Monro. The further away we got, the taller we stood, the faster we raced.

Eventually, after we'd run perhaps a tenth of a mile, even the sporadic gunfire on the hill stopped. I gave Conwall a sideways glance. Neither he nor I voiced anything. Stark was dead. Or he wasn't.

It was about time to split up. "Which way do you want to go?" I huffed and puffed.

Danger prowled in all directions. A hundred enemy warriors stood between us and William Henry. To the right, east, only a narrow corridor separated us from the lake. That really only left two possible choices, straight ahead toward French-held territory or westward.

"Left," Conwall proclaimed.

"Alright," I muttered, pulling to a temporary halt. We shook hands for the briefest of moments. "God speed," I said.

"You, too," he said. "See you at the fort, turd." Then he spun and bolted deeper in the dark woods west of Lake George.

I watched him go for just a second. The sounds of a hundred rustling feet brought me from my reverie.

Northward, I ran. Until my lungs burned, I ran.

Then I ran some more.

CHAPTER 33

Across hills and over low mountains I raced, hurtling without pause on legs that felt more flaccid with every passing second. Down into valleys, I plunged, only to climb back out to skitter across smooth limestone outcroppings. Lungs searing, I glanced eastward from one of those rocky portions of my trail. There was Northwest Bay. More than a mile had slipped into my wake since we'd first encountered the tribesmen.

And I was spent. My stride was getting sloppy. I tripped more frequently. Twice I slipped on melting ice and snow that lay nestled in mountain fissures.

Still, hooting calls of brave warriors chased me down. To stop would mean torture, death, or enslavement. Or, it would mean physically watching as my own organs were served for dinner to the members of their party. I'd been a firsthand witness to all of those particular, peculiar brutalities of the tribes and their personal ways of war. And so, I'd try anything to avoid being a recipient of their cruelty.

Running on, I looked up to the left. The slope was steep. That was no way of escape. I looked ahead. The wilderness never ended. I could run to Quebec, and still the warriors would run me down like the pack of wolves they were. Again, I glanced rightward toward the lake waters. The cliff dropped straight down so that the tops of the trees were level with my feet.

I skidded to a halt and checked the way I'd come. A half score voices echoed up the path. In ten seconds, they'd appear from the notch I'd just left and be upon me. I slung the Bess over my shoulder, took one more breath, and leapt off the ledge.

And found my legs couldn't produce the potent jump I had thought. My shins hit the top of the white pine I had hoped to vault. Its soft wood did not break. But as it bent, my torso continued unhindered while my feet slowed. I somersaulted, smacking into the trunk of another long-needled pine. Then I really began falling. My left shoulder struck a branch, which had the dizzying effect of rolling me right-side-up. I hooked my right arm around another branch. It was from a maple that had reached into the pine's territory. That limb cracked free. On I tumbled.

Another needled limb snaked its way between the Bess and my back. My weapon slid down the branch toward the trunk. The strap held. I found myself yanked hard until I rammed into the trunk once again. Then, pinching my elbow tightly to my side, I dangled there, some twenty feet from the forest floor.

The voices were above me now. I peered up at the ledge, praying that Providence had somehow masked the unholy racket I'd made in my fall.

The pack of trackers stopped at the exact spot from which I'd jumped. Some peered ahead. Others craned to get a look up the slope. A couple sprawled out on their bellies and gazed down the face of the ledge.

"Did you hear that?" their leader asked. He was Potawatomi, from deep in the pays d'en haut. And though he wore a Catholic cross about his neck, his flesh was decorated with all of the tattoos one would expect of a warrior who was practiced in the art of killing. Something told me he had only a rudimentary understanding of his Christian pendant's symbolism. "Run ahead. See if a stick is broken on the path."

One of his Potawatomi brethren raced ahead and scouted for signs of the broken branch they'd heard so clearly. "Nothing," he called back.

All the men on their bellies had to do was lift their eyes a few degrees. There I was. At most, my leaping, falling, and bouncing had placed a rod between us. I was obscured by little more than needles and branches. My dress blended in with the environment. But all they had to do was look.

The man on the right did. He lifted his head. Though thankfully, he did not look into the forest. Instead, he focused above me, on the treetops. "Do you suppose he jumped?" he asked.

One of those staring up the slope to the west scraped his fingers across the dirt. A small avalanche of leaves and earth rolled onto his feet. "He didn't go this way," he announced and turned, crawling down with the others on the ledge.

I was afraid to move, lest they catch sight. But the strap from the Bess was digging a ditch into my armpit and my strength was nearly gone from clinging so tightly. I carefully used my toes until I found a branch to stand on. As I gently set my weight on it, the limb slowly drooped.

"There!" called one of the Potawatomi. The tuft of limp needles at the end of my foothold had sagged by a yard. He followed the needles to the branch, saw my feet, and then locked eyes with me.

I blew his brains all over the leader behind him. That time at least, the French pistol's aim was true.

I exchanged the pistol for my knife. As my pursuers began to realize what happened, I cut the strap that held me in place. Then, teetering for just a moment, I pressed my back against the tree and wrenched the Bess down from the branches above. She'd been bred for war and knew right where to go. Her rump found my shoulder. I took aim down her sleek lines. Her speeding ball punched into the belly of a crouching warrior. He doubled over and, before his comrades could snag him, slipped off the ledge and crashed headlong onto a rock below.

An arrow rattled in the bark next to my neck. I dropped to my backside and slid to the next branch. A musket ball raced through my buckskins, punctured my food pack, and exited safely out the other side before it, too, found a home in the tree. Their vengeance was getting too close. So, I abandoned caution and, clinging with one hand to a lower bough, swung down. A heartbeat later I dropped to the ground.

Two of them had jumped into the trees above. One had been more graceful than I. He swiftly and deftly shimmied down. On the other hand, the other warrior toppled and tumbled until he cracked his neck next to me in the dirt. I exerted no effort to see him dispatched.

Two more men climbed down the cliff face while the other four planted themselves above and loaded their muskets. I had just the blink of an eye to fully turn the tables in their chase. Unbelievably sore, I hobbled over the base of the cliff while reloading the Bess. I aimed straight up. *Cr-crack!* The ball ripped into the warrior's heel and shattered his ankle. He gave a high-pitched shriek and plummeted. I skipped out of the way as both of his legs shattered.

"Faster!" the leader ordered the men still descending to me. The one in the pine leapt down to a branch on an adjacent tree so that the trunk of the first would shield him in case I shot again.

The man on the cliff wall, hesitated. Then he began climbing up.

Decisions made under such conditions are either right or wrong. They allow no time for delay. For to delay, well, that is to guarantee a wrong course of action.

I deemed the man on the wall craven or prudent. I didn't care which. I spun and limped away from the cliff just as a pair of musket blasts from above poured their contents over the edge. They blasted chunks out of the tree I used for cover.

It was a race. The man in the tree already had his knife drawn. He scrambled downward. Without giving my movements a single thought, my hands rapidly reloaded the Bess. His feet hit the ground and he sprinted toward me, game to close the gap before I could finish.

He won. I dropped the ramrod and half-loaded musket while dodging what he hoped to be the fatal blow. His blade swooshed by, snagging my sleeve. I prepared to receive his immediate attack, but he was more judicious than that. Facing me from four feet away, he straddled my Bess and halted. His legs and arms were ready for action, but he stood there scowling. "Take your time and come down safely," he announced to his friends above. "He's not going anywhere fast."

I followed his gaze. A sharp maple branch stuck out from my thigh. Blood soaked my leg. He was right. I was going nowhere fast.

Unless.

I slipped my toe beneath the barrel of the grounded Bess and shoved it hard. The stock of the gun swung around and bashed my attacker in the calf while the steel barrel rammed into his shin. It was the split second of freedom I needed. I tore my tomahawk free and swept it at him. The bottom tip of the blade punctured the back of his hand. He dropped the knife. I advanced, slamming my knee into his snout. The head of the hatchet was soon buried into the small of his back.

"Yes," I called, panting. "Take your time." I rolled the dead warrior off the Bess and finished reloading her, careful to remain tucked behind a pine. "Though I'd prefer if you send one down at a time. That would be much more convenient."

The leader cursed. He knew that at least two more would die even if all five descended at once. "You are an English dog," he barked.

"You are righter than you know," I proclaimed, ramming the shot and powder into the short barrel of the pistol. "I am called Fierce Dog in these parts and over in the Western Wilderness. I eat the French and their Indian pets for supper."

"I know this name!" he called. I heard their feet pattering back and forth above as they searched for a direct line of sight. "It is the man who killed Pakanka."

"A dear friend of mine," I admitted. And he had been. War made thinking men into ignorant beasts. "Just think what I do to my enemies." I stole a quick tug from my canteen. My leg throbbed.

The leader laughed. "I've seen what you've done to my party today." He then paused before switching from his native tongue to French. He whispered to his fellow braves. "Circle down. I will talk." I heard them scamper down either side of the path, searching for a shortcut.

"You ought to know," the warrior went on. "The memories of my people are long. We do not forget insults. And my memory is longer than most. One day, I shall find your lodge. I will find your family. I will take your children and make them Potawatomi. I will take your wife as my own and she will bear me a dozen Potawatomi warriors. And I will take you. You will watch as I plant my seed in my new wife, season after season. You will become my slave. And when I am finished destroying your mind, I will put you in one of the great iron kettles that the French traders have brought to my people. We will make you into a broth and pour your warrior's heart into our own. We will be stronger for it."

I bent to swipe some of his comrade's food and ammunition. "I thank you for the compliment," I called, carefully creeping straight ahead so that I remained hidden. "But I've told you my name. Would you care to share yours? The man who will kill Fierce Dog will become famous and I'd like to be able to say I knew him when…"

"Claude Sturgeon!" he called proudly. "Of the Blood clan."

On I crept, squirreling around another tree and continuing my beeline path.

"But it is not good for Claude Sturgeon to kill a Fierce Dog," the Potawatomi said. "A dog has teeth, but he is docile, friendly. No. Today, I give you a new name. One that befits a warrior. And one that will bring the man who kills him glory."

With blood trickling, I hesitated. For many years I had strived to have a nickname bestowed upon me that would strike fear and awe into my enemies and allies alike. I'd been given monikers of ridicule by others. In a fit of rage, I'd given myself the title of Animosh Aakwaadizi, or Fierce Dog. Perhaps, the one called Sturgeon was to be the name-giver.

"What else can fly from peaks and safely alight in trees? He hunts efficiently by perching and scanning from boughs. Only when his quarry is most exposed, will he strike with deadly accuracy." He waited for my answer. But I was smart enough to not give away my new position. I tempted fate by merely waiting. "From that wound I spied in your leg, perhaps the former Fierce Dog has already passed to the hunting grounds beyond," Sturgeon guessed aloud. "If that is the case, it will not be the hide of a lowly dog that I carry in triumph to my village. It will be the bleeding scalp of Kestrel's Wing that adorns my belt."

I grinned, limping away rapidly now. After more than a decade in the wilderness, I had a nickname I could live with.

But first Kestrel's Wing had to survive the day.

CHAPTER 34

And night.

Not looking back or listening for the hostile tribesmen, I'd raced directly to Northwest Bay. Once at shore, I slipped into the freezing water and removed the sharp stick from my thigh. It took a fair amount of teeth-gritting and cursing under my breath to keep from shrieking in pain. Thankfully, however, the wound did not bleed much more than it already had. Soon it was cleansed and I had it dressed. Having got rid of all of my supplies, I had to saw away one of my sleeves to use as a bandage. The entire medical procedure lasted five minutes. Then I turned obliquely northward and plodded off again.

By dusk, I felt it was clear that I'd slipped away from Sturgeon's band of Potawatomi. To be safe, there would be no fire that night. I scaled a tree and curled in a bough, shivering, while eating barley bread and a chunk of dried maple sap that I'd swiped from my attackers. Soon, rain came to join me in my bunk. It was a long, long night, spent mostly in that aggravating, and exhausting state of half-sleep. Worry and dreams slipped in and out of my dazed mine. Where was Stark? Had Conwall made it to the fort? Would I ever see its embankments again?

I felt myself falling. My hand grabbed the crook of the tree just before I tumbled out. "Damn army," I muttered when I realized that the sun was still hidden. My eyes felt heavy. My mind felt squishy. I could try to sleep again. What was the use?

Instead, I carefully shimmied down the slick bark. Except for the frequent drips of water falling from the canopy to the floor, the earth and all that was in it was quiet. Quiet like the time within two hours of dawn. The nocturnal creatures had already stalked about on their nighttime foraging maneuvers and since returned to their nests. The diurnal beasts had not yet awakened. It was a good time for a wounded man to move, since even tribesmen occasionally fell asleep.

I struck off west, planning to move as far away from trouble as possible. My pace was slow. As near as I could tell, my wound had stayed closed. Though, with each footfall, it still felt like someone bludgeoned me with a smith's hammer.

A narrow brook crossed my path. I waded across, the cold waters momentarily numbing my injury and shriveling my manhood. Trembling from cold, I emerged, slogging up the other bank as silently as possible.

Smack!

The unmistakable sound of a fist striking flesh and bone was immediately followed by a sad groan. Another voice laughed in a mocking tone. They were nearby.

I sprawled out in the mud, frozen in place. It was there I rested for five minutes until I was sure no one had heard me. Satisfied, I slowly crawled back into the creek, having decided to disappear the way I'd come.

Smack!

"How's that, Mahican?" asked a new mocking voice. "What's it like to be made women by the Mohawk and then whores by the English?"

For better or worse, the Mahican were our allies against the French. I knew of only three in the area, Chingachgook, Uncas, and Amos Conwall.

Crunch!

The sound of a brutal punch reverberated through the pre-morning dark. Yet another man derided the prisoner. "Your flesh is as soft as your heart. My fist doesn't feel a thing as it strikes." *Crunch!*

The smart thing, the life-preserving thing to do would have been to slide into the brook, follow its frigid course to safety, and hump southward to Fort William Henry as quickly as my hobbled legs would take me. I sighed and slunk forward with noiseless stealth.

Soon, I had pressed myself into a tight crevice between two enormous rocks that rested on the forest floor, having fallen eons ago from a cliff above. The grove of trees I peered into was ancient, as ancient as the dirt from which they grew. Oaks as tall and straight as the heavens towered above. Their trunks were as broad as a merchant's ship. In their shadows, dozens of tribal warriors slumbered, tucked tightly under hides to keep away the wet and rain from the night before. I saw snoring Ottawa and Fox, each organized into their own little segment of the floor. There was a clutch of Menominee slumbering at the far end around a low fire. In the distance, outside my direct view, I could see flickering signs of a few more dying fires with the shapes of more warriors sleeping.

I should have smelled their smoke as I approached. My only explanation for missing the camp's signs was that I was not quite myself.

Smack!

To my left, with his arms stretched wide and tied with leather cord around one of those great trees, was the Mahican prisoner. He'd been stripped to his waist. His rump sat on a root. His legs stretched out in the dirt. Five Chippewa youths had gathered around him so that I could not see his face. They took turns smacking or punching him, giggling each time. "My turn! My turn!" proclaimed one. He stepped forward and brought his fist against the prisoner's cheek. It was a sickening thunk.

"No. It's our turn," huffed Claude Sturgeon. He and the survivors of his pursuit stepped into the firelight. "We need morning refreshment before we run north. Let us strike this dog to whet our appetites."

One of the Chippewa shoved Sturgeon away. "Potawatomi girls. You lost your prey. Go hungry."

As quick as a wink, one of Sturgeon's braves slipped a knife under the Chippewa lad's chin. "You didn't catch this one either," he growled, pressing up. "And yet you have your fun."

"No," said a muscled Mississauga. He led yet another band of warriors toward the prisoner. "We caught him. The Mahican is our trophy." This barrel-chested warrior marched right up to the prisoner and kicked him in the belly. The tribesman was rewarded with a spontaneous decoration of spittle and blood on his moccasin.

"My sons!" called a French priest, his raiment fluttering as he raced toward the scene. "We must cease these attacks upon an unarmed man!" He approached Sturgeon and pointed to his chest. "That cross, my son. Remember its meaning."

Sturgeon looked down. For just a moment, and no more, he appeared ashamed. But his pride flared. "We are not your sons if you would not give us the gift of trophies in war. And besides, he is unarmed because he was caught. That is his own fault." Claude shoved a hoof against the prisoner's knee.

"This is my trophy!" hissed the Mississauga. "He is not Père Roubaud's gift to give. Especially, to a pack of Potawatomi women."

"He is a child of God. The One God I told you about, Great River Mouth," Father Roubaud explained.

"A father gives gifts," Great River Mouth barked. It was an argument I'd heard from the tribes before. Many times. "And I will not accept a father that does not give gifts to his children." The big Mississauga man slammed his knee into the unseen face of the prisoner. The defeated man managed only a gasp. "And our French fathers, I will not accept them either, if they deny me this gift."

"No one is denying you anything!" snapped a Canadian warrior dressed in buckskins, but wrapped in the gray-white coat reminiscent of his countrymen. He shoved his way among the disparate parties, elbowing Father Roubaud. The newcomer's features were a mixture of French and Indian. His belt bristled with weapons. "This priest has not the power to do such a thing. And though my king has granted me the authority to do whatever I feel is right, I'll not deny anyone the trophies of war. We are allies in this war against the English. There is no need to bicker."

"We are allies with the French fathers only for convenience, Langlade," grumbled Sturgeon. He spat on the face of one of the Chippewa boys. "These children should go back to the pays d'en haut where they belong."

A shoving match ensued.

"You don't belong here either!" shouted Great River Mouth. He belted Sturgeon with the back of his hand.

"Everyone knows that!" proclaimed one of the Chippewa. "The Potawatomi women invite Chippewa men into their lodges just so they don't have to carry the seed of their own filthy men."

Great River Mouth back-handed the Chippewa. "Who said you could speak, foreigner?"

There was more shoving. Father Roubaud backed away, glancing worriedly at the suddenly warring factions and the injured captive. In a flash, a Chippewa drove a tomahawk into the groin of a Mississauga.

Langlade then had two pistols out and fully cocked before the fight could escalate further. The first was aimed at the Chippewa assailant. The second was pointed at the forehead of Great River Mouth. "You will not retaliate for that!"

The massive Mississauga crossed his eyes to gaze at the barrel. "Not now," he admitted. "But Great River Mouth always repays his debts. And I now owe these Chippewa children a great deal."

"Not under my command," Langlade hissed. He pressed the barrel forward, shoving Great River Mouth's head back, before he trained the gun on Claude Sturgeon. "You will go to where the rest of your men sleep," he ordered. "Your French fathers have blessed you with bountiful gifts. They have given you the chance to decorate your lodges with prizes from the hunt and warpath. Leave this prisoner alone."

"Ha!" quipped the Chippewa who held the bloody hatchet.

Langlade squeezed the trigger of the pistol that he had leveled at the Chippewa's head. It fired, sending bits of bone and brain onto the onlookers. "Charles," breathed the priest as the hatchet dropped from the dead man's hand. "You just murdered him."

The echoing sound awoke the rest of the camp just as the sun began to poke through the trees. Langlade lowered the cock of the unspent pistol and stuffed into his belt. The still smoking gun was reloaded a few seconds later as the tribesmen watched the strange man. The Canadian leader then bent and coolly sawed away the scalp of the young Chippewa man who'd been his ally only moments before. He tucked it into his belt. "Justice is done," he announced. "And the prize went to the man who carried it out. Now go. Break your fasts. We march north in a half hour."

All parties, except the priest, scowled at one another for a long while. Their stares were sharper than daggers. The lone Canadian did not back down. Soon, the young Chippewa braves ambled away, frequently looking at their fallen kinsman with the missing face. Sturgeon huffed, but led his Potawatomi in the opposite direction.

"And as to the welfare of the prisoner?" Roubaud asked.

"He is my prisoner. My prize," the Great River Mouth announced, growling at the man of the cloth.

Roubaud did not back down. He stepped chest to chest with the warrior. The priest was more than a head shorter, two score older, and perhaps five stone lighter. He turned the corners of his mouth sharply down so that the long moustache of his gray beard drooped. His bravery was admirable, if not foolish.

Langlade chuckled. "Père Roubaud, what do you expect to do if Great River Mouth decides to move you aside?"

"If it be God's will, he and a thousand other men could not move me," Roubaud snarled.

Great River Mouth roughly shoved the smaller man to the ground. He and Langlade laughed. "Off with you now, Father," the Canadian commander said. "Get something to eat. We leave soon."

Roubaud stood and tried in vain to scrape the mud from his robe. He glowered at Langlade before leaving in a huff.

Langlade then glanced over his shoulder at the captive. The Canadian nodded. "Yes. He is your prize. But look at him. He can no longer speak. He'll not be able to make the march. He's too badly beaten. I would have liked to question him. Montcalm would have wanted information."

"My prisoner. I can do what I wish," proclaimed the Mississauga. "I chose to beat him like the cur he is."

Langlade wore a disgusted look. "He's not going with us because I don't want to be slowed down. Just finish your business and take from him what you will." He tugged out a watch from a fob pocket. "Less than a half hour. We march to Carillon." The Canadian took a step away.

"Half-breed," the Mississauga hissed. "Running back to the French fort. You don't even know what you are!"

Langlade calmly plucked his fingers at the pistols in his belt. He turned and faced, nose-to-nose, with the bigger man. "As far as I can see there is no benefit to being pure blooded. My mother was Ottawa. My father French. But you, Great River Mouth? No matter the blood that pours through your veins, you will always be someone else's stupid, blunt tool. As you are mine, right now." While speaking, Langlade had let slip his manhood and begun pissing on his opponent's foot.

A frightful minute went by with no movement. Every muscle in the Mississauga man's body flexed in anger. But, for now at least, his opponent somehow wielded much power among the many tribes that had come under the banner of the French. Great River Mouth glanced around at the camp, much of whom had begun to stare, as if taunting the Mississauga warrior to react and discover the consequences. At last, Langlade tucked himself away and sauntered off.

When he'd gone, Great River Mouth let out a loud, rolling growl that lasted a good three heartbeats. He finished his outburst by swinging his giant mitts downward onto the prisoner. He punched and punched and punched, unleashing rage onto the only man he could. With his right fist, he thrashed the man until his knuckles were raw. Then he switched to his left. When both paws were tender, he kneed the prisoner. He kicked him. He finished by again firing up his arms, alternating punches and elbows.

Panting, Great River Mouth eventually rested his hands on his knees. By now, his comrades had gotten bored with his frustrated show of force. They sat nearby and ate breakfast around a newly rekindled campfire. They laughed and traded barbs.

Great River Mouth grunted as he stood up tall and unsheathed his knife. Without ceremony he harvested a black scalp from his captive. He held it up over his head, blood dripping down his arm, and gave a chilling war whoop.

The call was answered by his kinsmen only. None of the other tribes represented in the camp that morning gave a reply. Great River Mouth peered around at his tenuous allies and growled. Eventually, he skulked over to his fellow Mississauga and feasted on a humble breakfast of smoked trout, leaving his bloodied pulp of a prisoner dangling limply against the tree trunk.

Some minutes later, Langlade hastily came back through. As promised, he gathered up the amalgamation of warriors, cajoling some, threatening others, and struck off north.

While examining the bloodied prisoner from my hiding place, I listened to their retreating march for many minutes. From that distance and given his beating, I could not tell which Mahican had just been executed. And the man was most definitely dead. His chest did not rise and fall even once.

But when the coast was clear, I crawled out of my hovel and inched toward the limp figure. Every inch of his body was splattered with crimson. One arm had been torn from its shoulder socket, causing the joint to jut grotesquely outward. A pair of ribs, broken, stuck out from the skin on opposite sides of his torso. And the face? The face was devastated. Pulp mash for papermaking had a thicker consistency than what had so lately been that man's window to the world. The jaw was dislocated and half of it crushed. A cheekbone had been tramped flat so that what remained of the battered skin hung limp like a ship's sails on a windless day. The lid and skin around one eye were so swollen that they had closed up entirely around the orb. And the other eye had suffered a worse fate. One of the blows from Great River Mouth had torn the eyeball loose. The brute had then stuffed it between his victim's teeth and beaten it until it was mush and the teeth were set free.

I searched for an identifying mark, but there was none to be found. It was not long before I gave up and turned southward, fairly certain that I now had a clean route to Fort William Henry. That was when I saw something quite light against the browns of the rotted leaves and dirt. Bending, I brushed aside debris.

There I found a white, whalebone pipe. I plucked it up and gently set it on Amos Conwall's lap.

CHAPTER 35

Weeks upon weeks slipped by. Since returning to William Henry, I had not been tasked with going on a single scout. In fact, no one had been sent out to scour the woods. Because no one could.

I should back up.

My struggle of limping to safety lasted for three days after witnessing Conwall's execution. In that time, I'd navigated around just one more band of perhaps two score warriors. But even as I collapsed into the first shoots of our gardens growing to the west of the fort, I was informed that Monro had dispatched another ten and three trios of rangers after ours. Half of those men never returned.

Stark lay in the bunk next to me, bruised and battered but alive. "You can't blame the colonel for all this," he'd said.

"Sending us out in small batches was as good as slitting our throats," I hissed, propping myself up and using a bedroll as a pillow. My thigh had healed nicely. And I'd been granted an extra ration of rum each day.

Stark shrugged. "Honestly, Weber. All forty of us ranging together could have met the same fate. Worse maybe. The bands of Indians out there are thicker than the rats in York City. Each one of us could have wound up like Conwall."

He was right. But I didn't like it. Monro was a red-backed colonel and his orders had caused my friends and me to suffer. "Damn officers," I grumbled.

"I'm an officer," Stark said, sipping broth from a bowl. Somehow, he'd come away from our disastrous scout with little more than an illness and several prominent lumps.

"You're not a redcoat. I hate 'em. Every last one."

"Eyre?" he asked, wiping a drip away from his stubbled face.

"Not him. No. He's alright."

"Johnson?"

"Alright. Him, too."

"Turnwell? Bradstreet? Colonel Mercer?" he asked in rapid-fire.

"Alright. Alright," I acquiesced. "Some of them aren't bad. I still hate 'em. Damn redcoats."

Stark snickered. "Me, too," he admitted quietly. "Damn redcoats." We shared a laugh.

It had been many weeks since we'd left the infirmary. What few rangers left alive, ranged within one mile of the fort, spitting distance. Even that close, we saw ample signs of the enemy prowling about. They harvested game with impunity. In great numbers, bands of them camped, fearing no reprisals from us. The bodies of some of the sentries who'd been tasked with guarding our gardens and livestock had been discovered scalp-less. We even saw enemy canoes audaciously traversing Lake George time and again. But since our fleet had been destroyed, there was nothing we could do.

Parker's New Jersey men slaved away at the beach. "Not long," Colonel Parker promised. He and Monro stood on the rebuilt dock. Below them on the shore, on a rare break, I skipped stones over the lake waters with Johnny and some of the camp children. Hell. Though I'd had two wives and had twins living somewhere in the world, at that point in my life I wasn't much older than those lads.

Monro nodded. "Thank you for volunteering your men to do these labors, colonel."

"It must be done," Parker said. "I just hope you'll think of us when it comes time to put them to use on the lake. Let Weber be your eyes in the forest. Let New Jersey be your eyes on the water. Many of my men have experience in the rough seas of the Atlantic." Colonel Parker pointed to Lake George with a thumb. "This glass will be like floating in a water tub for them. And I've spoken with Lieutenant Stark. We've sketched out a map together and I am prepared for every cove and point we might come across."

Monro nodded again. "Quit selling me your credentials, Parker. I don't care who we get out there. But we must have eyes on the enemy again. I don't trust this Montcalm of theirs. I'm told he arrived at Oswego last year with nary a warning. A specter, he is!"

From what I'd seen of the little French general, he was formidable indeed.

"And we are blind," Parker agreed, gazing northward. At that moment, a pair of enemy canoes lazily danced from east to west across the waters. They were careful to stay well out of cannon range.

"And impotent," Monro groused. The Scotsman looked around to make sure no one was eavesdropping. I pretended to be thoroughly engrossed with the children. "I've petitioned General Webb a dozen times for more men from Edward. We stand at the extent of the English frontier and the season for war is near upon us. This is when we should be fully prepared to reach out and attack or successfully receive one ourselves."

"His reason for not acquiescing, sir?" Parker asked, diplomatically. He had turned in disgust from the sight on the lake and peered up to Titcomb. There, with Major Eyre's help, Colonel Frye had begun the arduous task of making the provincial camp into something truly entrenched. Every colonial man who wasn't toiling at the shore was hauling baskets of dirt onto a steadily growing breastwork.

"Oh, a midden has more sense," Monro grumbled. Then he glanced sharply toward me. I diligently selected a proper stone for a boy aged four. As I turned away, I grinned broadly, glad that I wasn't the only man in America who thought that a dung heap employed more logic than Major General Daniel Webb. "Forgive me, colonel," Monro added. "He's our commander while Lord Loudoun has begun his descent upon Louisbourg. We owe the man the respect due his position."

"Frustration," Parker said congenially. "The frustration momentarily got the better of you, sir. Consider the matter closed."

"Thank you," Monro said with a formal bow. But when he raised his face, he showed a devilish grin. "Though the man in question can be quite witless, can he not?"

Parker smiled at his commander. "His sense is as fugacious as a fart in the wind." They shared a laugh. "Have you heard of Loudoun's progress?" Parker then asked as their mirth rattled to a stuttering halt.

Monro shook his head. "Not much. I only found out about his destination two weeks ago. Same as you. It was a well-kept secret."

Parker nodded. "I'm told that Loudoun's embargo on trade had much to do with that. No ships were permitted to leave the seaboard for months. Upset a good many of my countrymen in New Jersey."

"Yes," Monro said. "For the cause, I suppose. But Virginia's warehouses swim in tobacco while cod rots on Boston's wharfs." His heels clicked as he ambled up the dock toward the fort. Parker followed closely behind. "As to the rumors that came with the latest dispatches from Fort Edward, I'm told Loudoun got a late start for want of supplies."

Parker nodded. "A perennial problem."

"They did eventually make sail, however," Monro said as they began crunching over the shingle. "Now they sit in Halifax, waiting for the weather to clear. And you know how the navy insists on having the weather gauge."

"Aye, sir," Parker quipped. The pair then circled around west of the fort to check the progress of our gardens. Militiamen had been put to work in the fields. From the beach I could see their naked backs bent over as they tore out weeds. Those backs were tanned now that summer had come. The men of European descent had boiled to a nice copper color. The men whose ancestors had hailed from Africa had charred from brown to black. All of them wore a thick layer of sweat that glistened in the sun.

"Did you hear that, Ephraim?" Johnny Anson chirped as he launched a flat stone that got one, two, then three skips before sinking below the surface. "Loudoun is going to finally take the fight to the Frogs! Damn, that will be nice to see them get what's coming to them!"

"What about us?" I asked the boy.

He shrugged. "You saw what happened to the Frogs when they attacked this fort. Why, Major Eyre has made it in-pregnant."

"Impregnable," I said.

"Yes, that," he said without skipping a beat. "I swear, we've engineered this place to withstand anything. No one will set foot into it unless we invite them."

"You remember that Rigaud wasn't able to bring even one piece of artillery," I said. Another set of enemy canoes swept across the lake. I wished for Turnwell to take just one shot, just to see if he could shove some lead through them. The guns remained silent.

"So?" Johnny asked, as if an eighteen-pound ball of iron flying at you at unseen speeds was nothing to worry about.

"So," I huffed. "When Montcalm shows up and begins battering us with heavy guns. We'll need reinforcements. For all I hate them, British regulars know how to fight French regulars. Well, Loudoun has the best regulars with him. Near all of them on this continent. Monro was given the 35th Regiment. They just formed last year and are virgins when it comes to war. That leaves only the regulars at Fort Edward."

"Just fifteen or sixteen miles away. If we call, they can be here in less than a day," Johnny announced loudly.

I shook my head. "They won't come. They'll never come. I know this Webb. He'll never stick his neck out of his shell."

Johnny scoffed. "Who'll need them? The major's walls could take a beating for three days and three nights from whatever the Frogs bring and show nary a scratch."

I dropped the stones I carried and ambled to the fort to rejoin my rangers. Johnny Anson was a good lad. And for all his experience with death in his short life, he just didn't understand that Major Eyre's fort could not win a battle by itself. "I fear these walls might have to endure just such a beating, Johnny. And since we are blind and deaf in these woods, I fear they might have to take that beating sooner than later. Just when we are not prepared to receive it."

"Men from the woods!" shouted a sentry from the fort's nearest bastion. I froze and peered up at him. He pointed to the western woods, out past the glacis, gardens, and into a swamp.

Two men, appearing thin and sickly, waded knee deep in the stagnant green waters. They leaned on one another as crutches. If either one of them were taken away, the other would crumble below the surface.

A drummer from within the fort began playing and regular soldiers as well as provincials raced to and fro, reporting to the positions assigned to them for battle. "Come on," I told Johnny, hiking my Bess from where it leaned. "We'd best see the colonels safely into the fort."

Monro and Parker had not retreated in the face of the newcomers. Instead, they had walked further northwestward. They stood at the very edge of our gardens, peering at the ghostly men in the swamp and into the forest beyond. Nothing else stirred.

"We don't know what they're about, colonels," I warned, standing among a row of beans. "Could be meant to draw us out." I reached a hand to Monro.

He swatted me roughly. "I'm old!" he shouted. "But I am neither infirm nor feeble minded."

"At least advance to the rear of the garden, sirs," I suggested.

Parker and Monro exchanged glances and soon wordlessly walked back across the now workerless fields. The drumming had ceased. In its place, from both the provincial camp and the fort proper, officers' voices bellowed orders. "Anson," Colonel Monro growled as we walked. "Get inside. Have Major Eyre send out a company of men to be at my side."

Always eager to run, the boy shot off like flame from a muzzle.

And we parked ourselves close enough to the fort that we could disappear inside quickly if necessary. But the colonels weren't so close to the escape route as to appear frightened by the apparitions that slowly approached.

As many as five tense minutes passed. The pair of men stumbled through the swamp. They fell, both of their heads fully submerging before they came up spitting and gasping. None of us moved. A trick of the tribesmen was to release captives and then ambush those who would come to their aid. Or, they could be French deserters. Or, tribesmen themselves. They were so filthy and disheveled that it was impossible to tell. Or. Or. Or. We'd find out soon enough.

"Behind me," Monro said without turning as his guards arrived. "Shoulder arms. We don't need to panic." He craned up toward the battlements. "Any movement beyond them, private?" he asked the nearest man.

"No, sir, colonel," the man answered, cautiously staring into the forest with all his might.

The oncoming men fell onto their bellies at the swamp's edge. They laid there sprawled out for another minute, panting. One began to crawl, wobbling. Then the other. Soon, they used one another to climb to their feet. They entered the farthest garden and didn't seem to note or care about rows. Their path meandered, sometimes continuing between two ranks of peas for a fathom before they half-fell through one and, out of simplicity, maintained that direction.

One of the men began to weep aloud when they set foot on the gently sloping glacis. His sobs grew in volume the closer they came. He tried to call to us, but his voice was hoarse. He coughed with such fits that both of the newcomers tumbled yet again.

"I've not seen anything like this," Monro said. "Can a man truly be this ill and still able to move at all? It must be an act."

I squinted to the woods and saw nothing. Colonel Parker hollered up to the walls, asking if the men perched there could make heads or tails of what was going on. From all points of the compass, the eyeballs on the battlements reported that the coast was clear.

At last, the two men came near. I've said they were filthy. The soil itself is cleaner than were they. Layers of dirt and sweat and the-Lord-knows-what covered them from head to toe. They were nearly naked. One wore what looked like buckskin trousers. But both legs of the pants had been torn away. His shirt and jacket were long gone. If he had one rib showing through his skin, he had a hundred. A ratted beard grew wild in all directions. The other man wore the breeches of a soldier. At one time they'd been white. Now the tattered cloth was stained with grime and blood and a few other bodily fluids. His whiskers had grown in wiry. His long hair was stuck in his eyes and against his face.

The man in buckskins forced a grin and let go of his companion. He reached his arms out wide in greeting. "Ephraim!" he croaked as they both fell onto the packed earth.

Parker and Monro each looked at me. "You know these men?"

I shook my head. "They are strangers."

CHAPTER 36

A dead sentry here. A scalped ranger there. A vanished dog here. A captured scout there. Several more weeks went by. In that time, our ranging was forcibly shrunk into an ever-smaller circle around the fort. And in ones or twos, our garrison was winnowed down by invisible, bloody hands that hid among the trees.

Surely though, we weren't completely inept. Our depleted, yet active, rangers managed to hack off a little flesh from the enemy as they did the same to us. Those rangers and sentries brought in from the forest the occasional tribesman or Canadian prisoner over those long, summer days. In exchange for food and a quart of wine, these men always provided small bits of intelligence on the enemy. For it was a certainty that most men preferred pleasure to pain, food to hunger. And the image of a defiantly silent captive, be he white or red, was as much a myth as any concocted by the novelists and newspapermen from the east.

But, in truth, every clue or hint the prisoners offered had to be weighed against the likelihood that they were spies sent to misinform us. Therefore, it was the evidence provided by those two specters from the swamp that gave the garrison and its officers the most concern.

The man who'd worn the buckskins with missing pant legs was none other than Thomas Brown, the ranger taken during the battle on snowshoes. Even after he'd been bathed, fed, and shaved, I could not hope to recognize him. Thin to begin with, I believe he'd lost three stone. His flesh was puckered with poorly healing wounds as he lay in our infirmary. And as the man who was his closest friend, I sat stationed in a chair next to his bed.

"The Ottawa argued over me," Brown had said when he was again able to speak. It had taken many days of rations to get him to that point. Even so, his hands would tremble. Emotion would well up at the most unexpected moments. He would cry, falling silent for several minutes before he was able to continue. "One chief wanted to boil me outside Ticonderoga and share my flesh with his warriors. He even took the time to find an interpreter to make sure I understood his plans. Another chief planned to take me back to his village and enslave me." Again, he wept. "A young one got so angry during one disagreement over my fate that he drew his knife and began to scalp me." Brown lifted his bangs from his forehead and showed us a mean scar that had sliced clean through his widow's peak. "But still another warrior wanted to drag me to the French and sell me for as much rum as he could get. It was his greed that put a halt to my scalping."

"But Providence was watching me that day. Their scuffle brought attention from a Frenchman, a priest. He took pity on me," Brown said. "Father Roubaud. I'll never forget him. I wish I knew what he said to them. He yelled fiercely with a red face, waving arms, and balled fists. I think some of them thought he was mad. Eventually they gave up and left. That's when Roubaud knelt to where I cowered. He offered me a sip of claret before he took me inside the fort. I'd not be here if it weren't for him. I love that man." A torrential downpour of tears soaked his cheeks.

"What did you tell them, boy?" Monro asked gently. Several officers clogged the room to hear the tale. Lieutenants and captains were there. Majors and provincial colonels. Rows and rows of coats with shined buttons. "The Frenchmen inside Fort Carillon questioned you, no doubt."

Brown nodded, wiping away the mess. He sat up a little straighter. "I answered their questions, colonel. But I did my best to fib. I swore to them that we were four thousand men at Fort William Henry and twelve thousand at Edward. I said we grew stronger each day."

Monro chuckled. I patted Brown's hand for encouragement. Stark settled on his knee by the bed and set a hand on the bony shoulder of his ranger. "You really told them that?"

Brown nodded. He managed to screw up one side of his mouth in a proud smile.

Stark himself teared up. "As good a lie as any. If the Frogs believe it, that will give them pause." Stark glanced up at Monro. "We might be safe from attack, yet."

Monro looked wary. "How did you escape, lad?"

Brown shrugged. "Another sign of Providence. I was held in a storage room." He pointed to the bed next to him. "He managed to get away from where they held him. He found me at dusk. There was no moon. We slipped out before the gate was sealed for the night."

"Fine work," said the colonel. Monro then turned to the other escapee. "What about it, Mr. Baker? What did you tell the Frogs?"

The pair had been captured together and they'd escaped together. Robert Baker had been a member of the 44th Regiment when he'd volunteered to gather a little glory on Rogers' raid in the winter. Upon his return to William Henry, the only indication of his branch of service had been the tattered remains of his unit's breeches. The laundresses decided to burn them, saying there was nothing of the cloth worth salvaging.

"I don't know if they believed me or not," Baker said. He was a harder man that Brown. If he felt worry or fright at the memory of his ordeal, he hid it well. "I doubled the number in each garrison when I answered. I told Montcalm and Bougainville about our commanding artillery and ample supplies. I also said that Major Eyre planned to launch a surprise attack this year. Figured that I'd keep them guessing."

"Would that be true," Eyre lamented. "Could that be true?" he asked Monro.

The new commander shook his head. "Not until I know what we're facing. We can't go marching off into an infested jungle with no idea what awaits us."

"But it could help Lord Loudoun's assault on Louisbourg if the Frogs suddenly had to defend on two fronts," Eyre suggested.

Monro agreed. "Aye. But what do we face?"

Brown lifted a shriveled, weak hand. "I did my best to count during my stay, sirs." All eyes fell upon him in anticipation. "Near as I could tell, Montcalm has 8,000 men in and around Ticonderoga."

Monro gasped. Eyre murmured. Stark whistled. Frye, Parker, and a few other officers chattered.

Baker quickly agreed. "It could even be half again as many. And the regiments? All the best are represented, colonel. Their colors are proudly displayed all over the camps. La Reine.

Languedoc. Guyenne. Béarn. La Sarre. Royal Roussillon. Others. Not to mention troupe de terre and troupes de la marine and militia and Indians from a dozen tribes."

"Eight to twelve thousand?" Monro muttered. He looked at Major Eyre.

Eyre shook his head. "Those are the best-trained and best-equipped regiments in New France. No possible way for us to attack, sir. Even if we stole every one of Edward's men, we'd be swallowed up outside the walls before we let loose one cannon shot."

"And even if we brought the local Mohawk back into the Covenant Chain with us," I said. "The buggers would have us two-to-one."

"And Canada has had a couple bad harvests. The fact that Montcalm is willing to use his precious supplies to feed so many warriors right now means…" Stark began.

"An attack on William Henry is coming," Monro finished. The Scotsman scowled. "They could have even more warriors there by now." The colonel suddenly turned the discussion into an impromptu council of war. "Suggestions?" Monro asked his assembled officers.

"Clear fields of fire for the Titcomb camp," Eyre clipped efficiently. "Double the number of men assembling the hornwork. Petition Edward for more cannons and ammunition, immediately. Bring excess up from Albany if need be."

"Have Webb send more men to finish the boats as rapidly as possible," Parker said. "A hundred would go a long way. Even though we cannot control the forests just yet, if we can patrol the waters around the fort, we can prevent the French from landing artillery. Weber tells me there is no road to speak of between here and Ticonderoga. The water must be controlled."

"Have General Webb call up the militia," Colonel Frye offered. "New Hampshire, Massachusetts, and New York men could bolster our numbers."

Monro listened intently to all of their suggestions. He nodded approvingly. In some regards, I was forced to admit that he was not the ass I had initially thought him to be. "Others?" Monro asked, scanning the room.

"Sir," Turnwell spoke up.

"What, son?"

"We could use more brass guns, sir," the lieutenant said. "We have four, but they are smaller, 9-pounders. All our heavy cannons, including the two 32-pounders, are iron. I don't need to tell you what happens to iron barrels if we find ourselves in a real siege."

Monro understood. "I'll ask General Webb, but don't get your hopes up on that, lad. Everyone is more comfortable with a big brass in his bed."

"Thank you for passing the request on, colonel," Turnwell said in a formal tone.

"More?" Monro asked one last time, surveying his officers.

"Why not abandon the fort, sir?" Baker squeaked from his sickbed. "Fall back and fortify Edward?"

All eyes, including the whimpering Brown's, darted to the recovering soldier. Monro glowered. His speech became slow and harsh. "I'll choose to believe that such a cowardly idea is caused by the effects of your suffering, Mr. Baker. Don't ever suggest such a thing to me or to my officers again. If you utter those words to any man, woman, or child in the garrison, I shall bring you up on charges of cowardice in the face of the enemy. Do you understand?"

"I just thought that it might be safer…" Baker began.

Monro's face flushed red. His mouth contorted into a wretched, jagged line.

Baker blinked. "I do understand, sir. Not another word, colonel. Sorry, sir. I beg your pardon, sir."

"Not another word on it," Monro repeated through his teeth. Then he faced his audience, taking a moment to calm himself. "I'll give my decision on the morrow. Until then, perform as you've been, nay, better than you've been. Get the men humping. Build the breastwork around the camp. Get those boats in the water." After patting Brown on the head and glaring at Baker, the colonel marched out.

Just like that, the meeting was adjourned. Officers and men were suddenly ready to valiantly meet and thwart an enemy that was perhaps four times our strength.

But it might have been too late.

Baker's timorous lips had already flapped. And everyone knows the breeze that comes from a coward's mouth blows harder than any gale. You see, a pair of ensigns at the rear had heard Baker's craven idea. As they filed out, they babbled to one another about the odds we might be up against. Later that night, they prattled on again. This time they shared their worry with a few of the laundresses, who then fretted to their husbands, who whined to their mates, who muttered to the boys in camp, who squawked to Johnny, who told me that a full half of the camp and fort was apoplectic with worry over what was coming. Half the garrison wanted to go scrambling off to Webb and beg for his protection.

But you know my feelings about Webb. I'd sooner risk life and limb than plead with that man for anything.

And the French were more than willing to give me that chance.

CHAPTER 37

General Webb declined to send even a single extra soldier or worker. He called no militia. He forwarded no ammunition. He certainly felt no obligation to send extra cannons, brass or otherwise. He made no effort to reach out to the Indian Superintendent to recruit the Iroquois back into our fold. I suppose in some ways the constipated turd feared an attack in his own neck of the woods. Or, he was happy to know that doing nothing would allow him to risk nothing. Or, it might have bruised his English ego to allow a local Scottish colonel to house a greater number of guns than he brandished in his headquarters. Whatever the reasons, Webb remained an ass.

Nonetheless, Monro was faced with a choice that had bemused commanders before him and will likely continue to do so for eternity. How to utilize his precious few advantages to stave off myriad of threats. He might spread his resources over several tasks. Or, he could concentrate his efforts and finish one important assignment before moving on to the next. In the end, the choice was his and his alone, and based on incomplete intelligence and scarce labor. I am glad the decision was not mine. For, I cannot say, even with the benefit of years and the hindsight of knowing the exact result, what would have been better… or worse.

Monro shifted Frye's men, who'd been working diligently on the breastwork, to the shipbuilding beach. Better to prevent a landing altogether than have to fend one off that's already happened. To my mind, it seems as good a plan today as it did then.

With twice as many backs sawing planks from our supply of logs, shaping knees or strakes, and assembling everything from the bows to the transoms and rudders, out tiny armada was finally ready to make way. It was late July of 1757 that we finally left William Henry's wharf behind.

Two bay boats were propelled under sail. Given the haste of their construction and our limited number of experienced shipwrights, they were handsome crafts. Each was a double-masted, single-decked affair with room enough for more than thirty men and their supplies. Had we had any to spare, a pair of swivel guns would have looked keen upon each of their gunwales. But they were naked of any artillery.

A sweltering breeze brought swamp-like air up from the south and pushed the bay boats crisply, their prows cutting proudly through King George's newly reclaimed waters. Colonel Parker and his New Jersey Blues predominated in the sailboats, hauling the gaff, standing tall and balanced behind the planking like experienced seamen.

I, on the other hand, was stuck among the men, rangers, and other provincials. My seafaring craft of choice had always been a canoe, which suited my free spirit. On my knees I could single-handedly guide a canoe into a space as small as a penny. But rowing in time while facing backward with other inexperienced men? The joy of skipping in a birchbark was replaced with the drudgery of back breaking toil. I'd suddenly found my bottom glued to a thwart in one of our twenty new longboats. Parker's Blues had called the tubs whaleboats due to their shapes and sizes, though I doubted we'd find any whales in Lake George. I had said as much to Colonel Parker. He laughed and called me a landlubber.

Our expedition was dubbed a scout-in-force. But I'd never been on a scout with more than three hundred armed me. To me, we were a small army, capable of driving all but the largest foes away. We were clearly a strenuous effort from Monro to, not only see what was happening in the deep environs north of the fort, but firmly establish English supremacy on the water. That day, at least, we saw no Indian canoes brazenly gallivanting over the lake. Our flotilla had scared them away. And so, despite the heat and my awkward rowing, it was forming up to be a grand day.

"Did you hear that?" Brown asked. He was youthful back then and had recovered quickly. Since his return, he'd gained some twenty pounds. The only lingering effect from his imprisonment seemed to be an occasional twitching hand. Nonetheless, once the heroic lad was upright, he'd promptly volunteered to go a ranging. Stark and Monro happily acquiesced.

My back was hard at the oar, attempting to keep time with the other rangers when I perked my ears to hear what Brown was mumbling about. I heard creaking. The oar shaft eased back and forth atop the gunwale. I heard more creaking as the same shaft wedged against the fore or aft thole pins that created the oar stays. I heard loud slaps as the paddle blades were sloppily plunged into the lake's surface by novice seamen who were more suited to fighting on dry land. In the neighboring boat, I heard a pair of provincials hounding Baker for suggesting that we abandon the fort. Another pair defended his ideas.

"Mr. Weber!" shouted Colonel Parker from the nearest bay boat. The steady, but hot, wind had allowed their oars to be stowed. Other than several sets of eyes as lookouts, most of his Blues snoozed. The bay boats tacked rapidly, their pilots exhibiting much joy as they swooped about, to stay back in line with the rest of us. Parker's hair blew in the breeze and his tanned face was filled with delight. "You rangers row like women. Are you afflicted with a touch of the rheumatism?"

"And your Blues float as good as turds in a creek," I shouted, to the delight of my boat-mates. A New Jersey man who lounged next to Parker reached into a pouch. He pulled out a single lead shot and threw it at me over the waters. His aim was true. It pinged me in the temple.

Parker laughed. "Turds who can pinpoint a target." Their craft began slowly peeling away. "Eyes open," he called to his lookouts.

"No, Ephraim," Brown tried again. "That. Did you hear that?"

"You cluck like a hen," I scolded. "Of course, we're being watched from the shore. We've probably been seen by a hundred or more enemy. Good, I say. Let them scurry back to their rats' nest and inform the General Rat Montcalm that we mean business. I'd like to go one summer without seeing bodies pile up around me."

"Listen," Brown insisted, smacking my shoulder.

"Thomas Brown," I grumbled. "It's hot. We're not twenty minutes out. We've got a long day of rowing. Shut up."

"Ya," said Nero. He tugged on an oar in the bow of our boat. "Shut up, Brown. Are you trying to make us nervous like Baker over there?"

"No," Brown huffed. "I'm no coward."

"No one said you were," huffed Nero. He let out a big sigh as he rowed, shaking his head and scattering sweat onto us from the tips of his curly hair. "But I've got a question for you all. How can I freeze my ass off all winter? And not a mile from here, how can I nearly die, falling through ice?" he swore a time or two. "But a few months later, in the same exact place, I'm sweating so much my tits are as wet as a newly freshened cow's udder."

"I didn't know you had tits," said the man on the thwart directly aft of him. He lifted his oar from the water and spun to look. "I haven't seen an unmarried woman in a year. Show me those udders of yours."

We all stopped rowing and peered ahead to young Nero. Our boat's progress slowed. He loosened the thong that tied the top of his shirt and flashed his hairy chest, wiggling this way and that. He received a few hoots and hollers.

"Aw," I complained, stretching across the other men to him. I gripped his nipple and twisted hard. "I've seen bigger tits on a hare. Next time, don't get me all excited." He smacked my forehead with an open palm.

"Get rowing, boys," Stark said as his boat glided past. He reached out his oar and gently racked the Nero's shoulder.

We settled to our places, laughing.

"That!" Brown insisted before we resumed our noisy rowing. "Shh. Do you hear it now?"

I realized then that Brown wasn't panicking over nothing. I did hear something. "Wait. Wait," I said, grasping another ranger's oar before he could row. A heartbeat later, we all heard Brown's mysterious sound and craned our heads forward to listen.

A faint musket report, distant. Another musket report, feeble as could be, echoed. Then more and more, miniature cracks breaking the summer calm.

"Do you think it's the Frogs drilling?" Brown asked. He squinted to hear better.

I shook my head. "There's no order to it. That's a battle. Too sporadic to be some damned Frog regiment drilling."

"Camp Indians then?" someone suggested. "Celebrating liquor rations from the French?"

"Maybe," I guessed. The good Lord knows that I'd seen plenty of provincial soldiers spend a day's worth of ammunition just to rejoice over an extra drink of whisky. "No. That's a battle," I said firmly, setting my mind. "Lieutenant!"

Stark turned from his place at the tiller. With wide eyes, I pointed to my ear.

"Oars up," he barked. "Silence." His command was relayed from one boat to another. "Somebody's fighting," Stark said as we drifted together.

"Up around Ticonderoga," I said. There was an occasional cannon blast. Confused, we all looked at one another for answers.

"Can't be any of ours," Brown whispered. "We're the first men who've gotten this far from William Henry in months."

"Aye," answered Stark. "Can't be General Webb from Fort Edward. He'd have had to come through William Henry."

"And he's a coward," I added.

Stark frowned, but said nothing. "Could be provincials or militia from New Hampshire," he guessed. "They're always fighting over here."

I shook my head as Parker's bay boat skidded closer on its tack. "Don't think so, lieutenant. New Hampshire men are likely to shoot at New Yorkers or tribesmen over territory. But they'd never go up against a French fort."

"You and your rangers tired, Mr. Stark?" Colonel Parker jested.

Stark wiggled the lobe of his ear. "Somebody's fighting up a Ticonderoga."

Parker and his Blues leaned out over the gunwales, listening. Parker smiled. "Maybe we'll find her reduced when we get there."

"But who?" Brown asked.

"Mohawk?" I guessed. "We haven't seen hide nor hair of them all summer. And this is as much their hunting grounds as it is ours."

Stark agreed. "The Mohawk might be operating without approval from Onondaga. The Cayuga and the Tuscarora are far enough away and may not care. But I know the Mohawk have got to be lathered up over the foreign tribesmen marching all over their ancestral lands."

Colonel Parker pushed himself upright as his pilot again cut away. "It makes no difference what we hear. We need to prove that we own this lake. And I aim to lay eyes on our enemy so that Monro and Eyre know better what we face." He cheerily waved to us as they peeled westward.

We rangers sat still, bobbing and listening to the distant confrontation for another minute or so. Lieutenant Stark sighed. "The colonel is right. We've got nothing but echoes to report back on now. We've a job to do. Get your oars in the water and take us to that battle."

Only, it would come to us.

CHAPTER 38

All indications of the distant battle faded away after just fifteen minutes. The rest of that hot Saturday was spent tugging at the oar and watching the never-ending forest slip past on the shoreline. I saw no sign of man, but was confident that man's eyes observed our every move. Within a day or two the state of our progress would be conveyed all the way up to Montcalm. In time, a day or two after that, we all understood that the old general might mount some attack against us. Until then, there was nothing for us to do but press on.

Our anchors slipped below the surface and tugged against the silty bottom just before nightfall. We'd traveled relatively swiftly, having sailed past the mouth of Northwest Bay on the first day alone. Parker deemed camping on the land unsafe even for our great numbers. As such, ropes were then used to lash our crafts together in the center of the lake for stability as the sun set over the Western Wilderness. Our armada had made it to just south of one of the narrowest sections of Lake George and set about eating, drinking, and setting the watch. I ate a small loaf of bread that had been baked in the fort's ovens before we left. It was made from barley grown near Albany. The flour had given the bread a bitter taste so I assumed that their summer had been as warm and wet as ours. I wondered how Hannah and her children had fared since I'd seen them. A mood of melancholy set in.

"Your mouth was buttoned for the rest of the day," Stark whispered. He and I padded quietly over the deck of one of the bay boats while serving on the second watch. The two largest crafts had been placed on the outsides of our floating fortress to better protect the men should a stray canoe or bullet come from shore. "I've come to understand that means you are thinking." He peered into the darkness at the nearest, western shore as most of our cohorts snored behind us.

"Thinking about warm, soft bread… and women," I admitted.

The lieutenant chuckled. "Both can be delightful. The softer the better. But it's best not to think of such marvelous creatures when they are so very far away. Might take your mind from the task at hand."

"Thank Providence," I muttered, swatting a mosquito that had found the flesh of my neck a tasty snack.

Stark thought about it. "You've got a point there, Ephraim." He sighed wistfully. "I thought one day I'd farm. With Rachel Fookett."

I glanced at his grinning face. His mind was miles away. "Who's she?" I asked.

"Prey brought in by another hunter, I'm afraid," Stark said. "There's such a thing as taking too long, being too cautious while on the chase."

I laughed, quietly though sardonically. "I've never had that problem." My musket rested in my hands and in the crook of an elbow. "How old do you think I am, lieutenant?"

Just one of his shoulders went up. "Older than me, I guess. A score and eight?" he speculated. My body was lithe and small, wiry. But I'm sure my flesh, which was sprinkled with countless scars, appeared even older than his guess.

"Twenty-one. I know that by most measures I'm a pup just set loose on the world. But I've been on my own for, I don't know, fifteen years. Was married to a Miami girl, prettiest thing on this earth. Feisty. Could outwork all the men in her village except her father, the chief."

"Was?" Stark asked softly. "What happened?"

"She and the baby she carried were murdered at Pickawillany by a Frenchman," I said. I noticed that when I thought about it, there was still a sore spot deep down. But I could at last utter the words without breaking into tears.

"Sorry," he said. Then he mustered up one of those stupid things that all men say when they don't know what to say. "At least you had that short time with her."

"Hmmph," I muttered. "A short time is all I get. A few years later I was set to get married to a little girl from Williamsburg. She was feisty, too, but in a different way. I suppose I attract a certain type of woman. Anyway, one thing led to another and we had twins, a boy and a girl. Ephraim is being raised by my parents. The girl?" I shrugged. "A well-to-do family in Philadelphia is seeing after her. Heaven knows I can't take care of a grown woman, let alone a baby girl. I suppose it's all for the best."

"And their mother?" Stark asked. He rarely peeled his eyes from the shore, but he did take a moment to study my face. "She's unable to care for them?"

"Dead, like so many others. She was killed when the Western Delaware rose up after Braddock's defeat. I buried her myself, blood soaking my buckskins."

A long stretch of silence interceded on our conversation. Boats and ropes creaking against one other made the only series of sounds above the great hum of crickets from the forest. "You have lived a short, full life, Ephraim," Stark managed to say.

"Yep," I grunted. "Now you might have some idea why I'll not stop breathing until I kill every last Frenchman. And if any tribesman decides to ally with the Frogs, they'll find my steel cold and sharp in their bellies."

"Uh-huh," the lieutenant admitted. "I guess when you think of women, it only hones you in on your job rather than taking your mind away from it."

"Aye," I said. "Unless my mind drifts off to Hannah Wellbore. Then I think the same thoughts as any single man."

That lifted his spirits a little. "A long, lost, young love?"

"No," I said, leaning out over the gunwale. "In Albany. Twice a widow. A good ten years my senior with lots of little mouths to feed."

"Sounds like a real catch," Stark quipped.

I chuckled with him. "She is."

"Let me guess. She's feisty."

"Fierce and feisty," I whispered, squinting. "She once slammed her fist into my face. Laid me flat on my back." I pointed to shore. "I thought I saw movement. Just there."

Stark examined the pitch-black woods. "Did you deserve it?"

"Of course," I mumbled, before shedding the small talk. "There's a glint."

"I saw it, too," Stark said. "We figured we'd be watched. This is as far north as any Englishman has been since our raid to Lake Champlain over winter."

"Runners are probably headed to Ticonderoga as we speak."

"No doubt," Lieutenant Stark admitted. No attack came. We saw no more movement. He lazily ambled northward toward the bow to scan in another direction.

I wandered southward. "At least they can't get artillery down here fast enough to cause us any problems," I said over my shoulder.

"Uh-huh," Stark said, absentmindedly or filled with hope, I don't know which. And we continued our watch.

But cannons weren't the only possible danger in the vicinity.

CHAPTER 39

Soon enough, I slept like a corpse after the men of the third watch relieved us. Before shutting my eyes, I'd filled my belly with drink and a smattering of food. And there was something soothing about the rock of the whaleboat below and the evening breeze blowing across my skin as it came down the lake.

"Come on, Ephraim," Brown said, shaking me. "You already missed breakfast."

I grumbled a short string of curse words at him as I sat up, realizing that my spine was sore from spending a few hours wedged against the corner of a thwart.

"Take the oars, men," Stark called, filled with vigor. I blinked and saw that all the anchors had been weighed and the boats untied. They'd begun to bob away from one another. A dozen or so of Parker's Blues scurried about on his bay boats to make sail. "Make way to the foot of the lake."

Our longboat started inching northward. I felt nauseous. "What's wrong, Weber?" shouted Baker from the boat that bobbed at port. He was enjoying himself. "Too much rum last night?"

My head hurt. In truth, in addition to eating I had gambled a little with a man from New Hampshire after my watch. I remembered breaking into the rum stores at some point when the officers had all fallen asleep. But I didn't drink that much. My mouth tasted like dry rags. Perhaps, I had consumed a few too many mugs. My stomach chewed on itself. Alright. The fact is that I drank far too much. Even as we pulled away from our anchorage, I could see the discarded cask bobbing at the lake's surface. My bowels gurgled.

"No," I grumbled tersely. "I did not drink too much rum last night."

A few of the men laughed at me, knowing the truth. I think I lost a month of wages in a game of loo.

"It was your mother," I growled to Baker. "She paddled out to the canoe last night and kept me awake. Do you know how she ever got that flexible?" The men in the nearest three boats guffawed.

"You bastard!" Baker shouted, lifting his oar for a strike over the waters.

"Baker!" Stark barked. "Blade in the drink. Now. You, too, Weber."

Baker slammed the shaft of his oar between the thole pins and put his back to work while incessantly grousing. I rustled through my pack for breakfast. "Weber!" Stark warned. "If you want to drink spirits as to forget, you risk forgetting a meal. Put the sack down. Hands on the oar."

I went to work, grumbling about officers. This result seemed to cheer up Baker considerably.

We passed through the narrowest bottleneck of the lake. A fat, short peninsula stuck out from the west so that there was little more than half a mile separating it from the eastern shore. As such, the hills and trees still shaded much of our passageway from the crimson rising sun. It was actually a little chilly that morning and, despite my otherwise self-induced poor health, the rowing activity served to warm my muscles, if not my mind.

Parker's boat had skipped ten or twenty rods ahead of the main column of whaleboats. Meanwhile, its counterpart, the other bay boat, found itself momentarily trapped in our midst. The Blues that crewed the bigger craft swore at those of us who held them up. The rangers and other landlubbers from our longboats launched plenty of unholy oaths right back at them.

It was shaping up to be a fine morning.

"Aw, hell! It's Christmas," shouted a ranger. "A canoe full of savages seems to want to die today."

He faced southward, as did all the rowers. All I had to do was look up and see that he pointed at the tip of that fat, western peninsula. A long canoe, billowing with ten warriors, each splashed in paint, emerged from around the corner. Kneeling tall in the prow was a Potawatomi warrior with a large cross around his neck. His eyes seemed to pick me out among the hundreds of my companions. He and his kinsmen paddled fearlessly toward us.

"I hope they mean to surrender," Brown said, instantly remembering his last encounter with our tribal cousins.

"Unlikely," I said.

"Weber!" called Stark. "Use some of those language skills of yours. Warn them off!" A hundred muskets were already aimed at their rapidly approaching birchbark. "Even the tribesmen are not foolish enough to commit suicide on such a beautiful morning."

I spread my feet wide for balance and stood, dropping the grip of my oar against the leaky bottom of the boat. I then quickly plucked up my Bess and used her for further support, leaning her butt against the thwart. "Claude Sturgeon!" I shouted.

"Kestrel's Wing!" called the warrior. "I am overjoyed to see you today."

"And I, you," I proclaimed. "While it is not much sport, it shall do my heart good to watch you die with a hundred balls of lead peppering your chest. For, I saw that you took part in the murder of my friend, Amos Conwall."

He stood quickly, momentarily rocking his canoe. But he and the others were experienced and their progress did not slow. He gave his breast, which was decorated with a mixture of black ash and red clay, a single pound with the side of his fist. "The Mahican deserve cowards' deaths. Just like the English. I shall give it to them."

I turned to face Stark. "I guess they wish to die."

Stark was already nodding since Sturgeon's tone could not be misinterpreted. Then his eyes widened as he looked past me to the canoe. "Just like on land, boys!" he called, hefting his gun. "Pick good targets! Conserve ammunition!"

I spun to see what had suddenly caused Stark's alarm. Over Sturgeon's shoulder, fifty more canoes, all bristling with Indian and Canadian warriors veritably leapt from their hiding places on the concealed bank of the peninsula. With every passing second, they closed off any hope we might have of escaping via a southerly route. They were nimble. Oh, how I longed for a canoe beneath me rather than the tub with which I was stuck.

A great war whoop echoed. Yet, it did not come from the attackers on the lake. Even as musket balls began ripping at the flesh of men and wood of boats, I craned northward. At least twenty more enemy canoes had just launched from ahead. Already, Parker's Blues had begun a furious fire fight.

I felt the hot hiss of lead zip past my ear and crouched to a knee. Without thinking, the Bess was at my shoulder. I leveled her at the tall prow of the lead canoe, knowing that its thin skin would do nothing to stop the hurtling ball I'd send to Sturgeon. An instant later, the shot sliced a shallow gash in his arm and burrowed into the warrior behind him. Sturgeon beat his chest again and aimed his own musket in my direction. His counterstrike shattered the oar of the man next to me.

"Half of you row!" Stark screamed as he kept firing. "Take us to the eastern shore." He knew we were not marines. Our realm of war was the forest or, at least canoes. And if we wanted to survive the confrontation, we'd best even the field. "The other half of you, slow them down. Aim small!"

In a clunky fashion we began to advance toward the east. Whaleboat bumped into longboat. Oars tangled as half of our crews frantically loaded and fired as quickly as their hands could move. The second bay boat, the one that had been trapped among us, used its advantage of sail. It sped northward through us, scattering the smaller boats. It then immediately diverted on an arching course to the west, its pilot leaning heavily on the tiller. Spray sprinkled its New Jersey men as they knelt against the gunwale, sending and receiving gifts of burning musket balls.

Still, our foes closed. A pair of canoes had overtaken the slowest longboat, attacking it from either side. Warriors leapt aboard, hacking down the rangers one-by-one. The victors didn't even take time to claim their rightful war trophies. Instead, they abandoned the bobbing coffin and rejoined their canoes.

There were plenty of other men from whom to seize martial glory.

The sun, a big ball burning red and ominous, crested the trees. It and the hundreds, or thousands, of musket shot instantly warmed the air. My chest grew tight and I could have died from thirst. Still, unrelenting, I fired and reloaded. I don't know who in my boat set his back to the oars. I know only that we slowly crept eastward.

Our tubs were slow. But a canoe on the waves is swift as a hawk on the wing. Sturgeon gained. Other warriors gained. I saw Great River Mouth leaning out over the lake's surface. His massive arm ripped a tomahawk from the skull of a ranger after he'd just lodged it there. Another full boat of my friends, dead.

"Watch it!" Baker yelled from behind. He had been paddling manically. His craft rammed another, capsizing the second. A heartbeat later, I watched as the heads of the rangers and scouts emerged from the lake. A quick count told me they'd all survived. But none had managed to keep any guns. They splashed toward Baker's and a few other longboats. Baker used the blade of his oar to shove them away. "You'll put us in the lake, too. Stay back!" An instant later, he managed to row his boat safely out of their reach.

In the place of Baker's boat came Langlade's canoe. He and his Indians opened fire or launched spears at the helpless, treading Englishmen as if they were mere fish. Each of them was dead in seconds.

By now Parker's bay boat had spun around toward us. They were engaged in a running battle with the second company of enemy on their tail. Thankfully, despite a foul headwind, their experienced seamen managed to ably work the sails and keep the boat running on a close reach. Colonel Parker was waving to the captain of the other bay boat. He then cupped his hands over his mouth. "Keep going. Run through them!"

The captain waved his understanding and instructed the pilot to keep his new southerly course. Flecks and splinters erupted from the hull as they came under intense fire. Still, they plowed forward. And a second later, their bow crunched over a foe's canoe, sending its passengers diving away. The bay boat had been the first to escape through the bottleneck.

But we experienced little more success. I heard more firing. This time from between us and the eastern shore. Those damned canoes had beaten us to our goal. We were nearly encircled.

That is when Baker stood, shooting his empty hands in the air. "We're beat!" he shouted. His fellow crewmen would not argue. They knelt, balancing awkwardly on the floating boat, likewise surrendering. Then another boat surrendered. And another.

"Don't you give up," I hissed to my mates.

"Not a chance in hell," Brown huffed. He pulled with all his might against that oar. I dropped my Bess and joined him. We all did. Our boat skipped ahead of one that surrendered. "Come on!" Brown encouraged.

Stark's boat ceased returning fire as well. They all put their backs into it. Their feet shoved against the hull as they yanked those oars ever faster. The lieutenant's longboat slammed through a canoe, knocking it over. We followed the path he made. Some four other longboats chased after us.

The rest had surrendered.

And from my thwart, I had a bird's-eye view of the mercy they were shown. War clubs were hammered into the guts of unarmed men. Arrows puckered their buckskins. The butts of muskets cracked skulls. The crews of two boats abandoned their death trap, preferring to take their chances with swimming to shore. To a man, they were pursued and brutally killed below the gentle waves.

The prow of our boat struck the shore just as I watched Parker's big boat slip through the gauntlet toward safety. "You'll not fly away so easily!" taunted Sturgeon. His canoe had sliced a swath of death through our armada as he had never given up his chase of me. "I'll see Kestrel's Wing and his feathers clipped yet today."

There was no time for me to offer a snide remark. Instead, I snatched my gear and splashed into the dark forest with my comrades.

I'd been awake for a total of fifteen minutes.

CHAPTER 40

And within fifteen minutes more, we were captured and trussed. Though not all of us were so fortunate as to be merely bound.

The tribesmen and Canadians had a sunrise, lopsided victory to celebrate. Only a handful of their men had been harmed in any way. Our rum stores were immediately set upon as if it was the first sustenance seen by starving men in months. A massive bonfire was kindled. Drunk warriors danced around it. A few of the sober ones built three great spits. I watched as a comrade of mine was slipped onto each of the spits while still drawing breath. The three shrieked and screamed. Their cries only became louder as their skin bubbled, puckered, and roasted. It was a full five minutes, an eternity it seemed, for the last of them to fall silent. Two hours later, the tribes from the pays d'en haut, especially the Fox clan of the Menominee, ate heartily. Perhaps it is unnecessary to mention, but it was a grotesque sight to watch as men used their fingers to pull off the baked muscle of their fellow man.

Great River Mouth and his Mississauga beat two men to death. These, too, were drawn-out affairs. The captors would drink rum for a while, then sing, chant, or fight among themselves. After a while, they'd resume the beatings. It became a game at one point. The warriors bet who could land the most punches in a row without drawing blood from his own knuckles. When each of the attackers had sufficiently raw knuckles, that aspect of the game was abandoned. It morphed into something else, cutting without killing. Knife blades and hatchet heads dripped with rich blood. Soon, the game changed again. With each turn in the rules, the outcomes for their victims became worse and worse. And there was no Father Roubaud to save them.

"Who are you?" Langlade asked. He once again appeared to be in command, having avoided taking part in the worst of the debauchery while sending out patrols to protect his impromptu camp. I was tied to a tree by the neck and hands. Sturgeon, my official captor, had beaten me until I was woozy. Now my leg muscles faltered and the leather cords dug hard at my skin.

"King Louis XV of France," I sputtered.

Stark chuckled. He was similarly bound against a maple next to me so that we were part of a long line of captives. Thomas Brown was tied next to him. Brown's mind was frayed as he recalled the tortures of his first round of captivity. He whimpered. Many of the other battered prisoners did likewise. As far as I'd been able to count, a hundred of us had been killed, close to a hundred fifty had been captured, and fifty or sixty had escaped in the bay boats. Of all the disasters I'd been a part of over the years, Parker's scout stood out.

Langlade fixed the lieutenant with an icy stare. He brought his pair of pistols from his belt and pressed the muzzles through our pinched lips. The barrels rattled our teeth. "How do you like this, Louis?" he asked.

I offered a garbled answer. Langlade withdrew the piece. "Quoi?"

He'd cut the lining of my mouth. I tasted iron. "I said that I'm not really comfortable having a big rod thrust in my mouth like you Canadian sodomites."

Langlade flipped the pistol in his hand, grasping its short barrel. With a cocked arm, he raised it.

"Stop!" Sturgeon shouted. He marched over from where he'd been drinking with his clansmen to face the Canadian. "I gave you permission to question my slave. But I want him alive and untouched…" He grinned evilly and studied his own balled fist, which was emblazoned with cuts from his previous round of beating me. "Except by me, of course."

"You took a half dozen other prisoners," Langlade said, sliding the pistol from Stark's mouth. Both guns went to his belt.

"But *he* is my prize," Sturgeon answered, patting my cheek with his palm

"What makes him special?" Langlade asked.

Sturgeon acted as if he were offended. "This is Kestrel's Wing."

"Never heard of him," Langlade admitted. He examined me from head to foot. "Not much to speak of."

"I'm also called Weber," I growled, spitting blood with my words. "I'm Fierce Dog. Butcher of Frogs. Killer of Delaware. Friend to the Mohawk."

Langlade momentarily puzzled over my many monikers. Then he gave up and teased instead. "Perhaps not a friend of the Mohawk for long. Had they not attacked Fort Carillon yesterday, we never would have seen you!" He and Sturgeon shared a joyful laugh. "The only reason we were out in such force was to try to cut off their escape. That band of Mohawk got away." He threw up his hands, grinning. "But in so doing, they gave us a bigger prize… you."

Stark and I shared a sideways glance. "Good," bluffed the lieutenant. "I hope that party of Mohawk we sent slaughtered a thousand of you."

Langlade chuckled. "You didn't send them."

Lieutenant Stark growled. "Believe that if you will. But when our renewed Covenant Chain with the Mohawk and all the Iroquois bears its teeth, it will be you, not I, who is sorry."

The Canadian man's confidence slipped a degree. Though he regained it quickly. "If yesterday's assault proves to be the first-fruits of your Covenant Chain with Onondaga, I shall welcome it by the bushels. Your fearsome Mohawk raiding party managed to kill and scalp a grand total of two Frenchmen and wound two others. They successfully slipped away. But as I've said, they stirred up our beehive so that we could descend upon you." Langlade drew his knife while making a playful buzzing sound with his lips. He pricked Stark with the tip, then me. "And our stingers are sharp!"

Sturgeon didn't seem to mind. In fact, for the next several minutes, he joined the Canadian in taunting us. They poked at us with rigid fingers. They prodded us with elbows. For far too many times, the muzzles of guns were firmly pressed against our foreheads. And though Brown and the others were momentarily spared from any attacks, they whimpered all the more.

"Come now," Langlade said patiently. He smiled. It was not an uncomely grin. But all I could see was a Gallic-speaking monster. "Talk to me. One colonist to another. Tell me the truth about the fort and its garrison. Tell me about supplies and troop movements. Come now," he pleaded. "Help me and I'll gladly help you. Why, I promise that I'll buy you from Claude. I'll resell you to the French at Carillon. And you'll spend the rest of the war safely in Quebec or Montreal, eating and sleeping."

"No," Sturgeon and I both said at the same time.

Langlade shook his head. "Huh. You two agree on that. Must be made for each other."

"I'll tell you," croaked a prisoner's voice from down past Brown. I couldn't crane my head to see, but even though it was hoarse and filled with fright, I recognized it as coming from Baker. "I'll answer all your questions if you turn me over to the French. I'll not be a captive of the Indians again."

"Looks like you already are!" quipped Great River Mouth. He rested on fallen log with his elbows setting easily upon his knees. His fellow Mississauga laughed. Other nearby tribesmen joined in.

"No," insisted Baker. "I'll do whatever you ask. Just don't make me go with them. I'll guide you. I'll serve Montcalm. Please. Please. Please."

Through his own tears, Thomas Brown sniffed. "Shut up Robert! Don't do it."

Langlade gave me a last, derisive glance before he ambled down the line of prisoners to Baker. "But he already has done it, son. Once before. This will be his second round."

"You shut up!" Baker hissed.

Langlade made pouty lips. "Aw. Ashamed to admit that you told us everything we wanted to know during your last captivity?" Then his face flashed true astonishment. "I bet you were lauded for escaping. Perhaps even like a hero for sneaking away under the Frogs' noses. Frogs, right? La grenouille? That is what you call all of us?"

"What's he talking about, Robert?" Brown asked.

"Nothing. He's just telling tales."

"Test me," Langlade boasted. He then launched in to a detailed description of Fort William Henry both inside and out. The Canadian described things that only someone who had been garrisoned inside over the past winter could have known. He knew the schedules of watch. He knew the names of the officers from top to bottom. From Major Eyre to Lieutenant Turnwell. "Now, I'm sure my information is a tad stale. We've seen the small host of provincials encamped outside the walls. So, we could use an update if you'd be so kind, Mr. Baker."

"I thought we suffered together," Brown cried.

"Oh, don't be so hard on the man," Langlade tutted. "For those first several days you did. It was not until Père Roubaud brought you both inside Carillon that things swiftly changed. You ended up in a real bed, did you not, Robert?"

"Coward," Stark muttered.

"So be it," Baker declared. "Cut me loose and keep me from the clutches of the tribesmen. You'll get your information. I'll be your damned guide, if you wish."

CHAPTER 41

Three-quarters or more of the Indian and Canadian camp was fully inebriated by dusk. Our captors had eaten their fill of, well, us and snoozed wherever they'd fallen. The great bonfire had at last died down. Ribs and a trio of charred skulls rested in the embers below what remained of the spindly cooking spits.

Baker slept soundly, curled under a blanket provided to him by one of Langlade's fellow Canadians. He was in full view of every other prisoner and I believe our glares gave him enough guilt that he had to roll over and face away.

All afternoon he had chattered with Langlade. For his part, the Canadian proved his military acuteness by his questions, inquiring about approaches, higher ground within the provincial camp, weak portions of the growing breastwork, concerns that had ever been voiced by Monro. Baker answered in as much detail as he could for an enlisted man. He drew pictures, dictated numbers and artillery disposition to a second Canadian who could write. The three shared wine and bread. They ate from our stores of provisions that had been packed for our failed scout-in-force.

In my mind's eye, I murdered the bastard a hundred times over.

"Lieutenant Stark," came a whisper.

I must have fallen asleep, for the sound jarred me against my bonds. Being awake immediately returned me from my oblivious bliss. Every joint ached. My eyes burned and I could not do something as simple as rub them. My stomach was acid raw. The last nourishment I'd consumed had been loads of rum and a few bites of food during my unsavory gambling activities. I groaned.

"Shut up, Weber," rasped the voice. "You want to get us all killed?"

"Baker?" I asked.

"What do you want?" Stark asked him.

Baker flashed a knife in the dim light. "If I cut you loose, can you stand on your own?"

"Long enough to kill you," Stark said.

"I'm serious, lieutenant."

"So am I."

"Lieutenant. Think. I cut you loose and then you men sneak out of here to the boats."

Stark's eyes darted around the camp. All was quiet. "Where'd you get the knife?"

"The, uh, chefs left it by the fire," he answered sheepishly.

After one, quick, last glance at his surroundings, Stark nodded. He wobbled a time or two after the cords no longer held him up. Baker had to press a hand into the lieutenant's chest to steady him. "Cut the others free," he ordered, unsteadily pushing himself back against the tree trunk. "I need a moment."

Baker nodded. When our eyes met, I curled my lip at him, he at me. Nonetheless, he crept over and severed my bonds. Had he not supported me with his strength, I would have collapsed to the ground. "Don't give us away," he muttered in my ear.

"You already have," I hissed back. He left me wavering.

"Was this your plan all along?" Brown asked quietly as his thongs were cut.

Baker's guilty look said it all. "Let's just get out of here," he whispered. "You don't want to end up in the cook pot, do you?"

"No," Brown said firmly as Stark and I deftly plucked up our weapons. "Thank you, Robert."

"No time for that," Baker said, stepping toward the next captive. "You can thank me later."

"No, I can't," Brown rumbled. With snake-strike quickness, he stole the knife from Baker's grasp and rammed the tip between his ribs, up to the hilt. Baker opened his mouth in terror and offered a gurgling gasp before slumping to the ground. He roiled there for a full second. "Because you'll be dead."

The slight increase in noise stirred an Ottawa man who lounged nearby. With his arms crossed at his chest and leaning against a rock, he cracked open one eye, glanced at us, and promptly closed it. It took five more heartbeats for the image he'd glimpsed to be interpreted in his alcohol-infused mind.

The three of us who were free used that precious time. With three knives working, we cut away man after man.

"What?" asked the Ottawa in garbled speech. He crawled slowly to his knees.

Brown took a step to snuff him out.

"Leave him," Stark rasped. "Get this first batch to the boats. And watch for sentries. Kill them quietly."

Brown and the others obeyed quickly. After snatching what weapons they could from the nearest heap, Brown led a pack of six men to the shore. The drunk Ottawa warrior swooned. The next time I glanced over my shoulder, he was sprawled out over the ground flat on his face.

"Wait," Stark whispered as he cut. "We advance in packs to the canoes."

Cr-crack! Cr-crack! Blood-curdling screams. Brown's voice shouted. The sound of oars rattling against hulls or the sound of birchbark canoes skittering into the lake made a racket fit to wake the dead.

It worked.

The formerly dead warriors of the camp found themselves resurrected in that instant.

"Run, Lieutenant Stark. Go, Ephraim!" shouted some of the men who remained tied to trees.

"Don't leave without me," whispered the captive I'd just approached. Behind me in the camp, war whoops had begun to sound. Pattering feet raced toward us. A musket blast called its warning even as its projectile blasted into the collarbone of the man I was about to free. His crimson oozed, quickly covering his body like a death shroud.

"Time to go, Weber," Stark hissed. He'd spun and loosed one shot at the oncoming foe.

Those of us freed, sprinted toward the lake, burning past the rest of the prisoners. "God speed," I heard one man call. "Give 'em hell, lieutenant!" cheered another. But if I'm honest, most of them stood in silent reflection, perhaps jealous of our liberty, as they pondered the reprisals they were destined to suffer due to our escape.

Stark and I were no fools. We raced past the line of longboats and leapt over a brace of dead tribesmen who'd been guarding the fleet and into waiting canoes. Three men tumbled in with us. The others followed our lead, scrambling to shove the swift crafts into the water. We gathered energy, from where I know not, and plunged those paddles below the surface, willing the canoe forward. In just a second, our little boats were a yard, then a rod away from shore. In the faint, reflecting moonlight, we chased after Brown's set of canoes. They angled on a southward course toward the lake's center.

A spear hummed over the stern and buried its head into the back of the man kneeling in front of me. He crumpled, shrieking. "Lie still!" I shouted. "You'll tip us!" Still shouting, he managed to curl himself into a ball and merely quiver as the rest of us paddled.

Five or ten musket blasts followed us from shore. But none of the other boats put to sea.

"No!" growled Langlade as I heard a pursuit boat try to dip into the water. "Let them run to their nest. We have what we need and you have plenty of other trophies." The canoe rattled back up the shore. You could hear the disappointment in the way the tribesmen let it scrape loudly. "You have killed my new friend, Englishmen. I was just becoming fond of Monsieur Baker," called Langlade. I peered back and he stood with ankle-deep water lapping around him.

"Birds of a feather," I sang mockingly. "I'd expect cowards to flock together."

Langlade paid me no attention. "But I shall put his dear instruction to work. And his sacrifice will be avenged. Rest assured, King Louis, we will see one another soon. Very soon."

"Kestrel's Wing!" shouted Sturgeon. "I will again have my captive. We will make slaves of the Yankees."

"And dinner!" shrieked Great River Mouth. "We will feast on the hearts of the English!"

"Bon voyage," Langlade bid us in a most sickening tone.

We were sent off to the joyous, haunting calls of war whoops.

CHAPTER 42

The sun was high and sizzling by the time we arrived at the southern tip of Lake George. Whenever any day was in its prime, the activity at Fort William Henry was likewise to be found at its apex. But more than ever, the day after Parker's disastrous scout, men, as thick and bustling as carpenter ants, raced about with determination. Someone or something had lit a fire in their bellies. Every able-bodied Englishman or ally was hard at work.

Since I'd left on the scout, Eyre and Monro had decided to stack another three feet of stout timbers at the top of our walls. Slick, tired laborers and glistening beasts of burden lugged the logs from the forest across the desolate glacis. Draught horses and broad-chested men heaved on ropes that were strung over pulleys to draw the timbers up the bastions. Once at the top, young Johnny Anson was among those workers who leaned their pitiful weights against long, massive bars to help pry the logs into their final resting place.

Other sweating soldiers toiled with shovels at the shore, scooping up baskets full of sand. The baskets were stacked in wagons and then the wagons were hauled around and inside the fort's main gate. Nearby, workers demolished one of the outside sheds we'd just built to replace those that had been set to the torch in Rigaud's raid over the winter. The small barn's planks and rafters were thrown into the lake in order to deprive besieging foes from any extra cover. Similarly, a train of men, and even a few boys and women, carried armfuls of firewood from the fort. They traveled against the flow of wagons from the beach, unceremoniously plopping their cargo into the lake.

Atop the bastions, Turnwell and his fellow artillerymen ran through the grueling process of switching gun placement. I saw that every single one of the heaviest, fattest cannons now faced out over the lake. The northwest bastion especially bristled with a most terrifying array of iron.

Fully spent, we tumbled out of our canoes and plodded past the only two crafts that had survived the bloody ambush. Parker's two bay boats bobbed at the shingle. One of the sails was half-unfurled. It caused the boat to pull tightly against its ropes and continually bump against its small dock. Packs and supplies still sat piled up on its long, flat deck, an indication that the survivors had wasted no time in scurrying into the fort to report on the disaster.

Stark glanced at the untended vittles. "Empty the canoes," he ordered. "Once you have that gear stowed inside, come back out and unload everything of use from the bay boats. Brown, see it done."

Brown nodded. The rest of the weary men groaned, but made no other complaint.

"Weber, with me," Stark said. With a surprising burst of energy, he hiked up his weapons and marched to the east side of the fort. He quickly overtook a wagon full of sand, and then another. I ran after him.

A wagon that was heading down toward the beach pulled to a halt. "Ephraim Weber!" called the teamster. Itch was accompanied by Sarah Belle. Upon seeing me, she let a few joyous yips fly, pawing at her master with excitement. "The word spreads around these parts like wildfire. That you were among the dead."

"Sorry to disappoint you," I said.

"No disappointment!" he insisted, shaking his head so that his dilapidated hat flopped. Then Itch peered over the lake. "But you gave 'em hell, I imagine. Where are the rest of the survivors?"

"This is it," Stark said. He peered up at the pair. "You are a teamster from Fort Edward, aren't you?"

"Right you are," Itch assured him. "And so's my girl, here. Better companion than any wife. All she needs are scraps and a scratch and ol' Belle will be more devoted than a nun on Christmas."

Stark pointed to the frenetic activity that filled the clearing. The road was clogged with provincial workers who slogged at a blistering pace. They carried logs, branches, rocks, earth, planks, crates, and much more to enforce the humble breastwork that surrounded the encampment. Brass cannons were hauled into strategic places along the embrasures, in a concerted effort to make the low-rising Titcomb's Mount hazardous to the enemy. Frye's men and Parker's surviving Blues toiled together to fortify every spare section of the large camp outside the main fort's walls. "Have you and these other workers finally been sent to us from General Webb?"

"No, sir, lieutenant," Itch answered, apologizing. "I haul things from here to there. That's the extent of my abilities. It's mere happenstance that I and a few other drivers came on such a busy day. Sarah Belle and I brought in a load of salted pork. That Major Eyre of yours took one look at my cart and put me on this train. Back and forth. Sand inside. Junk outside." With a bony thumb he pointed to his wagon bed. It was filled with fractured beams, bent nails, shorn pegs, and split planks. "I'm to dump this in the lake and then return with a load of sand."

"Move it, teamster!" shouted a red-backed captain who trooped from the fort. His tone was as sharp as any whip that had been brandished by Pharaoh's Egyptians all those years ago.

"Of course, sire," Itch said, giving the man an insubordinate royal flourish. Then he clicked his tongue and snapped the reins. After moving ahead a mere foot, Itch hauled back and the beasts stopped. "Almost forgot, Ephraim." He reached beneath his hard seat and pulled out two folded letters. "Saw these sticking out of the mail back at Edward. Knew I was coming out here today and thought I'd be neighborly and see them to your hand. But then I heard you'd been killed. My! What a sad moment. Then I wondered, what does a man do with a dead man's mail? Glad I found you. Thought I might have to read it myself. Then I remembered I don't read so well."

"Come on, Weber," Stark barked. "We need to report what we know and get our backs into fortifying this place. I'm sure Colonel Monro can use every man he can find."

I reached up and snatched the letters, stuffing them into my shirt without so much as a glance. "Thanks, Itch. And you delivered my mail for Rogers?"

His reins snapped across the horse's backs. "Not a hitch was had," he assured me. "Rogers got your package." He gave a terse yank of his head toward the fort. "Better follow after the lieutenant there, boy. And make sure somebody lets me know when General Webb is ready to leave. I'll want to head back with his guard. Woods is dangerous these days. And I like my hair just where it sits."

Stark and I both stopped in our tracks. "Webb is here?" I asked.

Itch cackled. "Think I'm not sure who he is? I know him. I drove my little team down the portage road today and I was not ever more than three rods behind him."

Lieutenant Stark looked at me. "Better late than never," he said. "It'll be good to have his help, at least the extra manpower his personal escort brings." He turned and jogged toward the gate.

I followed him. But my legs, my Bess, and my heart suddenly weighed a thousand pounds. Somehow, Daniel Webb had weaseled his way back into my life.

CHAPTER 43

Except for the sick or injured, every single man, woman, child, or beast was busy. Stark and I found the parade ground of the fort filled with parties of workers running hither and yon. Sets of carpenters tore off shingles and rafters from the barracks and storage buildings inside. They threw debris into the wagons of teamsters visiting from Fort Edwards down below.

"Every item that is easily flammable and might remain unreachable during a siege!" Major Eyre calmly instructed the workers. He stood at the edge of a wall walk. Then he called to the nearest waiting driver. "See that everything is soaked in the lake."

"Yes, sir!" the idle teamster shouted from his seat.

Eyre pivoted, cupping his hands around his mouth. "Simeon. Jesse."

Two shirtless workers who had been feverishly loading the arms of men and women with firewood, paused, struggling to straighten their aching backs. "Yes, major?" called Simeon. He wiped a dirty arm across his dirty brow.

"How much longer until we can shift you and your train to other tasks?" Eyre asked.

Jesse glanced at the dwindling pile. "An hour, sir," he guessed.

"Good," Eyre stated. "Not a single piece of tinder or kindling is to be left inside these walls. We don't want to give the Frogs any help."

"No, sir," said Jesse. "Everything is being drenched in the lake."

"Fine. See me when you are done."

"Sir!" agreed Simeon. Then he and Jesse bent their backs to the assigned task. The train of human carts resumed its circular march. It was a shameful waste of a dozen racks of seasoned firewood. And if a siege came and if we survived it, there were two possible outcomes. We'd either have a lot of chopping and splitting to do this fall or a lot of damp firewood that would smoke awfully during the winter months. I suppose either of those was preferable to not surviving a siege.

"How deep?" called Eyre, pivoting in yet another direction. He faced down to those scrambling atop a magazine tucked beneath a casement. "Daniel! How deep is the sand?"

Daniel, a sergeant in the 35th, stood next to a wagon that was being unloaded of its baskets of sand. He inserted a long rod into an enormous heap of sand, marking the depth with pinched fingers. "We've covered it with another foot, sir," he said, reading the staff after it was pulled free.

Eyre glanced out over Lake George. "Montcalm may bring howitzers and mortars. I would if I was going to come all this way. Give me at least four more feet to protect our ammunition stores from exploding shells."

"Yes, sir," said the sergeant. "No aid to the enemy, sir."

Eyre's smart eyes scanned the rest of his lively work site. They fixed on us. "I saw your return in those canoes, Lieutenant Stark and Private Weber. Welcome back."

"It's good to be back, sir," Stark answered. "I'm sure Colonel Parker has already given his report."

"Indeed," Eyre said. "As soon as Colonel Monro and I heard it, we set about making these preparations. He and I expect a siege at any moment. And with our brief control of the lake all but evaporated, we cannot hope to prevent a landing. Our physical defenses must be exemplary."

"Aye, sir," Stark replied. "And where is the colonel? Ephraim and I have news to add."

Eyre pointed to the building that contained the headquarters. Its roof was already dismantled. "Colonel Monro is conferring with General Webb in there." Guarding the door was a small company of regulars from Fort Edward. They stood at solemn attention, a fixed set of points among the hustle and bustle.

"General Webb hurried here after the news of our dreadful scout. Do you think we'll finally get more men and guns?" I asked Major Eyre.

Eyre paused, choosing his words carefully. He suddenly looked like a Philadelphia attorney who was too smart for his own good. It was utterly out of character for the capable engineer. "I believe it is fair to say that the timing of the general's arrival was something of an accident. His visit might amount to an impromptu inspection. We'd already begun our efforts at strengthening our position in earnest."

"And the men and guns?" I pressed.

"General Webb is disposed favorably toward our position, I'm sure," Eyre said, stealing a glance down to Webb's soldiers. It was a chicken manure answer intended to convey little from a normally plain-spoken man.

But it expressed all Stark and I needed to know. "Come on, Ephraim. Leave the major alone. Maybe we can help explain the gravity of the situation to the general."

We tipped our hats to Eyre and crossed the yard. "Scouts with recent enemy contact to report immediately to General Webb and Colonel Monro," Stark said sternly to the ensign in charge of the company. In silent answer, the young man's eyes indicated we could pass through their ranks.

"I guess the tribesmen don't like the way you taste, Weber!" Lieutenant Turnwell called down from his terre-plein. Behind him, one of his mighty guns slowly made its trek from one bastion to another. A dozen men used ropes and pulleys to see its move completed. Turnwell, his uniform in perfect order with his black horse hair stock cinched tightly, grinned mightily, expecting a harsh comeback, I'm sure.

But despite my nature, I was unable to oblige. I could think only of those captives who were roasted above the bonfire. I pictured the way those Indian teeth tore at them during the drunken reverie. "A small blessing," I said. Turnwell frowned. And I followed Stark as he ducked inside.

"Saints alive!" Webb screamed when we entered the narrow hall. Despite the roof's removal, it was still dim because the upper floor served as a thick canopy, allowing only slices of sunlight to penetrate through its cracks. "This is what I'm talking about Monro!" The general stood in profile at the end of the hall. He faced into the fort commander's office. "Do you see! No, you can't see! Of course. Perhaps you'll never see! You drunk Scotsman!" He pointed down the hall to us. "Invaded by colonial scouts without so much as a warning or announcement. What type of place is this?"

My blood rose in hot anger. "It was your personal guard who let us in! Besides, we have news to report to the colonel." Stark stealthily stepped down hard on my toe to remind me of my place.

Webb squinted, finally recognizing me. "I knew we should have hanged you when given the chance! If only my dear friend, Prince William Augustus, had any idea that this is what his father's great army has come to... Why, he'd give me the authority to straighten it out! He was the Butcher of Culloden, you understand? Perhaps I should write him and ask that he join me in draining this army of its weakest blood! A nest of Jacobites! Saints alive! I'm leaving!"

"General!" Monro shouted from within as Webb plodded down the hall toward us. Stark and I pressed up against the walls to allow him to pass. "General Webb!" the colonel called as he raced into the hall. He was followed by Colonels Parker and Frye and a few more officers. "We need those troops we discussed."

Webb stopped right between Stark and I. He spun, his shoulders brushing our chests. "I'll send you the men you require! But I shouldn't. With how you and your predecessor have commanded this fort, it's a wonder it hasn't failed yet. Sloppiness! Eyre allows all of the buildings torched. And you? Look at this! I arrive and find men running around like fowl without their heads!"

"We are preparing for a possible siege, general," Monro explained. His face shone as brightly as his red coat in the dark hallway. It was clearly all he could do to hold his tongue from saying anything further.

I had no such control. "Major Eyre defended William Henry with expertise. I'm sure Colonel Monro and he will perform perfectly should another siege come our way."

"I wasn't talking to you, private!" Webb scolded. "What is this place? Does everyone think they have a say? This isn't a republic and you are no Roman senator. Perhaps I should inquire of the seamstress. Maybe she'll tell me how I ought to command. Or, maybe she has suggestions as to troop disposition or rations. Or, better yet, I'll ask one of those mulattos you have working out there. Or, one of the Indians you like to send out scouting so much. Or, the worst of the lot, perhaps I'll ask a colonial what he thinks. Saints alive! They all think they have a say. And you, Colonel Monro, you have fallen ill to the same malady that affects the rest. All summer, you write me letter after letter suggesting I call the militia. You ask for men and materiel. You ask for cannons, provisions, and ammunition. You ask for wagons and workers. Well, do you think I was just placed in this position because I am friends with the prince?"

That is exactly what I thought. I'm fairly confident that the same conclusion was dawning on Colonel Monro.

"Nay, sir! I am an experienced officer in His Majesty's service," Webb rambled on at a breakneck pace. He never paused to breathe so that his face was rapidly approaching the shade of his own coat. His blazing cheeks faced off against Monro's like lines of troops on a battlefield. "And I know what my men need! And I'll give it to them when I deem it necessary. I'll call the militia when I am ready."

"Do you think the militia just materializes?" Monro barked at his commanding officer. "Even in Mother England, it takes days for the men to assemble. And here? It takes weeks for men to move such great distances!"

"You'll not interrupt me, sir!" Webb shouted, avoiding any attempt to answer the question. The general panted, shooting silent missiles at the colonel. "Did you hear me? Did you? You'll not interrupt me!"

"I heard you, General Webb," Monro said, reverting to his most homespun Scottish brogue. "I'd never dare interrupt a proper Englishman again."

"Oh, my friend Prince Billy should have slaughtered every last one of you rebel Scots while he had the chance! Jacobites! The whole lot of them!"

"I'm no rebel Scot, sir!" Monro growled.

"And yet you rebel against my authority!" Webb roared. He turned and ripped open the door. "I'm leaving! Follow me." He plunged out between his company of regulars.

Monro grunted a slew of curse words under his breath, but dutifully chased after his commanding officer, skating between us.

Parker and Frye followed. Stark and I, wide-eyed, formed the butt of the train.

"Look at this!" Webb was shrieking. His hand swept here and there. "Chaos. Who can lead under such chaos? No one. But I am asked to do just that. For king and country! These men should be forming up and preparing to march out and meet the enemy should the French be foolish enough to arrive."

"We are told there are 8,000 enemy in the vicinity," Monro said. "We can field no more than 2,000 able bodies. Why would we do something as foolish as leave this fortress? Major Eyre has built us a solid defense. And all this activity you see is not for naught. Major Eyre and these two provincial colonels and their men work tirelessly to further strengthen William Henry. So, I ask you, general, why would we leave this refuge? Is it because you intend to swell our ranks with so many men?"

"I don't skip to your beat! It is you who must answer me when I ask you something," Webb barked. "You'll get men. But you'll do with them as you like. I suppose you'll put them to work like common slaves or provincials. I'll run Fort Edward. You run this mess." He faced the ensign of his guard company. "Form the column. You take the van. See my horse prepared immediately. I'll ride at the center." The ensign and his men marched off smartly toward the stables. The general then faced Monro. "You'll provide me with a company of men from your garrison. I come all this way only to find out the woods are filled with savages and Frenchmen!"

"We made you aware of the grave situation over these many weeks," Monro said as calmly as he could. His face shook as a teapot ready to blow.

"Excuses!" Webb claimed, as he strode off after his guard. "And you men!" the general called to the teamsters who had accompanied his train down the portage road. "I'll have you come with me. I don't want to be shorthanded should I be required to face the enemy."

"At least leave their wagons so that we may finish our preparations on a timely basis," Monro pleaded.

"The wagons belong to the king, as does everything! I am his representative in this godforsaken place. The men and the wagons go with me." Webb stamped his foot like a petulant child. "Speak up to me once more and you'll not have the men you so desire. Any questions?"

"No, sir," Monro said through gritted teeth.

Webb said nothing more. He tramped off to the assembling horses.

Colonel Monro cinched his mouth tightly. His silence was joined by the rest of ours. For, Webb had a way of ruining joyous times and making bad days worse.

"Colonel Monro?" Stark asked gently when Webb had already mounted his horse and trotted out the gate. His regulars had begun stripping the train of *Fort Edward's* wagons.

Monro swallowed. "It's good to have you back, lieutenant," he said quietly. "I feared I'd lost you."

"Thank you, sir," Stark said. "Many of our number were killed and taken captive. The Indians performed despicable acts."

"What are you waiting for Colonel Monro?" Webb shouted. He'd returned to the gate. His horse pranced and stomped, taking the cue for its emotions from those of its rider. "I want a company of your men to march at the rear of my column. Where are they? I see none assembling!"

"Pleased to provide them to you, sir!" Monro said with a tip of his hat and slight furrow in his shadowed brow. Webb harrumphed, snapping the tips of his reins against his beast's withers. Then he again cantered off.

"Colonel Frye," Monro muttered. "Give him a company of your Massachusetts men. Select those who aren't so exhausted that they are unable to carry a musket."

"Our progress on Titcomb will slow further," Frye warned.

Monro shook his head. "It can't be helped. Not when the king has sent his son's horse's ass to rule and ruin our theater of war."

Frye smiled sadly. "I'll see it done, colonel." Frye marched off to the encampment.

Monro sighed heavily and then walked to a set of stairs that took him to the wall walk. We ambled at his heels. "What else to report, lieutenant?" he asked Stark.

"Baker was captured," Stark began.

"The coward?"

"Yes. And he gave away every single bit of information he had. He drew maps. He listed our supplies, guns, ammunition, everything," Stark answered.

"I hope I see him one day," Monro hissed, tapping the hilt of his sword. "I'd like to use this to pin a medal to Baker's chest."

"Already done, sir," I said. "Before we escaped, Private Brown saw him properly rewarded for his treason."

Monro stopped us at the top of the step. He scanned over the scores of men scrambling about. A pair of tears welled in the colonel's eyes. "The general can go to hell. I'll take one Brown for a hundred Webbs. The general hides his cowardice and ignorance behind bluster. Brown admits his fear and dives headlong into danger anyway." He studied our faces. "Each one of you does the same. I'm proud of you."

"Thank you, sir," we said quietly, glancing away to allow Monro a chance to dry his eyes.

His countenance had firmed by the time I looked upon him again. Resolute, stood the old officer. "If I am to have a say in the matter, we shall not give up an inch of His Majesty's land. I'll fight tooth and nail. I'll not cease in prodding Webb to action. Damn the consequences. May I count on you? Are you with me?"

"Sir," we answered.

"Then Webb be damned. Get your backs to it and let's prepare to give any Frogs who are foolish enough to come this way a welcome they'll never forget."

"Aye, sir," we said in our various ways, all grinning.

We left the colonel, his arms clasped behind his back, watching over his men. He strolled atop the wall walk, pausing once to watch Webb's entourage disappear into the forest. What passed through his mind was no mystery.

I'd gone back and forth, once thinking Monro another ass wrapped in a red coat and on another occasion finding him capable. Perhaps he was one of those. Perhaps neither. Or both. I'm not sure. But at that moment it was clear he was an enemy of Webb. And that made him a friend of mine.

CHAPTER 44

Young bucks with no experience taking up arms often regale me with their tales of martial glory. They tell me what they expect to find when serving at the spear's tip in the army of the fields or navy of the seas. Cavalry charges. Sweeping maneuvers across rolling plains. Flawless execution. Brilliant volleys. Gallant stands. Swift turns about the enemy. Felling their masts. Prows plunging into giant valleys of waves. Prows bursting from the peaks of the next wave. Anything and everything. All of it very heroic. Those bucks go on and on, regurgitating the lies told them in women's novels and other mental smut. Then, inspired by such nonsense, they sign their marks on the recruiter's page. They're given a gun and little else. Then they find out what's what.

Labor. Work. Little sleep. Shoveling. Hauling. Dysentery. Lifting. Felling trees. Sawing logs (not the sleeping kind). Digging manure pits. Hunger. Rain. Mud. Snow. Rain. Mud. Mud. Mud. Heat. Humidity. Cleaning stables. Building walls. Tearing down walls. Lugging ammunition from one place to another and back again.

Those are the tasks that occupy a soldier's time more than any martial glory. Freezing while on guard duty. Boiling while on guard duty. Filling in pits. Weeding gardens. Those are things that a warrior does, even more than drilling.

And that is what we did for the next week. Major Eyre organized every task so that it was completed in the shortest time, with the smallest effort. He had made sure that the highest priorities were finished before he even contemplated taking on something less important. But by the evening of August second, the inhabitants of William Henry had done all we could and more. A barricade of stone, logs, and soil wrapped around the camp atop Titcomb. Six brass field pieces and four swivels watched over the encampment's walls. A modestly protected walkway led between the fort's gate and the camp's entrance. The corner bastions of William Henry were higher and stouter than ever. Our fields of fire were superb, not a pebble sat on the glacis or beach that could shelter the enemy. The French turds would have to construct their own cover. Anything flammable was long gone. Procedures were repeated again and again to make sure no soldier forgot his duty in the event of a siege.

Brown was tired and filthy. Anderson, Daniel, Simeon, and Jesse reeked of weeks-old sweat. Johnny Anson leaned against a brass piece, barely able to keep his lids open. All enlisted men wavered from the strenuous effort they'd expended over the previous days. Officers, too, hadn't been given much in the way of preferential treatment. Certainly, no proper British officer would remove his coat and toil in the mud. But Frye and Parker, Eyre and Turnwell and the others had stayed awake night and day as the various shifts of their men readied the fort.

I'd escaped none of the work. However, I now sat on the camp's freshly minted embankment, sipping from a tin canteen with the night sky and a million stars hovering overhead. And I know I was weary, for it was water I drank. I had neither the taste nor stomach for liquor. The unceasing drudgery had punched it clean out of me. I almost welcomed the coming of the French, if only to relieve me from my current misery.

Monro, surrounded by a ring of three torches, stood on the parapet of the southeast bastion. Except for the fatigued sentries who guarded our fortress and camp, every other man faced him. The encampment was crowded. The yard in the fort behind the colonel was packed with listeners. I expected a lackluster speech.

"Men of William Henry," Monro began as expected. "And even our followers, those hardy women and children who've toiled beside my warriors. I. I'm at a loss for words. I've served in His Majesty's army for my entire life and nothing could have prepared me for what I have witnessed since my arrival in this remote place. You have taken every hardship thrown up in your way and trampled them. Sieges, raids, ambushes, scalping, kidnapping, dwindling supplies, recalcitrant officers have been brushed aside." He paused, a single finger set upon his clean-shaven chin, thinking.

"I have no clever words of thanks to offer. And I'm unable to bestow upon any of you the rich rewards you deserve. I cannot even command rum to fill your cups from here to eternity." With a merry nature, the men booed. Monro chuckled with them. "I would if I could, lads and lasses. Now, some of you might know that I was born in Ireland. But my father was a Scotsman. And for those of you who have been raised far from the Mother Country, I'd like to inform you that a Scotsman can tell a tale. Even one so ill-practiced as I. Even the English seem to agree with us in that regard. So, I beg of you to grant me the time to share a story with you. It shan't be eloquent. But it comes from the heart."

"Once, there was a lad no bigger than a grasshopper on Monday. He met the sons of those who served on his father's lands. The youths became fast friends, though they had little time to spend together. The children of servants devoted their days to great toil. The son of a lord, he spent his time learning. Nonetheless, one day the cadre hatched a plan to escape for a bit of adventure. After the lordling stole handfuls of warm buns from the kitchens, they set off to cause a fair amount of trouble."

Monro's story halted as he laughed to himself. "They started in town, skulking behind an inn until it was safe for a pair of them to sneak in and steal more vittles. The lordling had his first taste of whisky that day. Burned his throat fiercely and he's not touched it since."

The men hissed, laughing. The colonel quieted them. "Don't judge him too harshly. He was just a pint back then. Today, he likes a good wine, mind you. Nonetheless, after peeping in the clothier's rear window where a scantily clad grandmother was measured for a new dress, the youths found themselves ready for a little more satisfying and harrowing adventure. It turned out that the lordling's nanny had often told him about the wisps and jacks that came to life in the fens. Well, it might come as no surprise that into the desolate bogs went those poor souls." As quick as a whip's crack, Monro's mirth fled and his throat seized. "Four lads entered the fenland that day. Only one came out."

"Within the hour, with legs scratched and shoes muddy, they fell in with a lone traveler who was gifted with gab. He told outlandish stories of far away lands and ladies that captivated their young imaginations. With no other plans, they accompanied him. Only he had been friendly just to lure the lordling to his fellow travelers. The lot of them were bandits, common highwaymen, who'd taken up using the bogs as hideouts. The gabby one had recognized the rich lad as the son of a prominent man in the county. He was seized and bound in their camp. The other lads, a little more world wise, got away."

"For two full days, the little lord was moved from one place to another to avoid capture should anyone come looking. The thieves fed him little. He listened as they bickered about what to do with him. One bandit wanted to kill him, then and there, to pay back the rich for centuries of oppression. But greed overpowered their desire for bloody justice or revenge. They decided to ransom him. By the third night of his kidnapping, he and his captors had fallen into a routine. He slept. They drank. When they were fully inebriated, a hand slapped over the boy's mouth. He awoke, startled and terrified. But there knelt his friends! Though it would have been the smartest and safest thing for them to do, they'd not run home. The lordling's bonds were cut and they were off."

"Who knows how exactly things happened from there? They'd not traveled a rod distant from the fire, when one of the captors stirred. He called a warning to his fellow highwaymen. That is when the lads heard the tell-tale cock of leveled pistols. Their voices bellowed. *Not another step!* The little lord froze. Not his friends. They grabbed his quaking arms and shoved him in front of them. *Run*, they told him. He did. A half dozen flintlocks sparked to life. Those friends, all three of them, were his shield." Monro gazed down at his feet, shaking his head in sorrow. "I never stopped running. Like the child I was, I cried all the way home. Those bandits never found me in the dark. The bodies of my friends were never discovered, probably weighted down with rocks and sunk into the bog. The highwaymen, perhaps evil specters all along, were never seen. They certainly never felt the justice they deserved."

A long silence ensued. Burning torches sputtered. Previously exhausted men and women gaped up at their commander, waiting to hear more.

A runner jogged along the portage road toward the main gate, just as a faint song of fifes and drums greeted us from further east along the road. Monro, transported to a regrettable past, again looked upon us. "For all these years, I have wondered, why? Why would the children of servants risk their lives for a boy who had already been given so much in his young life? And over these past weeks I have finally come to the conclusion. They shared a common purpose. And ultimately, the reason is you." He pointed out over the crowds. "You are the reason I was saved. I faced a formidable foe in those bogs. And my friends preserved my life. Well, tonight maybe, or perhaps tomorrow, we may face a terrible enemy of our own. The tribesmen might be our wights. The French and Canadians may be the ghosts who attack. Know this! I will give my life if it means preserving any of yours. And should I survive where others perish, I will count my life forfeit. I intend to give my all in order to save you fine, admirable men and women." He straightened his back, standing at attention. "God save the king," Monro roared. "And may God bless his great subjects in America."

We cheered for our commander as the runner from the road emerged on the parapet with Monro. The colonel bent his ear as the messenger whispered. Monro nodded and dismissed him.

"Do you hear the music?" the colonel called to us, tamping down our shouts with outstretched arms. "I guess even a general at Fort Edward can tire of a lowly colonel's many pleas. I've just been told that we are being supported with fresh regulars from the 60th Royal American Regiment. Should Montcalm be struck with the desire to visit these shores, he will find them most unwelcome!"

His speech was rewarded with dozens of huzzahs. As Monro waved and descended to the platform inside, men in the camp, with arms locked at the elbows, danced merrily to the tune of the approaching army. Provincial musicians became inspired. They quickly ran to their tents and retrieved instruments. One man had a Spanish guitar with just three strings. Three men had drums. Five or six had flutes. They formed a band, unpracticed, but loud and jolly. A barrel of rum was soon tapped and shared. I found that my appetite for such spirits had returned.

"I love the colonel!" Brown declared, downing his mug. "To think he's survived the same type of trials as me!"

I slapped his back. "The old goat's growing on me, too." And he was. Monro didn't make all the right decisions. But he made some correct ones. And his heart was with his men. He lived for them. It made me want to live for him. He had vowed to die for us. I wasn't quite ready to make such a bold commitment.

Over the din of the impromptu celebrations, I heard shouts from the fort. I couldn't decipher what was said. Nor did I care. I danced with the wife of a New Hampshire officer. She was round with child and carried a baby against her chest. Her husband sat on a pile of cannon shot. He clapped in time, singing and laughing.

But within moments of hearing those calls, the forts drums battered loudly, ominously calling us to order. The merriment rattled to a close. Officers raced about, running into the fort. Not three minutes later, they raced back out, running to their charges. On the wall, Turnwell trotted to his gunmen. In the encampment, Parker ran to his Blues. Frye to his Massachusetts volunteers. Stark jogged to us as I swigged the last of my rum.

"Sentries on the north wall see great fires on the western shore," Lieutenant Stark said. "A host. An army. Sounds like Montcalm has come at last."

It was funny, really. The news caused me no concern. I had long expected it and so when the enemy came, I accepted it as inevitable. Besides, I had just discovered that I served a commander who gave a shit.

"What does he want with the rangers?" Brown asked, tossing his empty mug into a heap of other dishes.

"Sit tight in the camp for now. Help Frye hold it should an assault come," Stark answered.

Parker's New Jersey Blues had begun jogging toward the camp entrance at the end near the fort. "Where are they going?" I asked.

"Colonel Parker has volunteered to take his men to the boats. They'll scout the enemy from the lake," said Stark.

"Brave," Brown said.

"Or stupid," I muttered as they raced down to the shingle.

"Brave," Stark said sternly. "And don't forget it!" His eyes lifted toward the portage road where the lead elements of our relief force had emerged from the trees. "And here comes a welcome sight."

With nothing better to do, we watched them stream in. The 60th was in the van, marching smartly and in time to the music. Four abreast they came. Row after row. I counted fifty rows, two hundred regulars. It was a fine start, even though they were redbacks. Next followed the Massachusetts men that had accompanied Webb on his journey back to Fort Edward. They appeared well-fed and carried large packs of extra supplies on their backs, another welcome sign.

Then the army ended.

"That's it?" Brown whispered. "Two hundred redcoats and the return of our own men? Is this a joke?"

Stark huffed. "If it is, it's not funny."

CHAPTER 45

Colonel Parker of New Jersey had been braver than he was capable. Never again did I lay eyes on his two bay boats or the men with whom he sailed out onto the lake that night. Parker himself might as well have vanished, or never existed at all. One moment he was there, cheering on his men as they hoisted the sails. The next moment he and his crews were eaten by the night.

"Anderson!" Stark barked. It was morning. He strode swiftly across the camp on Titcomb as we leaned against the northern embankment, gaping toward the lake. "Get to Colonel Monro! He's got a message for you to deliver to General Webb. It's a plea for assistance, no doubt, so I don't have to tell you how important it is that you live to deliver it."

"Sir," Anderson rumbled in assent. He sped off to headquarters.

Stark took Anderson's place in the line. "Look at it," he marveled.

"I've never seen nothing like it," Brown whispered.

I could only shake my head in agreement. Floating on the placid lake were fifty and two hundred bateaux. They rode low in the water, indicating just how much cargo they carried. Man and beast. Food and ammunition. Tools and guns. Cannons, mortars, howitzers. The scows that held the artillery were tied together to create a giant floating dock. At least sixty boats carried glistening brass or drab black field guns which were lined up and ready to be disembarked. Just outside Turnwell's cannon range, the French flotilla bobbed its way toward the western shore, where thousand of their comrades, having made the trek over land, were there to greet them.

Anderson jogged by on the portage road while stuffing a message inside his shirt. "Be smart," Stark encouraged. "Fast and hidden. Our lives depend on it."

"And mine," Anderson quipped. When he got to the eastern edge of the camp, he ducked off the road into the woods to take a more concealed route.

Our eyes were quickly drawn back to the city roving atop Lake George. Weaving in and out of the French fleet of flat-bottomed boats were Indian canoes. A hundred and a half of them, filled with warriors from every known tribe except those of the Iroquois and the smattering number of tribes still allied with the English. A few of the boldest Indians paddled southward, well into cannon range, guessing that we'd not waste precious ammunition on a lone canoe. And they had judged rightly. Turnwell stayed his guns while those particular tribesmen alternated standing or sitting in the canoes, waving hatchets or muskets and shouting words we could not hope to hear. But we didn't really need to hear their derision and defiance. The sole, deadly intent of their visit was clear.

"How many?" Brown asked.

Stark shrugged. "Looks like all of them."

Brown nodded. "That's about right. Every last one."

We watched. We waited.

An hour later, sporadic musket fire erupted from the western side of the fort as Indians peppered the parapet with lead. I peered up and saw Eyre on the walk directing William Henry's response. For now, the major seemed content to send only musket or rifle fire in reply, keeping Turnwell's leash tight. Those of us in the camp remained vigilant, but idle.

It's a strange thing, really. A man can be nearly bored out of his mind even knowing that a battle is nigh. His death might be seconds or minutes away, and he knows it. But something about survival or stupidity or ignorance or spite or willful blindness allows him to suppress that basest notion of panic. Crouching behind the wall, I played whist with a handful of my companions. We lied, hummed tunes, or stole from one another.

"Lieutenant Stark!" boomed Colonel Monro's voice. It was surprisingly close. I scooped up my cards and winnings.

We turned from the embankment and there he was, in the camp with lowly provincials. "Shouldn't you be in the fort, sir?" asked Stark.

Monro sighed. "I'll be where I must for the sake of this command, lieutenant." The colonel then pointed to a small table that a woman used for preparing meals. It was marred with knife marks, stained with blood from her butchery of game, and decorated with round char patterns from the bottom of heated pots.

"I need the desk, ma'am." He waved down a provincial captain who happened by. "Find me a pen and ink, lad."

A moment later, the firefight still rattling from the west, Monro sat at the small table on the camp's worn-down lawn, scratching out a missive. "I need someone swift and cunning, Stark. I'll be damned if I can't get my messages through to General Webb. I'm sending them at intervals. And Webb be damned if they all arrive and he still cannot find it in his heart to send more men. Our sentries figure we face seven thousand."

It was not the number of men that caused me concern. It was those cannons. One-by-one, over a third of the Frog artillery had disappeared from the scows and into the woods. It wouldn't take General Montcalm and his aide Bougainville long to see the siege works dug. From there… Well, from there, it was only a matter of time before our walls and bodies failed.

"Nero!" Stark yelled. "Nero!"

The sharpshooting ranger from New Hampshire trotted from his position on the wall. He was narrow-framed so that his torso was straight like an arrow's shaft.

"Lieutenant?" asked the freedman.

"The colonel needs your speed."

"I've heard you were a crack shot at the siege last winter," the colonel said. "But are you fast?"

Nero nodded, staring earnestly with those strange green eyes. "Like a hare, sir."

"Good," Monro said. He glanced up to the fort where a wounded man's screams echoed down to our peaceful site. The colonel grumbled under his breath, then returned his focus to the page, speaking the last of his words one by one as he scratched them out. "And so, General Webb, I make no doubt that you will soon send us reinforcements. Your servant, Lieutenant Colonel George Monro." He folded the note and watched as Nero stuffed it in his boot. "Like a summer breeze, lad," the colonel encouraged Nero as the latter leapt over the hornwork. We watched him as he raced across the road, through our pasture for grazing animals and onto a path entirely separate from the one Anderson had selected. "Thank you," Monro said to the woman as he returned her table. He'd stained the sleeves of his red coat black at the elbows from leaning on its damp surface.

"What goes on yonder, colonel?" Stark asked.

"The Frogs have spent a good deal of the day moving supplies. From the fort, we can see they remain concentrated along the western shore. Eyre and I concur that it will take some time for them to chop through the forest and excavate trenches and shooting platforms. But what is *some time*? A day? Two?" He craned his head toward the eastern end of Titcomb. "In the meantime, they may try an all-out assault or escalade right here. Swing far around us to the south and then cut us off from communications and provisions from Fort Edward."

"If any ever come, sir," I muttered.

No sooner had I spoken than the crack of muskets opened up from the woods at the south and east. Only a few lead balls smacked into our walls or tore through tents. But many hit their intended targets, with dull, sickening thuds.

Thankfully not a man or woman was hit in that initial barrage. But the pigs were. The cows were hit. Mercilessly, the Indians and Canadians shot all four-legged creatures meant to make our lives more enjoyable or in any way sustain us. Dogs, lolling through the meadows, were shot. A few cats and their kittens were dispatched. Hooved and clawed beasts alike were slaughtered. Horses that had grazed with our livestock were cut down.

Colonel Frye was itching. "Permission to drive the bastards off, sir," he said, rushing from where his Massachusetts regiment was stationed to the east.

The colonel gave it no deliberation. He nodded sharply. "Do it. In strength before they completely cut us off. And get what's left of your rangers in the fight, Stark," he said as Frye raced off to organize a company of his colonial warriors.

A moment later we'd assembled at the eastern edge of the encampment, ducking behind the wall. "Stay low. Move fast. We're Americans," Frye said, looking into the face of each one of us. "We fight like the Indians. Don't get separated. Don't stray from your kin. Listen for me. And don't chase after the buggers too far. They'll want to draw us out and kill us one at a time. Understand?" he asked.

His men nodded. The rangers nodded.

As a signal, Frye pointed a finger at the New Hampshire men who leaned against the wall, firearms at the ready. Instantly, in rolling bursts of twenty muskets, they fired. *Cr-crack! Cr-crack!* With the covering fire as strong as it would ever be, we scampered over the embankment and ran headlong toward the unseen enemy that ducked from the sizzling lead.

We advanced over clear ground. Ten steps. Then twenty. It was ominously silent. Then shrill war whoops and razor-sharp hatchets greeted us at the forest's edge. I felt a musket ball tear through the satchel that was slung over my shoulder. The angry Caughnawaga who had sent it my way, lunged from his hiding place, a spiked war club lifted. I spun and pressed the trigger of my Land Pattern just as his belly rammed into the muzzle. His progress halted as he flopped onto the barrel. I heaved him off, just as another bellowing warrior emerged from my left. One of my hands snatched the pistol from my belt. I sent the ball flying. It smacked into the brave's shoulder, instantly crushing his collarbone so that his arm slumped and he dropped his tomahawk. Nonetheless, fearless or crazed, on came the painted brave, crashing into me, his momentum knocking us both down.

We rolled. I'd let go of my spent guns. One of my hands had found his throat and I lifted him up and away from me. The fingers of my other hand had discovered his bullet wound. Without instruction, my thumb buried itself all the way to the second knuckled into his bleeding flesh. He shrieked, spitting, growling, cursing with bared teeth.

Over we rolled again. Now he was beneath me. I hammered my knee into his groin. With his good fist, he rapped my ribs then squeezed my wrist just as I began choking him. He gurgled, trying to turn his mouth toward my arm. His teeth chomped the air, attempting to bite me. Desperate now, the tribesman willed his damaged arm to attack. It clumsily slapped at my face then my chest. Eventually, it awkwardly struck my belt and weakly seized upon my knife.

He withdrew it.

Had he been strong in that hand, I would not be alive today.

I jerked away, releasing him with both hands. My fist clouted the hand on his injured side and the knife fell on his belly. His good hand reached for it. I got there first, tilting the point into his fluttering stomach. Then gripping the hilt with both hands, I leaned down with all my weight. The blade slipped in as if there was nothing there to resist it. The point didn't stop until it hit a stone in the earth behind him.

Still, he lived. His legs had ceased flailing. His arms, he slumped to the side and he tipped his head back, mouth agape. With eyes wide, staring up at the leaves in the canopy, he mumbled a chant. I dropped my lips to his ear. "You died well enough," I whispered. Then I yanked the knife sideways until the blade caught on his lowest rib. It took another ten seconds for him to breathe his last.

And I was up.

The mayhem had moved ten yards further into the forest. So, I took a moment to reload both my short and long arms before I ran ahead. I found Brown and Frye at the head of a group of ten men. Across a clearing and through a gnarled mass of vines, they exchanged fire with an equal number of Canadians.

Frye looked at the blood that covered my buff and green buckskins. "You alright?" he asked.

"Uh-huh," I nodded. "Not the other guy."

"Good," Frye said. He chopped his hand like a hatchet toward the road. "Stark is at the portage now with a dozen or so others. I aim to run to him and support him as we roll up their flank. Drive them south, so they have to flee west. Understand?"

We jerked our heads up and down once. "Go!" Frye said, clutching his blood-red sword and pistol. "Frye on your right!" he called as musket shots tore at bark and leaves all around us. The Massachusetts soldier directly in front of me had his knee blown off. He crumpled so that I had to leap over him. On we ran.

"Ready?" Stark asked when we'd fallen in next to him for just a heartbeat.

"Now!" Frye ordered.

Twenty and three of us ran a few paces on the road toward distant Fort Edward and then cut southward into the forest. Brown was the first man to see an enemy. He stepped to the side, dropped to his knee, and fired. A Canadian militiaman absorbed the musket ball with his temple. He was dead before he rested on the ground.

"Monro!" called Frye, sword raised.

It was a war chant I'd never think to call. Yet, when your heart is ramming behind your ribs and your neck pulses with energy, sometimes you do strange things. I admit it. I cried the name of a British officer that day as I charged the enemy's right flank. The only defense I offer is that it was my lungs and lips that pressed the air and formed the words. My mind had little to do with it.

We pattered to a halt and nearly all of us opened fire at once. More than twenty hurtling balls of terror sailed through the air, delivering just what one would expect – chaos, fear, and death. I do not know if my aim was true or not. But a baker's dozen Canadians and tribesmen fell with that volley.

"Advance," Frye hissed. "Again."

Before the enemy knew what was happening, we'd run in among their numbers. To our right, more of our company arrived at the same time, pinning our foes in a salient of our making. The fighting was brutal. Frye's sword sung. A few of the Massachusetts men employed their bayonets to lethal effect. After discharging my pistol again, I resorted to my tomahawk. The heavy head battered my enemy. It crushed a warrior's eye. It split another's nose. It loosed an Abenaki's bowels – from his person. So much killing. In the space of sixty seconds, crimson became the dominate hue in God's verdant forest. The handle of my hatchet became slick with blood.

"Enough," Frye called.

A dead man in buckskins lay sprawled at my feet. I panted, quickly studying my surroundings, recovering from the myopia that prevails in battle. I saw Brown and a host of others looking shocked and relieved. We'd lived. All of us had lived. And we'd driven the enemy back. Their commands and footfalls could be heard racing away.

"Search the Canadians for any correspondence that might be of value," Stark snapped. He sheathed his knife and then efficiently reloaded his gun.

"And then we get back to the encampment," Frye said, cleaning his blade off with a handful of leaves. "Gather the wounded." A set of privates raced off.

Meanwhile, like rat claws, our fingers scrambled in and out of enemy pockets. We riffled through trousers, caps, and the linings of coats. "Here's something," I announced, pulling a wadded piece of paper from what looked like a captain in the Canadian provincial troops.

"Stow it," Frye said. "We're leaving."

I stuffed it into my shirt and felt other letters already occupying the pocket. Confused, I tugged them out. They were the ones delivered by Itch the day of Webb's visit. I'd been so occupied with menial labor that I had forgotten they were even there, proof, I suppose, that my hygiene was less than ideal.

"Weber," Stark barked. Already the other men had begun trotting or limping back to camp.

The Canadian note and my letters went back to my inside pocket. I hiked my gear and stood, gliding through the scattered remains that littered the forest floor. Then I froze, finally seeing something that had been there all along. I spun and returned to what had been my position at the end of the battle.

"Ephraim," Stark hissed. "No time for trophies. Let's go."

"It's Anderson," I said, staring down at the dead body clad in buckskins. With pale, stale eyes, he glared up at me. His scalp was missing. In the place where his hair had been, he wore a glistening, tight cap of scarlet.

Lieutenant Stark hurried over. "He didn't make it far," he lamented.

"And neither did his message," I said. I bent down and took the page from his pocket so the truth of our desperation could not fall into enemy hands.

"Let's pray Nero had better luck," the lieutenant whispered, setting his hand on my shoulder.

We peered into the deep, untamed forest. We heard only the remains of the retreating enemy.

Thus ended our first *victory* in the siege of William Henry.

CHAPTER 46

Back on Titcomb, Frye had already reported our minor triumph to Monro. The colonel held his hand out, waving me closer with impatient fingers. "You have correspondence from the enemy?"

I reached into my shirt pocket and gave him the blood-stained letter. Monro glanced at the note and quickly furrowed his brow. "This is in my own hand. Where did you get it?"

"Oh, sorry sir," I said, tugging out the other page, careful to avoid giving him my personal mail. My nose pointed to the woods. "Anderson didn't make it but ten rods. It was a silent kill. Arrow wound and scalped. Whoever took his life had been careless and not bothered to search him."

"And your man Nero?" Monro asked, immediately concerned.

Stark shrugged. "No sign."

"It's a big forest," Monro grumbled as he unfolded the note I'd taken from the Canadian officer.

"Is it worthwhile?" I asked, peeping over the tilted page. It could have been a love letter from his fiancé back in Quebec. Or, it may have been a list of items to buy next time the Canadian was within a hundred miles of civilization. Soap. Vittles. Wine.

Monro nodded. "I believe it authentic. Maybe actionable. Colonel Frye, Lieutenant Stark, join me. We will meet in your tent, Frye."

The trio of men strode off for a petite war council. I patted my breast pocket, remembering that I had letters of my own. "Mind if I go freshen up?" I asked Brown.

Thomas leaned against our wall sipping from a shiny canteen that flashed in the sun. He eyed me. The blood spatter from my enemies was drying on my face. "You've looked worse and have never been one to launder yourself, Ephraim," Brown muttered. "But I'll not complain if you are turning over a new leaf and aim to be clean."

"We'll watch the Frogs for you," said another ranger.

Five minutes later, I had found a relatively quiet corner on bustling Titcomb. I sat on the packed ground, knees pulled to my chest while wedged between our tarped ammunition stores and several vegetable crates that officers had turned into houses for their dogs. Only now, the meandering dogs lay dead out in the pasture with the other animals. The tiny huts were a reminder to me of what our camp might become should we fail to hold it.

With dirty fingers, I tugged out the first folded page and broke the seal.

June 29, 1757

My son, My namesake,

It was how my father often began his letters to me, not that he had ever written much. Would I someday address my own son in such a way? Would I write to him? He was a mere babe and a stranger to me now. Would he always be a stranger? Likely. Would little Ephraim write to me? Why ever would he? If he did, what would he say? I brushed the thoughts away just as a discernable lull in the fighting on the western end of the fort slowly sunk in. The gaps between musket blasts stretched to five seconds, then ten or more.

Joy, son. It is with joy that I pen this to you today. I know you have chosen a path for your life that I'd have never wished. You've stepped away from our Society of Friends and embraced the solutions of this world which preach that violence is the ultimate end and arbiter of problems. It frightens me so to think of what you and those other men: French, English, and Indian do to one another in the name of patriotism or honor or glory or greed or avarice. But I need not go on. For while you and your companions deal in that currency of death, I have had the blessing, the great fortune, to take part in something that was truly renewing to the soul. The only coins with which we dealt were goodness, fairness, life, and peace.

The Easton Conference has now ended. I believe the results that spring from its well of inspiration will do more to end this terrible war than all the shooting and maiming you've done as you range the wilderness.

I scoffed then, tearing my eyes from the page. It was so much in my father's character to chastise, to correct, even from more than a hundred miles away. My temperature rose. I felt the blood rise in my chest and bubble into my head. He angered me so. It was why I'd run away at age ten. He was so righteous. And it always made me feel so sinful, so unable to hit even the widest mark.

But even I had to admit, the man who had been so cursed to be my father lived according to his beliefs. There was no double-mindedness, or two-tonguedness about it. That particular Ephraim Weber had a certain honor about him that most men would admire. Though perhaps not his son.

Would my own son ever see something to admire in me? How could he?

As citizen members of the delegation from Pennsylvania, Israel Pemberton and I were able to aid our brothers, the Eastern Delaware. Chief Teedyuscung represented the Delaware. Despite his near constant drunkenness, we secured much of what he had hoped for. The Iroquois, of course, sent many representatives. They were initially against Teedyuscung's aims. After all, they expect the Delaware people to be little more than their vassals at all times. The Penn Family descendants were there, as always advocating for the most beneficial terms of taxation and land ownership that tie back to their great ancestor, that first recipient of the generous grant of Penn's Woods from the then king. That Irishman trader, George Croghan, who initially took you in when you ran away, was in attendance. Upon learning my name, he exclaimed colorfully for a good long while. He remains very fond of you, though he stated often that he cannot understand why you ever left the employ of his lucrative business for the miserably destitute life of a soldier. Mr. Croghan served as the crown's Indian representative.

My reason for detailing all of these disparate parties was so that you might see that even with all the opposing objectives and viewpoints, determined, peace-loving men may come to pragmatic, beneficial solutions. No one got everything. Everyone got something.

The dreaded Walking Purchase will be reviewed by another acquaintance of yours, Sir William Johnson. He is fair, but partial to the Iroquois cause, I'm afraid. Nonetheless, this pleased many of the participants.

The government of Pennsylvania, represented by Governor Denny, will pay for towns, houses, and a trading post in the Wyoming Valley for the Eastern Delaware peoples. They need manufactured goods dearly. This will go a long way in providing for their needs.

Under the aegis of Onondaga, Chief Teedyuscung has signed his name to a formal peace agreement between his nation and Britain! His spirited grandson, Gideon Calf, too, supports peace. He returned to our area after being gone for some time last summer. I believe his journey helped the young man understand the importance of peace. Peace! The war may soon be over! Praise our Maker.

Who could argue with the notion of praising our Maker? No one with any sense, of course. And none of those things my father listed were bad. But neither were they, in and of themselves, capable of ending the war. The bloodlust of men on all sides had reached a full lather. I'll tell you, when a tired mare has spent her energy racing across the countryside and found herself soaked with foamy lather, the only way for her misery to end is death. It was the same with the War of the Two Tongues. Death, much of it, was to be the toll exacted before the conflict could end. The Western Delaware remained arrayed against Great Britain and her colonies. Hundreds of their warriors raided what was left of the frontier with impunity. And there was that little issue of the recalcitrant Frogs. My father's little conference in Easton made no mention of them, their intentions, or their king's pride.

So, perhaps I will see you soon, my son. Despite our differences, I long for your return. Your son grows. There are ivory white teeth in his mouth. He grins in a crooked sort of way.

His mother must have been a lovely woman, for when I do not see you in his face, there is something ever-so comely about him and his expressions. To a girl, your sisters Caroline, Eleanor, and Harriet dote on him. Tad and little Ephraim play more like brothers than uncle and nephew. Only Hiram and Frederick are too busy keeping up with the farm to pay Ephraim much attention, I'm afraid.

Before I close, I fear I must return to a topic from my last letter. I was decidedly vague then, but vow to simply state the facts, as raw as they are. Your mother no longer lives among us. She yet lives in the flesh. But her spirit is consumed by spirits. Drink has taken her more than ever. Her sorrow that was seeded at Trudie's death has only deepened over the years. The wife of my youth has discovered some twisted pleasure in wallowing in its misery. Unfortunately, she has found a fellow mourner who freely chooses to writhe and welter about in his misfortune. My Dottie has taken up residence in a lodge with Teedyuscung. I admit that writing the words is painful. Speaking them brings me to tears. Tears, son. They bring me nearly as much grief as when Trudie was taken from us far too early and when you ran away. Grief and sorrow define my lot. Nevertheless, Providence is good.

Trudie's death was a tragedy that ripples through our lives to this day. I know the pain from it built up in you for so long that five years later you ran. But you mustn't blame yourself. You were but a child, eating like a child with children's teeth and reasoning like a child with a child's mind.

I bid you well. Return home at your earliest convenience.

Your Decent Father
Ephraim Weber

Blame myself? Why would I do that? I hadn't killed my sister. But I know who had. And I knew that my parents and that rat, Teedyuscung, had pressed for forgiveness rather than justice. The culprit was at large, prancing and singing in the world while Trudie rotted in a cold grave.

The old man was right about one thing, though. The murder of Trudie, right before my eyes, still cast its shadowy effects in my life. It was why I had run away – not guilt, but anger. I couldn't look at those other members of my family as they went about their daily lives, as if there was not a huge void where happy Gertrude hadn't before existed.

I fiddled with the page and bowed my head, preferring to squeeze my eyes shut rather than let in the day's light. The dark behind my lids was fine company to the dark musings of my mind. I'm sure a tear, or two, fell as I thought about the siblings I'd already lost forever and the others, the younger ones, I'd never really get to know.

A man should take care of his family. My cuckold father seemed to have failed. I was already failing – had failed – time and again. Dead wives. Missing children. Grief and sorrow, they seemed to be everyone's lot.

"Private Weber!" It was Colonel Monro.

"He went to wash the blood off his face, colonel," Brown said. "Should be back shortly."

My shoulders sunk and I stuffed the letter into my pocket. Sorrow, anger, resentment. None of them had any place in that encampment. I spat in my palms and rubbed the spittle all over my face to clean a little of the grime off – and to hide the fact that I had wept.

"You called for me, sir?" I asked, jogging out from my hiding spot.

Monro, Stark, and Frye frowned. "I did," the colonel agreed.

"You need a lesson in washing," Frye said.

"That's just as clean as he gets," Stark said, smiling. "We've got a job for you, Ephraim."

Monro had already gathered up his erstwhile butcher table that he used as a desk. The pen and ink were soon had and a page produced.

"Running to Fort Edward with another message?" I guessed. The rattle of musket fire from the fort and her enemies suddenly halted entirely. We all looked in what had been the direction of the battle and saw nothing of note.

"Aye, lad," Monro said, soon writing with exemplar penmanship despite the speed with which the nib gamboled across the paper. "Lieutenant Stark says you are the best scout we have. Enterprising and adaptive. I fear we need that sort of fellow right now. That note you found on the Canadian was from Montcalm's aide to their militia and Indians. The dead man was a part of only the earliest force to make contact with us. The French are sending over two thousand men around and against this very camp. Anytime now." He paused, writing ever faster. "We do not know if either of our first two communications got through. It is imperative to try again. You must try again. And you must succeed. General Webb must be made aware of what is happening here and what will be inevitable if he does not act immediately."

The colonel then clamped his mouth shut and muttered to himself as he wrote.

"Godspeed, Ephraim," Brown said. "But you'll be fine. You're the best we've got."

"I know," I said with a wry smile. Though I didn't feel that much confidence. Two thousand enemy souls were a lot to avoid.

"I would therefore," Monro said, reading as he finished. "Be glad if the whole army was marched to us post haste before General Montcalm has a chance to dig his siege works and put our fortification to the test." The page was swiftly folded, sealed, and pressed into my hand. Monro stood, approaching me. "When you get there, General Webb will bluster to you, lad. He'll tell you that he's already done all he could. He'll tell you he's just called in the militia! The regulars he sent from the 60th reported this tidbit to me last night. As if calling the militia weeks late will do anything to help our situation here!" The colonel raised his arms out wide and then let them slap his thighs in frustration. "By the time the militia assembles in this remote place, this will all be over. I want you to inform the general what you've seen with your own eyes. We face an ungodly host. It is imperative that he dispatch his full army at once. Together, we may crush Montcalm between us."

"I'll tell the general, sir," I assured him. Stark then handed me a full canteen of water. I gave him my empty one. I accepted a few extra musket balls in my pouch and made sure I had a morsel or two to eat. The others formed a semi-circle, facing me. They each offered a manly nod of encouragement.

But when I set my hand on the embankment to scale it, I hesitated. It was not out of cowardice. I merely had a thought about men and families and responsibilities. I remembered a man who had entrusted the care of his son to me.

"Colonel Monro, sir?" I asked.

"Haste, boy," he encouraged. "We may only have a minute before our foes return in force."

"Aye, sir. Johnny Anson has come to know these parts very well, sir. He's young, fast, small. Sir, if you insist, I'll happily go to Edward. But I was thinking that if we can get Johnny out of this mess at his young age, it might be worth it. Send him to Fort Edward for safe keeping. He's not afraid of the enemy here. Though, let's be honest. He should be."

I awaited the flare of a British colonel's anger for questioning his command. I waited for Monro's face to redden and his Scottish roots to show plain. Instead, he turned to Stark. "You know the boy?"

"Well enough," Stark said, eyeing me. "If Weber says he's good in the woods, he's good."

"Fine," Monro huffed. He pointed to the central, rounded hump of Titcomb where the camp followers lived. "As it is, we shouldn't have to protect all these women and children. But men want their families around. Lord knows, I'd like to see my daughters again. But I'd never want them to be in the midst of such peril." The colonel's head bobbed as he became more confident in his decision. "Yes. And maybe Anson can find a way to carry our desperate message. Let's get this boy through the gauntlet and to safety so he can again see his parents."

I said nothing of the fact that both of Johnny's parents were already dead.

Five minutes later Johnny stood before us. Monro, agitated by the delay, plucked the message from my hand and gave it to the eager boy. The colonel then gave him the same speech he'd given me. When he finished, Johnny stood still and rose his right hand. "I do swear, colonel, solemnly. I swear! I swear. I will run the crookedest, fastest, hiddenest course ever set upon between here and Edward. Webb will get this message. Or, I'll die trying."

"Don't do that, son," Monro scolded as Johnny bounded over the wall. He ran jackrabbit quick across the portage road. He put a foot on the flank of a dead cow and leapt into the air, as happy as any lad out to play might be. But just as Monro and Stark began to voice a protest, the boy made himself small. He skulked around the fallen beasts almost entirely unseen. By the time he skittered into the forest, Johnny was a mere blur.

Two years earlier, Johnny Anson had used his innate tracking skills to locate where a band of Frenchmen, Indians, and Canadians had held a large band of our comrades as captives. His success then had led to a great victory and a very gory pond, made red with French blood. I was fairly certain that lightning could strike the same spot twice.

"I pray for the lad's success," Monro whispered.

"For his sake and ours," Brown mumbled.

"Colonel Monro!" called a voice.

Major Eyre and several attendants chased up the spine of the camp. "You've left the fort?" Monro asked, suddenly worried. We peered up at the ramparts to find that nothing was amiss. Smart sentries stood at the ready and under no duress. Their brilliant red coats remained untarnished. Behind them, atop a tall spruce pole at the fort's center, the Union Jack still flapped lazily in the breeze.

"Emissaries, sir," Eyre explained. "From the French. Under a red flag of truce. They've approached the fort and ask to speak with you. Shall I have them taken into your headquarters?"

Monro shook his head. "I'll not have one French turd set his grimy foot inside my fort!" He slammed his fist on his butcher's table. "Here. Bring them to me here. And they'll see where a British soldier holds court. With the blood of his supper under his arms!"

Eyre nodded crisply. He and his followers spun on their heels.

"You think they mean to surrender?" Brown asked. "After what we just gave them in the woods?" It was idiotic, but the young man tried. And he was fair with a gun and knife.

"No, son," Monro answered. "As bloody as it was, that was nothing. The battle is only now just about to begin. We'll exchange words instead of swords." He plopped down on his stool and waited for his guests.

CHAPTER 47

"Welcome," Monro said with a friendly, grandfatherly tone after the emissaries had been led to face him. The colonel played up his soiled, bloodied sleeves to the hilt, leaning back with crossed arms to show them off. It was a silent threat, implying that he was comfortable drawing blood from his enemies and then rolling in it. At the same time, he carried the professional air one would expect of a confident officer in the British army. "You've met Major Eyre. This is Colonel Frye. I am Lieutenant Colonel George Monro, commander of His Majesty's, King George II, forces at Fort William Henry. The rest of my command staff could not attend at such short notice, I'm afraid. Might I inquire of your names and the reason for your visit?"

A man in his late twenties with an impeccable, white uniform and chubby cheeks set his hand upon his breast and bowed with formal dignity. "I am Captain Louis-Antoine de Bougainville, aide-de-camp to my general, Montcalm." I had met Bougainville before, under similar circumstances, during the surrender of Fort Oswego to Montcalm. Though a Frog, I had found him to be honorable. He recognized me and we shared a dignified nod. In that flash of a second, he solemnly, wordlessly apologized for the heinous crimes committed by his allies after the hostilities in that prior engagement were to have ceased.

Bougainville then indicated the man standing at his side. "This is Lieutenant Charles Michel de Langlade of our troupes de terre." Langlade, too, recognized me from our more recent meeting. The look he gave Stark, Brown, and me was anything but hospitable. He had a bit of revenge on his mind.

"Such a small band of ambassadors?" Monro observed. He aimlessly patted one forearm with the opposite hand. "With so many wayward French and Indian soldiers, I thought your general would have sent more representatives, in case you became confused when we gave you directions. It's neither here nor there, I suppose. We will do all in our power so you might find your way to Fort Carillon." It was a tedious, though necessary, dance.

Captain Bougainville agreed. "Oui. Only the two of us. We originally considered sending a single representative from each of the forces arrayed around you today, but it was quite rightly pointed out that your small fort and encampment, even when taken together, could hardly hold us all. Dozens of tribes have provided His Most Christian Majesty with assistance against the unprovoked aggression of our British neighbors."

Monro smiled thinly. "I see. But let us agree, at least today, that it is the French who have set foot on lands controlled by the King of Great Britain."

Bougainville agreed with a half-hearted shrug. "Sometimes, during these types of conflicts, even the righteous must perform acts that he'd otherwise find distasteful." My sanguine opinion of him was waning.

"True. So very true," Monro lamented with a sing-song groan. "But we have an opportunity to forgo such atrocities here and now, do we not?"

"We do, colonel," Bougainville admitted brightly. "I'm so glad we see the inevitability of our situation so clearly and in the same light."

"I, too," Monro said brusquely. "Here are *our* terms of *your* surrender." He stared, unflinching, at the captain. "You will leave ten French officers behind. They will remain safe and sound in our custody until we have confirmation that every single man in your armies has retreated to Ticonderoga. One of those hostages will be released for every month we confirm that there is no further French incursion on Lake George or into our forests. None of you will engage in any conflict against King George's forces for a period of two years. You will abandon your artillery where it stands, save one field piece of your choosing. With it, and the rest of your host fully intact, you may march away, playing whatever gay tune you wish and flying those banners and colors that might lighten your hearts during the somber return home."

Monro's audacity had caught Bougainville by surprise. Yet, more than anything, the captain was a gentleman. He cleared his throat, while straightening his coat. "Thank you for being so well prepared, Colonel Monro. Rest assured, I shall convey your wishes to General Montcalm in their entirety. However, I must warn you that I have had the privilege of working with him for a long time. It is fair to assume he will not be disposed to agreeing to those terms."

Colonel Monro shrugged. "As you say, sometimes in war men are forced into actions that they might otherwise think unconscionable. For your sake and those of your comrades, I beg of you to take that as a warning, captain."

With a sweep of his hand, Monro then indicated the provincials who surrounded him. "These men are sharpshooters, sir. They hit what they aim at. I'm sure you've had the misfortune of seeing the damage a lead ball does to a man's innards." Brown beamed with pride while the colonel then pointed to the battlements. "And those men are the finest gunners in the world. With pinpoint accuracy, they can send two, hell, three shots a minute onto the cowering heads of any foe. Ask Rigaud. I believe he experienced just such a spanking when he mistakenly tried an escalade against our cannons last winter."

Captain Bougainville frowned thoughtfully. Then, as if uncertain, he glanced at Langlade, before he determined to speak his mind. "Colonel Monro. We've exchanged healthy barbs as is expected of men of our station. But I must be frank. And I hope you will take my words in the spirit they are intended. I abhor this war and all its grisly effects. Your man Weber knows that I am a member of your Royal Society of London. I would like nothing more than to once again sail to the fair shores of your Mother Country and engage in great academic discourse of a mathematical variety. I bear no ill will to you and your fellow Englishmen."

"I'm a Scot," Monro hissed.

"And your king's other subjects," Bougainville added diplomatically. "Please, sir. Reconsider. My general has sent me to convey a warning to you. There is no sinister, secret threat hidden in its words. We are 8,000 men, all capable of wielding a weapon of war. Each muzzle will be honed in on you and your fort, sir. You are terribly outnumbered and will soon be cut off. Please. Might we come to an agreement on terms? Surrender before any more blood is shed. Do so, and we will be better able to restrain our rather numerous, and oft times, murderous Indians. Do not, and well, colonel, I fear our ability to contain the actions of agitated warriors later will be severely curtailed, if not eliminated entirely."

Save his eyes, the colonel froze instantly. Monro blinked once. He blinked twice. Then he rose straight up from his stool, leaving his grubby arms folded for another half minute. He chose to hold his tongue. But it was clear to everyone, French or English, Canadian or American, that he was growing red with anger. Monro dropped his palms to his side, slowly clenching and unclenching them. "Captain Bougainville," he said calmly, his voice wavering or teetering on the precipice of rage. His teeth ground as he spoke. "Over the course of our brief encounter here today, I had marked you as one of those rare men who values truth and honor. A man who does not stoop to baseless, heedless, needless bickering, back-biting, or stabbing." The colonel scrunched his lips together in anger. They moved about over top his teeth as if they struggled to keep some terrible word or expression from unleashing itself on the world.

The index finger of Monro's hand then wagged vigorously, accusingly at the captain. "But you, sir, are the worst example of a Frenchman I have ever met! You are all the worst qualities I have ever seen in those goose-eaters. And if you have long represented this Montcalm, this general, this feckless, reckless, rash Frog officer, then that must mean that he, too, is a dreadful example of a military officer. He has none of the decency or integrity that one would consider ascribing to officers from Spain's corps all the way to Prussia's staff. You and your leader are wastes, sir. You tell him that! How dare you and this shit-eating Canadian come as guests into my fortifications and then threaten me and my men with massacre! Massacre! You tell me that should we fight and lose honestly and honorably, you will unleash your savages to cut the hair of our women? To tear off the arms of our children! How dare you, sir! How dare you. Surrender now, you say, or else your allies will pillage and rape! How dare you! It is the victor's role to protect the defeated. How dare you imply otherwise!" Monro clamped his hands on the table and tossed it over. It tumbled against Bougainville's white stockings, marring them with a hint of red. "Well, sir, you tell General Montcalm that when we prove victorious in this little encounter, we will make damn sure you are not abused in any manner. That our provincials and our Indians will treat you with the respect that is deserved of all fighting men. So, unless you yourselves stoop to some low cellar that would make such fair treatment unworthy, you may count on it. We intend to resist your efforts to the last extremity!" His face shook with rage. His collar had loosened. His gorget rattled. "Get these, these snakes, these rats, these French Pox-riddled beasts out of my sight." He spun, kicked the stool out of his way, and stormed into the heart of the camp where all eyes followed him.

After the requisite time of awkward silence passed, Major Eyre cleared his throat. "Captain Bougainville," he said crisply. "Do you and your guest require any sustenance before we see you safely returned to your camp?"

Bougainville glanced around at the officers and men glaring at him. "No. Thank you, Major Eyre. Please tell your colonel that he may have misconstrued my meaning. English is my second language."

Eyre used his hand to indicate the way they should take toward the gate. "I'll not convey that or anything else to him, captain. For we've all heard the tales of how well General Montcalm controls his armies. Some of us in this fort have lived the terror and butchery of Fort Oswego's surrender. Any goodwill you may have hoped to gain has vanished with your thinly veiled, unjustified threat. Shall we?" he asked, flipping his wrist to bid Bougainville and Langlade move.

"Mr. Weber?" Bougainville pleaded. "You know that neither the general nor I wished for Oswego."

I carefully set the butt of my Bess on the ground and leaned on her. "Yet a massacre is exactly what happened is it not?" I asked. "And then you come threatening the same thing again." I shook my head in worry. "You'd better hope you win, captain. Because if you don't, every Englishman within a day's ride will make sure they make the creeks run with French blood. And I'll be at the lead."

"Captain. Lieutenant," Eyre insisted. "Leave. Now."

The news of their threats had already zoomed throughout the camp. If stares filled with hatred could actually become daggers, those two foes would have been pierced ten thousand times as they marched toward the French lines.

CHAPTER 48

Several probing attacks materialized from the woods that evening. We'd begun to think that the correspondence I'd taken off the dead Canadian was incorrect or a bluff because the strikes were half-hearted affairs. I'm happy to report that Frye's encampment on Titcomb resisted ably. Not one of the enemy had set foot within a rod our muskets, field pieces, and swivels. By first light on the next morning, it seemed our foes had all but given up hope of rushing over our prickly walls.

Still, they lurked in the woods. We saw shadows and flashes as they darted from one cover to the next. Yet, a dozen or more Indians, French, and Canadians lay dead in the clearing between us and the forest, serving as reminders to their surviving allies as to what awaited them should they decide to venture forth once again. And with summer's heat coming, those bodies would soon become even more macabre warnings. By evenfall they'd plump and pucker. After another forty-eight hours, the reeking gases building up inside would cause them to burst.

Conversely, on the inside of our low embankment, our bodies remained intact and our spirits buoyed. Just one of our number had been wounded during the raids when a ricochet lodged in his shoulder. He'd been carried promptly into the fort's infirmary for treatment. Soon thereafter, a note to Frye from the physician said he'd extracted the lead ball and the fellow would live a full life. Even now, the patient likely sat up in his bed sipping tea and visiting with the women of the camp who often volunteered in the hospital. He didn't have it so bad.

Above him, past the thick timbers that protected the injured and sick soldiers in the infirmary, Turnwell's guns had roared to life. By the time the cock had crowed, hundreds of pounds of solid or exploding shells had been heaved onto French heads. It was a great, thunderous racket, awe inspiring and frightful. And since we wanted for a breeze, choking plumes of smoke billowed about, lingering, clinging to and hanging low over the fort. With each spent round, the cloud grew thicker and thicker, until it appeared that the sky had descended upon us, setting a fat haze over us like a heavy cloak.

"Do you know what is going on over there?" Brown asked. We'd rotated around the camp, guarding different sections of the wall at different times. Fortunately, I was able to stay with my rangers, who were becoming more like brothers to me with every passing day. They were the kind of brothers I liked to dislike and loved to abuse.

"How would I know?" I asked. "I've been stuck next to you all night. And its talk, talk, talk."

"Haven't heard any reports," Stark answered, giving me a quick, disappointed glance. He gnawed on a piece of tough, salted pork while peering into the southern woods.

"Sorry," I told Stark. "I didn't know we were in the business of answering stupid questions." I then wheeled from my position, cocking my head. "If you listen carefully when Brown isn't yapping, you can tell that the Frogs aren't answering Turnwell, yet."

"Likely haven't had time to set up any platforms or trenches," Stark surmised, shaking his head in mild disgust. I had a knack for exasperating others.

"Soon enough," I grunted. I reached over and stole the last slice of pork he had remaining. He'd just taken a bite and was drawing it away from his mouth. "I'm hungry," I said, stuffing the meat between my teeth.

Laughing, Stark reached two fingers past my lips and fought to grab hold of his breakfast. I swatted at his arm while nipping at his dirty hand.

Brown laughed. Then a lone musket blast from the woods rang out. A puff of dirt kicked up from the wall and pelted him with dust. Dirt splattered his eyes and he ducked away, falling to his knees.

All our heads stooped a little lower as Stark withdrew his arm. "You hit?" Stark asked.

"I don't know," Brown groaned, reaching for his canteen to wash out his eyes.

"You'd know it," I told him, grasping the pork between my front teeth and showing it off to Stark.

"Did anyone see where that came from?" Frye asked scrambling to our position.

"Just there," said a New Hampshire fellow who manned the nearest swivel.

"Then give them a taste of your grape!" Colonel Frye insisted. "I've already informed your fellow gunners. Four rounds, well placed. No more."

The gunner grinned. He and his small crew went to work. Soon their smoldering botefeux kissed the touch hole. *B-boom!* The edge of the forest was peppered with shot as the rest of our southern and eastern facing artillery opened up with salvos.

"Stark," said Frye, tugging Brown to his feet. "Colonel Monro wants to make it clear to the Frogs that it is dangerous for them to lurk about. It's our job to prevent a complete envelopment if we can." Monro had decided to stay in the camp for the time being. It was where the enemy had approached the closest and he'd taken over Frye's tent as his command post. Throughout the night I had heard and seen Monro striding fearlessly along the wall in full view of the enemy, daring them to shoot. They never had. And though most all of the soldiers he spoke to were lowly provincials, the red-backed colonel had nothing but encouragement upon his lips.

"Massachusetts is sallying out from the east end," Frye continued. "I don't want to be flanked. You take command of two hundred men along the south wall. Advance no more, no less than fifty yards and drive anything and everything you see away. We spring off after this man's fourth round. Rally back to Titcomb. Understand?"

B-boom! The second round of canister pelted the distant trees. Three brass field pieces added their noise and lead to the mix, decimating any living creature foolish enough to cower in the first ten feet of woodland. I heard more than one distant groan. Several curse words in the French or Algonquian tongues flared.

"Aye," answered Stark. Frye then marched to his Massachusetts fighters, preparing to jump. "You," Stark said, choosing a New Hampshire sergeant at random. "Find me forty volunteers. Be quick. We leave on my command." He then repeated that five more times, selecting a colonial private here, an ensign there.

B-boom!

"Stay together. Move as one. Don't get separated! On my mark," Stark shouted as his hastily arranged company settled along the wall.

B-boom! The last cannon blast from the camp echoed for three seconds.

"Now!" called Stark, his command exactly matching the timing of Frye's. Four hundred men clambered over the wall, shouting or grunting, as the case may be, for courage. Painted faces or white coats popped in our path from behind trees. The woods before us erupted with musket fire, clumps of smoke swelling around the clusters of troops who had ducked from our initial barrage. A dull thud announced that a nearby New Hampshire man was hit. He gasped. I heard his musket clatter to the ground as he tumbled. Onward, we advanced.

After their first volley, the enemy did not attempt to hold us off. They jumped to their feet and ran. We shot the slowest ones in the back. The next slowest ones, we caught up to in the woods, cutting them down with hatchets, bayonets, or knives. Next to me, Stark peered over his shoulder. The camp we'd just vacated was barely visible through the brush. "Keep pressing them!" he encouraged, reloading his piece. Our small cadre of rangers did likewise. "Move ahead orderly!" Stark screamed angrily when some of the men broke from our skirmish line and chased after a lone foe here or there.

It had happened before. It would happen again. When men of all stripes found momentum on their side as they'd begun to kill the enemy with ease, they no longer thought. They were simply incapable of thinking rationally or cautiously. On the contrary, it was only repetition, drilling, punishment, and much shouting that could get them to break off from the scent of freshly spilled blood. Though they were hardy mountain men and all-around solid companions, our New Hampshire brethren had endured little in the way of training or experience. On they raced, shooting the odd Frenchman, hacking the isolated tribesman.

Stark growled a string of incomprehensible curses. "After them!" he barked to those of us left in the skirmish line, perhaps half of his two hundred. "Stick together. Reel them in."

Crouching, we jogged ahead among the virgin forest. Along with the New Hampshire zealots, the shooting and stabbing and punching sounds of our small skirmish had moved ahead of our position. We stepped over the scattered enemy soldiers we'd already killed or wounded. "Over there," Brown said, pointing to the southeast. A huge racket had erupted.

"Frye will have to take care of that," Stark muttered of the unseen threat. "We have one job. Retrieve our men. Forward."

We shuffled swiftly over the level terrain. I knew the forest well there. For the most part, tall, rounded mountains and hills grew up from the shores of Lake George. But at the southern tip where Fort William Henry lay, there was a broad, flattish plain. Even with the trees, our visibility was clear. We were fairly confident in our ability to retreat safely to Titcomb just as we passed through Frye's limit of fifty yards, then sixty, then seventy. The clatter and screaming of intense, personal combat grew louder. The New Hampshire provincials had stirred up some trouble.

Stark's hand went up. He dropped to a knee and, in a ragged line, we followed suit, leveling our guns. Another twenty yards ahead we saw that the enemy had regrouped and turned back upon their pursuers. Our New Hampshire comrades were being cut down from two sides. Only a handful had wizened to their predicament and escaped. "Hold your fire! Don't shoot them!" Stark barked as the frightened New Hampshire men hurtled toward us. Frustrated, he slapped the butt of his musket against the dirt. "Get them back in line!" They were promptly tackled and roughly slapped into place.

A smattering of the enemy had noted our presence, but their slaughter continued unabated. "They'll turn on us when they're done," I warned Stark.

"Not if we run now," Brown said.

"Can't do that," Stark grumbled. "And we can't shoot at them without killing our own. Fix bayonets if you've got 'em!" he shouted. There was clattering up and down our line. Men without bayonets abandoned their muskets in the dirt and yanked free knives or tomahawks. "Up! Forward! March!"

It was the farthest twenty yards I had ever walked. Stark shouted the entire way, screaming for us to draw in tighter. "One chance!" he warned. "Break them. Gather our friends and advance to camp!" I stepped around a tree that had come in my path. "Get your ass against me, Weber!" Stark bellowed. I cinched next to him.

"Miss me?" I asked.

"Not the time, Ephraim," he growled. Five yards separated us from the talons of our foe. Still, the enemy had begun to suffer from their own case of bloodlust. They drained those poor, surrounded New Hampshire fellows with ease. Only one, then six, then twenty truly noted our arrival by preparing to receive us. And despite their vigilance, they died, poked by our long-shanked socket blades, cleaved by hatchets.

That is when it turned into an ugly business. Hundreds of men, of varying races and sides, found themselves pressed together in chaotic carnage. A man fell against my arm. I swept him off, stabbing him in the chest before I looked. I cannot say whether he was friend or foe. On came another, crimson splattered on his face. With a vicious backhanded swing, the rear of my ax head dislodged a half score of his teeth. He slipped down out of view.

Suddenly Langlade was upon me. From where he'd sprung, I cannot say. On my back now, I peered up into his deadly intense eyes. I'd dropped my tomahawk and, with both hands, held his cocked hand at arm's length. He held a dripping blade. We shook and struggled. His other hand had formed a fist. It felt like iron as it rained down upon my snout. I saw a flashing light with every strike. He was stronger than he looked. And he knew his way around a scrap. He was every bit as resourceful as me. Perhaps more so.

Langlade's knee found my groin. A sudden bout of weakness shivered from by guts to my head. His knife drove to within a hand's breadth from my chin. He drew back his knee again. One more blow would bring about my demise.

With my left hand, I shoved his knife-wielding hand over my head. My right hand dropped to my belt and I tugged free that inaccurate, ornate, perhaps life-saving, French pistol. But

Langlade was swift, and good. He diverted his knee from by groin to the cocked gun. They connected just as my swooning mind willed my finger to squeeze the trigger. The pistol jerked. But it fired.

I was blinded by the pan and muzzle flashes an inch or two from my face. My ears hummed. But Langlade's weight was no longer pressing down upon me. I rolled to the side and snatched up my hatchet. By the time I was on my knees, I saw that Langlade was staggering into a coalescing body of his men. When he peeked back at me, I saw his face was mottled black from burst powder and one ear dripped blood.

"Carry the living!" Stark yelled. An even greater din had erupted. I'd heard it before. I've described it before. It was a tribal war whoop, amplified by thousands of synchronous voices. Normally shrill enough to make your hairs stand on end and your arms sprout goose bumps, my momentary deaf condition had turned the calls into rolling, booming, thunderous chants. "We'll have to leave the dead."

Rubbing my eyes, I stood, wobbling. My head rung. I couldn't tell from which direction the reinforced enemy came. I saw only that we'd successfully driven them off from our immediate position. "Here, Weber," Stark said. He'd come with a wounded man's arm slung over his shoulder. "Put him on your back." I bent obediently and when the lieutenant tossed him against me, I seized the man's leg and hoisted myself upright. Stark forcibly spun me around. "That way. Just keep walking. We'll get the rest." After I weakly crouched to retrieve my musket, I had to concentrate to place one foot in front of the other. Stark, carrying a man of his own, prodded me from behind. "Move. Faster." My muddled mind swam.

There were others in a similar state. Rescuers and wounded alike moaned as we retreated. Many had to lug injured cargo. Eventually, we staggered to camp. We handed the suffering over the wall first. There, the Massachusetts men, who had already returned, carried them and began hustling them to the camp's impromptu field hospital. There would be too many for the fort's meager facilities. A moment later, we tumbled over the embankment.

"What took so long?" Frye asked. He stooped over Stark and I as we panted against the wall. Monro stood next to the provincial colonel. Brown had made it back alive and mostly well. He tipped his head back and closed his eyes, basking in the blazing sun. "What little resistance we met on the east was driven back in a hurry."

"Ours too. But then they proved a little stiffer," said Stark, sipping water. Sweat and dirt and black-red blood caked in his knuckles. He said nothing about the poor showing of our New Hampshire companions, which was well and good since their folly had already exacted a heavy toll. Many of them had paid with their lives.

"What do you make of it?" Monro asked, tilting his head to the sound of our approaching enemies. "Will we have open communications with Fort Edward?"

Frye nodded hastily. "From what I saw, colonel, if we can sortie out a few times a day, we may be able to keep the hounds at bay."

Stark was shaking his head. "No, sir." He pointed to the wall upon which his head rested. "That is finally the sound of all those reinforcements mentioned in that letter. The full complement of tribesmen has made the trek around and are here at last. They outnumber us greatly."

Musket shots promptly fell upon the encampment from the south, from the east, and even from the north where the tribesmen had swarmed around the small pasture opposite the portage road. Only our western edge, nearly abutting the fort, was currently free from fire. The Indians hooted as specks of stone exploded and bodies of our men crunched.

"Give them a dose of it right back!" Monro hissed to his gunners. *B-boom! B-boom!* Field pieces and swivel guns belched forth flame, smoke, and shot. Entire regiments of provincials leaned against the walls and returned fire. A great battle had come upon us.

A musket ball ripped through the silk pad of Colonel Monro's epaulet. He dropped to a knee, tearing the dangling bullion fringe free.

"Sorry, colonel," said Colonel Frye, seeing with his own eyes the size of the tribal and Canadian armies. "Looks like we won't be able to conduct any sorties after all."

"No," groused Monro. He stuck his head up, shot whizzing by, sizzling the air. "No one is leaving Titcomb or the fort. I pray little Anson and Nero got through."

"And Webb will listen," I added. Monro raised a bushy eyebrow, but spoke no words.

The furious battle only grew in strength, both sides surging in anger. Not a fraction of a second went by without the *cr-crack* of a musket or rifle, or the *b-boom* of our big guns. And all the while, Turnwell's artillery in the fort snarled with unceasing vigor. The smoke was pungent as the camp was filled with a gaseous residue of burnt sulfur. Our white cloud grew and grew, until it joined with that of the fort. It seemed that little of the sun's light could get through the haze. Only the heat of the day managed to sink into our camp. Minute by minute, the air around us came to resemble the inside of a boiling, stifling cauldron.

"You'd best get inside the fort, colonel," suggested Stark.

Monro furrowed his brow. "This is where the most dangerous fight is. This is where a commander ought to be."

"True," admitted Stark. "But this camp can fall and the fort still stand."

"Then I'll prevent it from falling. You'll prevent it from falling," Colonel Monro insisted.

Frye pointed to the gate at Titcomb's west end. It was only a few dozen steps from the fort's own access. Despite a recent awakening of the artillery situated on William Henry's southeast bastion, enemy warriors on the south had begun to spray the area with musket fire. "But we may not be able to get you back through that gauntlet should the need or time arise."

Monro weighed his options. Again, he shook his head in the negative. "Major Eyre and Turnwell and the rest of my regulars are more than capable. They know their duty."

"Aye, sir," I said. "They know theirs. But do you know yours! I dare say that there was a day when I thought they could do their jobs a fair amount better without you in their midst. Why do we need another redcoat around here? That's what I wondered when you showed up."

"Weber," Stark warned.

"Spit it out, boy," Monro hissed. "What do you mean, *do I know my duty*?"

"We face Indians out here. Indians and Canadians, mostly. Leave that job to the provincials, sir. Frye can handle it. Leave the rangers to it. We fight like they do. But on the other side of that fine fort that you and Major Eyre recently bolstered are French engineers and Canadian laborers. Even now they dig and dig. Their damn trenches! European sieges are something I don't pretend to understand, colonel. I've never seen one properly defended. I'd say we ought to put up our best officer against the Frog's best damned general. So, I say, get your Scot ass in there and give 'em hell, colonel, sir."

"Private Weber!" Stark yelled.

Monro patted his shoulder, tutting. "It's alright, lieutenant. The boy speaks the truth, colorfully, yes. But it's the truth, nonetheless."

"So, you'll go?" Frye asked.

"I'll go," Monro agreed, smiling. "After all, I've got to see that Montcalm and his Frogs are handed their hats and their heads. If we can stop their siege works, their attack on Titcomb will have to crumble." He slapped my chest with the back of his hand. "Come on lad, we're making a run for it."

"Me, sir?" I asked. "I'm a ranger, better suited to fighting out here."

He gave me a wink. "Any lad bold enough to tell a colonel what for like that, is a lad I want with me."

"Careful, colonel," Stark warned as I crawled up to join Monro. "He doesn't ever know when to shut up."

Monro's eyes twinkled. "Oh, that means there's hope. We'll make a good Scot out of him yet."

"I'm German, colonel," I said as we sped toward the gate.

"So's our *English* king. And in that case, perhaps I'll just use you as musket fodder for my race to William Henry. One less German might do the world some good." Then, with a hail of gunfire around him, Monro shoved open the stout fence and ran across the way. Pebbles flew. Puffs of dust billowed. One of the tails of his coat was pierced. “Open the gate!” he shouted to the men behind the fort’s walls. It swung out no more than two feet and he scrambled inside. A moment later he stuck his head back outside, the wooden gate splintering from musket fire. “Are you coming, or not?” In he went.

“Damned redcoats,” I grumbled.

And I ran.

CHAPTER 49

Just as my bleached sight and muffled hearing from the battle in the woods at last fully recovered, I joined Colonel Monro upon William Henry's northwest bastion. Turnwell's guns rumbled, reverberating the meaty oak planks that formed the terre-plein below my feet. The packed earth that held them up from below shook to such a degree, I feared it might rattle loose from the foundations of the world set down by Providence so long ago. It was a silly thing, but I thought we might rattle right off the earth. *B-boom! P-poof!*

The squat iron mortar gasped with fire and smoke, sending its shot, which was packed with explosives, hurtling on a high arcing path. In those days, a mortar's trajectory was fixed at 45 degrees. Therefore, the size of the charge was varied to reach the target. And the breech of this particular royal mortar had been packed to the limit, blasting the ball to its maximum distance. I saw only a streak of light as its burning fuse sputtered on the way down, eventually punching the ground. A second later, as terrified laborers scattered, it exploded, sending scorching fragments of iron in all directions while carving out a generous crater. Four Canadians fell. Two did not ever climb back to their feet. And, in the fort, the mortar crew frantically reloaded, while Turnwell hung a plumb line to refine its aim.

The terrifying 18-pounder fired at that moment. Its invisible ball flew with a white, smoky tail. In the blink of an eye, a shallow trench was carved by the flying lead. It may have hit a buried rock or perhaps fate had decreed it skip at the next moment. The racing shot climbed steadily and sheared off a man's arm, so that for a lingering moment, his detached hand still gripped a shovel. The ball's path did not stop until it shattered two great trees that had likely been growing since before the founding of Jamestown. And, like the workings of a fine timepiece, the cannon's barrel was probed, sponged, and reloaded. Our gunners were exemplary that day.

The mortar rumbled. The cannon boomed, sending a finger of flame up from the touch hole and, of course, a slithering tongue of fire out the muzzle. And more of our cannons split the air. *P-poof! B-boom! B-boom!*

Still, the French engineers kept their Canadian laborers toiling. About a thousand yards away, picks swung, shovels swept. Baskets were filled with dirt, but they were not hauled away. No. The engineers made sure everything was properly employed. Filthy workers tipped the baskets up to fill gabions that had been constructed on the spot using woven branches. These cages would soon form a protective wall around the foremost French camp. And more activity fluttered. Timber was felled. Timber was split. By man and beast, timber was dragged. But my eyes kept going back to those diggers. Inch by dreadful inch their ditches got deeper and longer.

"New France is filled with nothing but wuchaks!" I shouted in order to hear myself over the din.

"What?" Monro shouted back, leaning.

"Wuchaks!" I repeated over the snarling, one-sided battle. "It's what the tribesmen call a groundhog."

"Woodchucks?" he asked.

"Close enough!"

"Have we slowed their progress at all?" Monro asked when Major Eyre had found us.

Despite the stifling smoke and relative chaos, the major was the picture of order. "Turnwell knows his aim and his guns, sir. He's laying in shot with deadly accuracy."

"Not what I asked."

"I'm sure you see the same thing I see, colonel," Eyre admitted. He guided us to an open crenel in the parapet. "Montcalm is digging a parallel trench to set in his first guns. From there, his Canadians will dig a perpendicular trench toward our walls while those guns blaze. Then, new guns will be set at point-blank range to completely reduce our fortifications."

"Can we stop it?" Monro asked.

"If we allow it to go on too long, no, colonel," Eyre said. "Absent outside assistance for the besieged, the besieger always wins."

"Then we must halt their progress now, discourage them now, and send them packing now," Monro clipped.

"No word from General Webb, sir?" Eyre asked.

Monro frowned in answer.

"That is what we feared," Turnwell said as he approached. His myriad of crews functioned at a break-neck pace, their sunburnt backs slathered with sweat and grime. "I've given my gunners orders to be merciless in their swiftness. No time for cooling the pieces until twenty-four shots have been fired."

"Even for the iron guns?" Monro asked, aghast.

"Sir," Turnwell said with an affirmative nod.

"But that is twice the allowed amount when firing constantly!" Monro snapped. "Did you approve of this?" he asked Eyre.

"Yes, sir," Eyre answered calmly. "Without hope of relief from Edward, we must drive them away within a day, no more than two. To do so, every extra round Mr. Turnwell can fire is most welcome."

Monro scratched his chin. It was stubbled white and gray as he had not taken the time to shave that morning. "Balance the need for speed against our concern for iron fatigue?"

Turnwell and Eyre agreed.

"It must be done," growled the colonel. He stole a glance at the destruction wrought by Turnwell. We followed his gaze, wondering if our efforts would be enough. Yard by inexorable yard, the parallel ditch dug by the French lengthened. "Keep it up," he ordered. "Weber, with me."

Turnwell and I shared a funny look. His side of the inaudible conversation asked, *what are you doing here? With Monro?* In answer, I cryptically raised both my eyebrows as if I was privy to some important tidbit that Turnwell was not. Not knowing would make the lieutenant truly mad. His face wrenched up. Then, chuckling, I trotted after the colonel.

"Damn Webb," he was muttering when I caught up to him on the wall walk. He wound his way through the southwest bastion, that fired upon the French positions as well, but with less effectiveness given the difficult angle. "Damn bonny friends of the prince," Monro mumbled, as he ignored the toiling crews. His chin then tipped down as he studied the floor while deep in thought, sauntering along the southern wall.

We halted at the southeast bastion. It had temporarily opened fire on the Indians and Canadians assaulting Titcomb. They'd had luck driving back most of the attackers from being able to shower the gates with musket balls. But they couldn't reach the enemy's onslaught against the south and east ends of the encampment without risking firing at the heads of our own soldiers. The guns idly clicked as they cooled in silence.

"What do you think, Mr. Weber?" Monro asked when he was through pondering.

"Sir? I'm a simple woodsman. Give me my tomahawk and I can wriggle free of any scrape. Sieges are for educated men like you."

He chuckled sardonically. "Hmmph. Ephraim, I'm an old officer. I've seen a lot in my time. And I've learned a lot in my time."

"There you go, sir," I said.

Monro shook his head. "All of my experience has been in the Mother Country, Mr. Weber. Thank God, it has been a time of peace on our native soil. But it means that my experience is in logistics, moving men and materiel from here to there. I understand order and discipline, morale and fatigue. I can get soldiers to do things."

"See? There you go, sir," I repeated. It was never good to have a commander second-guess his abilities. Lack of confidence was almost as dangerous as to be stuck with a leader who over-estimated his talents.

"You're not listening, Weber. I'm an old officer who's earned little respect. I've never served in the field. My career has been unremarkable."

"That can be good, sir. You've made no mistakes."

He grinned. "What do you think of our counter to the siege?"

I scanned the horizon in all directions. Two very different kinds of battles raged around us. "At Oswego, we turned our guns and shot right over the heads of our garrison."

Monro again glanced at the now silent cannons in the southeast bastion. "You were desperate. Did it work?"

"It was scary as hell when Turnwell sent his lead sailing. Thought my cap might be torn from my head from the wind. We were pelted with bits of wadding and smoke." Then I nodded. "But, yes, it worked. The only reason we surrendered when we did was because Colonel Mercer was killed."

Colonel Monro shook his head. "Too much risk to our own souls to fire down toward them," he said, strolling the walk toward the northeast bastion. At least he could still be decisive. I'd served other commanders who froze with vacillation whenever the bullets began to fly.

On our right, in the woods past the meadow that was filled with our dead livestock, trails of smoke began to rise. Hundreds of them. I pointed them out to the colonel. "Some of the Indians must have broken off from the battle below. They are making their camps for the night, sir. Right along the portage road. There can be no doubt. No message will ever get through now."

We halted at the next bastion. The artillery on the northern face roared, shooting over a corner of the lake onto the main French position. The guns on the eastern face remained silent. There was nothing for them to shoot at except trees and campfires. "I expect the Indians to assault the camp from the north soon enough," Monro told a pair of idle gun chiefs. "When that occurs, today or tomorrow, consider it a standing order to resist them with all you've got."

"It'll be good to get in the fight, sir!" one of the chiefs chirped with a smart salute.

And then a tremendous explosion, centered on our northwest, fighting bastion, tore through the afternoon. It was a far cry louder than anything Turnwell had heretofore been able to produce. The sound of metal shattering or tearing into a million pieces was unmistakable. As were the screams of its victims.

A small amount of debris had sailed all the way across the fort's diameter. It had poked several small holes through the waving Union Jack before tinkling at our feet. Bitter smoke wafted as I watched three men helped up and away from the destruction. The bottom half of their trousers were torn and burnt away. Their legs were lashed with trails of crimson. The remains of two other gunners were dragged away in at least seven separate pieces.

"The French are already shooting?" shrieked one of the idle gunners who had suddenly ducked for cover.

The colonel, unmoving, didn't so much as glance to inspect the mess. He merely shook his head. "No. Who needs the Frogs? That is what iron fatigue will do to us, lads."

B-boom! B-boom! B-boom! On rolled our other guns.

"Where's Webb?" the colonel asked as he peered down the portage road that disappeared into the forest.

CHAPTER 50

How right the colonel had been. In the fort, the next day of the siege was much like the previous. Unrelenting, our gunners shot at the growing French works. A Canadian laborer had his torso split in two. A French engineer lost a leg. On our terre-plein, a dozen Englishmen were injured and five killed when the iron 18-pounder in the northwest bastion finally gave way to stress. Its heated, clicking, and smoking remains were heaved over the parapet or down into the yard. An hour passed before one of the unused guns from the eastern face of the northeast bastion was finally trundled into place.

Fortunately, it was never needed in its original position. For, the Indians' attack through our pasture had failed to materialize. In fact, their assault on Titcomb as whole waned. To be sure, musket fire continued unabated at the embankment from three sides. But the volume of shot was much reduced. I believe one incident in particular captures just what was going on in the tribal camps that caused the fading vigor of the barrage.

I'd been stuck inside the fort for twenty-four hours. Monro wanted me around, *in case he needed me*. In the meantime, there was nothing for me to do but watch. If I offered my assistance to the artillery crews, at best, I'd be in the way. At worst, I'd contribute an error which might kill me along with several others. I could not lay atop the parapet to snipe at the enemy. They were too distant for my smooth bore musket to accomplish anything but waste ammunition. So, I stared at my fellow rangers down in the camp working in shifts to keep the wandering enemy at bay.

During a brief lull below. A bold Caughnawaga chief emerged, naked except for his loin cloth and war paint. He was highly decorated with feathers, ribbons, and grease in his tufted hair. In one hand, the warrior held aloft a spiked war club, emblazoned with a color of scarlet that could only come from man. In his other extended hand, he shook a crinkled page, also wet with blood. He screamed and shrieked defiantly. He gestured and strutted like a cockerel. Our rangers and Massachusetts men on the embankment were like me. They watched him, curious, not firing.

But when the warrior grew bored with his own antics and turned to leave, he was confronted by another fighter. This one was Mississauga. Great River Mouth ran headlong into the Caughnawaga chief and they both went into the dust, tumbling, scrapping over the shred of paper. Punching and biting one another, they rolled over a dead hog.

A brace of Caughnawaga emerged then to aid their chief. They were swiftly followed by a pair of Mississauga. Then, bizarrely, a half dozen Ottawa ran out, fighting against the other two factions. They were joined by Chippewa, Menominee, Western Delaware, and Sauk. A brawl, centered on the page, kicked up tufts of dried grass.

Frye and Stark allowed the infighting to evolve for a solid minute. But then, a single, pointed volley from Titcomb, drove the survivors scurrying back toward their own hidden camps. Seven tribesmen lay dead, among them Great River Mouth. It was not a completely satisfying end to the man who had beaten Amos Conwall to death with his bare hands. But at least Great River Mouth and his fellow Mississauga had not triumphed in their fight. As far as I could tell, the original Caughnawaga chief had retained the paper prize, whatever it was.

"Natives are fighting among themselves," Monro observed as he joined me at the eastern wall.

"They're men, same as us. My pa would say they're fallen, same as us. They've been killing one another since long before our forefathers came to these shores," I said. "Murder comes from somewhere deep in a man's darkest greedy, prideful soul."

The colonel patted a balled fist softly against the parapet. "As long is it keeps them from an attack on Titcomb, I don't care if they're men or beasts. It helps us preserve ammunition."

I peeked over my shoulder. The newly placed 18-pounder had fired nonstop for nearly an hour. "And nothing we do seems to stop the French from digging?"

He crossed his arms and casually leaned against the wall, observing Turnwell and his crews. "Nothing. Yet. But Turnwell is a keelie himself. The aim of an eagle and the heart of a lion."

"And sometimes as prickly as a porcupine."

"Be that as it may," Monro sighed. "With each round he pours atop their heads, he's killing one, two, perhaps four Frenchmen. Eventually, even old Montcalm must relent. And Major Eyre is an observant man. He insists that their pace of trenching has slowed. Never underestimate esprit de corps, or lack of it, and its effect on the mission." He bobbed his head from side-to-side, thinking. "Another afternoon of our barrage, might send them back to their boats."

"Hope so," I muttered, resting my chin on my folded arms atop the wall. I gazed outward, seeing nothing in particular, just the top of the canopy of a never-ending forest. "Be nice to move about the woods again. Been a long time since we had free reign."

"Aye," Monro said. I caught him studying my profile. "You miss being out there with your chaps?" he guessed.

"Yes, sir," I admitted.

"Good lad," the colonel said with a confident, curt nod. "But I want a ranger in here. Especially one who will tell me what he thinks. This continent, and its ruggedness, I think it seeps into your bones from your youth. You know, you Yankees have a way about you."

"We do, sir," I said absentmindedly. Things grew quiet between us. Except for the growl of our artillery, that is. "You once said you had children, colonel. They must be grown and wed by now. Grandchildren?"

He grinned, wistfully, immediately lost in fond recollection. "Daughters. Two. Cora and Alice. Neither are wed, the oldest, Cora much to my eternal chagrin. Though I currently have hopes of marrying Alice off to a promising Major Heyward. He spends his time hustling between York City and Albany for Lord Loudoun. I expect them to give me a troop of grandsons."

Like moss on an old rock, the colonel was growing on me. "When you and the major return home to the Mother Country, I hope that your wish comes true."

He scoffed. "You know young ladies, Ephraim. They have plans other than those of their fathers. And with the girls' mothers dead these many years, they hear no other voice of reason but mine."

"Mothers?"

"Two wives, dead," he sighed.

"Me, too, sir."

He gaped at me. "At your age?"

I frowned. "It's a rugged continent, colonel. You said so yourself."

"Aye," he groaned, watching the fluid, brutal dance of his gunners.

"So, I assume that your Alice doesn't want to marry Major Heyward?" I asked. "What about your Cora?"

He chuckled. "Goodness. No, lad. You've got it wrong. Alice rarely tells me her mind. It is not because she is independent and strong-willed. No. She's quiet, demure. It's hard to know what she is thinking behind her smart, doe eyes. But were I to guess, I believe she might wed the major right in York City before I'm even aware."

"She's here?" I asked. "In the middle of a war?"

"Not here, per se. Cora, the independent one, insisted on making the voyage with me last year. And wherever Cora goes, Alice follows. I did prevail upon them to take up residence, and stay, in York City. The Lord knows I make it my business to keep my location a secret from them so they don't get it in their minds to visit."

"They would get a noisy welcome now," I said.

"Dreadful," Monro admitted. "But I'm sure we don't have to worry about that." He clapped my back. "A widower, huh? Someday, when this is all over, I'll introduce you to my Cora. She's spirited, yet solemn, but kind. She'll make a fine companion to a fortunate man."

"I like a feisty woman, sir," I admitted. Then, I rolled against the parapet so I faced across the grounds with him. "Truly, it's kind of you, colonel. But I don't think I'm much good for women."

"Ha!" he laughed. "No man is good for woman. Look at us slaughtering one another. But man and woman is as the Lord intended, so it is." Turnwell had dispatched a runner. The boy zipped between gunners and workers, who carried shot and powder on the walk. The lad made eye contact with Monro and struck off a direct course toward us.

I smiled. "You're right, sir. I should like to meet her."

"Hold your horses, lad. In time. In time. First thing is first. Let's beat the pants off these Frogs."

"Colonel," the boy rasped after he thundered to a stop. "Lieutenant Turnwell and Major Eyre say there is something going on over at the French camp. You'll want to see it."

"Very well," Monro said, pushing himself upright. "Come, Mr. Weber. The time for you to meet Cora may soon be upon us."

For a brief moment the call of our guns came to a halt. Their heated iron and brass groaned, stretched, creaked, clicked, clacked, and sighed during the well-earned break. If the mercury had hit ninety elsewhere, in the immediate proximity of those beasts, it had surely soared into triple digits.

We took turns peering through a pair of spyglasses. Monro's was a fair instrument, but its lenses, even the internal ones, had somehow been smudged over the years. It was like looking through a curtain. Major Eyre's on the other hand was a fine specimen. He carried it in a stiff, boiled leather case that was buffed to a shine. The wood tubes appeared to be at least a decade old and oft-handled, with hand oils having worn down the finish. But the brass and lens themselves? The way it smoothly glided when it was telescoped in or out? The real working parts of the device were exquisite. It was just what I would expect from an engineer of Eyre's caliber.

"That's the same Indian, is it not?" Monro asked, handing off Eyre's scope to me.

It took me a moment to find the man in question on a field filled with the enemy. For the first time in the siege, Indians had joined their allies on the northwest corner. "That's him," I agreed, passing the glass to Turnwell. Monro had quietly stowed his since no one wanted to use it. "Caughnawaga. See the markings?"

"What's that he's carrying?" Turnwell asked. "It's a speck of red at the end of his arm. A scalp?"

"Can't tell from this distance," I admitted. "But when the colonel and I saw him on the other side of the fort, he held a sheet of paper that was smattered with blood."

"And it must be important," Monro explained. "The tribesmen fought ferociously to see who could claim the honor of holding it."

"One of your letters to Webb?" Major Eyre guessed.

Monro pursed his lips. "Likely," he sighed. "But was it Nero or Johnny? I hate to think of losing either."

No one dared say aloud, though we all thought it, that both of the messengers may have been killed.

"Or maybe it is a letter from Montcalm, granting the savages the right to trophies should we fall," Turnwell suggested. "That would be enough to cause a stir."

"Do you know the Caughnawaga chief?" Monro asked.

"I know one of them, a blood-thirsty monster named Collière. But that's not him. Don't know this one. Every band has a chief, you know. Every chief wants to call himself a king."

Monro snatched the glass from Turnwell. He placed it to his eye and leaned into the crenel. "He seems to be done with his act. He and his fellow tribesmen are dancing their way into the French camp. What?" he gasped. "There's the old dog himself. Montcalm. He's out among his engineers."

"Pulling back, sir?" Eyre suggested. "Turnwell and our gunners have put them through hell. Until this moment, there has been no sign that we'd cease."

Monro collapsed the glass and handed it off to Eyre. "We can hope. We can pray that our own defense has been enough." He peered up at the sun as it slowly descended in the west. "Tonight, under the cover of darkness, Montcalm may be able to admit he's been licked and fall back north with his army somewhat intact, if not his dignity."

"Aye, sir," said the officers, wearing genuine smiles.

"But in the meantime, Mr. Turnwell," Monro said, making his way toward the steps. "I don't want a second to go by when I don't hear your men hurling shot at the enemy. Sometimes, a stupid Frog needs a fair bit of encouragement."

CHAPTER 51

It was precisely 6:00 am on August 6. I remember it clearly because each of them, Major Eyre, Colonel Monro, and Lieutenant Turnwell had pulled watches from their fob pockets and considered the slender hands creeping across their clock faces. When the long hand pointed up and the short hand directly down, Turnwell set his own hands upon the shoulders of two crew chiefs and whispered, "Let's test your calculations, shall we?"

Two howitzers cracked open the morning in an abrupt fashion when the gunners set their smoldering linstocks against the touch holes. The short-barreled guns had been packed with light charges and angled strangely low. The reason for this peculiar orientation was quickly answered as their hollow shots began falling as soon as they cleared the dry moat. The balls smacked into the wall of the approaching trench, bounced back and forth twice, killing a man from momentum alone. Then they bounded another two rods along the floor of the trench before each exploded.

"Fine work, lieutenant," Monro complimented.

But, for the first time in the entire siege, our guns received a reply from those of the French. I watched in horror as nine, yes nine, puffs of brilliant white smoke sprang directly toward us from the muzzles of Frog artillery. Another massive cloud billowed upward – from a Coehorn mortar. And by the time I actually heard the cannon reports and could hope to react, their projectiles had begun finding their way among us.

With splinters the length of a man's arm flying in all directions, one ball tore off five inches of our parapet. The shot's momentum carried it up and over the fort until it landed somewhere amidst the dead animals in our pasture. But those jagged, sharp shards of wood impaled faces, necks, and arms. Other solid shot pelted our earthen and stone walls, rattling my teeth as well as the ground. Then, as we all ducked for cover, it seemed an eternity while we waited for the mortar round to finish its journey.

I heard a growing whistle. A heartbeat later, the shot hammered down onto what had been the bare second floor of

Monro's headquarters. It punched a hole clean through native planks that had been sawn at a full four inches thick. Later, when I would have cause to run an errand to the colonel's office, I would find that the ball had bored another three feet through the floor and into the hard-packed dirt below.

We stood as the enemy reloaded. Already, our gunners were dragging their injured brethren away and reserves poured in to take over. "The Frogs didn't quit after we dumped iron into them!" Turnwell shouted to his crews. "Reload and make them regret that poor decision!"

B-boom! Boom! Boom! Cannons and howitzers blazed.

"If anything," Monro muttered angrily. "Since that Indian's antics yesterday, the French have increased their pace of digging. One battery is in place and active." He ventured a peek over the wall. "Another day, and they'll have a second."

Eyre, careful to not be overheard by the men, nodded. "It is a matter of time now. I've built this fort to withhold all manners of assaults. But it is not invincible. There is no such thing."

"I can see that, major," Monro conceded. "Do all you can to keep her in condition. Perhaps General Webb will come through."

"Yes, sir," Eyre said with a tip of his hat. He did well hiding his disbelief in Webb's ability or interest in offering assistance. "I'll see that the carpenters are prepared and arranged for quick duty should anything require shoring."

"Very good," Monro said as I glanced toward the French works.

My eyes went wide. I gripped their shoulders and forcefully shoved them down as I watched the long, smoking botefeux of the French descend. By the time our knees had bent, the parapet was bombarded with solid shot. Sections of the fraising was torn away like it had been made of mending thread rather than solid six-inch ash poles sharpened to points. The curtain wall shuddered.

And even as the shock faded, I had to keep pressure on the officers' backs to prevent them from standing. I knew another shot from the mortar must be coming. Then Eyre and Monro heard it. They had the sense to keep down. The French mortar chief had adjusted his charge downward. The round from the Coehorn traveled a shorter distance than the first. It smacked on the very top of the parapet. I watched it as it bounced, rolling quite slowly in the air over our heads before it slammed down in the parade ground. It smashed a chicken to little more than a splotch of feathers. Then, it grossly broke a laundress' leg who had been hurrying with a pail of water before it cracked against the foundation of our well.

B-boom! B-boom! Boom! B-boom! Boooom! So answered Turnwell. Our early morning conversation with our new neighbors was devolving into a brutal exchange.

"Sirs," I said when we stood upright and surveyed the dust spattered across our coats. "I think you'll both want to see this." Out of habit, they peered toward the Canadian wuchaks. "This way, please," I said, running down the steps to the yard. Curious, the pair followed me past the crunched remains of the chicken. We ambled by a set of women who were helping the wounded laundress to the infirmary. She sobbed as she looked down at her mangled limb. Then we stood over the spent ball.

"A 32-pounder," Eyre said. "Likely the biggest gun they brought."

"What about it, lad?" Monro asked.

"We haven't shot any 32-pounders in that direction," I said. Then I set my foot against the ball. The heat from its firing radiated through the sole as I rolled it out of the crumpled well foundation toward me. We were greeted by a familiar marking.

"The devils!" Monro growled, barely able to contain his rage.

"Good eyes, Mr. Weber," Eyre commended.

"Don't laud me too much, major," I warned as I scraped a patch of dirt from my shoe into the grooves of the small broad arrow that had been cast in the ball. "I was a participant in each of the battles where that may have been taken."

"The fall of Oswego," Monro lamented.

"And Braddock's March," Eyre added. "They're shooting our own ordnance back at us."

"Salt in the wounds," Monro said, gripping the hilt of his sword in anger.

Crash! Crunch! Shatter! Another volley from the French cannons struck the fort. A lone 6-pound shot sailed over the wall and snapped the top of the flagpole off. The detached section of tree went tumbling in one direction. The Union Jack fluttered in the other.

"Catch that before it touches the ground, Mr. Weber," Monro bellowed.

I ran, clearing a trough of water and bounding a tuft of straw. The flag wavered softly into my arms.

By the time I returned to the base of the pole, Eyre had already found a carpenter whose mighty moustache may have hidden a small livestock operation. From the looks of his facial hair, he kept enough crumbs tucked away in it to feed himself and a herd of cattle for an entire day. Nonetheless, the man, tools in hand, had already propped up a ladder. "Scramble up there and see our nation's banner is properly displayed, lest the French get the wrong idea," Eyre ordered.

"Of course, sir," clipped the man with a sloppy salute.

"And make the blasted pole taller than it was!" Monro added. "That'll give our men down on Titcomb a little boost."

"Good as done, colonel," the carpenter said. He jogged off to what remained of his supply of lumber. He'd managed to convince the officers to hold back a small stack from the lake just in case he had to make repairs. Once he threw back the tarpaulin, his fingers rapidly pattered down their sawn ends until he selected a straight, knot-free board, two by four by eight. Nails jiggled in his pouch as he hastily returned to us with his prize. His hammer clattered in his belt. "Will this due, sirs?" he asked.

"It doesn't have to be neat," Monro agreed. "Get the Jack affixed and get your head back down here."

B-boom! B-boom! Turnwell's cannons and howitzers roared.

At the grommeted end of the flag, the carpenter carefully nailed the Jack's blue, white, and red material to the new board with short, fat-headed brads while I prevented our Mother Country's sacred banner from touching the dirt. Next, he started four sixteen penny nails at the other end of his board by driving them halfway through. Then, short pole in hand, he scaled his ladder. I steadied the base as it bounced against the flexible, upright flagstaff. He had to stand on the very end of the ladder rails while perched on his toes just to reach the tip of the broken staff. But his forearms were as strong as iron straps and he could hold the long board straight up in the air. Two whacks apiece from his hammer drove each nail into place.

Our efforts had become something of a spectacle to the fort's and lower camp's defenders. When the flag again snapped in the breeze, tugging against the pole, thousands of men gave a hearty cheer. His patriotic enthusiasm brimming, the moustachioed carpenter stayed put and pumped his hammer in answer.

I heard a round of distant thunder rumbling from the west. Before my eyes could blink, the carpenter's head evaporated into a crimson mist. The 12-pound cannonball that had claimed it crashed into the inside of the parapet of the east wall. Meanwhile, the dead man's hammer plummeted, nearly striking Eyre's foot. The carpenter's body slid like thick melting tar along the flagstaff, folded in two, and then tumbled backward down the ladder. I dove out of the way just as it landed between us with a thud.

It was then that thousands upon thousands of distant French voices sounded their own hoorays.

CHAPTER 52

By noon on the following day, it had become clear that Titcomb's Mount would remain intact. Very few of the gray and white uniforms favored by the Canadian provincial forces or the dingy, mismatched attire of their militiamen rushed about below. Most of their colonial regiments had been called back to the main efforts of the French siege. Digging and digging. Canadians, the damn wuchaks! Meanwhile, the thousands of tribesmen remaining in the vicinity of the encampment seemed content to occupy their time by taking potshots at Frye's little military village.

Yet the brave colonial colonel could do nothing to alter his situation. Though our camp held a greater number of inhabitants than did the fort's garrison of regulars, it would find itself fighting against an enemy at superior strength should it decide to sortie out against the Indians. All Frye and Stark could do to hasten victory was wait to exploit some, as yet unseen, opportunity.

The same, fading hope prevailed inside William Henry. On the terre-plein, Turnwell's artillerymen hustled as ever, while we scanned the horizon for some prospect for triumph. Our cannons, howitzers, and mortars belched. But with every passing hour since the carpenter had lost his head, our zealous gunnery officer had fewer weapons with which to work. Four more cannons and three swivels had suffered from fatigue. One moment they'd sat still on their thick stocks, earnestly performing their destructive function. The next instant, the tired iron beasts burst, shooting knobs, necks, trunnions, bits of barrels, and muzzles in all directions. It was quite an act of Providence that only sixteen men were wounded and seven killed from the explosions.

As our force of artillery waned, the enemy's increased. Now, whenever the French guns fired in a coordinated fashion, I counted seventeen cannon, two mortars, and two howitzers. And if there was anyone who cared to quibble about the exact numbers arrayed against us, our walls and morale accurately tallied the strain the French guns wrought in sagging timbers and sullen countenances.

"A red flag, sir," Eyre reported. He clutched his spyglass next to the long row of polished buttons on his coat.

"A truce?" Monro's interest immediately perked. He and I had been visiting the injured, who had begun to pile up in the dark, sheltered hospital. Since the start of the conflict, the reek of human frailty had sunk into every corner of the dismal establishment. One man, in particular, had a seeping wound that stank of such extended corruption as to cause my barley cake breakfast to demand release through the same way it had entered.

"Methinks," Eyre answered. "They've taken the time to remove the French flag, with its white field, and replace it with a long red banner."

"The mythical oriflamme?" Monro asked, disgusted.

"Hardly," Eyre said. "It looks little more than a tattered rag. Besides, the flag bearer approaches with just a single officer and a platoon of fifteen grenadiers."

Monro patted a bedridden, unconscious man's hand and stood from where he knelt on the packed earth floor. "Difficult to storm our little castle and take no prisoners with scarce more than a dozen. Even Montcalm has to know that."

"I dare say, colonel."

"Very good," Monro clipped. "Instruct Mr. Turnwell and all our sharpshooters to let them approach the gate. Send a message to Frye. He is to see that no harm comes to our guests as they pass between the camp and our walls."

"Escort them inside the fort?" Eyre asked.

"Not until each one of the Frogs is blindfolded. Even an idiotic Frenchman can tell our secrets. I'll have none of them lay eyes on the destruction they have inflicted."

The sun was high when we assembled to receive the emissary and his guards. As you might have come to expect by now, it was hot. Humidity was the norm that summer. Sweltering, Monro stood, this time in a freshly cleaned uniform, crisp from his shined boots up to his recently groomed hair and brushed hat. About three yards behind him, the limp Union Jack hung from its makeshift flagstaff. Two hundred British regulars, as clean as fighting men could be, held themselves at rigid attention, muskets shouldered, behind the pole, opposite our gate. On the ramparts above, the rest of the garrison stood, facing the guests. We put on an impressive display of martial prowess for the blind men. Yet, it was a precaution in case one or two of the visitors peeked through a gap in their eye covering. Our bodies would block the views they might steal of our shattered buildings and blown artillery.

"You," Monro said as the emissary was carefully led over the threshold. It was not a genial greeting. It was an accusation.

Bougainville followed the sound of the colonel's voice and came to halt a dozen feet away. He wound himself up straight and proud, his chest and chin up, his arms and shoulders down. His uniform was in pristine condition, white shirt with a ruffled white cravat. His coat was dark blue, dare I say, almost Prussian. It had fine, gold embroidery at the seams. The turnbacks and lapels were pale white with soft, powdered, rose-colored flowers set amidst delicate green vines and three-petaled, sapphire lilies. Someone had tied his blindfold exceptionally tight. The band pushed Bougainville's already chubby cheeks into miniature mounds. I giggled to myself. Even a dignified man looked ridiculous in a blindfold.

Before responding to Monro's barb, the French captain waited until he heard the last of his white-bedecked platoon of grenadiers settle in place. "It is I," Bougainville said. He lifted his hat and bowed.

And though his counterpart could not see it, Monro returned the gesture. "I thought we had made it clear that you were to avoid seeking refuge with us again unless there had been a discernable softening of your former, aggressive posture. Am I to conclude that such a change of heart has, in fact, occurred and you've only come to bid me your respects before you and your troupe depart?"

I felt sorry for Bougainville. It was true that he and his men had been killing us for days. It was also true that he and his men had killed hundreds more during the siege of Oswego. But it was just as true that Captain Bougainville had allowed me to keep my bladed weapons after Oswego's surrender. They'd helped me stay alive in the massacre that followed.

"Colonel Monro, some moments ago, when I heard news that my general wished to correspond with you, I volunteered in an instant. Our peoples may be at odds, at war. But that need not mean that two gentlemen must allow a misunderstanding to threaten their personal relationship. Before I convey the wishes of General Montcalm, I beg of you to accept my sincere apology. My behavior at our earlier meeting was never intended to be anything other than cordial. And I take it as my personal failing that I permitted sentiments to fall from my lips that could, in any way, be construed as threatening. Upon reflection, my choice of words was deficient. I meant, and mean, only to express my earnest respect for you and your men. Nothing can sway me from that position."

Monro smiled affectionately at the younger man. "Good captain, I accept your apology. But it is I who behaved and spoke rashly. Might we forget the incident? Might we, as men, as officers of our kings, start anew."

"Très bien!" Bougainville exclaimed. He grinned broadly, further bunching his cheeks.

"Now then, sir," Monro said. "You mentioned that you carried correspondence from General Montcalm…"

"Oui," he said, reaching to an inner pocket of his coat. Bougainville revealed a small, folded letter. But before he extended it to the colonel, he blindly looked up at the surrounding fort. In a raised voice, he shouted, "My general has asked that I extend a message to your colonel and to you men as defenders of this fort. He compliments you. Your defense has been admirable, your firing unrelenting, your tenacity under return bombardment has been heroic."

"But?" Monro asked.

Bougainville shook his head. "There is nothing further in that regard, colonel. C'est tout."

The colonel pointed to the note in Bougainville's hand. "The letter must express the general's desire for terms. I must tell you, with my entire garrison bearing witness, that we have no intention of surrendering, no matter what Montcalm's pen has spun."

The French captain again indicated his answer with a shake of the head. "My general does not pretend to demand terms from those who are exhibiting such a spirited defense." He lifted the letter and held it out. "This is not from my dear general. May I approach to see it delivered to your hand personally, colonel?"

"You may. Ephraim," Monro indicated with a yank of his head.

I trotted forward and took the blind man's hand, guiding him within arm's reach of the colonel. The paper passed from French hands to Scot. It was wrinkled and splattered with blood. "There," Bougainville breathed. "My duty is complete. You'll find that to be an express letter, sir. We inadvertently intercepted it. I admit that it was opened when it fell into my possession and I read the correspondence obviously deemed private. But I had a dual duty to accomplish. To discover to whom the wayward letter belonged. And to my beloved Mother France. I believe you will understand fully once you view its contents."

Monro stuffed the letter into his own pocket. "Thank you, captain. I shall signal for you should I require anything further. In the meantime, it may be best that you remain in your camp."

"Until this bloody conflict is over," Bougainville added.

"And then we may enjoy a rich glass together. And a toast to shared experiences," Monro said cheerily. "Ephraim, see the captain and his men to the glacis."

"Sir," I said.

After they'd blindly filed out the gate and discarded their blindfolds in a small pile, I ambled beside Bougainville as we rounded the southern end of the fort. Peering into the nearest woods, I saw a hundred shadowed, painted braves staring back. And as we turned the southwest bastion, I saw on the western wall what the French could see from their point of view. The casement timbers were buckled and battered, straining to hold back the monstrous pile of dirt behind them. Spent solid shot peeked back at me like the eyes of a hundred cyclops lodged in the curtain.

I accompanied the Frenchmen as they descended the gentle slope of the glacis. "Mr. Weber," Bougainville warned. "Unless you have decided to join the more righteous side in this great conflict, I shall be forced to blindfold you should you wish to continue on this path."

"Not much more," I assured him. We reached the edge of the gardens and I stooped to harvest peppers. "I noticed these from the ramparts. They made my mouth water."

"Go back and hide in those ramparts," said a sergeant in the grenadiers, bold now that he wasn't among redcoats. "We'll blast you down here soon enough."

"Sergeant!" Bougainville scolded. "There is simply no need to be so discourteous!"

"I'm sorry, captain," said the man's voice. But his face said otherwise.

"Gather what you can carry, Mr. Weber," Bougainville encouraged. He stood waiting over me rather than continue to his camp.

"Do you need something, sir?" I asked when I stood tall, with more than a dozen ripened vegetables spilling from my arms.

"Ephraim," he began sheepishly. Then he hurriedly dismissed his men. It took a fair amount of cajoling to get them to leave the captain alone with me. "Ephraim," the captain said again. "I was distraught over the calamity at Fort Oswego. So was General Montcalm."

"I know," I said. His regret could not bring back Reverend Button or Rupert, both brutally slain long after the fight had been officially called off. "I believe you."

He rested his hand upon his breast. "It warms my heart, it does. Nonetheless, what I said the other day. The topic that caused so much torment."

"About the Indian slaughter?"

"Yes. It was no threat."

"I understand. I think the colonel does, too."

He gripped my arm passionately, nearly causing every morsel of my harvest to tumble. "It was no threat, Ephraim. But it just as well may happen. Do you understand? Hundreds upon hundreds more of the tribesmen have joined our campaign. I'd like to believe it is because they support our cause."

"But they don't," I said. "They rallied because Chief Collière and the Indians from Oswego's fall have spread tales of easy war trophies once an English fort surrenders."

Amazed, he stared at me. "That is it exactly."

"What will you do about it, should it come to that? What will Montcalm do?"

"Even now, we have held council fires for our allies. By day, we meet. Under the stars, we meet. We explain through interpreters time and again what our intentions are should we prove victorious."

"And you can't be certain of their understanding or compliance. Especially of those tribes that have come all the way from the pays d'en haut. They are a foreign bunch, for the most part."

"Indeed," Bougainville agreed, releasing me. He sighed. "We do all we can. But please, Ephraim. Take the necessary precautions to prevent such a tragedy." In truth, neither he nor I knew what those precautions could have possibly been.

"I guess we'd better win, then," I said. We exchanged awkward, sad smiles and I left him alone in the gardens.

Every last pepper was stolen from my hands before I had taken ten steps back into the fort. "You were gone a long time. What was that all about?" Eyre asked after I'd sought him out in the commander's offices.

"I've met the captain a handful of times now. He inquired of my family," I lied. No need to dredge up the subject that would set Monro, and everyone else, on fire.

"Courteous man," Eyre said, respectfully, though non-committedly. He stood at the small window that looked out into the parade yard.

Colonel Monro sat at his desk, scratching out a missive on a fresh page in overly large handwriting. Next to it was the unfolded, bloody letter given him by Bougainville. "May I ask which letter that was? It's clear that it was what caused the Caughnawaga chief to be so agitated two days ago. Was it Nero who carried it, or Johnny? I'd like to know whom to mourn." Then I steeled myself for the answer.

"Neither," Monro answered. He snapped his quill in half when he angrily hammered a sharp period at the end of his page. "See those displayed on the gate for all to see," the colonel told Eyre, handing him both the blood-spattered note and his freshly penned memorandum.

"Sir," Eyre answered before departing.

Monro rose and advanced to the window, quietly watching his major find a carpenter to nail up the notices.

"Sir," I ventured quietly.

"What!" he snapped with a menacing, sideways glance.

"The bloody correspondence, sir. May I ask what it was?"

"No!" Monro hissed. "It's not your place to ask, Private Weber!" He roughly clasped his hands at his back and walked around the room, lost in thought. "But it is my prerogative to share it with whomever I deem appropriate. And you'll find out as soon as you approach the gate, assuming you can read."

"Fine, sir," I said. "Do you need me here, sir?" I asked, inching for the door.

He threw up his hands. "Webb answered me. That's the damned letter, Ephraim. They intercepted Webb's answer to my repeated requests for troops. They killed the messenger."

"Are you sure it's genuine, sir?" I asked.

"I compared the handwriting to the other banal orders I've received from the esteemed general. It is in Webb's hand."

I looked expectantly at the colonel, almost afraid to ask for Webb's reply. But Monro was ready to discharge some of his anger and required no encouragement. "The ass!" he called, stepping around the hole in the floor from the mortar round. "He's a bag of wind, incapable of outsmarting a lintel. Do you know what he says?" Monro asked. "Do you want to know? You don't. Because to know what shit comes from that man's mind and mouth is to be fouled with it yourself. I'm afraid I shall never be rid of his stench. For the rest of my life, I shall be tainted by his inane decisions!"

I stood quietly, proud mostly that I managed to keep my mouth clamped rather than agree with the colonel. Though I did concur, there was a certain order to complaints. I was not permitted to complain about a general to a colonel. Even one who had asked me to be honest with him.

Monro grumbled for a time. Outside, I watched as men who were currently idle in the garrison raced to the gate to read the new posting. The colonel then leaned one hand against the wall and stared down at the floor. "At noon on August the fourth, before William Henry had so much as received a single cannonade from our enemy, that imbecile who so improbably occupies Fort Edward's headquarters wrote, and I quote, *I do not think it prudent to attempt a junction or to assist you at the present time. Furthermore, in light of the large force reported against you, and that I am unfortunately subjected to delays from the militia, you, colonel, might consider making the best terms of capitulation possible."*

"He suggested capitulation almost before the outset!" I gasped. "And Montcalm knows it!"

"That's not the worst of it!" Monro shouted, arms flailing. "That flatulent-souled turkey has the audacity to cite a delay in the militia as one of his chief reasons for not reinforcing us when he disregarded all advice to call it up earlier!"

"Treasonous," I whispered.

"You said it, Weber," Monro snapped. Then, as if his anger had been blown out like a candle, he straightened himself, shaking off his rage. "It matters not," the colonel insisted. "Even though some in this army think otherwise, we still have a duty to perform."

"And we won't capitulate?" I asked, thinking of Bougainville's heartfelt warning.

"No, Mr. Weber. And that very fact was covered in my personal letter to the garrison. In no uncertain terms, I've explained what will happen to any man or officer who suggests surrender."

Whistling, hollow-shelled howitzer rounds fell into the fort then. The bombardment had been renewed, the truce officially over. After two thuds echoed from the main firing bastion and one second passed, the burning wicks in the French rounds reached the powder buried inside. They erupted. Then there was a massive secondary eruption.

The men who had been reading the notes nailed to the door spun and raced toward the carnage. "They've hit an ammunition box!" they called. A third explosion then a fourth explosion, each centered on the bastion, followed. Then, I heard the anguishing shrieks of wounded soldiers.

Monro set his hat upon his crown. "We have work to do. Come Mr. Weber."

I chased after him into the hall and followed him into the yard. Men, ablaze, fell from the wall walk where a gaggle of boys had brought blankets and buckets of water. Other injured souls, pimpled with shrapnel, crawled limply out of harm's way, dying from their wounds before they had made it four feet. The rescuers worked frantically, braving flames and gruesome, stomach-churning sights.

The colonel pointed out those men and women who pulled others free from the debris even as the bombardment from the French continued. "They have taken to heart my warning, lad. They will inspire others so that none of us exhibits cowardice in the face of our foes."

"What happens if someone does?" I asked.

Monro examined me. "A young man like you has nothing to worry about. My threat is hardly necessary." His eyes followed the contours of the fort. "But after seeing Webb's traitorous reply, some of our weaker brethren may have needed a little coaxing. I merely explained that anyone who runs afoul of my edict will be hanged over the walls by the neck until dead to show the French what we do to cowards."

Then Monro slowly walked the step and directed the recovery efforts.

CHAPTER 53

Thus far, we'd been free from nocturnal cannonades. Not so, the night after our truce. And I suppose it was the natural progression of men's hearts in war, to move deeper into the dark forest of carnage, devoting more hours to the destruction of the enemy. As such, from the gloaming to the cock's crow, William Henry endured constant bombardment. The energetic Mr. Turnwell, returned the eerie favor with his remaining guns. It was a holy hell, at times brighter than the midday sky. The racket, the screams, the sulfur made for a frantic phase of the battle. All night through, with muskets in hand, we ran the wall walks, preparing and waiting for some type of daring escalade that never materialized. We shot at shadows of shadows. By morning we were run ragged, sleepy. Our vigilance had waned. Even the French seemed tired, allowing the persistence of their bombardment to fade – a welcome Godsend.

An optimist would have said that there was one more trivial blessing. For, the mercury had finally dropped a few degrees. Had a thermometer existed anywhere within two hundred miles, I'd bet that it read seventy-five degrees, as cool as anytime during the siege. Yet, it was one of those maddening periods when a man can be simultaneously wet, hot, and cold, shivering and sweating. And since I've never been accused of being an optimist, I complained more about the weather that night than the killing inflicted upon us by the French.

Predawn arrived as what was dark, began to take on qualities of form and color. The mercury dropped a little more. It remained humid while the sun had not yet crested the eastern horizon. The faintest of faint breezes rolled in from the lake, lifting the limp Jack and inch or two before it dropped. The mercury fell again, into an almost enjoyable range.

"Maybe you can shut up now," Turnwell said to me. A company of infantrymen snored against the parapet. I should have been among them. "I've seen men who've lost limbs that complain less than you."

"The only reason you don't complain is that a *Turd* is *well* wherever he goes, Turdwell."

"How original," he retorted.

"Then you prefer, Shitwell?"

"Shut up," he said laughing. His momentary pleasant demeaner fled. "Fire!" he screamed at one of his few remaining crews. "Damn it! Gun chief! Fire! Fire! What are you waiting for? A one-armed grandmother can reload faster than that man you've got posted at the rammer!"

The man in question yanked the rammer free and turned, covering the ear that faced the gun. "Fire!" shouted the gun's chief.

"That's more like it!" Turnwell complimented with a swift nod. He left the exhausted men to their repetitive chores and ambled along the northern walk that led toward the northeast bastion in order to check on the sole working piece of artillery that snoozed there. I trailed along after him, but pulled up short at a crenellation in the works. Turnwell noted and came back to me. "I heard that you had Anson take one of the colonel's messages instead of you."

"Yep," I said, peering over the lake.

"I can't decide if it was cowardly or heroic to let him go in your place."

"Yep," I admitted, feeling guilty. "Me, neither. At first, I thought it a blessing to get the boy out. He's good in the forest. But, well, you know…" I said, glancing toward the lingering smoke from hundreds of Indian cookfires in the eastern woods.

"I know," he said. "I'm sure he made it through the gauntlet."

"One of them did. Nero or Johnny. Webb got at least one of the letters demanding troops. How else would he know to decline?"

"Or both messengers made it," Turnwell suggested.

"Optimist," I rasped as a curse.

He gave a single chuckle. "Fog's coming in. Thick." I followed his gaze. The rounded hills surrounding Lake George had begun to stick out of a blanket of fog. The newly formed, dense cover itself slowly descended down the lake, drawing closer and closer to us. The lieutenant checked the progress of the rising sun as it spread its orange glow at the tips of the trees. "The

French might use its cover for an escalade. I'll warn the captain of the 60th on the western wall."

I glanced to the eastern wall that faced the Indians and smattering of Canadian troops. The foot soldiers there slumbered with just as much vigor as their counterparts on the west. "I'll tell Monro."

I found Monro inspecting our gunpowder stores. "Fog's coming in, colonel," I reported. "Might be that escalade will finally come."

He lazily kicked at an empty keg of powder. It made the sound of a hollow drum that echoed off the thick walls as it rolled against a stack of others. There were frighteningly few left in the cavernous storehouse. "Such a thing might not be all that bad," said the colonel. "Kill enough of them in one swoop. The arithmetic of feeding all those troops and sustaining the siege might catch up with Montcalm. The French aren't invincible, you understand? He might have to retreat."

I studied the room that had once been stacked from floor to ceiling and from wall to wall with enough gunpowder to set the world ablaze. "Colonel Frye can probably spare some powder from the camp," I offered. "They haven't used as much as we thought."

Monro nodded as he walked out the door, waiting for me to follow and latch it shut. "See some of his excess hauled over, Mr. Weber. I'm going to the eastern walk to inspect this cloud phenomenon of yours."

We parted company, he springing up the eastern steps, me to the gate. I'd already begun feeling water droplets forming on my face. The fog was settling in fast around us, growing in heft from the ground up. "Looks like your prediction for the weather was correct, Mr. Weber," Monro said from directly above me. The fog had enveloped us so rapidly that he appeared as little more than an apparition. "Now we'll see if you were right about an all-out French assault." He began gently waking his weary infantrymen.

Just as I opened my mouth to respond, a smattering of musket fire burst from the eastern woods. It was answered by haphazard small arms fire, until finally a cacophony of shots broke out. Indian hoots followed. French screams called out. More shooting. More calls, some in English. There were women's voices, but they didn't sound like they originated in the camp. All of it, the shouts, the shots, the whoops, like a swarm of bees moving together, drew near.

"Be ready to lay into them, men!" Monro called as a hundred black-spatterdashed feet rubbed sleep from their eyes and positioned themselves along the walk. "Select a target, aim, and drop the dogs!"

"Damn fine work, Ephraim!" Monro added. I chuckled to myself. It wasn't every day that I got credit for another man's work. Though the opposite had occurred on several occasions. And I wasn't about to confess that it had been Turnwell's sharp eyes and mind that had seen us prepared.

"Father! Father! It's Alice. Save us, your daughters!" The call came from less than two rods away on the other side of the curtain wall.

"Alice?" Monro asked, confusion apparent in his voice. "Alice? My daughters? No! What? Alice? Cora? Here?"

"We're here, father!" said another woman's voice.

"Cora? What in blazes?"

"We are pursued, father. Help us!" shrieked Alice. "These men, they've helped us. But we are almost lost."

"Hold your fire!" Monro barked with more authority than I'd ever heard from even the fiery Scot. "Muskets down." The colonel came scrambling down the stairs. "Sixtieth! Outside the gate. All of you. Do not harm my daughters or their rescuers! See them encircled and brought inside."

A wave of red-clad warriors immediately vacated the western wall and washed around me. The massive gates, not the small man door that was set in the big gates, crashed open from their weight and they poured outside. Sword drawn, Monro followed at their heels, fixing me with an angry look when we bumped into one another in the fog. "The enemy indeed! You nearly got my daughters killed!" And he huffed off outside while I dumbly stood in place on the parade ground.

There were more chaotic screams from man and woman. Monro's charged voice boomed above all others, directing the men of the 60th to form up and fire a volley into the thick fog bank to discourage the noisy pursuers. Scores of muskets fired with perfect simultaneity, creating a sharp, long-reverberating *cr-crack*! Less than two minutes later the colonel led the way into the fort with a fatigued young woman under each arm. He pulled them close. They clung to him, pressing their messed hair against his chest. One had fair features. The other was of darker complexion. From the strength of her nose and broadened cheek bones, I'd guess her to be mulatto. Their skirts were soiled and torn in places. Their faces were splattered with the grime from a long trail. Bruises decorated their arms.

Chasing closely after them was a major in the British army. This man was a fine specimen, large shoulders and a confident face. He was fit, but carried a little bulk in his jowls that made him appear to be older than he was. The rest of his features clearly indicated he was little past one score and five. All the while he raced, his eyes never tore from the back of the lighter haired sister. *He must be Major Heyward*, I thought. *She must be Alice*.

Then a most strange figure emerged from the bank of fog. It was Reverend Elisha Burton, resurrected! At least that is what my mind told my eyes that they saw. Tall and gangly. A hatchet nose with fragile spectacles perched on its bridge. I ran up to him. "Reverend Button!" I exclaimed in spite of myself.

The man reacted just as I'd have expected Button. He jumped, his voice rising in a trill. "Dear! I do not know what more my heart can take of this strange place! Specters attack from the clouds both inside and outside the fort!"

"I saw you shot and killed," I gasped. "Last year!"

His hands patted down his own chest, probing every tatter in his coat for a hole in his flesh. "Dear! I'd think I would have remembered such horror. The pain, I'd think, would be unforgettable. Goodness. I wasn't shot. Though a year ago I did have a nasty fall down a flight of church steps."

"Then you are a minister!" I marveled. "Resurrected. Reincarnated. Whatever it is called. You are Elisha Burton!"

"I am not resurrected!" he insisted. "Though, I'd like to think of myself as born again." He then attempted, unsuccessfully, to calm himself. His large hands trembled.

Countless stray hairs jutted out from beneath his hat, which was askew. His voice quivered. "I am no minister. A psalmist," he answered. "A psalmist who requires a rest. Now, sir, I must respectfully insist that you allow me to pass. I am a stranger to you. A stranger who feels faint."

I stepped aside and let the twin of the man I'd known drift into the fog that choked the parade ground.

"Strange one," said a familiar voice. I turned to see Chingachgook enter the fort. He was followed by his son and the famous Hawkeye. "His incessant singing makes the distant mountains aware of our approach long before we can even see them." It was yet another trait that made me feel the lanky Methodist minister had come back to life.

"Oh, it's not as bad as all that," Hawkeye countered. He set his hands upon his hips, allowing his long, rifled piece to rest on the ground while leaning against his chest. "Well, it probably is, but we've all got our gifts from Providence, you see. My voice can't carry a tune. But my eye, and aim, is true. We've all gifts."

I shook their hands, welcoming them as the redcoats returned inside, having driven off the small band of Canadians and Indians who had chased the party to our walls. "Have you raised the funds for the wife?" I asked Uncas after releasing his grasp.

"Weber!" Monro bellowed as he emerged from the fog bank. "I told you to gather powder. You may talk of Indian weddings another time!" He pointed a firm finger at Uncas. "You! I want to talk to you!" Then he marched off toward his headquarters.

Uncas looked to me for explanation. I gave him my favorite answer to most questions – I shrugged, then silently crept out the gate to make the mad dash toward Titcomb.

CHAPTER 54

Frye's stash of powder had dwindled only modestly since I had sat next to it reading the infuriating letter from my father. And the Massachusetts colonel understood that the battle would now be won or lost at William Henry and not upon the walls of his encampment. The Indians, as sane men, would not attempt to exuberantly attack a fortified position if they did not have direct support of artillery. He gave generously from his stores.

I recruited Brown from his lounging among the rangers to assist in my chore. He and I made multiple trips back and forth, clumsily rolling casks of powder from the camp to the fort's gate. Unfortunately, as we worked, the sun climbed higher along with the mercury. It burned off our cover of fog so that we hustled to and fro while under a hailstorm of musket shot. Twice, one of the kegs I rolled along the rough patch of ground between the doors was pierced by shot from the tribesmen. The impacts made me momentarily freeze and panic as I waited for a spark to send the staves, and me, flying to bits. I'm here writing. No such tragedy occurred.

Yet, even as we tipped the hundred-pound containers up in the storehouse, Turnwell's gunners rolled them down, and began dispensing the explosive mixture into a variety of charges. "At this rate, these new kegs won't last long," Brown, the master of stating the obvious, observed.

"Can't you bring any more?" asked Simeon as he carefully sealed a measured amount of powder in a bag that would be blasted over the French in a matter of minutes. With two hands, he set it in the ammunition crate he'd lugged from the ramparts.

"Stark and Frye need something with which to discourage the Indians from storming the embankments," Brown answered. "Elsewise, they'll resort to throwing rocks."

Simeon had already filled another pouch and cinched it closed. "Well, we'll have to spit at the Frogs soon enough if this is all you can spare." He set the bag in place and, with his smudged, practiced hands, set about filling the next in his stack. Meanwhile, another soldier clattered his way down the steps with yet another empty crate.

B-boom! B-boom! Turnwell's remaining artillery barked. *Crash! Crunch!* Montcalm's gunners punched holes into Eyre's labor of love.

Brown extended his hand. "I best get back to the rangers."

Our filthy palms embraced. "Be over there as soon as I can. But right now, I've got to find Monro."

"I bet he has you doing important things," Brown said as we stepped up and out of the powder room. "Private Ephraim Weber," he said with equal parts sarcasm and admiration. "Working for a colonel in the regular army!"

"He likes me so much, I'm going to marry his daughter," I bragged. The glimpse I'd captured of Cora had been brief. But she appeared comely, sharing the features with her womanly kind that drew men to them. I'm ashamed to admit it, but at that moment, had I been asked, I would have responded to a certain query by saying, *Hannah who*?

Brown grinned. "Don't that beat all?"

"I just have a way with women," I quipped, flashing what I thought a charming smile.

"And their fathers, I guess," said Brown jogging to the gate for his break across the killing zone.

"Mr. Weber?" I turned to face Major Heyward – his chest actually. He was a big man. He'd cleaned his face and run a comb through his hair since his return. Yet, his uniform still bore a coat of trail residue. "Colonel Monro bids me bring you to him." Without awaiting a response, he spun and noiselessly guided me into the headquarters building and down the hall past the commander's office. I noticed that the colonel's desk was stacked with sacks, kilderkins, and rundlets of dry goods or bottles of wine. Several chests had been moved inside as well. Fort records and items as diverse as herbs and vegetables were heaped about. Only a tiny rabbit path of floor space remained for a man to sneak between the towering cliffs of sundries. We then slipped by two other rooms with doors ajar that had likewise been suddenly relegated to storage room status. Then, Heyward's hand lifted the latch on the actual storeroom door.

Monro stood in the now-empty room's center. Since I had left to gather the gunpowder, bags of sand had been filled, transported to, and then stacked along the walls of the room. A single lantern flickered in the dim space, illuminating the crowd that had gathered. It hung from a hook hastily driven into a naked timber in the ceiling. As such, the lamp rocked gently from the constant rupture from guns. Cora and Alice rested on a roughhewn bench set against one wall of sandbags. They leaned against one another for what seemed physical and emotional support, clutching hands. Heyward moved immediately to Alice, who released her sister and set her head against the major's shoulder.

"What of the gunpowder supplies?" Monro asked.

"Low," I said. Monro's disgusted response prompted me to explain. "Frye is left with enough to fight off one, perhaps two, full attacks by the enemy. If they had to employ every musket and larger gun in the camp…" My voice trailed.

"And the fort's?" the colonel asked.

"Not much better, sir. At the rate Simeon and his laborers were filling and hauling charge bags, we've got one day left."

Monro bit his lip. He looked at his daughters and probably asked the same question he'd already asked them a dozen times. "What would possibly make you think it wise to visit me here?"

Alice sat up a little taller. "Your last letter said that you wished to see us, father. We thought it might be a nice diversion for you."

"It's a diversion alright," he snapped. "And how did you find out where I'd be."

Alice guiltily looked to her betrothed. Monro's eyes were instantly ablaze, sending their flame to the young major. Heyward squared his shoulders. "Colonel, I merely said that much of my dealings up the Hudson dealt with supplying your post. It was too much to say, I know, sir. But I was unaware of their attempt to come until it was too late. I discovered they were at Fort Edward when I arrived from York City to Albany. Well, I raced to Edward."

"And no one at Edward thought to warn you away?" Monro asked, astonished.

Cora spoke. "General Webb mentioned that there had been some trouble of late. But Major Heyward agreed to accompany us. And the general provided us a guide."

"Le Renard Subtil," Hawkeye said derisively.

"Magua," Chingachgook growled. "A fox of a man with the principles of a snake."

"Magua betrayed us," Heyward explained. "We would have been killed had it not been for these three men."

Chingachgook and Hawkeye stood tall. Uncas shied from the scrutiny. "I am in your debt, gentlemen," said Monro. "You've saved my most precious possessions on this earth." He bent down and placed a kiss on the head of each girl.

"If I might ask, colonel," Hawkeye began. "Why have you not informed Webb of your plight. He sits just fifteen miles down the road. Your powder stores could certainly last long enough for him to muster his army and trap the enemy between it and your walls."

"I thank you again for your assistance, woodsman," Monro answered stiffly. "But I have already done what you suggest multiple times. The general has decided to forgo dispatching assistance."

The pair of Mahicans and Hawkeye looked at one another, speaking without words. "Then you need all the help you can get. Mind if we join your men on the wall. I'm fair with this rifle," Hawkeye said. "And my companions can likely outshoot all but the best marksmen in your bunch."

"You are welcome to help where you will," Monro said. "But first, break your fast. We have ample food."

"Thank you, colonel," said Chingachgook. He took to the door and led the others out.

They passed Major Eyre on the way in. The colonel did not have to open his mouth to receive the news he had to share. Without referring to any notes, the engineer dove in. "Another mortar has exploded from fatigue, colonel. Thirteen men killed. Two crates of powder destroyed. We have just five working guns and I'm certain that Mr. Weber has informed you of our dire situation with regard to gunpowder. The Canadian diggers…"

"Woodchucks," Monro groused.

"Close enough," I said.

"The Canadians have dug to the swamp. While under a constant barrage and while sustaining heavy casualties, they've built a bridge over the swamp. Since then, they've dug through our gardens, sir. They are within 150 yards of our walls."

"A lazy-eyed child could hit a target that close," I murmured.

"And they have," Eyre went on, undeterred. "On the north and west, our walls have been reduced by three full feet. Casements are damaged. The sand we poured over the bunkers have helped, but much of it now lays scattered over the yard from exploding shells. It wouldn't take a large round to penetrate the last of our powder stores and send it up in a fury. And, sir, I might add, that I am sorry for failing to construct a fort that might have been equal to the task."

Monro gripped his engineer's elbow. "Your fort is a marvel, Major Eyre. Would it be that *I* were up to the task of defending her in the manner she deserved."

"Thank you, colonel," Eyre said.

The colonel again turned to his daughters, each lovely in her own unique way. I imagined what it would be like to marry Cora. Without the fog obscuring her features, I could see that my initial guess had been correct. Colonel Monro's first wife had been of African descent. Had I been a man who frequented the Georgia colony or spent time in the maddening cities on the coast, that fact might have bothered me. For men and women jabber and gossip and chat about things they do not understand. I'd not want to submit Cora or any woman to such needless scrutiny.

But I was a woodsman and her heritage worried me none. As long as she favored the divine nature of Providence, I believed a man and wife could surmount any differences. After all, I'd been married to a Miami woman. I'd been married to a merchant's daughter from Williamsburg. Why not someone whose roots sprang from yet another continent?

"You will stay here," Monro said, fixing the pair of women with a fatherly gaze. "This is the safest place in the fort, tucked against our earthen walls." His hands affectionately stroked their cheeks and he peered into their eyes, I believe, seeing their mothers youthful, alive, and well at that moment.

Then he again became a commander. "Heyward, Eyre, and Weber," Monro clipped, moving for the door. "Gather for me all the officers from the camp and the fort. We will meet in private in what remains of the enlisted men's barracks." He tugged out his watch. "Five minutes." Then he was gone.

"What of me?" asked a nervous voice from a darkened corner. I hadn't even noticed the spindly psalmist was in the room.

Heyward gave Alice a look. She interpreted his meaning. "Oh, David, please stay with us and keep us company. I do not know how we should ever get through this dreadful day without you to lift our spirits."

"But if the men are required to defend you with brute force, I must lend my strength to the noble task," he said with dubious confidence.

Major Heyward smiled approvingly at his betrothed. "Mr. Gamut," he said. "It is the most noble task a man can think of to protect the, the…"

"The fragile sensibilities of the fairer sex," Cora finished for him. Though fair (as in beauty, not hue), Cora did not in any manner appear to have fragile sensibilities. She was frightened to be sure, as would any normal person. But both Cora and her sister held themselves with dignified composure.

The psalmist's voice and limbs still quaked with terror. He seemed the only person in the room willing to believe the fib that he was somehow brave for staying behind in the storeroom with the Monro sisters. "Then I shall set my shoulder to the yoke of that noblest of duties," Gamut answered with relief.

Heyward led us out the door, careful to tightly latch its great oak planks tightly to the jamb. He clearly believed Alice to be a precious possession he wished to keep safe from all harm. Monro had two such possessions. And now, even I felt like I had something quite special to preserve.

If only Cora had known it. And her father had actually meant what he said.

CHAPTER 55

I believed it was a solid, nearly unassailable claim that when a daughter was born to a man, his heart softened. That mangled mass of tissue in his chest became progressively gentler over the years as the little girl grew and matured and became a woman in her own right. Because of the gift of her life, his heart was at last able to see the glint of decency that had always remained around him, but had been so difficult to perceive before her arrival. His mellowed heart now realized that he had a part to play in preserving goodness. For these reasons, daughters, women were deserving of great praise.

And I wonder how I would have matured differently had it been my daughter, not my son, that I had successfully recovered from that Philadelphian brothel the prior year. Would my cold heart have melted under the gaze of her blameless eyes? Would I have fled the foolish carnage and adventure that I seemed to so crave? Would I have remained on my parents' farm, raising my daughter along with hogs and cattle?

A day earlier, Monro had been sincere when he had threatened hanging anyone over the walls who so much as suggested surrendering to the French. Now, Lieutenant Colonel George Monro's heretofore rigid heart had been tenderized by the precipitous arrival of both of his genial daughters. He suddenly thought of preserving a future for them and others. At the meeting of his officers, he was among those advocating for and voting in favor of capitulation.

The final tally proved to be unanimous.

At 6:00 am the following morning, the Union Jack, that had so gallantly waved atop our flagstaff throughout the bloody strife, was replaced with a white banner of parley. Our cannons had been blazing for five straight days. The French had bombarded us for seventy-two terrifying hours. And as quick as a man snaps his fingers, the field fell silent. The gentle lap of Lake George could again be heard. A flock of gulls soared overhead.

Many capable representatives were sent from among our officers to discuss the terms of our surrender with our foes encamped across the glacis. The estimable Major Eyre made the trek over the pock-marked ground as our chief negotiator. The heroic Colonel Frye and passionate Major Heyward joined him. Lieutenant Stark embodied those clad in the simpler green and buckskin uniforms. Others, whom I have thus far never had cause to mention in my memoirs went along as well. There was a certain Captain Rudolphus Faesch, who was Swiss by birth, but served in the Royal American Regiment. Faesch's heritage meant he was fluent in French. He was accompanied by the commander of his regiment, Colonel John Young. Young was required to travel by horseback since he'd sustained a grievous wound from the shrapnel of an exploding mortar. And finally, as one of the few men capable of understanding the myriad of tribal languages, I was dispatched with those more notable men.

In short, it was nothing like the capitulation of Fort Necessity when the entirety of the English negotiating party had been comprised of two men, who at the time had only modest knowledge of French. I had been one of those envoys. Unbeknownst to us and Colonel Washington, we encouraged him to inscribe his signature to a page in which he admitted to committing several international crimes. After the Necessity debacle, it was that linguistic disadvantage that played the chief role in just how our own people came to view our ineptitude. Thankfully, I felt confident that such a bleak outcome was unlikely in this case. My use of French and Indian tongues had become better than my native English.

"Colonel Monro tells me that you are to wed his daughter, Alice," I said to Heyward. Surrounded by a small set of guards from the 60th, our column was a narrow snake working its way to the conference. We'd just walked through what was left of the fort's gardens. The well-tended rows were a thing of the past. Mounds of excavated clay, tracks of ditches, and heaps of exploded bits of logs, limbs, and vegetation fertilized the land. "Congratulations."

The brooding demeanor Heyward had painted upon his face for the coming discussions, relaxed. "Thank you. I'm unashamed to admit I am delighted. I dare say that Alice is as well."

"She looks it," I said. The way the pair had looked at one another in the supply room spoke volumes about their devotion. I had once looked upon Tahki with such eyes. And Bess.

"You talk of weddings at a time like this?" Stark asked through the side of his mouth. He marched directly in front of me. "We go to meet face-to-face with the enemy."

"Only a few moments, lieutenant. Then I'll have your man's mind back where it belongs," Heyward explained. Then he sighed out a great breath, allowing his cheeks to puff. "Now that I am certain Alice will be safe from the cannonade or a storming of the fort, I feel absolute relief. That's how it is when you care for someone more than you do your own life. I will encourage her to go home and wait for me there." We crossed the shoddily constructed bridge the French engineers had seen built to span the swamp. "I should like that Cora accompanies her, for both their sakes. But I'm told that a new suitor has come into the picture. Cora may linger in America."

If I wasn't filthy and sunburnt, the major may have noticed I blushed. I found a spring in my step that hadn't been there in many long months. "Then Colonel Monro has spoken to you about him?"

"Yes," Heyward said. We'd begun to pass through the outskirts of the French camp. Dirty laborers took well-deserved naps in their trenches, shovels still in hand. Artillery officers and men tended to tired guns, moving powder boxes and shot into place just in case our truce didn't hold. "We discussed him just before I was sent to bring you to the store room."

"And Cora is pleased?" I was almost afraid to ask. I hadn't even spoken a word to the raven-haired woman. Though, if Cora had been informed of her father's plans, she'd given me no queer or quizzical glances when we had shared the small space within the sand-bagged room.

"Tentatively so, I would say," Heyward admitted. "She's not voiced it, but I believe she is concerned about a mixing of the races."

I nodded. "There is wisdom in caution," I pontificated. "But might not the support of her father go a long way?"

Major Heyward grinned as our band of negotiators began to file between unwelcoming, twin lines of smartly garbed French grenadiers standing at attention, arms shouldered. “He does have a persuasive streak,” he admitted. “But of the two, I think she favors the union more than he.”

I shook my head in joyous disbelief, beaming like a young lad who had innocently fallen in love with the face of his tutor or the baker’s wife down the lane. At that moment, I realized that Providence had such a firm grasp upon my future happiness, that I should never question His wisdom. To think that I had had to endure the heart-wrenching losses of two wives and been witness to military tragedy upon calamity to wind up there upon the shores of Lake George, surrendering to be sure, but perhaps gaining a wife to whom I’d be wed for decades. From our union, her womb, might spring a dozen lads and lasses. Goodness from loss. The eternal way of Providence.

“I shall be glad to become acquainted with her,” I proclaimed. The shade of the forest began to fall around us and we passed ever deeper into the camp. Every stray stick or twig had been cleared from the forest floor, used for building gabions and cookfires. Thousands of idle troops loitered, curious to see whether or not their English foes really were two-headed wyverns.

“And I shall be honored to introduce you,” he proclaimed.

“It might be best if I allow Colonel Monro the honor.”

Major Heyward nodded his agreement. “You are a practical man with good sense of propriety, I see. While you’re at it, you may want to inquire of Uncas, the Mahican, before you visit with Miss Cora.”

I chuckled. “Uncas hardly says a word to his father and friends. I should think he would sooner skitter into a badger’s sett than come face-to-face with one as comely as Cora.”

Heyward joined in my mirth. “That was my impression of the lad as well. But, as with many men, he was able to find his courage when it came to love.”

“So, he did gather the money for his bride price? He sold enough pelts?”

We were near the end of the long lines of French soldiers. At their terminus, a wide, circular clearing beneath the vast canopy opened between the waters of Lake George on the right and a stagnant pond on the left. A low fire sent up wisps of smoke at the clearing's center.

"I don't know anything about a bride price," Heyward said. "Should the colonel agree to the match, I think that he would be happy to provide Uncas and Cora with a generous gift rather than the other way around."

"No, no," I said. "Uncas is marrying some Delaware princess."

"Not anymore," Heyward said.

"Uncas and Cora?" I asked.

"Yes," Heyward answered with a shrug. "Who did you think we were talking about marrying Cora?"

"Monro said that I…" I stuttered.

"Ephraim," Stark warned as we entered the ring of verbal contest. "Later."

"But I…" For once, I was at a loss for words.

Opposite our point of entry sat General Montcalm, wearing a green coat with yellow accents at the seams. His stark white breeches were tucked into the tops of his black leather riding boots, which were polished until they shined like a mirror. He was bracketed by Captain Bougainville, looking equally as grand, and Langlade, who had arrived in decidedly rougher attire. At least a dozen other French and Canadian officers surrounded them, creating an impressive aura of military attentiveness. Even Père Roubaud, his gray beard spilling over his shirt, had a place at the edge of the delegation. In some ways, the father acted as a bridge between cultures. To the Europeans on his right, he spoke French. To the Indians on his left, he spoke with an Algonquian dialect.

Chiefs, major and minor, from two dozen tribes stood or squatted about. Sturgeon was among them. The Caughnawaga chief who had held aloft the bloody letter from Webb had a seat nearby.

"Magua," Heyward grumbled, referring to a third scarred warrior who sneered viciously at our arrival. And he wasn't the only surly one. Fifty or more other frowning faces of tribesmen stared at us as we set our rumps on logs, bundles of hay, overturned barrels, or plump sacks that had been arranged for just this sort of meeting.

When our party had settled, Montcalm stood abruptly. Every one of his officers joined him in the gesture. He was a small man in stature, but his presence was large, exuding control over man, beast, and even the elements as was expected of a god of the battlefield. He chivalrously plucked off his green hat and swept it to his waist, slowly bending low. Bougainville and the others repeated the motion a heartbeat later and returned to their standing positions in the same instant as their commander.

Montcalm tucked his hat under his left arm. "What an honor you grant me by visiting this camp," he said with disarming charm through an interpreter. "For the remainder of my days, I shall count it as my undeserved privilege to have faced you in this contest. Your defense has been most spirited and carried out with a moral rectitude I would expect from proud Englishmen. And at this time, if it pleases you, and your esteemed commander, Colonel Monro, I should be further grateful to do all I may to see our two parties agree to terms that we might put an end to these hostilities." His opening remarks were a far cry more complimentary than when he'd chastised our lackluster defenses at Fort Oswego.

Colonel Young, wavering atop his horse, muttered a few things to Captain Faesch, who was to act as our chief interpreter. "Tell him, thank you," grunted the colonel, in obvious pain, blood seeping through his bandages. "Inform him that Major Eyre will be our main spokesman."

After Faesch had conveyed the colonel's response, he looked to Eyre for direction. Our chief engineer began, with Faesch speaking only a word or two behind.

"It is I who toiled to construct the fort you've seen daily through your glass, General Montcalm. Two of your predecessors have come against it, the first, when William Henry was but a pile of dirt and sticks. Both failed. But you, sir, have persevered. And for that achievement, I congratulate you. And Colonel Monro sends his regards, as well."

"It is I who must congratulate you, major," Montcalm said. There was not a hint of sarcasm present. This old man from Old

Europe had an old sense of nobility that forced me to admire him. "Never have I seen mere timbers, stone, and earth withstand such a constant barrage at such close range. Your engineering brilliance has cost His Most Christian Majesty much in the way of manpower and treasure. Nonetheless, I give you my endearing respect."

"Thank you," answered Eyre. He solemnly glanced about the motley ring of warriors, steeling himself for what he was about to admit. "Colonel Monro has authorized us, as his representatives, to arrange for the orderly surrender of the garrison. We've come to treat with you in a forthright manner and would be obliged if you vow to do the same."

"There is no need to be concerned, major," Montcalm assured him, taking the time to study each one of us. I'm sure he recognized me from our encounter under identical circumstances the prior year. He lifted his eyebrow and tipped his head in salute. "In a show of good faith, I will offer you the terms that you'd likely hope for yourselves were you permitted to speak first. In light of your valiant efforts, I will grant you all the honors of war. First, all personal effects, including small arms, and a single bronze field piece will be retained by you and your men. I grant the entire garrison, from your Colonel to your camp followers, safe passage to Fort Edward. Your wounded, who may be unable to travel, will be placed under the care of our best physicians and freely returned to the nearest English outpost when they have fully recovered. And the stipulations we must levy are no more than what you may expect. Each one of you will take the role of a non-combatant for a period of eighteen months. All stores of war within and about your fort, including gunpowder, cannons, and unspent shot are to become the property of King Louis. All French prisoners currently in the hands of the English will be returned to Fort Carillon in three months' time. And finally, as a mark of my true esteem, I will require only one British officer stay behind as my guest until the escort of French troops which will take your garrison to Fort Edward has returned safely. Should you accede to my proposal, I recommend a transfer of the fort into our possession by midday."

Nearly a score of interpreters rattled off his words in English, Iroquois, and the myriad of Algonquian tongues from Ojibwe to Fox to Lenape to Abenaki and on and on. Father Roubaud spoke to a particular band of warriors who stared at him with rapt attention. He was the type of man who expressed himself with his hands. They seemed a vital accompaniment to his voice. Other priests translated to other packs. Several Canadian officers had organized their designated companies of tribal warriors into neat rows. The gray clad men informed their near naked charges of Montcalm's terms.

"You," moaned Colonel Young. He winced, leaning over his horse's withers. "Weber, you understand all that's being said over there?"

"Most of it," I assured him as I perked my ears to what had become a back and forth exchange between interpreters and Indians.

"What are they saying?" Young asked as Eyre and Faesch continued the discussions with Montcalm.

"It just so happens that understanding the words they are saying isn't all that important in this case," I said.

The colonel gasped haltingly as he twisted in his creaking saddle to observe the side show. He watched for a full minute before slowly fixing his gaze back to me. An involuntary moan escaped as he said, "None too happy, are they?"

I peeked around him. Sturgeon caught my glance. He snarled. The one that Heyward had named as Magua, too, curled his lip the more of the terms he heard.

That is when the Caughnawaga chief, who'd brandished the bloody letter, brushed past his tribal brethren and shoved his way into the center of the circle. He faced his back to us as he stood tall and addressed Montcalm, interrupting Colonel Frye, who'd been in the middle of an exchange with the French corps of officers. The chief fluidly danced between employing French and his native Iroquois.

"What's he saying?" Eyre asked Captain Faesch.

The Swiss man shrugged. "I'm only getting every other word."

"Tell him, Weber," Stark ordered.

I'd been listening intently, but struggled to remember the angry chief's opening. "My great French father, I am Kanectagon," I interpreted. "A chief in a line of chiefs, a sachem to my people, who had lived among the woods and rivers of what the British name as New England and the Mohawk call Iroquoia. But my people, your dedicated Caughnawaga, were driven away to your Canada, not by the English and their Yankee kin. No. It was our own confederation of tribes, the Iroquois, who sent us away. From beneath the Tree of Great Peace, Onondaga said that we had no place among them, that our conversion to the true Catholic faith gave us more in common with our French fathers than own former brothers like the Cayuga, Oneida, or Seneca."

Kanectagon continued. "And one hundred autumns ago, we went. I am the sixth chief in my line to have lived among the Canadians and Frenchmen and towns. My fathers before me have served His Most Christian Majesty in all manners. I, and my own band of braves contribute our blood and honor to the cause of Louis, king, and our father, General Montcalm. I ask the general to recall that it was I, as his child, who brought him the blood-soaked letter that gave him the confidence to continue his siege without fear of an assault from the coward, Webb."

Though I agreed with the words, saying them out loud with so many officers about, drew more than one scowl. "You're not editorializing a paper, Weber," Stark warned.

"I'm just repeating what he says," I answered.

"Shut up," Stark grumbled. "Just keep talking."

"And so," I said, jumping back into Kanectagon's speech midstream. "I ask my father, Montcalm, to consider his children, the Caughnawaga. The terms you offer deprive my warriors of trophies and of glory. We will get no captives to sacrifice or enslave. We will take no scalps. We will get no treasure. Yet, we have given our time and risked our lives for His Most Christian Majesty's glory. Would your king not want you to share in the spoils of victory with those whose hearts are forever with his?"

"His king has no heart!" screeched Magua. "For I have eaten it from his chest." He spat in the face of the nearest Catholic priest and huffed off.

Sturgeon held out his hands to calm his fellow Potawatomi as they chanted their agreement. "Listen! Listen! Listen for our father's words. He is wise and good. And though the Caughnawaga is a tribe without a home and without honor, let Montcalm answer Kanectagon's question!"

Kanectagon nodded half-hearted thanks to Sturgeon. Claude, apparently friends with precious few of his fellow tribesmen, fixed him with a slit-eyed stare. Kanectagon again faced Montcalm, pleading. "Father, will you not answer?"

Montcalm was visibly ruffled. Normally polished in all ways, his face had twisted in discomfort. "Chief Kanectagon, I thank you for reminding me of the dedication of your people and of yours personally. Rest assured, your father will always look upon you with the proud eyes one would expect. As to your present sacrifices, you and your men have been fed with the best of our provisions. No more, no less than Canadians and Frenchmen. You and your men have been supplied with ample ammunition. I am a father who treats all of his children equally. And, upon the conclusion of this campaign you will return to your villages as heroes and with the eternal gratitude of your king."

Again, the interpreters buzzed among the tribes. In pairs, or in groups of three, Indians got up and walked out, their disgust apparent. Sturgeon grabbed ahold of the large cross that dangled from his neck and yanked until its cord snapped. He marched up to Roubaud and hammered it into the old man's chest. "If, after a century, this bit of wood has not helped the Caughnawaga dogs earn gifts from the Onontio, I will not waste another moment with it." He roughly shoved the priest away with one hand. Sturgeon's fellow Potawatomi brazenly did the same thing, one-by-one, following after their leader as he retired into the woods.

"You tell this Montcalm that he'd better get his savages under control," Young grunted to Faesch. "You tell him we don't shy away from war. We're Englishmen. But you tell him that all of his graces can go to hell, if he thinks he can allow a band of naked Indians to cut us down when we are unarmed."

Faesch dutifully relayed the message. Bougainville appeared ill at the turn of events. Langlade leaned his back against a tree, wearing a curious grin as he waited to hear Montcalm's response.

The little general called out loudly, in English. "Colonel Young, your concerns do not fall on deaf ears. For, where would be a man's honor if he allowed others, even his children among the tribes, to alter his promises? He would have none, I say. And I further say, promise, and swear to you, my gallant foes, that, should you agree to the terms I've offered, they will be followed in exacting detail."

"Like at Oswego?" I asked.

Montcalm appeared less than calm. A shot of embarrassment jolted him. Yet, he managed to ignore my barb. Instead, he turned to face the Indian representatives who remained. "My children, your father is concluding a peace, do you not trust your father?"

"We trust our father," came a few, less than resounding, replies.

"Bien," said Montcalm. "Then you will return to your camps and allow your French fathers and Canadian brothers to orchestrate the surrender. You will remain among us as valued companies of warriors. Then, when the time comes, we will march home. You will have tales of this great siege and the battles that accompanied it to share around your council fires for the rest of your lives. There shall reside your lasting glory, in the stories you tell to your progeny."

After the tribesmen, led reluctantly by Kanectagon, made their oaths to obey the terms of the agreement, Montcalm returned his focus to us. "Will that suffice, Colonel Young?"

The colonel's attention had waxed and waned with his level of pain. He managed a grunt. Nearby, Frye, Eyre, Heyward, and Stark whispered as the defeated Kanectagon plodded into the crowd.

"We have little choice," rasped Major Heyward. "The woman and I skirted their camps on the way in. They are far too numerous."

"I trust not in Montcalm's ability to hold the reins of his allies," Eyre said.

"Then let us tell him that we'll carry his terms to Monro in order to confer. Meanwhile, we send another letter to Webb," suggested Frye. "Webb cannot possibly let us surrender when there is a blatant threat of Oswego all over again."

"He can," I murmured. "He will."

"Shut up, Weber," Stark said. "But he's right. We'll get no help from Webb at this stage. At least nothing that can possibly arrive in time."

Eyre studied the worn faces of his men. He took a longing look over his shoulder. The mangled outline of Fort William Henry could be seen through the trees. The heads or caps of a hundred or more curious Englishmen stuck above the parapet, watching for signs of our negotiation's progress.

The major made a snap decision. He spun back toward the fire, straightening his jacket and hat. He took three broad steps away from his cadre of officers and brought himself to stiff attention. Without command, we did likewise. So did Montcalm and his staff. In a single, fluid motion, Eyre drew his sword and carefully grasped the blade near the hilt. With chin held high, he extended the grip toward the dying embers and Montcalm.

In response, the French general leaned to Bougainville and whispered in his ear. The trusted captain then left his side and marched around the fire, halting directly in front of Eyre. His hand reached for and took the sword. He swept it once in a clockwise manner. He swept it once in a counterclockwise direction, ending with the blade in front of his nose. "A fine specimen, Major Eyre," Bougainville said. "General Montcalm accepts your surrender." He changed his grasp so that he now held the blade near the hilt. "But not your sword. My general keeps his word, monsieur. You and your men may keep all of your personal arms."

Eyre smiled sadly, nodding to the general across the way. He took his sword and slid it home at his side. "We will await your arrival at our open gates," he said to Montcalm. The opposing men noiselessly bowed to one another and Eyre led us back the way we'd come.

Atop his beast, Young was unconscious, blood wetting his horse.

The officers mumbled about what might happen once the French took over the fort.

And after all that, the only thing I could think to say was, "What do you mean Uncas is marrying Cora?"

CHAPTER 56

To the somber beat of our lads' drums, we filed out through the gates of William Henry.

And into the camp at Titcomb. Despite the brevity of the march, with General Montcalm and thousands of Frenchmen and Canadians staring at our shamed forms, it was a time of deep reflection. Since my first involvement with this War of the Two Tongues, I had been certain that the righteous cause and that of the English were one and the same. It had been the French and Indian attacks at peaceful Pickawillany that had started it. It had been the brash seizure of the new English fort situated at the Forks of Ohio that had further stretched our frayed relations. And then, it was the Frog's pursuit of Washington's force and our humiliating destruction at Necessity that sealed the fate of the world into a state of conflict.

Since then, our noble cause had suffered under the twin fronts of military defeat and brutal Indian raids. Thousands of citizens in Pennsylvania and Virginia had been slaughtered in their homes by roving bands of Delaware, Shawnee, and even those southern tribes of which I had no direct knowledge. The middle colonies had given up even trying to keep the peace, withdrawing to within a hundred miles of the seaboard. Braddock's disastrous march had further emboldened our foes. The ruthless destruction of Fort Bull and all its inhabitants, the lamentable Fall of Oswego and the massacre that followed – these debacles had been the norm for almost every campaigning season. Only Sir William Johnson's improbably victory in the Battle of Lake George could be considered a success. Wins at the Battle of the Bloody Pond and Eyre's repulse of Rigaud's winter raid were minor compared to our long list of defeats.

How could a cause, if truly righteous, be thwarted at every turn?

Then the psalmist, David Gamut, answered the question that I had thought been uttered merely in my mind. "I imagine that the Most Holy High God of Providence wonders the same thing at times," he said. "Surely your kin among the Quaker folk of Pennsylvania have considered that in answer to your age-old question."

Monro and his daughters had led the column on its short trek. And with still more regular red-backed soldiers filing out from the battered walls of William Henry, the colonel had begun to organize the full order of march to Fort Edward within Camp Titcomb. Also within the confines of our former encampment were several hundred French and Canadian soldiers, who were meant to keep order.

"I'm sure I don't understand your meaning," I told the broomstick of a man.

He tutted. "Oh, I am disappointed in your Society of Friends that they have never conveyed this wisdom to one of their sons."

"In their defense, my attendance at Sunday meetings has been irregular."

He set a bony hand of comfort upon my shoulder. "Look how aged Moses was before he came to know the Lord. You are young, Mr. Weber. There is much time for you to delve into the Word of God."

"Uh-huh," I muttered, as I studied our surroundings, I was pleasantly surprised that there was not a single tribesman within the camp. The oaths most had taken under the watchful eyes of Montcalm and Kanectagon had had the desired effect. And even those who had ventured from their Indian fires north of the portage road, were few in number. Le Renard Subtil leaned a shoulder against the curtain wall of William Henry. His weapons were securely at his belt, but his perpetual scowl was difficult to read. Only a small band of his followers lingered nearby. There was nowhere near enough of them to cause trouble, even to an army of Englishmen who had vowed to keep their personal arms sheathed.

"And so, you see, the eternal plan of Providence has been for mankind's redemption from our fall. God's cause is the most noble ever conceived, to grant freedom and peace and forgiveness to each one of us, those who in no way deserve it," Gamut explained.

"What does that have to do with us?" I asked. A pebble hit my chest and bounced to the dirt. My eyes followed the path it had taken to find me. Claude Sturgeon and his pack of miscreants guffawed at the other end.

"Everything," David insisted. "God's most righteous cause is hindered year-in and year-out, by us! How much more so are the so-called righteous plans of mankind! In fact, I would be surprised if any virtuous plan, apart from Providence, could hope to succeed in the present, fallen state of the world."

The end of our column had passed beneath the flagpole in the fort. The lifeless banner of truce pointed to them as would an accusing finger. Montcalm peeped inside, saw the last of them, and withdrew. With him, he led Bougainville, and twenty senior French officers on the journey to his distant camp, where all of his accoutrements of command and style had remained.

"Are you saying that our cause in this war may still be just, even if we lose?" I asked.

"That and more," Gamut assured me. "Even in a man's personal life, just because he loses a prize to someone else, as long as he maintains his integrity, he may still win."

"Are you sure your name didn't used to be Button?" I asked.

He bunched the skin of his face into a stack of loose wrinkles. "I am not reincarnated, Mr. Weber."

I held up my hands in surrender. "So you insist!"

"David!" called Heyward. He stood next to Monro, who was mounted on a horse borrowed from Montcalm, in the van of the column now assembling inside the camp. "The colonel and I may be occupied during our march. Would you be so kind as to escort the Monro sisters?"

"Yes, major," answered the psalmist eagerly. "I believe I proved myself capable of such valiant deeds during my stand in the store room."

Heyward chuckled and returned to his business of jockeying men and women into place. After an advance guard of Frenchmen, Monro and his daughters and the regulars would go first. Followed by the provincial warriors. Followed by rangers, there may have been a half dozen of us left. Followed by militia. Followed by women and children. Followed by the wounded.

And finally, yet another company of Frenchmen would guard the rear.

I attended the psalmist to his lovely charges. "The major is a good man," I told Alice. "I wish you much happiness."

I had never introduced myself to her. The golden-haired Monro daughter cinched herself up into what was considered a polite posture and extended her hand. "Duncan makes me ever so delighted. Thank you for your well wishes, sir."

"That's no, sir," proclaimed Hawkeye, approaching along the length of the column. "That's Kestrel's Wing." His omnipresent Mahican companions followed. Chingachgook stayed with the famed marksman, while Uncas peeled away. He clasped hands with Cora. Their foreheads tipped toward one another, though each had the propriety to keep a finger's breadth of air between them.

"You heard my new name?" I asked, deciding that I could maintain my integrity without offering personal well-wishes to the Mahican and Cora. Besides, at that moment, any felicitations that I would speak to the happy pair would be forced and fictitious.

"A good name is rather to be chosen than great riches," the renowned hunter said.

"Wonderful use of the Word, Hawkeye!" exclaimed David.

"And some might dare call my companions and I heathens!" he declared.

Our heads instinctually turned toward a rising ruckus from the within the fort's walls. The last Englishman had vacated it, but no Frenchman had yet entered. A small company of Frogs was forming up to do just that. But there were shouts of terror and cries of pain. I heard a war whoop, then another. Normally, a hundred or a thousand would answer those first ones. None came. There were, in fact, no tribesmen nearby. Magua's and Sturgeon's bands had vanished.

Father Roubaud, panic-stricken, pushed his way through the forming French soldiers. "Mes fils!" he shouted in stern warning. "You mustn't do this!" He passed into the fort, disappearing toward the chilling sounds.

"What's going on?" Stark said, running to us. He had Brown in tow.

"A battle in the fort," Chingachgook answered.

"But there's no one left," Cora said.

"The wounded," Hawkeye and I said in one breath.

I ran to the nearest Frenchman. "You must stop this!" I demanded, pointing to the gate. "Montcalm gave his word."

"Get in line," the Frenchman answered, unmoving. He didn't so much as twitch his eyes, to me or toward the unholy sounds. But he was not deaf. His ears couldn't hide from the screams.

Monro trotted up. "I hear slaughter," he accused. "What is the meaning of this! Our wounded were to be treated with dignity and care!"

The young French private managed enough respect to glance up to the colonel. "I am to remain at my post, sir. As far as I can see, we are honoring our bargain. I and my fellow men are not constables to the tribes."

Monro swore and snapped the tips of his reins against his horse, driving it out of the camp and onto the road. He trotted next to the marching company of French warriors as they filed into William Henry. "Get in there and put an end to this! Punish the perpetrators!"

A sergeant uncaringly studied the defeated colonel. "My orders are to immediately take control of the fort and its munitions, sir. I've been told nothing about suppressing a band of raging tribesmen." When Monro attempted to guide his beast through the yawning gates, the sergeant spun on his heel and put up a hand. "Sir, I have strict instructions to allow no Englishman within these walls, except for those injured, who are already present."

"There will be no injured present if you don't do something!" Monro shouted.

Roubaud then emerged from one of the ammunition casements that had held our overflow of wounded. He was splattered in blood but appeared unhurt. Yet, he was dazed. His hands, wet with crimson, were held at his sides. His eyes were forlorn, crazed. "C'est tout," he cried. "Ils sont morts."

"All?" asked Monro.

"Tous?" asked the sergeant who, for that moment, was not the unfeeling Frog I had taken him to be.

"Tous," nodded the priest. Roubaud set himself on a rambling path that terminated at the feet of Monro's horse. He plopped down on his rump against the gate, shaking his head.

The colonel yanked the reins of his beast and began trotting along the gaping corps of French and Canadians. "An officer with integrity!" he shouted. "Give me an officer! Someone, come and hear my demands! This is unconscionable! Fetch me Montcalm!" Inside the fort, the sergeant had begun distributing his men up the steps and into the structures. The yard was momentarily empty.

"Should we make a run for it? Kill the bastards?" asked Brown.

"Too late," whispered Chingachgook. From the infirmary emerged Le Renard Subtil. He had two scalps fastened to his belt. They were fresh, dripping the blood of their former owners down his naked thigh. In one hand he carried a knife. In his other, with his fingers interlaced among shocks of long, thick hair, he carried an entire head of a woman. I recognized what was left of her as the laundress with the leg that had been snapped by the hurtling cannonball.

Cora and Alice gasped, turning away. Gamut turned an ill shade of green.

More warriors emerged from casements or barracks or the infirmary. They marched into the yard, carrying shoes or stockings stripped off of the men and women they'd killed. A Potawatomi had a pile of candlesticks pressed tightly against his chest. Over his head, Sturgeon swung a pocket watch at the end of its chain. He released it and it crashed into one of Magua's men. A scuffle broke out. Noses were broken, even an arm or two. But then, as quickly as it had begun, it snuffed out. The butcherers gathered up their ill-gotten trophies and giddily ran onto the portage road.

"Those men ought to be hanged!" Heyward shouted, shaking the French ensign in charge of the camp's guard.

But nothing happened. No one did anything. More Frenchmen methodically filed inside the fort. Our guards remained unbending.

"Major Eyre!" shouted Monro. He'd approached the embankment. "Get the goose-eating guards moving. And get our column on the march. Abandon all provisions except those essential to the march. We don't want this to turn into a massacre. I'm going to find Montcalm!"

"Sir!" clipped Eyre, who immediately conferred with his French counterpart for the march.

"Massacre?" asked Sturgeon as the colonel rode away. He and Magua shared an evil grin. For once, the foreign tribesmen seemed to agree on something, as unspoken as it was. Sturgeon shoved his stolen goods into the filled hands of his kinsmen. "Take these trophies to the camps. Pass them out. Tell Kanectagon and his followers that there are even more to be found for those willing to shed the yoke of their French masters for just an afternoon."

Magua did the same. Then the pair of men fearlessly led what remained of their bands directly into the camp. "You must put a stop to this!" Heyward demanded of the ensign.

"Your train is leaving, major," said the impassive young man.

"En avant, marche!" screamed a captain at the head of the French portion of the column.

Row-by-row, the victorious army began departing the camp. Once outside the low gate, they made an abrupt right turn, nearly a full about-face, to snake their way onto the portage road. Row-by-row, our British regulars dutifully followed, with Eyre at their head. I held my place next to Stark, at first allowing our position in the column to come to us.

The smattering of roving tribesmen walked right past the redcoats, paying them no mind. Instead, they kicked over crates of chickens, stealing fowl and eggs, and kept on their way. "David and I will stay with the women," Heyward assured Uncas, who looked pitifully at Cora as she stepped forward. "It is safest to stay at our designated places in the column." With every second, the French van pulled further and further away down the road.

More redcoats filed by inside the camp as they looped onto the road, the 60th Regiment, the 35th. Turnwell and his blackened artillerymen came next. One of them had stolen a rammer as a souvenir. Left one-legged from a hurtling ball, he used it as a crutch. Turnwell pulled the reins of the ungainly horse that hauled the token cannon Monro had been allowed to keep.

Uncas gaped hopelessly at the receding form of the woman he considered his betrothed. "You may join us," Stark offered. He pointed with a thumb and began walking in the opposite direction of the column to find our places.

"Thank you," Chingachgook said, gently pulling his pitiful son toward the rear. "By the time the sun sets, my Uncas, you and I will treat with Chief Monro. You will have your bride. Our race may continue."

Uncas smiled sheepishly and trailed after Stark. "Keep your eyes pinned front," the lieutenant warned us as a half score new tribal warriors arrived from the Indian camp. They leapt over the unguarded embankment and rustled through untended baggage, fanning out with Magua and Sturgeon to find the best treasures. "Don't look at them. They won't look at you. I want no trouble. The battle is over and lost. Our job is to get to Edward."

"Aye, sir," chirped Brown.

The very front of our column was now passing the embankment on the road. Magua took note of Heyward and the comely companions he'd betrayed. Clutching a woman's dress and a sack of flour, he called to them. "Dark-haired daughter of Monro. My lodge still has a place for you!" He dropped his goods and ran to the low wall, reaching over it and grasping her dress with his bloody hands.

She screamed, "Away," and tugged free. Cora looked down in horror at the streak of crimson across her skirts.

Le Renard Subtil croaked with wicked laughter. "It is red, but it comes from white veins!"

I diverted from the rest. "Weber!" Stark barked. "Ignore it. Weber!"

"You ignore it. Keep going!" I told him.

"Brown!" Stark hissed. I looked back to see that my fellow ranger had followed me. Uncas chased after him, Chingachgook and Hawkeye on the Mahican lad's tail.

"Keep your hands off!" I growled, forcefully yanking Magua around by the shoulder. Quick as a wink he pulled a knife up with a cocked arm.

"Non!" shouted a Canadian guard from within the camp. "No killing!"

Magua froze momentarily as a trio of St. Etienne muskets leveled in his direction. He flashed a smile filled with worn yellow teeth and patted me on my crown. Then without further confrontation, he tucked his knife away and returned to his looting, careful to roughly brush against Brown, then Uncas, then Chingachgook, then Hawkeye as he wound deeper into the camp.

"Is it impossible for you to follow orders?" Stark asked when I returned.

"Sometimes you have to act impulsively for love," Uncas answered, boldly for him. Hawkeye chuckled.

Several minutes went by with only minor instances of arguments as the camp was looted by an ever-growing mass of young braves. They were warriors who'd been filled with bloodlust from the previous days of battle. Then they'd suddenly been made greedy by today's stories of easy glory to be had within the camp and fort. Spectacles were plucked from a man's nose. Then the Indians returned their attention to the discarded tents and liquor stores. Kegs were cracked open and their contents poured down thirsty gullets. News spread. More tribesmen came. Some of them left the camp, arms full of merchandise and scurrying so they might hide their ill-gotten goods and return for more. A woman's shawl was tugged right off her shoulders. Still more warriors arrived, seemingly more than had attacked the camp at any time during the battle. Painted warriors, brave and coward alike, came for prizes.

Eventually, all the goods that could be stolen, lifted, or consumed had been. And still more roving warriors showed up in camp. Late to the party, Kanectagon led a hundred Caughnawaga. His band inserted itself behind the rangers as we began to move out. "Stop," he told the militiamen at our rear. "Give us your weapons and clothes." None of them budged. So, Kanectagon tugged out his war club and repeated the order.

"No bloodshed!" hissed a Frenchman.

"I mean to shed no blood," Kanectagon answered. "Why would I want to soil my new clothes?"

The French guard laughed. "Give him your clothes," he told the militiamen and then continued his patrol through the camp that was growing more chaotic with each passing moment.

"They can stand to march barefoot," Stark warned us, careful to give me a stern glare. "As long as they are safe, keep marching."

"And if they are not safe?" I asked.

"Keep marching," Stark answered.

Soon, except for a long shirt here or a pair of breeches there. The militiamen were bare-chested, bare-legged, or completely nude. Huddled and ashamed, they waddled back into the order of march, under constant derision from the victors, who joyously tried on their new garb.

Next followed the women and children. "Give us your clothes," ordered Sturgeon, who'd appeared suddenly. He had a drum slung over one shoulder and a fife stuck into his belt. The handle of a wicker basket was nestled in the crook of his arm.

"Never!" barked a defiant cook. She clutched a family blanket around her ample midsection.

"Then we will take you along with them," yelled Sturgeon. He grabbed the sleeve of the woman in question and yanked her away. Each one of his fellow Potawatomi snatched a woman for themselves. More than one child was wrenched from her mother's arms. In some cases, the Potawatomi war band had one captive to each hand, dragging the thrashing children and women by the hair.

Naked husbands in the militia turned and, with only their bare hands as weapons, advanced on the thieves.

I need not tell you what was the result.

Eight naked colonists were cut down in a heartbeat. They'd been bashed with clubs or hacked with tomahawks. Blades flashed, flicking streaks of scarlet throughout the camp. More of the militiamen died as the women and children were thrown over the low wall and tied to nearby trees. A crying baby was smashed against the ground until it breathed no more.

Then, as fast as a spark ignites dry tinder, the bloodlust of men surged. At once, without warning, it hammered from our hearts and into our muscles, bypassing our minds so that our bodies might do the most damage to those enemies we suddenly hated more than ever.

A war whoop sounded. Some say it was Magua's voice that made the screeching appeal for violence. Others name Kanectagon as the minstrel of the macabre music. But I've also heard tell that it was Sturgeon, Turned Hand, Weasel's Grin, Onchonow, or Stone Steel who made the fateful cry. It doesn't matter. Because, while they had pillaged the fort's hospitals, there had been no one to hear the call. This time, more than a thousand armed, young tribesmen were crammed in and about Titcomb. They answered with their own ghoulish chants.

Hatchets crashed against skulls. They chopped through arms upheld in defense. Knives stabbed or filleted. Painted braves flashed from here to there, dragging captives of all ages into the woods. Those who fought back with too much effort were summarily executed and scalped. Another baby was killed, hurled into the stampeding mess. Muskets fired. Some shots came from my fellow rangers. Frye's provincial soldiers loaded and shot in a haphazard fashion. Some blasts had even rung out from among the Indians, which at that moment had now truly come to embody the word, *savage*.

In fact, there were only two bands of warriors on the field that day that did not use their weapons. The Canadians in our camp carefully backed away, slithering over the walls to safety. The Frogs, too, vanished. Hoarfrost, melted and evaporated on a sunny day, left a more meaningful trace. Meant to shelter us from just such a tragedy, our guards protected none but themselves.

The order of the march disintegrated. Tribesmen were among us. Or, perhaps, we were among them. An Ottawa was upon me, reaching for the pistol in my belt. My Bess was strapped to my back and momentarily out of reach. I whacked his forearm with a balled fist and used my other hand to drive my tomahawk up into his chest.

"To the militia!" I heard Colonel Frye call from his place among the Massachusetts and New York troops. "Protect them and the women!" But the Indians had begun to insert themselves among his own men, chopping and chanting. Some of his soldiers stayed and fought, losing their lives and clothing. Others panicked and ran up the road, slamming into the backs of the heretofore unmolested regular soldiers.

About two yards distant from me, an Abenaki dropped to his knee. He wheeled back his arm and launched a spinning hatchet. I blocked it, just barely, with the musket I'd just unslung and leveled the muzzle in his direction. He smiled, crinkling the layers of clay and ash he'd used to paint himself. Then, he stood slowly, and boldly stuck out his tattooed chest. "That's not loaded," he bragged. "Montcalm told the English to travel with their pieces clean and free from powder. And the English are good, obedient dogs."

"And Montcalm told his allies to treat us with respect," I said, squeezing the trigger. The angular flint struck the Bess' frizzen, sending a shower of sparks into my primed pan. An instant later the powder packed at the back of the barrel ignited and sent a lead ball into the warrior's cheek, turning half his face to shredded meat. "Don't forget," I told the corpse. "Dogs have teeth." I never traveled in the forest without a fresh load of dry powder and shot in the morning.

Then, strange as it sounds, I was struck by an enchanting force that might have come from one of those old fairy tales told in our old countries. I was confused. For, over the din of battle I heard a strained voice singing in the highest tones available to mankind. In its quality and passion, the voice belonged to none other than Reverend Button. My heart grew heavy. I had not been able to prevent his death at Fort Oswego. Button haunted me through the psalmist.

"Cora!" shouted Uncas, his call returning me to reality. The brave Mahican warrior dashed the head of a Potawatomi against a rock in the wall, leapt to the road, and raced toward the van. Without hesitation, Hawkeye and Chingachgook dumped the men with whom they'd grappled and chased after him.

By now, the tribesmen had emptied their camps entirely. Warriors from a dozen clans fell upon the regulars. The French soldiers at the lead, seeing their fellow regular soldiers assaulted, finally reacted. They ceased their march and turned, running back to their aid.

But they could not reach the besieged British soldiers. For, fifty or a hundred or two hundred terrified redcoats ran into them head-on as they clamored for safety. Some frightened Englishmen ran straight down the road, not looking back, as they disappeared toward Fort Edward. Others ran into the woods. And there were still many tribesmen who had yet to claim their military trophies. These deprived men were willing to chase their prey in a game of deadly pursuit.

Among that scene of madness was Alice, Cora, and Gamut. Heyward fought off a pair of Chippewa with his sword. He used the butt of his pistol as a club. Gamut stood rigid, sheltering the women behind him. His eyes were closed as he faced an onslaught of blood-spattered warriors. And he sang at the top of his lungs. He was Button. To this day, I swear to you, he was Elisha Burton, Reverend Button, as back from the dead as the risen Christ. And as mad as it sounds, the experienced braves he faced at that moment, shied away. Whether they thought him crazed or charmed, I do not know.

But Magua was drawn to his melodic cries. "You will be my wife!" he demanded of Cora after he had slipped past Heyward.

"Never!" Cora shrieked defiantly. Uncas and his companions struggled through the melee. With every step they took, fighting parties tumbled in their path or menacing Mississauga tried to kill them. More women were murdered, men and children, too.

Alice's face raced pale and she collapsed from fright. Magua peered toward the fort and saw that Monro had finally been able to bring Montcalm and a dozen French officers with him from the west. Seeing his window of opportunity fading, Magua scooped up Alice and tossed her listless form over his shoulder. He bolted for the forest.

"Alice!" Cora shrieked. She grabbed Gamut's sleeve and they went chasing after.

"Cora!" Uncas shouted.

"Cora!" I said, leaping the wall.

Only to be met by Sturgeon. He bid me no formal welcome. The back of his hand cracked my lip and I rolled, upright but stumbling, barely catching myself with the butt of my musket rammed into the dirt.

"Ephraim!" shrieked Brown. I saw him being hoisted over the heads of four Ottawa warriors, the very clan that had captured him at our battle on snowshoes. He was bound from head to foot. His face, oh, his face, was grief stricken. And they slipped into the forest amidst a train of fifty other prisoners.

The bottom of Sturgeon's moccasin kicked my rump. This time there was no preventing my fall. I tucked my head, somersaulting. I thought I would wind up on my feet, but Sturgeon had already pounced. His elbow locked around my neck and the blade of his knife flashed before my eyes. "The plumage of Kestrel's Wing will decorate my wigwam for all my days."

I reached back and seized his calf, tugging with all my might. Down he went, shaving a section of my scalp with his sharp blade. Now, I was upon him. The heel of my palm rammed into his windpipe. The muzzle of Tahki's French pistol punched into his belly. It discharged its blunt missile.

He struggled all the more, cursing and spitting. Blood churned from the gaping hole in his stomach. Sturgeon screamed, clutching my ears with both hands. He wrenched them. He twisted them, pulling my forehead hard against his own. My head rang. Stars danced before my eyes. I pulled my knife from its home at my belt and slipped it between his ribs. Sturgeon grunted. He winced and whined, clawing madly at my flesh and eyes with his filthy fingernails. Yet, with each stroke, he lost strength. He was sapped of it. Two minutes later, with much whimpering, he breathed his last, gurgling breath.

I stood, coming face-to-face with Langlade. I panicked, grasping for any of my weapons, which seemed to delight the Ottawa Canadian. But he was no threat. He chuckled, unmoving, with his hands resting on his twin pistols. "Pity," he sighed. "I saw all the excitement and came over to watch you die. It looks like it was a wasted trip."

"Why don't you try to do it yourself," I snarled, flicking his wounded ear.

He didn't budge as I went about gathering my scattered weapons. The arrival of the highest-ranking French officers seemed to have had the desired effect. From the dying clamor, it was clear that the worst of the battle had begun rumbling to a close. Langlade used the top of his head to point down the road. "My French father would not like it if one of his Canadians took part in a massacre." His tone was filled with oozing mockery.

"If you did nothing to stop it, you're just as guilty."

"Langlade!" screamed Montcalm. The general had forcibly taken a captive from an Indian's hands. Then, perversely, rather than lose their prizes, other tribesmen killed their prisoners and stole their scalps before Montcalm could intervene. "Langlade, control your divisions!"

Langlade gave me a smug tip of his hat and took his time returning to where his mixed force of Canadians and Indians had begun to coalesce. Many of the tribesmen under his command sported new red coats or hunting shirts.

Meanwhile, the little general had a gloved hand clutched around Kanectagon's neck. The Caughnawaga was a head and a half taller and four stone heavier than the Frenchman. Yet, Montcalm was undeterred. He drove forward, pressing the wide-eyed Indian against the wall of our former camp. "You swore to me. I am your father. Liar! You swore!"

Kanectagon held his blood-red hands at his sides, stating calmly, "You denied your children the honors of war."

"Honor?" Montcalm retorted. His anger was piqued, his face blazing. "Where is the honor in killing an unarmed man? A child could do it. In fact, that is what you are, a cosseted child. Not a child worthy of having a French father and French king. All of you are overindulged children, screeching at your mother's knees!"

Over the whole of the grounds, similar scenes played themselves out. Officers barked. And, for the most part, the tribesmen, tired from their exertion, complied.

They did so only because they'd already claimed their valuable prizes. Hundreds of English and freedman captives could be heard shouting in the woods as they were dragged back to Indian camps or even beyond, already beginning their long journey to the pays d'en haut. Scores of warm scalps hung from belts or were proudly displayed at the ends of makeshift poles. Trinkets, brooches, vests, rings, waistcoats, breeches, folding razors, trousers and toiletries, skirts, children, hatchets and hens, muskets, plates and pistols, swords, belts and boots, cookpots, forks, thimbles and thread, and more, so much more. Everything that was not attached to human flesh was taken. And in many cases, even human flesh had been ripped free.

"Take your so-called warriors with you!" Montcalm went on as Colonel Monro frantically searched among the dead for any sign of his daughters. "Return to your hovels and never come back!"

Kanectagon frowned. "Vaudreuil will be displeased."

"The governor general can follow you to hell if he wishes!" Montcalm snapped. "Never has a French soldier needed such allies any less than he does now!" He gave the Caughnawaga chief one last shove and strode off, stepping over spilt blood and scattered chests.

I flopped to my bottom in the road. But rather than steadily feel my breathing calm and return to normal, it raced. My heart pounded in my chest. I felt queasy. My temples thundered. Never had I felt this way after a battle. Even after the Oswego massacre, I hadn't panicked.

But the massacre at William Henry was different. It all happened in the span of two minutes, a blunt shock to the very soul. In all my time at war on the frontier, it was some of the most personal fighting I'd seen. Personal because it struck so indiscriminately against the weak as well as the strong. From where I sat, I counted four babies, all who had not yet reached the age to walk, dead. The corpses of twelve women, their skirts and bodices stripped off so that the areas of their bodies rightly reserved for modesty were on full display. And still, there were more sights within my field of view that I dare not etch onto the printed page.

My hands trembled uncontrollably. And I cried.

EPILOGUE

It took two sleepless days for me to make the short trek to Fort Edward. There was no French escort, no waving standard under which to march, no music, no fanfare, and no orderly column. The tribesmen, now completely loose from their French masters, patrolled the road with exacting dedication and wholesale butchery. I stuck to paths, known only to me, that were no wider than what would permit a rabbit to pass unscathed. Stark and I led a motley assembly of five militiamen, one New York provincial soldier, three regulars, and a woman and her child over the hilly terrain.

After the massacre (I've decided that I am unable and quite unwilling to refer to it as a battle), I had no contact with Hawkeye, the two Mahican men, Gamut, Monro, Heyward, or the two sisters. The forest, and history, had swallowed them whole. I have waited for near fifty years to discover what became of them. Suffice it to say, I never married Cora. Though, when I am not in a surly mood – rare, to be sure – I like to imagine that she and Uncas have a full brood of grandchildren galloping around the creeks and lakes of what we used to call Iroquoia. Such notions are pure fantasy.

"I swear! I do swear!" screamed Johnny Anson when we entered Edward's busy yard. He rattled down the white painted steps from the wall walk. "Ten men came from William Henry yesterday. Only ten, when it was supposed to be a couple thousand! They wore only breeches! I swear. They were crazed with fear, I tell you." He rambled a mile a minute. "Half a company of regulars came in during the night. They had all their clothing, but none of their weapons, even though that snake, Montcalm said they could keep their arms! What happened to their muskets? They told of a massacre. I swear, was it bloody?"

At the mention of the carnage, the child of the woman we'd led to safety cried against her shoulder. She, herself whimpered, as she set a course to where the other camp followers who had managed to survive had begun to congregate. I counted four other women and twice as many children. Each of them appeared bewildered.

Wordlessly, the other men with whom I had made the journey split off in separate directions, not a one thinking it important to report to a commander of any kind. With heavy eyes, Stark patted my shoulder and crawled under a set of stairs. He was asleep a minute later.

Johnny dug a half-nibbled pear from his pocket. "You look hungry. Are there many more of you left? How did you get through? I barely made it through myself. With all the time I wasted hiding and ducking and crawling, it took me half a day to get here. Must have been worse for you."

I roughly grabbed the lad's head and tugged it to my chest. I gave him a hug. He allowed it without a fight, but did not return the gesture. He was like so many in those days. Johnny had known a tough life from a young age, so he was accustomed to pain and hardship. Peace, plenty, and privilege were as foreign to him as a merchant from Cathay. "Good to see you made it," I said. "I'm sorry I sent you alone."

He pushed away, shaking his head energetically. His poker-straight hair flopped and flapped. "It would have been more dangerous to stay. I'm glad I came when I did."

I offered a sleepy smile. "So am I." I examined my surroundings. "Did Nero make it with his message."

"I did," called Nero, approaching. "I heard a few rangers had just come in and wanted to see for myself. Where's Stark?"

I embraced the freedman the same as I had Johnny. Nero reciprocated, slapping my back a time or two. Then I pointed to the buff and green curled up ball of Stark. Nero chuckled. "The lieutenant knew I was fast. Had to be. I had to run, full-churn, the whole way here. Had a band of blood-hungry savages on my trail the entire way. But I gave Webb that message." Nero tousled Johnny's hair. "So did Anson."

"Lot of good it did," I grumbled. "A garrison of French soldiers would have come to our aid quicker than what that turd Webb did."

A hot tongue licked my hand. I stooped to scrub Sarah Belle's ears. "She likes you," Itch called. "Makes me jealous, you know. She'd like to marry you. But I keep telling her that she's mine. We made our vows to one another all those years ago. She can't leave me just because a younger man comes around. Not right!"

I hugged Itch. It felt an odd thing to do, but even after experiencing so much war in my short life, William Henry had created images in my mind that I could not erase. They are still there, at night when I close my eyes, during the day when I rest in the privy. Those bloody scenes unfold anytime I allow my mind to rest or veer away from some task at hand.

Itch hugged me back. Though he reeked of horse manure and stale sweat, I welcomed his awkward embrace. "I see he's an affectionate one, Sarah," he told his dog. "But that don't make it right, what you're thinking. You and I, we're sticking together." He snapped his fingers and the pair trotted off to help unload a string of bateaux that had just slid into the shingle with supplies from Albany.

I gazed at the flotilla, with its guards. I saw the eyes of the rivermen who had piloted the vessels northward up the Hudson. It was clear that they'd heard of the fall of William Henry. In a matter of days, papers in all of the colonies would include details of yet another debacle for our cause. And those rough bateaux men were fearful. They were eager to deliver their goods and quickly scurry the way they'd come. I'd never seen a group of men work so efficiently.

"I think I'll join them," I said, following after Itch and Sarah Belle.

"Who?" Nero asked.

"Them," I mumbled cryptically. "I'll find some ale, some rum, some whisky, some wine. Maybe all of it. Something. Get drunk. And sleep. I'll sleep for days."

"Where are you going?" Johnny asked.

"Home," I said.

"You can't go home," the boy retorted, chasing after me. "Loudoun made you a regular! You leave now, you're a deserter."

Nero, a shade wiser than the lad, slapped a hand over Johnny's mouth. "Let him be, Anson. Sometimes a man has things to do."

"Thanks," I said, returning to shake the freedman's hand.

Johnny wriggled free of his grasp. "But you love ranging and scouting! You wouldn't have it any other way."

"I do love it," I admitted. "At least I did."

"But what about all that stuff you wrote to Rogers? Loudoun wants you to help train regulars to be rangers. Did you ever hear back from Rogers?"

"I only heard from my father," I said patting my breast pocket. But then I reached in, tugging out the corner of a letter I'd never read. My days and nights had been nonstop battle since I'd received it. "This might be from Rogers now."

"What's it say?" Johnny asked.

I tucked it back. "It's waited this long. It can wait a little longer. See you."

"See you," Nero said.

"Oh, I swear," Johnny exclaimed. He ran to me. This time he gave me a bear hug. It had only the strength of a cub, but felt good. And though Johnny was less than a decade younger than I, his embrace gave me a twinge of guilt. I suddenly realized that I'd never hugged my own son. It was time to remedy that error.

"Goodbye," I said, leaving them alone in a fort that was quickly preparing to receive what they expected to be Montcalm's next strike.

As I slumped my way down to the shingle, I passed a straggling column of regulars who had emerged from the wooded road. There were more than forty. All were bruised and dirty. Less than half had managed to retain their red coats. Between them, there was no more than six muskets… and one cannon. "Turnwell?" I asked.

Lieutenant Turnwell looked up from his burden. He and eight other men had hitched themselves to the tongue of the cannon and acted as draught horses. "We bargained with a band of Iowa on the road. Had to use hand signals. We gave them our horse," he explained. A tear leaked down his face and he choked back his emotions. "Good to see you."

A jolt, fleeting, hit me. I normally would have said something cruel to the man. Instead, I kept true to my new form. I embraced him. It just happened. "You, too," I said, soon pulling away.

"I'll see you inside," he croaked, as he and his fellow beasts of burden laid their shoulders into the harness.

"Yep," I answered. "See you inside."

Grudgingly slow, they entered the heavily guarded gate. I turned and peered down the shadowed portage road. There were no terrifying French grenadiers charging. There were no screaming Ottawa advancing. For these facts, I was pleased. Yet neither was there any sign of any other survivors. There had been many more outside Titcomb. But fifteen miles was an infinite distance to travel when there was nothing between you and a scalping but your frazzled wits.

"General Webb is sending me to Fort Frederick," I lied to a private who stood guard at the bank. I patted my breast pocket. "I have a letter for Abercromby."

The private was at first disinterested. He nodded, saying only, "Fine. At this rate, they'll leave soon. But I don't think the general is in Albany."

"Of course, Abercromby's not in Albany," I said, climbing aboard a rapidly emptying scow. I plucked a bottle of wine from a crate carried by a laborer. A menacing scowl quieted the boy before he could serve up any protest. "That fat ass of a general is probably locked in a butcher's shop eating all the choicest cuts as well as the offal."

The private tamped down a smirk. "Still," he said trying not to laugh. "General Webb ought to know where Abercromby is located. Are you sure you're supposed to be here?"

"General Webb should also know that its treason to be cowardly in the face of the enemy, yet he exhibited that trait in spades these past few weeks. So, I'd not hold the man in such high esteem if I were you. It makes sense that the buffoon does not know where his commanding officers are."

The private stared at me, dumbstruck. "Then, uh, carry on." Boldness had its advantages.

I settled onto the deck, tossing my gear into a disorganized heap. Then I broke the seal of the letter I'd yet to read. My name was roundly penned in a woman's hand, a fair woman's hand. Sipping my wine, I devoured her words, as I had long desired to devour her lips. The drink as well as the affection I inferred from her penmanship warmed my needy soul.

Upon finishing her note, my outburst of laughter startled the private. I folded the page and stuffed it into my pocket, chuckling quite madly. "I thought that was for General Abercromby," he accused.

"No," I said simply. "That one was for me. Came in the post."

The private nodded knowingly. "As rare as it is, it's good to get word from home. You must have received fine news."

"That?" I asked, tapping my pocket. "No. That was terrible news. Turns out that all the work I did over the winter, slaving through snow, fighting, shooting, freezing, shivering, soaking and then keeping track of it all, then organizing, winnowing, and writing… well, it turns out that the man I was helping, stole it from me. He published it himself and claimed all the credit."

The private sized me up, studying my forest buckskins and green leggings. "You're a ranger?"

"Was," I said.

He peeped over his shoulder to make sure no one watched and set the butt of his musket carefully down among the stones. He pulled a pamphlet out of his pocket. "Rogers' Rules of Ranging," he explained. "Just came out. Bought a copy before I left York City."

"Yep, I suppose a lot of folks will give him more credit than he deserves," I sighed, leaning back and tipping my hat over my eyes.

"When you did it all," he opined.

I sat up and lifted the brim of my hat, staring him in the eye. "No. I just penned them. Those rules, though, they're known by most frontiersmen. And Rogers? He's good and all. But I'd give ten Rogers for one Stark or Brown or Anderson or Nero or Conwall."

"Who are they?"

I shrugged, reclining. "Men like me. Men like you. Men who do all the work and dying and get none of the credit. Not when shivering toads like Webb or saggy-titted cows like Abercromby are around."

He gave me just a few seconds of peace. "So, if it was such bad news, why did you laugh?"

"Because," I said. "It was written by the woman I am going to marry."

THE END

(Dear Reader-See Historical Remarks to separate fact from fiction)

HISTORICAL REMARKS

Lord Loudoun had taken over from Governor Shirley as Supreme Commander of the British effort in North America in early 1756. Shirley's dominion itself was utterly brief and disastrous after he had secured the job following the death of General Braddock. The rotating doors of generals, recalcitrant and stingy colonial assemblies, inefficient provision systems, immense distances through virgin forest, often independent provincial troops, and willful ignorance by the entire corps of British officers had conspired to make the early years of the Seven Years' War decidedly grim for King George II.

As such, Loudoun had his hands full at the start. By most accounts he was a capable administrator and tirelessly diligent. He vowed to intelligently utilize the British war machine in a manner which would highlight its strengths. Therefore, after years of terrible defeats in the interior of the forbidding American continent, he focused his offensive efforts toward the sea. He would seize the French stronghold of Louisbourg in 1757. From there, if necessary, it is clear that Loudoun planned to steadily move up the St. Lawrence with ships and marines and foot soldiers to conquer Quebec and Montreal, ending the North American war once and for all.

Given the shift of his focus away from retaking Fort Duquesne, Fort Bull, and Fort Oswego or even striking out from Fort Edward and Fort William Henry, these interior domains or campaigns might again contend with insufficient supplies of troops and materiel. Enter Colonel Bradstreet. As I've depicted in this and previous works, his proficiency with managing bateaux men and routes and trains of wagons or packhorses proved invaluable to the British cause. Through his efforts, 1757 marks the first time in the war that British outposts did not suffer from starvation conditions. But he could not conjure men from clay.

Loudoun's growing fleet in New York Harbor was taking every extra regiment of red-clad warriors. It was a miracle at all that Forts William Henry and Edward were granted even the small number of regulars stationed there. The plan was to fill the British forts with a few companies of trained redcoats and supplement them with provincial troops. Then, if needed, the local governors and or military rulers were to call in the militia for short periods of time. The interior forts had no bold offensive strategies for 1757. At best they were to skirmish and cause trouble for the French in the Lake George and Lake Champlain areas. At worst, they were to hold the line while Loudoun took Louisbourg.

However, after a long-delayed start, the weather proved uncooperative for the Louisbourg expedition. After hundreds of ships and thousands of men bobbed about idly in the harbor at Halifax for many weeks, the entire attack was called off. Loudoun's bad luck meant that the only thing his massive, well-orchestrated undertaking had accomplished was to restrict the number of warriors available for fighting in the interior.

While Lord Loudoun toiled in Albany and York City during the winter of 1756 to 1757, Robert Rogers was busy instigating trouble for the French cause using his famous tactics of irregular warfare. Operating out of Fort William Henry, he and a couple hundred of his rangers (veterans of the unit went on to form what has become today's US Army Rangers and even the Queen's York Rangers of Canada) traveled across frozen Lake George. There were many hardships and injuries during the first night alone when a dozen or so had to turn back.

Rogers had come to rely on bold maneuvers and adherence to his Rules of Ranging for all of his previous successes. Unfortunately, his fate took a dark turn during their scout and raid in that bitter cold. They had made it north of Fort Carillon and did attack a sledge trotting across frozen Lake Champlain. However, as depicted, a slower band of French sleds fell upon them. Rogers won that small engagement, driving the enemy south to Carillon. He then violated one of his guidelines by exactly tracing his steps in order to get away before the whole of the garrison fell upon him and his small troupe. What followed has become known as the First Battle on Snowshoes. Lieutenant Stark (who has much fame yet to earn in his own right – in this war and the next) properly deployed his force on a rise. They were able to defiantly hold off the ambushers for several hours until they were finally able to slip away after dark before reinforcements could arrive.

Rogers was badly wounded. The ranger, Thomas Brown, and the regular, Robert Baker, were taken as Ottawa hostages. The rangers were forced to kill all of their French or Canadian captives.

Then, just weeks later, apparently inspired by Rogers, Rigaud led a much larger army southward over the ice. Without artillery, there was never really a true risk to Fort William Henry itself. But after four days of fighting – sorties and escalades – there were no wooden structures left standing outside the fort's walls. The most significant of those possessions destroyed was the entire Lake George fleet of tiny warships – sloops, whaleboats, etc. For the time being, William Henry was stuck on its shores.

But the British still had their scouts and rangers, operating under Lieutenant Stark after Rogers was sent away to recover. They ranged far and wide, keeping tabs on the enemy and their own environs. Yet, these brave men were steadily overwhelmed by the immense numbers of foreign tribesmen who began to arrive as the sun stayed longer and snow turned to rain. I say "foreign" because they were. Tribesmen from beyond the Great Lakes had heard stories all winter long about the easy war trophies that many Indians had taken after the Fall of Oswego. They'd been told that they'd be "swimming in brandy" if they made the trek. They came in droves onto land that had historically been Iroquois, English, or Dutch.

From the time Colonel Monro arrived and onward, the British ability to scout even just a mile or two was completely thwarted. The woods were veritably controlled by bands of disparate tribes, not really working in concert with one another or the French. Canadians, mostly under Langlade and several others, attempted to maintain order for their French king. My depiction of Amos Conwall's death by a beating was fiction, but based upon a story told by the French priest Father Roubaud about what he had witnessed during the main siege of William Henry itself. A Mahican ranger, allied with the English, was beaten nearly to death. The tribes, as many a man throughout history, were out for blood.

Compounding events was the fact that General Webb had assumed command in Fort Edward. He was the same Webb who had done little to reinforce Oswego and then panicked and destroyed Fort Bull for no reason the prior year. Staying true to form, this time Webb denied Monro's repeated requests for men and supplies from Fort Edward to bolster his garrison on Lake George.

Monro and Eyre and the other commanders at William Henry kept working throughout the summer. They steadily built a fortified camp on Titcomb, while rebuilding a small fleet of ships. Midway through their reconstruction project, two exhausted Englishmen arrived, having escaped from Fort Carillon. These men reported that Montcalm now had 8,000 men at his disposal and that number was growing every single day.

By the way, these two men were neither Baker nor Brown as I've shown. Thomas Brown was held as a captive for two years by the Ottawa. After he escaped, he wrote a pamphlet describing his trials that wound up being widely read after the war. And I honestly cannot say what ever became of Robert Baker.

The report from the escapees spurred Monro to even faster action. He beckoned for Webb to call in the New York militia so that they might allow more regulars to march from Edward to William Henry. He also increased the work rate on the fleet.

Colonel John Parker led five companies of New Jersey provincials and the remaining rangers north in the new boats on July 23. By the following morning, a Sunday, hundreds of his men were killed or captured in a brutal ambush. To this day, the promontory of land at which the one-sided battle occurred is referred to as Sabbath Day point. Men were killed as they surrendered or struggled to tread water. Unfortunately, the only reason that the enemy was in that location in such force was due to more bad luck for the British.

Unbeknownst to the British, a band of Mohawk warriors had attacked the camps outside Fort Carillon on Saturday. They did little damage, but put the garrison on high alert. Langlade, his Canadians, and many Indians were at the point only to cut off the Mohawk escape. All the captured rum stores were consumed in short order. A French report from Bougainville describes that three of the English prisoners were boiled, then eaten by tribesmen.

By the time the survivors limped back to William Henry, they found that Webb was visiting. Though his post was only fifteen miles down the portage road, it was his first visit the entire year. He quickly discovered that William Henry was now down to only 1,100 men and 80 women and children. The enemy that would likely descend upon them was many multiples of that number. Webb promptly left, promising reinforcements for the siege that was likely to come.

Out of the many thousands he commanded, he sent 200 regulars and 800 Massachusetts provincials under Colonel Frye. These men arrived about a week later, on the same evening as the enemy.

Other than minor changes, the siege of William Henry played out as I've described. It was as destructive as it was methodical. All reports state that Monro was inspiring in his defense. But he and his chief engineer Major Eyre understood the limitations of their fort and ammunition. Monro repeatedly sent runners through the dangerous gauntlet of enemy warriors to ask Webb to send a large force to destroy the enemy against his walls.

The Indians that surrounded Titcomb bickered and fought amongst themselves. The Caughnawaga Chief Kanectagon killed a messenger that carried Webb's letter of denial to Monro. General Montcalm was given the letter early in the siege and held it for several days as he pounded the fort, waiting to reveal it at the optimal time.

After being shown the blood-soaked letter from Webb that refused him any assistance, Monro was forced to capitulate. His opponent, Montcalm, was a soldier thoroughly believing in the structure of his command. He expected all forces to obey the terms of the fort's surrender. Unfortunately, there were thousands of foreign tribesmen who came for their own personal military glory.

Briefly, I must note that I have made two minor adjustments in this tale with regard to time and geography. Concerning geography, I have set the Titcomb encampment closer to the main gates of William Henry than it actually was. However, in the map of the Siege of William Henry, I remained faithful to the actual location.

Concerning time, I placed two separate events much closer together. My research tells me there were several hours between the massacre of the wounded inside Fort William Henry and the more famous massacre outside at the outset of the march. On the afternoon of August 9th, the fort itself was officially handed over to the French. After the British filed to Titcomb, but before the French could occupy the vacated premises, tribesmen fell upon about seventy wounded British men and women. Only a few were saved by French soldiers or missionaries.

On the morning of August 10th, the British on Titcomb formed up to be escorted to Fort Edward. Small groups of Indians, chafing because they'd been given no trophies, began demanding that men give up their arms, equipment, and clothing. Despite it being against the terms of capitulation, the victorious French did not intervene. Therefore, the vanquished were forced to comply.

News of their braves unexpected successes spread throughout the Indian camps which were essentially right across the road. More Indian warriors came. Then they began to take more than just personal items. The Indians were like their white cousins in that they viewed blacks as property. The tribesmen grabbed every black man, free or slave, and hauled him off. They seized all the women and children from the camp and dragged them to the forest, tying them to trees. For the most part, they had allowed the British regulars to file away unmolested. And since the militia and provincial troops were at the back of the filing train, they received the brunt of the assault.

Somehow, some way, a war whoop was sounded by someone. Chaos reigned for several minutes as Frye's regiment dissolved. Three to five hundred British men successfully fled to French priests, soldiers, or officers for refuge. About the same number of men were taken captive by Indians. 185 were killed in the rapid assault before Montcalm and his regulars could restore order. Survivors straggled into Fort Edward over the coming weeks. Only ten of the 80 women ever arrived.

This was the second time in two years that a victory by Montcalm was spoiled by wanton slaughter. He was horrified by what had happened and feared for his personal honor that he held so dear. It was too late. His reputation among his enemies soured.

NEVER again in the war would any victorious English army grant any French or Canadian army the honors of war in surrender.

A brief word about the word massacre. Several modern commentators have attempted to downplay the butchery and attacks as something other than massacre. They suggest that frightened provincials and regulars invented the idea of massacre to justify their embarrassing behavior as they broke ranks on the road. However, even using such authors' conservative numbers (which I have stated above) to account for casualties, it is safe to say that any rational human being or soldier, if standing in the midst of such rapid carnage, would only logically describe it as a massacre. All of the English correspondence at the time states that it was a dreadful massacre. Even the French, as they attempted to save face, admitted that it was uncalled-for butchery and thievery. As a result, a quarter of a millennium later, I believe that it was truly a massacre if there ever was one.

And the massacre tainted relations between Montcalm and his Indian fighters. He no longer wished to employ them. They no longer wished to serve a man who wouldn't freely give them war prizes. 1757 was the last time that droves of warriors came to support their French fathers. As the years passed in the long war, the English picked up more and more of the tribes that had lately been their enemies.

I mentioned the Easton Conference in a letter from Ephraim's father. It actually ended in August, while the siege of William Henry was in its final hours. It, too, helped bring more tribesmen into the English camp. Though the Eastern Delaware had been neutral throughout the struggle, when they concluded a formal peace with the crown, they brought with them the opportunity to corral their violent Western Delaware cousins, the Shawnee, and others. It was the results of the Easton Conference that helped pave the way for eventual victories on the American interior.

By the end of 1757, defeat had thus far led to more defeat for the British. And if you asked any colonial citizen or British subject even as late as 1758, they may have said that all hope was lost. Another commander, less able than the last, would take over in North America. The British cause in Europe would begin to suffer as the prince and his army were recalled from the Continent. From Europe to America, more defeats were yet to come.

Yet things were finally beginning to turn in their favor, though no single event could prove such a claim. A string of small things would work together, swiftly over the coming years. A new prime minister, with a radical new idea for waging the war, was named. Poor harvests in Canada had begun to exact their toll. Friction between the two most powerful men in New France escalated after the William Henry massacre. And British superiority over the seas finally began to tip the scales.

A final note about Monro. He survived the massacre, but died of natural causes just a couple months later. He had no daughters. I've taken the diversionary tale of Alice, Cora, and Magua straight from The Last of the Mohicans by James Fenimore Cooper, the first novel I ever read. Hawkeye, Chingachgook, and Uncas remain heroes of mine to this day and I felt joyfully obligated to include just a small part of their adventures in my novel.

I relied on many terrific works to guide the history of my tale. The most important of those, follow. *Crucible of War*, by Fred Anderson has become the modern-day classic on the French and Indian War. Also by Fred Anderson is *The War that made America*, which is a shortened version, but includes a few interesting details not mentioned in his longer tome. *Betrayals: Fort William Henry and the Massacre* by Ian Steele aided in my discussion of the events immediately surrounding William Henry's fall. Ron Chernow's *Washington: A Life* was instrumental in fleshing out details of the young man's first journeys westward. I also trusted *Firearms: An Illustrated History* from DK Books. Finally, *The Brown Bess* by Erik Goldstein and Stuart Mowbray was a magnificent reference on the ubiquitous musket. Any errors you spot in the yarn are my own.

ABOUT THE AUTHOR

Jason Born is a popular historical novelist. *The Long Fuse* is a series of novels that thrillingly captures the violent period of America's rise from ragtag colonies to independence. He is the author of *Lions & Devils,* a series which vividly describes the heroes and villains of the monstrous Islamic assault of Western Europe during the Eighth Century. Other works include *The Norseman Chronicles*, a multi-volume set detailing the gritty adventures of the faithful Viking, Halldorr, who desired only peace, but found only war in the Old and New Worlds. *The Wald Chronicles* set of historical novels centers on the rugged conflict and improbable outcome in Germania during the wars between the Roman legionaries and their tribal adversaries over 2,000 years ago. *League of the Lost Fountain* is his first work for kids of all ages. He has penned an historical fantasy called *Girl King* under the pseudonym, Emily Hawk. Jason lives in the Midwest with his wife and three children. If you enjoyed this work and would like to see more, Jason asks you to consider doing the following:

1. Please encourage your friends to buy a copy – and read it!
2. If you think the book deserves praise, please post a five-star review on Amazon and/or a five-star review on Goodreads.com.
3. Visit his website, www.authorjasonborn.com. There, you can submit your email address to receive an occasional update on his latest novels.

Made in the
USA
Columbia, SC